W9-CBX-130

THE IRON SICKLE

Also by Martin Limón

Jade Lady Burning
Slicky Boys
Buddha's Money
The Door to Bitterness
The Wandering Ghost
G.I. Bones
Mr. Kill
The Joy Brigade
Nightmare Range

THE IRON SICKLE

SICKLE

Martin Limón

Published by
Soho Press, Inc.
853 Broadway
New York, NY 10003

Library of Congress Cataloging-in-Publication Data

Limón, Martin, 1948–
The iron sickle / Martin Limón.
p. cm

ISBN 978-1-61695-391-1
eISBN 978-1-61695-392-8

1. United States. Army Criminal Investigation Command—Fiction.
2. Murder—Investigation—Fiction. 3. Americans—Korea—Fiction. I. Title.
PS3562.I465I86 2014
813'.54—dc23   2014003813

Interior design by Janine Agro, Soho Press, Inc.

Printed in the United States of America

10 9 8 7 6 5 4 3 2 1

To my daughter, Michelle, with love and respect.

THE IRON SICKLE

-1-

The man with the iron sickle entered Yongsan Compound on a Monday morning in the middle of October at approximately zero seven forty-five. This is the hour when the bulk of the Korean workforce rushes through the pedestrian entrance at Gate Number Five toward the hundreds of jobs they fill in the headquarters of the 8th United States Army in Seoul, Republic of Korea.

He must've shown an ID card.

Most of the Korean workers wear them dangling from lanyards or clipped to their lapels. A contract-hire gate guard checked the identification of every person shuffling single file through the narrow passageway, a chore he'd performed every weekday for years. Interviewed later, he admitted he didn't have time to compare every card to every face. The crush of people was too great. So the ID card might've been a forgery or it might've been stolen, and there's at least the chance it might've been borrowed from someone else.

The weather that morning had been blustery, with cold rain splashing beneath the tires of the military vehicles and the big PX Ford Granada taxis rolling through the heavily guarded gate. An American MP wearing a rain-soaked poncho slowed each vehicle and peered inside, looking for unauthorized passengers. Occasionally, he ordered a driver to stop and pop open a trunk. If no contraband was found and all the passengers showed military or dependent identification, he waved them through.

At first it was thought the man with the sickle might've taken a cab onto the compound, but every PX taxi driver on duty that morning was questioned and not one admitted to taking on a non-US military fare. Dispatch records confirmed the main pickup points had been Niblo Barracks, the UN Compound, and Yongsan Compound South Post—US military installations, all—thereby corroborating their assertions. Korean taxis—often called "*kimchi* cabs"—are never allowed on US military compounds.

What we did know was the man with the sickle was tall for a Korean, a couple of inches short of six feet, and that he wore a rain-damp overcoat. After entering Gate Five, he made his way through the headquarters complex approximately a quarter mile to the 8th United States Army Claims Office. Many of the 8th Army headquarters buildings are long, stately, two-story brick edifices originally constructed during occupation by the Japanese Imperial Army. Since then, the 8th United States Army built cement block single-story offices in a row that runs behind the ornate headquarters building itself. These utilitarian constructs reach some two hundred yards to the 8th Army Judge Advocate General's Office. It was from amongst this row of buildings that the man with the sickle struck.

The sickle itself was a small farm implement the Koreans call a *naht*, a twelve-inch, crescent-shaped blade attached to a wooden handle about a foot and a half long. It is meant to be used with one hand, most often to cut rice shoots or to trim grass. But when this otherwise innocuous instrument is sharpened to a razor's edge, it can be used quite effectively for murder.

At approximately zero eight oh five, when the man with the sickle entered the front door of the 8th United States Army Claims Office, he was greeted respectfully by Mrs. Han Ok-mi, the receptionist. The man stood with his hands at his side, his overcoat buttoned, and nodded to Mrs. Han. She testified later that his speech was guttural, as if he was either extremely nervous or suffering from some sort of speech defect. She also noticed the right side of his lower lip was puffy and dark purple. Being a polite woman, she didn't stare at the deformity. The man with the sickle requested to see Mr. Barretsford, the civilian boss and the head of the 8th United States Army Claims Office. Mrs. Han asked if he had an appointment and then asked for his name, but both questions were dodged. Mrs. Han informed the man Mr. Barretsford hadn't yet arrived for work, but just as she was about to ask him to take a seat, Mr. C. Winston Barretsford barreled into the office, shucking off his raincoat and tossing his wet umbrella into a holder by the door. All the Korean employees stood. Barretsford smiled and waved a hello, then rushed into his office and shut his door. The man with the sickle asked again if he could speak to Mr. Barretsford, and Mrs. Han motioned for him to have a seat against the wall and told him she would let Mr. Barretsford know of his request.

The function of the Claims Office is to evaluate the validity of claims for reparations, compensation, and damages made by outside parties against the various units attached to USFK, United States Forces Korea. There are over fifty military compounds—infantry, air force, and even a naval facility down south at the port of Chinhae—and these units are constantly on the go, training and conducting military operations in defense of "Freedom's Frontier." During these operations things get broken. Rice fields are churned up by tank tracks; pear trees are knocked over by towed artillery pieces; pedestrians are injured when convoys careen down muddy country roads. Under the ROK/US Status of Forces Agreement, the injured parties are allowed to make formal claims for reimbursement. A system for adjudicating these claims was set up outside the Korean courts and, over the years, a cadre of attorneys who specialize in such claims has developed. These men follow the troops, search out victims, and solicit claims on behalf of the injured—or not so injured—parties. For a hefty fee, they apply for reimbursement from 8th Army. That Monday morning at the Claims Office, all the workers assumed that, even though they'd never seen him before, the man asking to see Mr. Barretsford was one of those attorneys.

Through the intercom Mr. Barretsford notified Mrs. Han that he would be in phone conference for at least a half hour, and if the man who wanted to see him wouldn't identify the claim he was there about, he would just have to wait.

Records at the Yongsan Compound telephone exchange later revealed Mr. Barretsford had been on the phone to his wife, Evelyn Barretsford, who lived in their quarters on South Post. His wife would testify they'd been arguing about whether or not they could afford another midtour leave back to the States during Christmas break since they'd just shelled out a bundle for a trip home during their daughter Cindy's summer vacation. Finally, after slamming down the phone, Mr. Barretsford called Mrs. Han and asked her to bring three files he was working on into the office. Ever efficient, Mrs. Han already had the files ready and immediately rose from her desk and walked into Barretsford's office. According to the other workers at the Claims Office, the man with the iron sickle followed, uninvited.

What happened inside the office is somewhat unclear. Mrs. Han suffered only minor cuts and bruises inflicted when she tried to intervene, but her testimony is hampered by the hysteria that is brought on every time the attack itself is mentioned. At the advice of her doctors, 8th Army law enforcement has not been allowed to interrogate her and can only go by what she managed to babble after the incident.

The physical evidence was clear. The main cause of death of Mr. C. Winston Barretsford was a six-inch slash across the neck. The cut was so surgical that Barretsford was almost certainly not expecting it. Anyone, if by nothing more than reflex, would've raised their hands and stepped back to ward off the blow. The man with the sickle must've whipped the sickle out of his coat and slashed Mr. Barretsford's throat in one lightning-quick motion. It happened so fast and so unexpectedly that Mrs. Han didn't even scream right away. The workers outside testified they first heard what sounded like the desk being shoved and then Mr. Barretsford's chair falling backwards. During those few seconds, the man with the sickle lunged around Barretsford's desk and slashed him again and again with the wickedly sharp *naht*.

By then Mrs. Han was screaming bloody murder and everything was being spattered with gore, up to and including the uppermost Venetian blinds. In all, the 8th Army coroner counted two dozen stab wounds, all delivered in rapid succession and all but the first superfluous because that one had neatly sliced Barretsford's carotid artery, damaging it beyond any hope of repair.

By the time the workers outside recovered from their initial shock, the man with the sickle was already walking quickly but not hurriedly out of the office. According to at least one eyewitness, his overcoat was once again buttoned, and he seemed to be holding something beneath it. After he left, everyone rushed into Barretsford's office.

Mrs. Han was still wide-eyed and screaming, and Mr. C. Winston Barretsford lay in a growing pool of his own blood. Life still pumped red from the gaping wound in his neck. Finally, an onlooker of some presence of mind called the Military Police.

-2-

The 8th United States Army was on lockdown.

I stood with an MP named Grimes on a low hill overlooking a drainage ditch that slithered darkly beneath jumbled concertina wire. The hour was zero six hundred on the morning after the attack. Grimes shifted the weight of his M-16 rifle in the crook of his arm, took another long drag on his cigarette, and stared beyond the chain-link fence at the shadows that enveloped the Yongsan district of Seoul.

"Commies," he told me. "They want to chase us out of Korea, so when we ain't looking, they kill as many of us as they can find."

"You think that's it?" I asked.

"Course that's it." He exhaled resolutely. "But we ain't going."

Already the general assumption was the man with the sickle had been an agent for the Democratic People's Republic of Korea, better known as North Korea. The honchos of 8th Army were convinced the assassin was a trained professional who had been sent south to create mayhem and drive a wedge between the US and our South Korean allies.

"They're tricky, those Commies," Grimes said.

My name is George Sueño. I'm an agent for the 8th United States

Army's Criminal Investigation Division. My partner, Ernie Bascom, and I had been drafted, along with every other CID agent and MP Investigator on the compound, to perform the duties of Sergeants of the Guard around the five-mile perimeter of the 8th Army headquarters compound. It was our job to patrol the fences and the gates every half hour to make sure the MPs and the contract-hire Korean gate guards were alert. We couldn't have another attack like the one at the Claims Office.

"Seen anything unusual?" I asked Grimes.

"If I did," he responded, "don't you think I'd report it?"

"I guess you would."

Without saying goodbye, I continued my rounds, strolling past the now-dark brick buildings of the headquarters complex, stopping to talk to the pacing Korean guards heavily bundled in hooded parkas, M-1 rifles slung over their shoulders. No one reported seeing anything unusual. All quiet on the Yongsan front. This extra security was a classic case of shutting the barn door after the horse has escaped. Many of us thought it was a waste of time. But the brass didn't, and in the army, only the opinions of those with eagles or stars on their shoulders truly count.

After finishing my circuit, I made my way back to the MP station and pushed through the swinging double doors. Ernie was already back, lounging on a wooden bench, a copy of the *Pacific Stars and Stripes* in front of him; this morning's edition, just flown in from Tokyo. With the back of his hand, Ernie slapped the paper.

"Nothing in here about the murder," he said.

"They haven't had time," I replied, shrugging off my field jacket. "Their deadline was something like noon yesterday."

"Barretsford was dead before that," Ernie said. "They knew about it."

Ernie was right. The editors at the *Stripes* office in Tokyo must've known about the brutal attack on C. Winston Barretsford before they went to press, and yet they'd chosen not to print the story. So far, our only source of information had been chatter amongst law enforcement personnel and the tight-lipped briefing we'd received when assigned to our sections along the perimeter. The radio and television outlets of the Armed Forces Korea Network had been completely mum about the man with the iron sickle. It was as if he hadn't existed.

"They're shutting the case down," Ernie said. "Total blackout. I bet even AP and UPI won't be able to pick up on it."

"Maybe not." I drew myself a mug of coffee out of the big metal urn the 8th Army chow hall had set up for us. It was barely warm but I'd been out in the cold so long it tasted good.

"No maybe about it," Ernie replied. "And you can bet the Korean papers won't say *boo*, not if the ROK government doesn't want them to."

The military dictatorship of President Park Chung-hee kept a tight control on their own news outlets: print, radio, and television. So tight they occasionally arrested a reporter without trial and threw him in jail to rot for as long as the regime saw fit.

"Okay," I said, sitting down on the bench next to Ernie. "So Eighth Army's keeping it buttoned up. That doesn't make Barretsford any less dead. And it doesn't make the guy with the sickle any less out there."

"That's my point," Ernie said. "So far we haven't found zilch. No evidence that would lead us to this guy. Not even any clue as to his motive. With publicity, maybe somebody who knows something would drop a dime on him."

"You mean ten *won*."

"Okay," Ernie replied. "Ten *won*."

I picked the paper up off the bench, sipped my coffee, and started reading the front page story about two cub reporters who were giving President Nixon hell. It was fun to read, like a soap opera, and it took my mind off our current troubles. After finishing my coffee, I put the paper down, slipped back into my field jacket, and trudged out into the still, dark morning to make my final round of the perimeter. When I returned, I waited until Ernie had finished his inspection tour on the far side of the compound, and we marched over to the 8th Army movie theater. Colonel Brace, the Provost Marshal, was giving a briefing for law enforcement personnel at zero eight hundred, and our attendance was not only requested but mandatory. At the entranceway to the theater, a colorful movie poster announced the upcoming re-release of Steve McQueen and Candice Bergen in *The Sand Pebbles*.

"Don't they ever get any new movies?" Ernie asked.

I didn't answer. We pushed through the double doors.

Just past the empty popcorn machine, Staff Sergeant Riley, the Admin NCO of the CID Detachment, was taking roll. His thin body looked lost in the neatly pressed folds of his khaki uniform. As GIs passed, he checked names off a list on a clipboard.

"Fill up the front rows," Riley growled. "The Colonel doesn't want to shout."

"Yes, Teacher," Ernie said.

Riley pursed his thin lips and jammed his pen toward the front of the theater as if to say, "Keep moving."

During the day when he was sober, Riley was one of the most efficient men I knew. At night, he pulled out a bottle of Old Overwart he kept hidden in the back of his wall locker and laid into it. After three or four shots, he was completely stupid, which was how he wanted to be when the sun was down anyway.

Contrary to Riley's orders, Ernie and I took seats in the seventh row from the front. More CID agents and MP investigators filtered in. After about three dozen of us had taken our seats, the murmured conversation started to subside. Finally, Colonel Brace strode down the aisle. Riley shouted, "On your *feet!*" and we all stood at the position of attention.

Colonel Brace stared at us for a moment from the stage, then told us to be seated. Riley switched on an overhead projector and soon the Colonel was droning on about crime statistics and the progress the command had made since he'd taken over as 8th Army Provost Marshal. A couple of guys were starting to snore when he finally got to the point.

He informed us we were going to apprehend the man with the iron sickle.

"The Korean National Police think this is their baby," Colonel Brace said, "but they've got another thing coming. I've just been in conference with the Chief of Staff, and he says this happened on our compound, to one of our own. A Department of Defense civilian, but still someone who those of us here are sworn to protect."

He glared around the quiet theater, as if daring anyone to contradict him. No one did. All fifty thousand GIs stationed in Korea, their dependents, and the DOD civilians fell under our jurisdiction.

"The KNPs will be involved. We might need their help off compound, but it's us who are going to catch this guy. Is that understood?"

A murmur of assent rose from the crowd. Then the Colonel started to give us our assignments. Most of the MP investigators were to start combing through the archives of the Claims Office, searching particularly for disgruntled applicants who'd had their claims denied and might still hold a grudge against Barretsford or against the 8th Army Claims Office in general. Some of the CID agents were to look into past cases of lost or stolen Korean employee identification cards. Others were assigned to track down forgery operations that might've provided the killer with a phony ID. Although they weren't at this meeting, Colonel Brace told us a half dozen counter-intelligence agents would be joining the effort, shaking down their informants, trying to gather information on whether or not the man with the sickle had been sent by the North Korean regime.

An MP investigator raised his hand and asked what exactly the KNPs would be up to.

"The Korean National Police," Colonel Brace replied, "are giving this case the highest priority. They've already started interrogating Korean employees and bus and cab drivers in the Yongsan area to see if they can discover how he reached the gate."

Ernie and I had yet to be given an assignment, and as it became more apparent the meeting was closing down, Ernie began to fidget. When the Colonel asked if we had any final questions, Ernie shot to his feet.

"What about us?" Ernie said. "Me and my partner here, Sueño?"

"Oh, yes," the Colonel replied. "See Staff Sergeant Riley after the meeting."

Some wise guy in the second row said, *sotto voce*, "The black market detail."

Everyone cracked up. Ernie flipped the guy the bird. The Colonel shouted, "Dismissed! Get out of here and get to work."

As everyone stood and started to file out, Riley shouted, as best he was able through his whiskey-ravaged throat, "I want a progress report every day before close of business."

Grumbles greeted the announcement. Colonel Brace marched out of the theater, and Ernie and I sat as the other investigators filed past. A few made snide remarks. To each one, Ernie raised his middle digit and replied, "Sit on it and rotate."

Finally, after everyone left, Riley walked over to us.

"You two are staying on the black market detail," he told us. "The Colonel doesn't want the commissary and PX overrun with *yobos* while we're chasing down the Barretsford case."

Yobo means girlfriend, a term used to refer, impolitely, to the Korean dependent wives of American servicemen.

"Why don't they want us on the case?" Ernie demanded.

"Colonel's orders," Riley said, jotting something down on his clipboard.

"I'll tell you why," Ernie said. "They don't want the truth. If they wanted the truth, they'd have us taking the lead. Sueño here is the only American investigator in the country who speaks Korean. I'm the only investigator who's not a brownnoser with a corncob stuck up his butt. What Eighth Army wants is to have the honchos manage every detail of this investigation from start to finish because they're afraid of where it might lead."

"The Provost Marshal is committed to getting to the bottom of this murder."

"As long as nobody's embarrassed," Ernie said.

Riley finished making notations on his clipboard and stuck his pencil behind his ear. "How long have you been in the army, Bascom?"

"Almost ten years."

"Two tours in Vietnam?"

"That's right."

"Then you know you go along to get along."

"Or better yet," Ernie said, "you fuck up and move up."

Riley ignored the insult. "Be at the commissary when it opens," he told us. "Make your presence known. And Sueño . . ." He turned toward me. "Try to convince your partner here to keep his mouth shut for once."

"I'll think about it," I said.

"Think quick," Riley told me. "You, too," he said, pointing at Ernie. He started to walk away.

"Who's been assigned to look into Barretsford's past?" I asked.

Riley stopped in his tracks. Slowly, he turned around and pointed his finger at me. "You'd better be quiet about that," he said. "It's already been decided that this had nothing to do with Barretsford's personal life. This was an outside attack."

"Decided by who?" I asked.

Riley shook his head. "Don't you two get it? You ask too many questions. That's why you're off the case."

He tucked his clipboard beneath his scrawny arm and stalked out of the theater.

Ernie and I sat in his jeep in the back row of the parking lot, sipping PX coffee we'd bought at the snack stand in front of the Yongsan Commissary. It was hot and tasted about as acidic as battery fluid. We watched customers, mostly Korean women, flow out of the commissary, trotting behind male baggers who pushed huge carts laden with freeze-dried coffee, soluble creamer, mayonnaise, concentrated orange drink, bottled maraschino cherries, and just about anything else that was imported and therefore highly prized on the black market.

Even twenty years after the devastation of the Korean War, Korean industry was still flat on its back. The government was working hard to rectify that situation, but for now they were concentrating on big ticket items like oil tankers, M-16 rifles, and the new Hyundai sedans that were zooming all over the city. Ladies' nylons, stereo equipment, and washing machines were luxury items their industrial plant could not yet produce.

After the groceries were loaded into the trunk of one of the black Ford Granada PX taxis, the female shoppers tipped the baggers and climbed into the backseats.

"Which one should we bust?" I asked.

"Let's finish our coffee first."

"Okay by me."

Earlier this morning, after leaving the 8th Army movie theater, we'd had no choice but to pass Gate Five. Without talking about it, we decided to loiter nearby beneath an old elm tree to watch the American

MPs and Korean gate guards check people and vehicles as they came through. Manpower had more than doubled since yesterday: four MPs and five gate guards. Each piece of identification had to be taken out of its holder, handed to the gate guard, examined, and then, in turn, handed to the MP. If any anomaly was noted, an entry was made in a ledger with the time, date, name, and serial number of the ID card. Apparently, much of the Korean workforce had decided not to show up today. If they had, there would've been a line a half mile long. As it was, only about a dozen workers waited patiently to enter.

Again without talking about it, Ernie and I sauntered casually across the street, strolling behind the brick headquarters and down the line of cement block buildings until we reached the Claims Office. It was still roped off with yellow crime tape, and the front door had been barred.

"Yesterday it was raining," I said. "If a guy arrived a little early and had to wait for the office to open, he wouldn't want to stand here on the sidewalk."

"No," Ernie replied, "he'd wait in *there*."

Behind us loomed the back entrance to one of the two-story brick buildings, this one belonging to the Logistics Command. Ernie and I stepped up on the porch and pushed through the door. Inside, a stairwell wound up to the second floor, and just past the foot of the stairs, a small snack stand had been set up. Most of the headquarters buildings had similar operations, sponsored by the PX.

An elderly Korean woman wore a loose smock and a white bandana enveloping her grey hair. A small man, maybe her husband, reached into a cardboard box and handed her wax-paper-wrapped rolls and doughnuts, which she set on display behind a plastic sneeze guard. The smell of percolating coffee gave the stand a homey air.

"*Anyonghaseiyo*?" I said in Korean.

The old woman bowed slightly and said, "*Nei. Anyonghaseiyo. Myol duhsi-geissoyo*?" What can I get for you?

I ordered a small coffee. Ernie bought a carton of orange juice.

After the old woman gave us our change, I said, "Yesterday, the man who waited here, did he order anything?"

Both of them stopped what they were doing, as if suddenly frozen by a cold wind from Manchuria. Finally, the old woman cleared her throat and said, "What do you mean?"

"I mean the Korean man who stepped in here yesterday morning to get out of the rain, just before eight o'clock. Did he order anything? Coffee maybe? Juice?"

The man and woman exchanged glances, and I guessed they must've worked together for many years.

"No," the old woman said. "He ordered nothing."

Bingo.

"Did he speak to you?" I asked.

"No." The old man spoke for the first time, straightening up from his chores. "He said nothing to us. He just stood there in front of the door, staring at the rain."

"What did he look like?"

Their description matched the one given by the employees of the Claims Office.

"Did you see him leave?" I asked.

"No, but I was glad when he did."

"Why?"

"He just stared out the window. He didn't move. Not one muscle the whole time he stood there."

"There was one thing that moved," the old woman corrected.

"What was that?" I asked.

"His lip. His lower lip. It was purple, puffed up, like something was wrong with it. The whole time he stood there it kept pulsating, like blood was pounding through it."

"Is that it?"

"No," she replied. "He kept sniffling, as if his nose were running. I kept thinking he was going to cry."

I tried more questions but stopped when I realized they had nothing else to tell us.

On our way back to the barracks, Ernie insisted we ought to tell Riley that none of the vaunted investigators who'd been assigned to the Barretsford case had thought to interview the couple who ran the PX snack stand across the pathway from the Claims Office.

"You just want to rub it in," I said.

"Why not?"

"Let's wait for them to come to us."

This crime wouldn't be solved on the American compound. Like an avenging warrior, the man with the iron sickle had emerged out of the vast city of Seoul. Eventually, if Colonel Brace wanted Americans to solve this case, he'd have to enlist someone who spoke Korean and wasn't afraid of snooping around back alleys and asking embarrassing questions. That would be us. Most of the other investigators were afraid to even venture off compound. They couldn't read the signs, Korean addresses made no sense to them, and not enough people out there spoke English. If you ventured too far from compound, toilets were hard to find; and when you did find one, it was often nothing more than a stinking square hole in a dirty cement floor. If you weren't limber enough to squat, you were in trouble.

And more importantly, most of our American colleagues were afraid to piss off their military superiors. Ernie and I sometimes tried not to piss off our superiors, but it rarely worked. Mostly we just didn't give a damn.

We sipped on our coffee for a while, each lost in thought, until suddenly Ernie said, "Whoa! Who's that?"

I glanced up. Barreling across the parking lot was an American woman, light brown hair uncovered in the drizzle. She was wearing only a long black dress covered by a grey sweater, and was dragging a little girl behind her who looked to be about eight or nine. The woman was thin but strong, as if she worked out regularly, and she was glaring at us, enraged. As she headed straight toward us, I realized who she was. Ernie did, too.

"Trouble," Ernie said, quickly climbing out of the jeep. I popped out of the passenger side and walked to the front of the jeep.

The woman marched up to Ernie and slapped his chest with her free hand.

"What are you *doing* here?" she asked.

Ernie stood with his mouth open, dumbfounded.

"You're CID!" she shouted. "You're supposed to be finding the man who murdered my husband. What are you *doing* here?" She glanced at the commissary, quickly turning back to us with an incredulous expression. "Are you worrying about the black market? Black *market*! At a time like this?" Her mouth hung open, and her eyes were scrunched in disbelief. "What is *wrong* with you people?"

This time she let go of her daughter's hand and launched at Ernie in earnest, reaching sharp nails toward his eyes. Just in time, he grabbed her wrists and leaned away from the assault, but she continued to come at him, throwing a knee to his groin, pushing him back onto the hood of the jeep, screaming at the top of her lungs. The little girl, Barretsford's daughter, Cindy, held both her hands to her mouth, her shoulders hunched in fear, crying.

I hurried around the jeep and grabbed Mrs. Evelyn Barretsford in a bear hug. Out of the corner of my eye, I saw that people were beginning to congregate in front of the commissary, and a few of them were trotting across the parking lot. In the distance, I heard the groan of an MP siren. By then, Mrs. Barretsford had started to calm down, and we let her go. She knelt and hugged her daughter, sobbing and saying, "You should be looking for *him*. You should be looking for the man who slaughtered by *husband*!"

A few other military dependent wives gathered around her, comforting her and her daughter, all the while shooting evil looks at us.

When the MPs arrived on the scene, even they gave us the business. "What are you doing here?" one of them asked. "You're CID. Maybe you should forget about the black market for a while and go out and solve some real crime."

"Get bent," Ernie told him.

The MP, a burly fellow, took a step forward, then stopped, apparently seeing the fire in Ernie's green eyes. The MP hesitated, shrugged, and turned back toward Mrs. Barretsford.

-3-

An hour later we were ordered to report to the Provost Marshal—immediately if not sooner. We found him out on the parade field in front of 8th Army headquarters, standing with a group of dignitaries on a white bunted podium. We skidded to a halt at the edge of the field.

"Too late," Ernie said.

A bass drum pounded and the United Nations Command Honor Guard marched onto the raked gravel. First out was a unit of the Republic of Korea Army with their green tunics and white hats, followed closely by the American honor guard in their shiny brass buttons and dress blue uniforms. Finally a platoon of Gurkhas from the British Army swung white-gloved fists resolutely forward as they strutted onto the field in their bright red blazers. A six-gun salute from a battery of 105mm howitzers blasted into the sky as sergeants shouted commands and the parade wound into formation in front of the podium. Smoke roiled across the field, cuing the 8th Army band to strike up first the Republic of Korea national anthem and then "The Star Spangled Banner."

"Who are they trying to impress?" Ernie asked.

"Some dignitaries from the UN," I said, "here on an inspection tour."

"Hope they watch out for guys with sickles."

A Korean general spoke first. I couldn't understand everything he said; the language was formal and used a vocabulary seldom heard in the red light district of Itaewon, but I picked up most of it. Every few sentences he paused, and a younger officer translated what he'd just said into English. The general expressed his gratitude to the countries of the United Nations for their support of the free Republic of Korea, both now and during their time of need some twenty years ago, when they'd been attacked by the forces of the North Korean Communists and the massed legions of Chairman Mao Tse-tung and the Red Chinese People's Army.

After a few more droning remarks by the American general, which were similarly translated into Korean, a plaque was presented to a UN civilian in a grey suit. Dutch, I believe he was. Then a half-dozen Korean women, decked out in full-skirted silk *hanbok*, placed leis over the heads of the smiling dignitaries. The pretty young women backed up and bowed deeply. More martial music blasted out, and the UN Honor Guard saluted with their silver bayoneted rifles. Then, to the accompaniment of a pounding drum, they marched smartly off the field.

The assembly was dismissed and Colonel Brace, along with many of the other dignitaries, hopped off the podium. After saluting a few generals and exchanging some smiling remarks, he motioned for us to meet him beneath a quivering elm tree. When he reached us, his demeanor had changed completely. His eyes were squinting, and he glanced away from us, setting both fists on his hips, as if manfully controlling his temper. Colonel Brace was a jogger who kept his weight down to anorexic levels as was the fashion of the 8th Army officer corps. He might have been much smaller than either of us, but his fists tightened as if he were preparing to spring forward and pummel us both.

"Where do you two guys get off," he said, "upsetting Mrs. Barretsford like that?"

"We didn't upset her," Ernie replied. "The fact that we were assigned to the black market detail is what upset her."

Colonel Brace shook his head slightly, as if he couldn't believe what he'd just heard. Finally, he said, "No 'sir' in that answer, Bascom?"

"Sir," Ernie said.

"You should've kept a low profile," he told us, "done your work without drawing attention to yourselves."

When neither of us answered, Colonel Brace continued. "I'm putting you back on Sergeant-of-the-Guard duty, effective immediately. Report to the MP Station after evening chow. You'll be on that detail every night until further notice."

"No more black market?" Ernie asked.

"No more black market. And end your questions with 'sir.' Is that understood?"

"Understood, sir," Ernie replied.

He stared at us for a while, as if amazed at the human wreckage he had to deal with. Finally, he shook his head again and said, "Dismissed."

Ernie and I saluted, maintained the position of attention, and waited for the colonel to stalk away. As we watched him go, Ernie chomped on his gum a little louder. Other than that, he showed no reaction to the butt chewing. We were used to being treated as if we were lower than whale shit. It's a leadership technique the officer corps uses. I believe at West Point they have a week-long seminar on the finer points.

When the colonel was out of sight, we returned to the narrow parking lot where we'd left our jeep. Ernie hopped in, but I hesitated to climb into the passenger seat. He looked up at me.

"I have work to do in the admin office," I told him.

He rolled his eyes. "Suit yourself. I'm going to catch some shut-eye before we start the night shift." The jeep's engine sputtered to life. Ernie backed out of the narrow space, shifted gears, and roared off in a cloud of carbon and grime.

Inside the CID office, Staff Sergeant Riley was busy shouting into the phone about some personnel transactions that had gone missing. The admin secretary, Miss Kim, industriously typed away on a stack of reports that had come in concerning the Barretsford case. She allowed me to read them, both the American ones and those from the Korean National Police. There wasn't much to see: a whole lot of interviews, plenty of harassed bus drivers and cabbies, and US officers and civilians who had known Barretsford. But nobody seemed to know anything about why he had been attacked. In the entire stack, there was no new information. When I finished, I placed the paperwork back on her desk and said, "*Komap-sumnida.*" Thank you.

She smiled in response.

Miss Kim was a gorgeous woman, tall and shapely. I liked the way she held herself: poised and self-aware while at the same time quiet and watchful. I had often been tempted to ask her out on a date. What held me back was not shyness but worse. She had once been close to my partner, Ernie. At the time, she thought the relationship was serious, but eventually she discovered that to Ernie Bascom, nothing is serious, neither life nor death and certainly not romance. Now she could barely stand the sight of him. I believed she still cared for him, and I figured if I made a concerted effort I could break through those emotions and win a place for myself in her affections. But there's something about the memory of another man—especially a man you know well—that can stop a romance from developing. Jealousy, it's called. So instead of asking her out, I was unfailingly polite to her, showing kindness whenever the opportunity arose. I brought her gifts: a rose, a small bottle of PX hand lotion, candy on holidays. She appreciated my thoughtfulness but I wasn't winning her heart. And I wasn't trying to—at least that's what I told myself.

I found a typewriter on a wooden field desk at the back of the office. I rolled a sheet of paper, along with three carbon onionskins— one green, one pink, and one yellow—into the carriage. Carefully, I started to type, first the date and then the subject: INTERVIEW AT THE PX SNACK STAND. And the case: C. WINSTON BARRETSFORD, HOMICIDE.

I typed out what the couple at the tiny snack stand across from the Claims Office had seen. An Asian man in his thirties, about five ten, a hundred and forty to a hundred and fifty pounds, with a deformed lower lip; well dressed, wearing a suit and a long overcoat and apparently holding something hidden beneath the coat. I described how he stood completely still, out of the rain, staring at the locked front door of the Claims Office. I even mentioned how his nose was running and how the old woman had speculated that he seemed to be staring at some far away vision. I described how he abruptly disappeared after the Claims Office opened at zero eight hundred. At the end of the report I typed my name, rank, and badge number. Then I pulled the four sheets out of the typewriter, peeled off the carbon, and signed my name at the bottom. The original would go to Colonel Brace; the green copy would stay in the CID file cabinet; the yellow copy would go to Lieutenant Pong, the Korean National Police Liaison officer; and the pink copy was mine, to be stashed in a dusty brown accordion file I kept in my wall locker back in the barracks.

I dropped the reports into Riley's in-basket, stuffed my copy into my pocket, and nodded my goodbye to Miss Kim.

Nobody else noticed me leave, which was good because if they'd asked me where I was going, I would've been reluctant to admit that I was on my way to see someone who my old drill sergeant in basic training would've referred to as an egghead.

■   ■   ■

The military doesn't trust intellectualism. The honchos of 8th Army only appreciate raw facts and actions based on those facts. Anyone who hunts for motive by delving into the recesses of the human mind is either laughed at or, more often, ignored.

I stood in a small office at the end of a long hallway in the western wing of the 121st Evacuation Hospital. The receptionist for Captain Leah Prevault was a punctilious Korean woman who'd probably been working in the hospital since before Christ was a corporal. She asked me if I had an appointment, and when I answered I didn't, she told me I'd have to make one. I reached across the counter and, before she could react, twisted the appointment book in my direction.

"Captain Prevault is free until two thirty," I said.

"Yes, but you still must make an appointment."

I pulled my badge out of my pocket and showed it to her. "Tell her it's a matter of life and death."

It never fails. Having lived in a police state for all of her life, the woman's face blanched and from somewhere in the folds of her skirt a handkerchief appeared. She swiveled on her chair and, holding the embroidered cloth to her nose, disappeared into a back room. Five minutes later, she was back.

"Captain Prevault will see you now," she said.

Captain Leah Prevault stood with her back to me as I entered the room, studying a book from a shelf behind her desk. She wore the neatly pressed tunic and skirt of a US Army captain. She put the book away, turned, and motioned for me to sit. She was a slender woman, not particularly tall but with long legs and arms she seemed to have to work at keeping under control. She sat at the same time I did and stared at me intently through horn-rimmed glasses, reminding me of a precocious adolescent examining a water bug that had just crawled out of a sewer. Her long brown hair had been pinned back so as not to interfere with her meticulous observation. She continued studying me, saying nothing.

The silence worked. I told her why I was there.

She cleared her throat and glanced briefly down at her Army-issue blotter. "I was wondering when you'd contact me," she said.

"You mean *me*?" I asked, pointing at my nose.

"Not you specifically."

"So no one else in law enforcement has bothered to ask you about the murder?"

"You're the first," she said.

I pulled my notebook out of my jacket pocket. Thumbing through it, I pretended to be reading from notes. I gave her the description of the Korean man who'd been seen waiting in front of the Claims Office.

"You think he's the killer?" she asked.

"Most likely," I said. "He matches the descriptions given by the workers inside the Claim Office, even down to the damaged lip."

"Why do you say 'damaged?'"

"It might've been a recent injury."

"But the woman at the snack stand said it appeared to her to be a permanent deformity."

"Thanks for pointing that out," I replied. "But I'm here to ask your help. Are you the only psychiatrist here at the one-two-one?"

"Yes. And after I return to the States, there'll be none."

"Why?"

"Budget cuts."

"Who will take on your case load?"

She shrugged. "The worst cases are shipped to Camp Zama. Or Tripler in Hawaii."

"Do you have any patients who match the description of the man who murdered the Claims Officer?"

"We don't do Koreans," she said.

"Who does?"

"There are a few practitioners on the economy. Not many. Most of the criminally insane would be handled by the Korean health service."

"You think he's criminally insane?"

"Either that or he's what everyone at the Officers Club says he is: a North Korean terrorist."

"But in your professional opinion, anyone who did what he did would have to be insane."

"Little doubt." She placed her hands in front of her chin, touching the tips of the long fingers together. "The attack was too unexpected, too brutal, to be anything else."

"Was he after Mr. Barretsford in particular, do you think?"

"Unlikely. If it was personal, between Mr. Barretsford and the killer, there would've been a moment of confrontation. A moment of taunting, a moment of blame, maybe even an attempt at humiliation. Instead, the killer went immediately to work, as if he wanted to blot Barretsford from the universe. The Eighth Army Claims Officer represented something to him. What exactly, I couldn't speculate— not without a thorough examination."

"Come on, Doctor. There's no way we can examine him. I need you to stick your neck out a little. What do you think motivates this guy?"

"Unofficially?"

"Unofficially," I said, nodding.

"Hatred," she said, without hesitation. "This man has been traumatized, deeply and probably repeatedly. For some reason the Chief of the Eighth Army Claims Office represented to him everything he loathes, everything that has caused him to suffer. Even if he's a North Korean agent, this is what motivated him. Hatred of a man who represented a system he's been programmed to hate."

I started to write that down in my notebook but she said, "Unofficial, remember?"

I stopped writing and stared for a moment at the blank page. "This Korean mental health service you mentioned, can you refer me to anyone there?"

"Wouldn't the Korean National Police already have checked them out?"

"Maybe," I replied, "but most of the thinking is the killer is a North Korean agent. Not a nut case." I realized my mistake and felt my face flush red. "Sorry."

Captain Prevault stared at me. Her face was narrow with a smooth complexion and not unattractive. If a GI stared at another GI like she was doing at me, he might get his nose punched. On her, it seemed normal. Disconcerting, but normal.

"They might be right," she said. "Even considering the gruesomeness of the crime scene, a North Korean agent might've done the same, if he were trying to spread terror."

"That's what the brass thinks, yes. The more gore, the more panic."

"But you don't?"

"I try to keep an open mind."

She smiled faintly. It was a nice smile. "An open mind is not good for promotion, not in this man's army."

"No," I agreed.

"What's the saying? Get along . . ."

"Go along to get along," I corrected.

"Yes, which is why I'll be getting out of the military soon." She swiveled on her chair, pulled out a drawer at the bottom of her desk, and appeared to be thumbing through some files. She stopped, lifted a clump of paper, stared at it for a moment, and then dropped it back into the folder. Closing the drawer, she turned back to me.

"I'll make some inquiries," she said. "Do you speak Korean?"

"Some," I replied.

"That will help. If the person I'm thinking of consents to talk to you, I'll let you know."

"Just give me his name," I said. "I'll find him."

She smiled a sad smile, as if I were hopelessly naïve. "That's not the way it works. Not in the civilian world and particularly not in the academic world. But I'll be quick about it. I understand the urgency."

I stood and thanked her and handed her my card. Without glancing at it, she placed it in the center of her desk. I considered offering my hand to shake but when she just kept studying me, I decided against it.

As I was leaving, she said, "Agent Sueño."

I turned.

"Did I pronounce your name right?"

She had pronounced the "n" as the "ny" in canyon.

"Yes. Very good."

"I would like to go on a date with you."

I fidgeted, unaccustomed to anyone being so direct.

She smiled. "I'm making you uncomfortable."

"It's just that I'm an enlisted man," I stammered. "And you're an officer."

"But in the CID, your ranks are classified. No one will ever know."

"I have guard duty tonight," I said, hating myself for my tone of voice. It was as if I were conjuring up an excuse that was my last line of defense. And maybe I was. The thought of going out with an American female officer was something I'd never even considered. We were constantly being warned against fraternization between ranks.

Captain Prevault continued to stare at me evenly, but the smooth complexion of her face took on just the shadow of a frown.

"Perhaps some other time then," she said.

"Perhaps," I agreed, not knowing what else to say. "Some other time."

I turned and fled from her office.

Grimes was surprised to see me.

"I thought they took you guys off of guard duty."

"Back on again," I said.

A steady drizzle spattered the mud around us. We wore army-issue rain gear: hooded plastic parkas over weather-resistant trousers that were held up by suspenders. We stared at the same filth-filled drainage canal we'd stared at the previous night, flushed now with rushing water. But instead of somber darkness beyond the concertina wire, there were rows of yellow lights about a quarter-mile in the distance and beyond them, flashing neon and cars whizzing through the rain.

"Curfew in less than an hour," Grimes said, tossing a still-burning cigarette butt into the dirt. It sizzled in the mud and went out. "Gets boring around here after that."

He was referring to the nationwide midnight-to-four A.M. curfew, slapped on by the ROK government supposedly to make it more difficult for North Korean spies to infiltrate the South. The real reason, I thought, was to provide a daily demonstration to the South Korean people that the military regime of President Pak Chung-hee was in complete control of their lives.

"We'll do a midnight commo check to make your life more interesting," I told Grimes.

Unconsciously, Grimes patted the walkie-talkie at his side. "Do that," he replied.

I nodded goodbye and walked off toward the next stop on my rounds. My pullover plastic boots sloshed in the mud. I kept thinking about Captain Prevault. She was an attractive woman, at least to me. Ernie would think she was too bookish and too plain, but he specialized in flashy women. I didn't. Maybe I should call her tomorrow, let her know that once they take me off this night shift guard duty, I'd have more time and maybe we could get together then. Maybe I could take her to a Buddhist temple out in the countryside, somewhere that would be new and interesting to someone of her intelligence—somewhere without a thousand GIs staring at us.

As I was daydreaming, I thought of Dr. Yong In-ja. She had been in charge of the Itaewon District Health Clinic, treating the dozens of Korean business girls who needed her help every week. I'd worked with her on a cold case, a case involving an American GI who'd been dead twenty years. One thing had led to another and during the investigation, Doc Yong and I had become close. Very close. She landed in trouble with the Korean authorities, trouble so serious she felt compelled to flee to North Korea, the homeland of her parents. Later, I'd seen her again, when I'd been sent up there to try to search for tunnels that led south beneath the DMZ. While there I discovered she'd given birth to Il-yong, our son. When the three of us returned to the South, her troubles began to multiply, and eventually she'd taken Il-yong and disappeared. It had been months now, and I'd received no word from her.

I was a professional cop. I could've searched for her, and I believed that if I searched long and hard enough, I'd find her. The only problem was that in so doing the Korean National Police almost certainly would take note of my investigation. A KNP report would be passed up the chain of command and eventually would reach someone who'd realize that I was searching for a fugitive—a highly sought-after fugitive.

I couldn't search for her because I couldn't risk leading the KNPs to her. If I did, and she was arrested, she'd face the possibility—the probability—of spending the rest of her life in prison.

Ernie kept telling me that it was her responsibility to contact me. If she was very careful, she could do it. But if she wouldn't make the effort, it meant she was finished with me, and I was therefore free to see other women. It had been months now and I'd heard nothing from her. Ernie was right. It was time to emerge from my shell and start to live again.

As I wallowed deep in this morose reverie, something whistled through the air. Reflexively, I ducked. Whatever it was splashed into the mud on the pathway in front of me. I leapt backward, thinking it was a grenade. In a moment of panic, I realized I had nowhere to hide. This was it. I was done for. For a few agonizing seconds, I waited for the ordnance to explode, for a thousand metal pellets to zing through the air and rip into my body, slicing me into a tattered patchwork of bloody shreds.

Nothing happened.

I stared at the lump in front of me. It lay inert. I stepped forward, pulled out my flashlight, and knelt to study it. Just a rock, a jagged chunk about half the size of a brick. I stepped to the ten-foot-high cement block wall and with both hands, pulled myself up so I could peek over the ledge through the rusty concertina wire.

Nothing. A bare alley. I lowered myself back to the ground.

Maybe some kids had run by on their way home before curfew. Maybe one of them had seen the rock, picked it up, and thrown it. Still, I hadn't heard any footsteps. No teenage giggling.

Someone had silently slipped down the alley; maybe they'd stood still and listened for my approach. Had they wanted to bop me on the head? Why would anyone do that? I lifted the rock and studied it. There was nothing special about it. I dropped it back into the mud.

About a half hour later, I returned to the MP Station. Ernie was dozing on the wooden bench. I pulled off my wet parka.

"Reveille," I said, without much enthusiasm. He cracked open an eye, groaned, crossed his arms, and leaned back on the bench, trying to get as comfortable as possible on the varnished wood.

I pulled off my wet overshoes, set them under the bench, and tromped in my combat boots toward the back counter to pull myself a cup of coffee before realizing the metal urn had been removed by the 8th Army chow hall. The sense of urgency surrounding the Barretsford case was dissipating, and as best I could tell from the MP rumor mill, little if any progress had been made on the investigation. No suspects, no clear motive, not even a murder weapon. Even if the 8th Army was dropping the ball, the KNPs would come up with something. Korea is a highly controlled society: everything's recorded, and the KNPs have plenty of manpower. By now, every bus driver and cabbie who'd entered the southern part of Seoul on that fateful morning had probably been interviewed. Somebody would've seen something. At least that's what I believed.

The information that had somehow leaked and that everyone was gossiping about concerned C. Winston Barretsford's personal life. Apparently, he'd been less than faithful to his good wife, Evelyn. Already, one of the massage parlor girls at the steam and cream behind the 8th Army Officers Club had admitted he'd been one of her regulars. Also, the Claims Office civilian driver revealed that Barretsford had made an inordinate number of so-called "inspection trips" up North to a suspect establishment in the red-light district of Yongju-gol.

All of this wasn't unusual. Civilians, officers, and GIs all took advantage of the sex trade in Korea. During the Korean War the country had been completely devastated. Most of the populace had been malnourished and many had literally starved to death. In the twenty years since, much progress had been made: a four-lane highway was built from the Port of Pusan in the extreme south of the country all the way to Seoul, high rise buildings were being constructed in urban centers, and state-of-the-art manufacturing plants were cropping up all over the countryside. Still, much of this wealth had yet to trickle down to the poor working classes in the cities or farmers in the agrarian countryside. Young men were required by law to perform military service from the ages of twenty to twenty-three. Young women, after finishing their schooling, sometimes found employment in the new industries that were coming into existence, but many of them didn't. Those who didn't were excess. Their families could no longer support them, and there was no gainful employment to be found. Many ended up in brothels catering to Korean or Japanese businessmen, and some ended up in the GI red light districts like Yongju-gol up north, or Itaewon here in Seoul. Few healthy American males with time on their hands and money in their pockets could resist the lure of the Korean sex trade, and C. Winston Barretsford hadn't been one of them.

So far, the 8th Army had made heroic efforts to keep this information from his wife. They'd also tried to keep it from the ladies of the Officers' Wives Club. This wasn't only motivated by concern for Mrs. Barretsford's feelings. The less the OWC knew about Itaewon and Yongju-gol, the 8th Army honchos believed, the better for everyone.

I was mulling these thoughts over and plotting the various ways I might be able to track down a cup of hot coffee when the Desk Sergeant called my name.

"Sueño!"

He sat behind the high reception counter of the MP Station, holding a phone receiver in his left hand and motioning frantically with his right hand for me to come running. I did.

"What is it?" I asked.

Instead of answering, he thrust the phone into my hand. I raised it to my ear and said, "Hello?"

The connection was bad, and the message was mostly garbled.

It was a GI shouting into a pay phone in Itaewon. Something about someone being hurt and there was blood everywhere and he thought one of the guys might be an MP.

The man was panicked. I knew I had to get information from him and get it quickly.

"Where?" I shouted.

He told me in front of the OB beer tent, one block off the MSR near the Itaewon Market.

"What's your name?" I shouted, but the line had already gone dead.

I slammed down the phone

"Ernie!" I shouted. "Let's go."

He was already up, tucking his fatigue shirt into his trousers and slipping on his field jacket. As we headed for the door, I called back to the Desk Sergeant, "An ambulance! At the southern end of the Itaewon Market. Now!"

We pushed through the big double doors and trotted through the drizzle, sloshing our way toward Ernie's jeep.

-4-

An hour and a half before the midnight curfew, the man with the iron sickle pushed through the rubberized curtain of a *pochang macha*, swiped rain off his shoulders, and sat heavily on a wooden stool, staring down at the grease-stained plank in front of him.

Pochang macha literally means "multiple product horse carriage." In ancient times, before modern retailing and petroleum-driven distribution systems, independent businessmen traveled from village to village throughout the Korean Peninsula carrying their goods in a cart pulled by an ox or a horse. In modern times, especially in the city of Seoul, the horses have gone by the wayside. The carts are now on rubber wheels and can be pushed on paved streets from destination to destination. Most of the *pochang macha* owners cook hot food—like cuttlefish stew or boiled pig's blood dumplings—and sell a lot of *soju*, a fiery rice liquor, and the cheaper *mokkolli*, a rice beer. They are also required to be licensed and inspected, but they have enough freedom to move from one area to another depending on where they can do the most business. When it rains or when it's cold outside, which is often in Korea, huge rubberized flaps are folded down to envelop the cart, which, given the warmth of the charcoal stove in the center, creates a cozy environment away from the hustle and bustle of the city streets.

This particular *pochang macha* just happened to be located one block south of the MSR, the Main Supply Route, in front of an alleyway that led into the open-air Itaewon Market. According to Mrs. Lee On-su, the owner of the cart, there were already two customers seated at the splintered wooden serving counter when the man with the deformed lip entered. Both of the men were still in work clothes. Each had ordered a tumbler of *soju*, the Korean working man's drink of choice, and a warm bowl of *dubu-jigei* ladled from a bubbling pot of scallions, fermented cabbage, and sliced bean curd. The *kibun* of Mrs. Lee's *pochang macha*, the good feeling she had so carefully tried to cultivate, was about to be shattered.

Outside, the village patrol sloshed through mud and rain.

Corporal Ricky P. Collingsworth and Senior Private Kwon Hyon-up, a US Army MP and a ROK Army *honbyong*, had been assigned to patrol the bars, brothels, and nightclubs of Itaewon. "The ville," as GIs call it, the red-light district set aside for foreigners, sits just off the MSR, about a half mile east of Yongsan Compound, the headquarters of the 8th United States Army. At night, Itaewon is packed with American soldiers and Korean "business girls" and the people who make their living waiting tables or tending bar or playing music, the support jobs in the manic world of sex, money, and good times.

Collingsworth and Kwon wore polished black helmets and Army-issue parkas to protect them from the rain. Still, the lower reaches of their fatigue trousers were damp and their combat boots were soaked through. According to the other MPs who worked the ville patrol, Collingsworth and Kwon were required to walk the same route every night, up to a half dozen times during their six-hour shift. In each barroom they entered, they made sure no brawls were about to erupt and then inspected the bathrooms, both male and female, and most importantly the back storage rooms and dark alleys behind the bars, to make sure no GIs were toking up or otherwise causing mischief. None of the Korean club owners objected; they appreciated the extra level of security. Besides, in a police state, objecting would've been futile.

"He ordered a bowl of *dubu-jigei*," Mrs. Lee On-su told me, her chubby face perspiring even now on this cold evening. We stood beneath an overhang, out of the rain. "He hardly touched it, just let it sit while he sipped on his *soju*."

"Did he drink much?" I asked.

"No. He just ordered the one glass. That's it. Then he sat there, staring down at his soup, not saying anything, just listening to the two other customers."

"What were they talking about?"

"*Chukgu*," she said. Soccer.

"And all three men were still there when the MPs came?"

"Yes. The Korean soldier peeked in first, holding back the flap and poking his nose in. Then the American."

"Did anyone pay any attention?"

"No. No one did. I'm used to them coming around every night when I'm in the Itaewon area, five or six times, so I just continued my work. My two customers kept talking about sports."

"What did the man with the deformed lip do?"

She thought about that for a moment. "I remember I was wondering if he was going to eat his soup before it got cold or if he was going to return it to me and ask that I replace it with a hot bowl. I do that for my customers. No problem at all. I just hate it when they want their money back. More soup is not a problem, but the money is hard to replace."

She was a husky woman, with calloused hands and a swarthy, sunburned face. Over her floor-length cotton dress she wore a thickly embroidered pullover wool sweater. She kept her thick arms crossed, as if she were suddenly freezing. The KNPs hadn't interviewed her yet. They'd been too busy cordoning off the area and calling in the ambulance to take the ROK soldier away. Corporal Ricky P. Collingsworth still lay there, covered by a rain-soaked tarp. The medics in the ambulance from the 121 had decided not to move him. They were waiting for the 8th Army Coroner.

"So what did he do when the MP poked his head in?" I asked, keeping her on track, "The man with the deformed lip?"

"He lifted his soup bowl to his mouth. The broth was already cold. I wondered if he liked it that way, but he didn't drink; he just held it there in front of his mouth, staring at the MP."

"Did the MP say anything to you or any of the customers?"

"No. He just backed away. And when the flap closed, the man with the deformed lip set his bowl back down." Mrs. Lee seemed slightly offended. She hugged her arms even tighter around her ample bosom. "He didn't drink any soup."

"What did he do then?"

"He reached in his pocket and set one thousand *won* on the counter. Too much money. He only owed me six hundred."

"Did he wait for his change?"

"No. He stood up, opened the flap, peeked outside, and walked off without a word."

"What was he wearing?"

"An overcoat. And beneath that a suit."

"Mrs. Lee, do you remember if he was carrying anything?"

She puzzled for a moment over the question. "No. No briefcase. A lot of the men who wear suits carry briefcases. Sometimes they drink too much *soju* and leave the briefcases beneath my cart. Then I have to search it and call them. What a headache."

"Was he carrying anything else?"

"Yes. Under his overcoat. I thought he might have been holding papers. Something he was trying to keep dry."

"But you never saw what it was?"

"No. But I remember now. He was still holding it when he left my cart."

"When did you hear the screams?"

"They weren't screams exactly. More like grunts. And curses."

"Was it his voice?"

"I'm not sure. He never talked."

"How did he order the *dubu-jigei* and the *soju*?"

"I offered," she said, "holding up a bowl with a ladle." She demonstrated. "He nodded. Then I set a tumbler in front of him, and he didn't object. He poured the *soju* himself from the bottle on the counter."

"But the grunts and the curses," I said, "how soon did they start after he left your cart?"

"Almost immediately," she said.

So the man with the deformed lip had stepped outside the rain-soaked flaps of the *pochang macha* and attacked Collingsworth and Kwon as they walked away. Could they have heard his footsteps approaching? Probably not. Not in this rain.

I stared at the canvas-covered body. The highly polished combat boots lay twisted at an odd angle. Half filled with water, the MP helmet lay tilted in a puddle of mud.

The small van of the 8th Army Coroner pulled up just a few feet away. The coroner climbed out and surveyed the scene, then pulled back the canvas and grimaced. He knelt and made a few checks, then stood, shaking his head.

Ernie helped him load the body into the back of the van.

I asked Mrs. Lee a few more questions, but she didn't seem to have any other information. I thanked her, handed her my card, and told her to call me if she thought of anything else, though I knew she probably never would, especially since it takes up to twenty minutes to be switched from the Seoul civilian phone lines to the 8th Army Yongsan Compound telephone exchange.

I was about to leave when she grabbed my arm. I turned.

"There is one more thing," she said. I waited. "When he walked out of my cart, it was the first time I noticed."

"What?"

"He walked funny."

"He limped?"

"Not exactly. He didn't favor one side over the other. Nothing like that. It was strange, unlike anything I've ever seen. He walked quickly but carefully, as if every step caused him pain. Like a barefoot man walking on glass."

I stared at her, waiting for more, but that was it. I thanked her again and walked toward the coroner's van, examining the ground as I did, noticing most of the blood had already been washed away by the rain.

Ernie turned to me. "Sharp instrument," he said. "Sliced across the front of the neck, so deep Collingsworth never had a chance."

"And the Korean?"

Ernie lifted a fiberglass helmet. The entire back section had been caved in. "Blunt trauma to the rear of the head. Knocked down. Stunned. Then as he was falling, our man apparently swung the sickle at Collingsworth and caught him across the throat."

"Quick work," I said.

"Expert work," Ernie added. "This guy's had a lot of practice."

I described to Ernie what the *pochang macha* proprietress had told me, concluding with his funny walk.

"Maybe he's got an extra sickle up his butt," Ernie said.

When the coroner's van drove away, the half dozen or so KNPs ordered the crowd of gawkers to disperse. Mostly they were people who lived in the immediate neighborhood, and they all scurried away quickly in order to avoid being cited for a curfew violation. The lone investigator from the Itaewon Police Station was a sergeant of inter-mediate rank who had called the ambulance for the injured ROK MP, surveyed the scene, and taken a few notes. Afterward, without both-ering to consult with us, he'd returned to the warm confines of the Itaewon Police Station.

"What about the two guys drinking *soju*?" Ernie asked.

"Disappeared," I said, "according to Mrs. Lee. She doesn't know who they are or how to get in touch with them."

"Do you believe her?"

I shrugged. "Yeah. This was only her second night in this area. It's unlikely she's developed any regulars yet."

We studied the dark shuttered doorways and the narrow alley that led toward the canvas-covered stalls of the Itaewon Market. Everything was locked but in a few hours, before dawn, farmers and vendors would appear, deals would be cut, and eventually the wooden stalls would be loaded with peaks of glimmering Napa cabbage, piles of white-fleshed Korean turnips, and schools of iced mackerel fresh from the Han River Estuary that emptied into the Yellow Sea.

"What?" Ernie asked.

"I was just thinking. Why here?"

Ernie shrugged. "It's Itaewon. Close to the ville. Plenty of American victims to choose from."

"Why Americans?"

"To spread terror. To show us that he can strike anywhere, on or off compound. Even against an armed MP who's trained to be alert."

"And he was careful not to cut the Korean MP."

"Just like at the Claims Office. Americans only. No Koreans killed, which is why that KNP investigator got out of here so quickly."

"Which way did he go?" I asked.

"The KNP?"

"No, not him, the man with the iron sickle. After knocking out the

Korean MP and almost slicing the head off of the American, which way did he go?"

Ernie turned slowly in a three hundred and sixty degree arc, studying the surroundings of the now-dark *pochang macha*. "Down that alley," he said, pointing into the long narrow darkness that led toward the center of the Itaewon Market.

"Yeah," I said. "That's where I would go. Did you bring your flashlight?"

"Of course." Ernie patted the side of his field jacket.

"Let's go then."

"After you, professor," he said.

Ernie was always needling me about the long hours I spent studying the Korean language. But it paid off. Tonight I'd been able to interview the proprietress of the *pochang macha* without having to wait for the English translation of the KNP report, a report that would have been self-serving and possibly full of flat-out lies. I pulled my flashlight out of my pocket, checked to see it was working, and led the way into long shadows.

Somehow the man with the iron sickle had bluffed his way onto Yongsan Compound, maybe with a fake ID, maybe with a stolen ID; we hadn't figured that part out yet. But out here, at a *pochang macha* on the edge of Itaewon, he wouldn't need to go to any such trouble. He'd known about the ville patrol, and he'd known that at least one of the MPs would be an American. Had he followed them earlier? Stalked them? Picked out his victim? Almost certainly. He couldn't have made such a clean, precise attack if he hadn't. So that meant someone in the area might've noticed him. But even if we found a witness, would it do us any good? We still wouldn't know who he was or where he came from or even what his motive was. We'd still be groping in the dark.

Ernie cursed.

"What?" I whispered.

"Stubbed my toe. Who leaves all this stuff lying around anyway?"

Ropes and stanchions anchored the canvas lean-tos that covered the wooden produce stands of the Itaewon Market. The rain had stopped and floating clouds revealed a half moon, which provided just enough silvery light for us to follow the long stalls that led ever deeper into the market.

"Why would he come back here?" Ernie asked.

"Just to get away without being seen," I said. "On the far side of the market is the main drag. From there he could blend into the crowd. Make his way to a bus stop or wave down a taxi."

"Maybe he's from around here."

"Maybe."

I switched on my flashlight and searched the area. Something wild and furry scurried into a gutter with a squeal, a reptilian tail scattering a pile of wilted turnip greens.

"*Rat*," Ernie said. "Hate those damn things."

"Wait a minute. What's that?" I pointed. The beam of Ernie's flashlight followed mine.

"Hell if I know," Ernie said.

There was a jumble of wooden crates, most of them flattened, thin slats held together by thick wire. One of the crates was standing upright, the slats of wood forming a teepee-like shape. Atop that, strands of wire had been woven into a flat, rectangular grill. The entire edifice stood about three feet tall.

"Christ," Ernie said.

Hanging from the construction was a dead rat, eviscerated and dangling from its back paws, thick blood seeping from red guts.

Ernie knelt, peering at the dead rodent. "Who would do a thing like this?"

Whoever had built the edifice had spent some time on it. Wires had been twisted, cut, and retied together, and the object itself had been placed against the wall where, in the daylight, it easily would be seen by anyone passing by. In the dark, however, it would be invisible without a flashlight.

I knelt and studied it more closely. The immediate area had been cleared of debris and blood from the rat had dripped into a sticky puddle.

"It's like a fetish," I said.

"A what?"

"A symbol. A totem."

That's when I saw it, through the wooden slats, on the ground in the center of the teepee.

"There's something in there," I said.

"Where?"

I pointed. Ernie saw it, too. "What is it?"

"Only one way to find out."

I warned Ernie to watch our backs. It was possible the whole point of the display was to mesmerize us, allowing for an attack from the rear. As he scanned the alley, I gingerly tilted the base of the teepee-like structure up, slipped my hand underneath, and grabbed the round object that lay flat on the ground. It felt like smooth wood. I pulled it out and allowed the teepee to fall back into position, wires rattling.

The round object fit neatly in the palm of my hand. I stood and held it out to Ernie, and he shone his flashlight on it. It was finely grained, as if it were made from walnut or cherry wood, and sanded so smoothly it almost shone. A serrated raised circle had been carved in the center, and around the edges there were tiny white marks, every fifth one slightly longer.

"A tuning knob," Ernie said, "like from a radio."

"Not a regular civilian radio," I said.

"No, a field radio. Like we used in Nam. Like every combat unit in the country uses."

"Maybe not a field radio," I said, "but some sort of electronic device."

"Right," Ernie agreed. "I can't be sure exactly what type of equipment it comes from but something like that."

I studied the object more closely. There didn't seem to be any marks or dents on it. But these things were usually made of plastic or sometimes metal, and they were stamped out by machinery. As I studied this one more closely I realized not every part of it was perfectly symmetrical. In some spots the lines had gone astray, as if the carver had needed to make allowances for the hardness of the wood.

"Why would anyone go to all the trouble to carve something like this?" I asked. "And then set this contraption up just to make sure we found it?"

"*Moolah* the hell out of me," Ernie said, "but we found it."

I slid the smooth knob into my pocket. "Maybe it has nothing to do with the attack on Collingsworth."

"Not likely," Ernie said. "Whoever did Collingsworth knew we'd walk up here and see his little arts and crafts project."

Yeah, not likely, I thought.

We left the wire and wood slat totem behind and kept walking. At the end of the long rows of stalls was another narrow alley lined with dirty brick walls. This one led to the main drag of Itaewon. Now, an hour past curfew, there was no glimmering neon; all was dark and quiet.

"Maybe he's waiting for us," Ernie said.

I scanned the alley with the beam of my flashlight. "No place for him to hide."

"Maybe down there," Ernie said.

"One way to find out," I said. "Let's go."

I switched off the flashlight and let the moonlight guide us into the alley. Step by step, we peered into the darkness around us. No monster popped out. At the end of the passageway, we paused, listening. When we heard nothing, we emerged onto the central street of Itaewon. All the red lights were off now, and everyone had gone to bed. Up above us on the steep hill loomed the unlit signs of the 007 Club and beyond that, the King Club. Below, at the intersection with the MSR, the UN Club sat silent and somber. Except for a few stray *ramyon* wrappers blown by the wind, nothing moved.

"So what now?" Ernie asked.

"This guy's jerking us around. He leaves an elaborate clue and then disappears. Probably thinks he's smart as hell."

"He is. Smart enough to get away with two murders."

"He hasn't gotten away with them yet."

We searched Itaewon for another half hour, to no avail. The streets were silent and empty. Finally, Ernie said, "So maybe I'll go visit Miss Ju."

"Isn't it sort of late, Ernie," I said, "to be barging in on her?"

Ernie glanced at me, puzzled. "What do you mean?"

"I mean is she expecting you?"

"What's that got to do with it?"

Miss Ju was a tall and gorgeous cocktail waitress with an elaborate hairdo and an affinity for exotic makeup. A couple of months ago when she'd first started working at the 007 Club she'd attracted so much attention that the owner had taken her off serving drinks and switched her to hostess for whichever table was spending the most money. For some perverse reason, she'd been attracted to Ernie. I'm not sure what it was. He didn't have much charm as far as I could see—in fact he was often downright rude to women, but for some reason they liked him. Maybe it was his pointed nose and his green eyes behind round-lensed glasses, or the way he was fascinated by whatever odd thing was plopped down in front of him. Or maybe it was the way he looked at life; as if there was nothing, ever, in any way more important than what was happening right now.

■ · ■　　■

"We're supposed to be on guard duty," I told him.

"When the call came in, we were the only investigators available. So now we're investigating. Screw guard duty."

Ernie was right. Once the honchos of 8th Army heard an MP had been murdered, that's all they'd be concerned with, not the sergeant-of-the-guard patrol. Still, I felt uncomfortable with him staying out here. It was possible the Provost Marshal had already been informed of the incident and he'd be waiting back at the compound for our report. Ernie read my mind.

"Tell the Colonel that I stayed out here to continue searching for the guy."

"He's not going to buy that."

"Who cares? He won't have any proof I didn't."

I was weakening. "What about your jeep?"

"It's parked in a safe place. And locked."

Actually, Ernie had rank on me. He was a Staff Sergeant, and I was only a buck sergeant, E-5. Still, I often played the role of the adult. Ernie liked that. It gave him someone to irritate.

"Okay," I said finally, "but you better be in early tomorrow. A whole lot of waste is going to hit the fan."

"Don't sweat the small stuff, Sueño. See you *mañana*."

As he started to walk away, I said, "What happens if Miss Ju is otherwise occupied?"

Ernie swung a left hook into the air. "I'll kick the guy out. Then I'll go find a different girl."

He probably would, too. Ernie cared less for the opinions of other people than anyone I'd ever known. It was his two tours in Vietnam that did it to him. Death is waiting. Why worry about anything else? In a few seconds, he was swallowed up by the jumble of passageways that led back into the tightly packed hooches that surrounded the main drag of Itaewon.

I stared up at the darkness. The half moon hovered overhead, surveying the silence. I turned and headed downhill. When I reached the MSR, I looked both ways, but there was no need. At this hour, because of the midnight-to-four curfew, all traffic had ceased. The walk back to the compound was slightly less than a mile. I put one combat boot in front of the other.

The façade of the Hamilton Hotel leered in front of me. I passed it and glanced down the narrow lanes leading off the MSR. No signs of life. In this area even the street lamps seemed to have died. I heard the scratch-like scurrying of vermin getting out of my way but they were too fast for me; I didn't see them. I half expected one of the military jeeps of the Korean National Police curfew patrol to loom out of the darkness but they didn't. It was an eerie feeling, like being the last person on earth, but I knew I wasn't. This area of town, like the rest of Seoul, would be crammed with people during the day; people buying and selling and driving and walking and shouting. The people were still here but they were indoors. Quiet. As if hiding from some great beast of the night. And then I heard it.

A cough, down one of the alleys. I stopped, stood silently for a moment, listening. When the cough wasn't repeated, I stepped forward and peered up the incline. Two-story cement block buildings lined the road. Farther uphill, brick walls surrounded homes with tiled roofs turned up at the edges like blackbirds ready for flight. Just beyond the overhang of a small store, a thick telephone pole rose from the cobbled street. Behind it, I saw movement. Someone was standing there, purposely hidden. Why would anyone be out at this hour? And why hide?

I checked to make sure my flashlight was in my pocket. When we'd left the compound earlier this evening, neither Ernie nor I had time to stop at the arms room and check out a weapon. But I probably wouldn't need one. Chances were this was just some husband who came home too late and was locked outside of his home by his wife. Or maybe it was a drunk who was afraid of being caught by the curfew police.

Or it could be the man with the iron sickle.

I stepped into the alley. Off to the side, I noticed a wooden crate of empty beer bottles of the Oriental Brewery. Thick, heavy things, a liter each. I grabbed one and held it in my right hand. Then I started uphill, holding my flashlight in my left, ready to click it on.

Whoever was standing behind the pole hadn't moved. Maybe they didn't realize I'd spotted them. I continued uphill, thinking about Mr. C. Winston Barretsford, the man who'd been brutally murdered right in his office, and Corporal Rickey Collingsworth, a young soldier barely out of his teens who'd had his life cut short.

I wished Ernie were there to back me up.

Suddenly, whoever had been lurking behind the telephone pole stepped out into the roadway, someone dressed all in black.

He was twenty yards above me, uphill at a steep incline, still too far away for me to charge. Too far away for me to reach him before he had a chance to whip out whatever he was holding beneath his overcoat. He stood perfectly still, staring at me, but in the dark shadow I couldn't make out his eyes or any facial features. I was thinking of what I would do if he came at me, maybe throw the beer bottle at him. Then, unexpectedly, he took an awkward, tilting step forward.

I held the bottle loosely in my hand, ready to wing it at him as soon as he came within range. I also pulled out the flashlight, ready to use that, too. I stepped toward him, angling for position in the narrow road and hoping for enough space to maneuver and to avoid the slashing iron of his curved blade.

-5-

Instead of continuing toward me, the man in black swiveled and disappeared into the dark mouth of an even narrower pedestrian walkway. I knew where it would lead. Back into the maze of walls and hooches that made every neighborhood in Seoul an indecipherable labyrinth. If he reached those impenetrable catacombs, I'd lose him. I shouted and started to run. It was too dark to be sure, but I thought the man had tightened his hold on the front of his coat and glanced back at me just before he stepped into the narrow walkway.

When I reached the opening, I stopped for a moment and stared into the darkness. He was already gone. Somewhere off in the distance, one pale bulb shone. The path ended about twenty yards in and then forked. I ran in, glanced to the right, and saw nothing, so I turned left and climbed uphill.

The pathway narrowed. I was forced to turn sideways in order to slide through. Spider webs at the top of the walls hung down and brushed against my ears. I swiped them away. Finally, the lane emerged onto a slightly wider passageway illuminated by a streetlamp. I walked toward the pale light, asking myself what in the hell I was doing. I wasn't armed, I was alone, nobody knew I was up here, and the man with the iron sickle was clearly leading me into some sort of ambush.

Situated the way I was, there was no way he could get at me. I'd see him before he could attack, and much of his advantage with the sickle would be nullified by the close quarters. He wouldn't be able to swing it effectively, and he certainly didn't have the element of surprise he had at the 8th Army Claims Office or outside of the *pochang macha*. Still, I had no idea what he was planning. Maybe nothing. Maybe he was just trying to get away. Maybe this wasn't even the same man, although he fit all the descriptions. It was too late to go back; I wasn't even sure I could find my way back to the MSR. So I plowed forward.

At last the path spilled out onto a street I knew. It was broad, two lanes, and ran parallel to the MSR over a row of hills that eventually led to a high-rent district on the edge of Namsan Mountain. I glanced up and down the dark street. Nothing. Nothing, that is, except for a three-wheeled pickup truck, locked and parked for the night, and next to that a pushcart. I knelt so I could see beneath the truck. No feet lurking. I raised myself and started to walk forward, and then I heard it: footsteps emerging from an alley to my right, an alley so narrow and so well hidden by shadow I hadn't noticed it.

Quickly, I backed toward the pushcart. I swiveled to search for the source of the footsteps but at the same time, fifty yards downhill, a pair of headlights appeared around a curve in the road. They were moving fast. The engine roared, and within seconds the headlights shone directly into my eyes, blinding me. I backed away from the mouth of the alley where I'd heard the footsteps, covering my eyes with my hand. Then the beam of the headlights swirled, and I saw him frozen in a brilliant tableau, staring directly at me—a face with a mangled lower lip, a face contorted with hatred. Held across the long black overcoat like a scepter, the *naht*, the short-handled sickle with the wickedly curved blade.

And then the alley went dark and the man was gone, disappearing in an instant. The driver of the vehicle stepped on the gas, making his engine roar. The headlights swung back toward me. I ducked behind the pickup truck, but it was too late. Whoever was driving pulled up on the far side of the truck, brakes squealed, and a door opened then slammed shut.

"Hold it right there!" An American MP appeared around the rear of the truck. He held a flashlight in one hand and a pistol in the other.

I froze, averting my eyes toward the alleyway.

He stared at me for a moment. "Sueño?" he asked.

I nodded.

"What the hell you doing up here?"

I didn't answer, considering whether or not to call for backup and try to cordon off the neighborhood and maybe trap the man with the iron sickle. But it was too late. Such an effort would take at least a half hour to set up. He had too much of a head start and the catacombs of Seoul were vast. Instead, I sighed and answered the MP's question. "It's a long story."

"Better be a good one. The Staff Duty Officer has a case of the big ass."

"So do I," I said. "Do you mind helping me check out that alley?"

I pointed to where I'd seen the man with the iron sickle. He aimed his flashlight. It was empty now, nothing but ancient brick and string-like cobwebs.

"You spot something down there?"

"Yeah. Come on."

He followed me into the maze. We spent a half hour chasing our tails. No sign of anything.

"What the hell are we looking for?" the MP asked.

I could've told him I saw the man with the iron sickle but I'm not sure he would've believed me. Every MP craves glory. If I claimed to have seen the most wanted man in 8th Army and had no evidence to back it up, I would be thought of as either hallucinating or, more likely, making up stories to make myself seem important. And I'd be asked the most embarrassing question of all: why didn't you take him down?

"Forget it," I said. "I thought I saw something. Guess I was mistaken."

We returned to the compound.

"Abandoning your post," the Staff Duty Officer said. "Absent without leave. Disobeying a general order. Need I go on?"

"No, sir," I said.

"Well, do you have anything to say for yourself?"

"A call came in just before midnight," I told him, "an MP under attack, bleeding, no one else was available."

"Burrows and Slabem were on call."

"By the time we got through to them and woke them up and they got dressed and found their vehicle and drove out to the ville, whatever was happening would've been all over."

"It was all over when you got there," he told me.

Not quite. The Korean MP was still alive and on his way to the hospital, and, as I found out later, the man with the iron sickle was still haunting the area. But instead of explaining, I kept quiet. When a military officer is angry, proving to him he's wrong just makes matters worse.

First Lieutenant Wilson was the 8th Army Staff Duty Officer for the evening. A leather armband designating him as such was strapped around his left shoulder. He kept rubbing his forehead and pushing his garrison cap backward over his cropped hair, as if he couldn't believe what he was hearing.

"The Provost Marshal has been informed," he told me. "Burrows and Slabem are out there right now at the Itaewon Police Station."

"Waiting for the police report," I said.

He studied me, suspicious of the insolence in my voice. "That's their job," he told me.

At their core, the Korean National Police are a political organization; their main reason for existence is to support the military dictatorship of President Park Chung-hee. Despite this fact, the honchos of 8th Army allow the KNPs to translate their own police reports into English. That's what CID agents Jake Burrows and Felix Slabem were waiting for now, the KNP English translation of the police report concerning the attack at the *pochang macha*. I doubted either Burrows or Slabem could read even one word of Korean. In the past, I'd gone to the trouble of comparing the Korean version of a KNP police report to the English version. Often the English version was watered down even more than the Korean version. Important information was left out in an effort not to upset 8th Army or in any way damage the special relationship between the US and Korea.

I considered explaining all this to Lieutenant Wilson, explaining the need for first hand information, the need for American cops capable of interviewing Korean witnesses, but I was too tired to go into it. Instead, I said, "Yes, sir."

Lieutenant Wilson pushed his cap back even further and rubbed his furrowed brow. "I'll let the Provost Marshal decide what to do with you. For now, I want you to finish your shift as sergeant of the guard." He checked his watch. "Two more hours until morning chow. I expect you out there, on patrol, until then. When you're properly relieved, report back here to the desk sergeant. He'll log you out."

Lieutenant Wilson asked me if I understood what he'd just told me, and I said I did. He was treating me like an idiot, and maybe there was some justification. In the army an experienced NCO who risks reprimand in order to do the right thing is suspected of either not understanding the situation or, more likely, of having gone mad.

■   ■   ■

I was starving by the time I was relieved from guard duty, but instead of making a beeline to the chow hall, I went back to Itaewon to search for Ernie. When I reached Miss Ju's hooch, I knew I must've found Ernie because the sliding latticework door in front of her room was hanging halfway out of its frame.

"Ernie?" I said, rapping on the edge of the wooden porch. A bleary-eyed Korean woman peered out from behind strips of shredded oil paper that had once been part of the door. She realized who I was and her eyes popped open. She raised her knee and stomped behind her at something. A man grunted. Ernie.

I reached into the hooch, sliding forward on my knees, and shook him.

"Reveille," I said. "The Provost Marshal wants to talk to us at zero eight hundred."

Ernie sat up and rubbed his eyes. As he got dressed, Miss Ju said, "You owe me money!"

"Money?" Ernie repeated in mock outrage. "I thought you *rubba* me too muchey."

She slipped on a robe and stood leaning against the broken door as Ernie slid into his trouser and tucked in his shirt. "Not that," she said. "Last night you come here, you punch Bobby, you break door. You gotta *pay!*"

"No, sweat-*ida*," Ernie said. "I'll get your money."

Miss Ju was a slender woman with permed black hair twisted in jumbled disarray. Still, she looked cute when she frowned. "When?" she asked. "When you get money?"

"As soon as I find Bobby," Ernie replied.

"You make *him* pay?"

"Sure. He's the one who broke the door, isn't he?"

"Yeah, because you *push*." She mimed a two-handed shove.

Ernie shrugged. "He shouldn't have complained when I told him to *karra chogi*."

"He don't wanna go. Why he gotta go just because you say he gotta go?"

"You wanted him to go, didn't you?"

"No. I want him stay. He not Cheap Charley like you."

"Women," Ernie said, turning to me, "who can understand them?" He finished lacing up his combat boots and stood up and grinned. "Life was simpler in Vietnam."

"You mean you just took women when you wanted them."

"Yeah. Later, they'd ask for money but the two things weren't associated, you know what I mean?" He shook his head. "Koreans are so mercenary."

As we left, Miss Ju stood with her cloth robe wrapped tightly around her slender torso, glaring at us. A few yards down the road, Ernie stopped and told me he forgot something, and he'd be right back. Before he left, he paused and said, "You wouldn't have twenty bucks you could loan me, would you?"

I did. I pulled out two blue ten-dollar military payment certificates and handed them to him.

"Thanks." He shoved the MPC in his pocket and returned to the hooch. He didn't want me to see him reimburse Miss Ju for the damage to her room. When he came back, he shrugged. "Don't want no hard feelings out here in the ville."

I slapped him on the back. "You did the right thing."

As we walked away, Ernie stuck his hands into his pockets and hunched his shoulders. "You're not going to tell anyone, are you?"

"About what?"

"About me paying Miss Ju for the damage."

"I wouldn't dream of it."

"Good. Riley'd never let me hear the end of it."

In the army, performing a good deed is considered to be a character flaw.

We stopped in the open-air Itaewon Market. Beams of early morning light filtered through canvas awnings and piles of fat fruit shone in their red and purple glory. Vendors and farmers bustled everywhere, jostling with the mostly female shoppers with their wire-handled baskets slung over chubby forearms. We found the stall where last night we'd discovered the dead rat, but the totem was gone. I asked the proprietor what he'd done with it.

"*Jui-sikki?*" he asked.

"Yes, a rat." I described the wood slat foundation and the twisted rectangle of wire.

He shook his head vehemently. "*An boayo.*" He hadn't seen anything.

"The guy must've doubled back last night," Ernie said.

That's when I told him about my encounter with the man in black on my way back to the compound. He didn't say anything, just shook his head and whistled.

The Provost Marshal kept us waiting for almost an hour. Ernie and I had showered, shaved, and changed into our dress green uniforms. The mood at the 8th Army MP Station and here at the CID headquarters was somber to say the least, what with one of our own lying dead at the 8th Army Morgue. I'd only had time to jolt back one cup of strong coffee in the CID admin office, and my stomach was growling.

When we were told to enter, we marched into his office and stood in front of the Provost Marshal's mahogany desk. Behind him, displayed on three poles, were the flags of the United States, the Republic of

Korea, and the United Nations Command. We saluted. He didn't salute back, just continued to glare at the paperwork in front of him. Without looking up, he said, "You left your posts."

Ernie spoke up. "An MP was dying out there, sir. We had to do something."

Instead of barking a rebuke, which is what I expected, Colonel Walter P. Brace, the Provost Marshal of the 8th United States Army said nothing. The silence grew long. Finally, he said, "The KNPs are asking for you." For a moment I wondered if Miss Ju had filed charges against Ernie for trashing her hooch, but then Colonel Brace continued. "Inspector Gil Kwon-up. You've worked with him before."

"Mr. Kill," Ernie said.

"Yes. The first murder was committed on compound, under our jurisdiction. The murder last night was committed off compound, under Korean jurisdiction. The KNPs are giving it their highest priority and assigning their most senior homicide investigator, this Mr. Kill. He asked for you, specifically, and his request has been approved by the Chief of Staff, Eighth Army."

"Both of us?" Ernie said.

"Yes, both of you. Apparently he was impressed with your work on that last case you worked on together."

The Colonel shuffled through more paperwork, as if he were trying to understand why his two most unreliable CID agents had been assigned to his highest profile case. Colonel Brace preferred investigators like Jake Burrows and Felix Slabem, who would never dare follow up on information that might prove embarrassing. He was worried about losing control of the investigation. Once Ernie and I were out there with the KNPs, Mr. Kill, and all the resources of the Korean law enforcement establishment at our disposal, the investigation would go wherever it went, regardless of whether

Colonel Brace wanted it to go there or not. The whole face-saving cover story of the man with the iron sickle being a North Korean agent might be blown sky high.

Colonel Brace shifted in his seat. Here it comes, I thought, as he began to speak in a deeper, more authoritative voice. "Now that one of our MPs has been killed, we're pulling all our agents off other cases. We're going to find this guy, and we're going to find him immediately. Is that understood?"

Ernie and I nodded.

Blood had rushed up from beneath Colonel Brace's tight collar and reddened his ears. "You might be working with the Korean National Police, temporarily, but you are first and foremost soldiers in the Eighth United States Army. Is that understood?"

Ernie and I nodded again.

"You'll turn in progress reports to Staff Sergeant Riley by close of business each and every day. Is *that* understood?"

We nodded again.

"All right, now get out there, and get me some results."

I would've been happy to get out of there, but Ernie knew the Provost Marshal was over a barrel. The decision to assign us temporarily to the Korean National Police had been made above his pay grade and now was our chance.

"How about our expense account?" Ernie said.

"What about it?" Colonel Brace asked.

When working an investigation, we were allowed to turn in receipts to reclaim expenses of up to fifty dollars a month.

"How about upping it to a hundred a month?" Ernie asked. "Each." Colonel Brace frowned.

"We'll be in downtown Seoul," Ernie continued, "working with Mr. Kill. Things are expensive down there."

"You'll be wherever the killer is," Colonel Brace said.

"Yes, sir," Ernie replied, "but if we let the KNPs pay for everything, Eighth Army loses face."

Colonel Brace continued frowning and shuffling through paperwork until finally he said, "Okay, approved. Tell Riley."

"Yes, sir."

We saluted and turned toward the door. Before we reached it, Colonel Brace said, "One more thing. Don't think that because you've received sponsorship from someone high up in the Korean government that you can go around me. All reports come through me and me alone. No contact with anyone outside the chain of command."

"Yes, sir," we said in unison. As quickly as we could, we escaped from his office.

Out in the hallway, Ernie asked, "What in the hell did you do to us, Sueño? Pissing off the Provost Marshal like that?"

"I didn't do anything."

"This Mr. Kill thinks highly of you. That's why he asked for you."

"He asked for you, too."

"Only because he knows you're no good without me."

I barked a laugh.

"You know it's true," Ernie said.

No one else could watch my back like Ernie. And I watched his. It was the way we worked.

In the admin office, Ernie told Staff Sergeant Riley about the increase in our monthly expense account.

"Getting over again, eh Bascom?"

"We'll be hobnobbing with the elite," Ernie said. "Got to keep up appearances."

"You? The elite? This I've got to see."

"Just keep the money flowing, Riley. Me and Sueño, we'll take care of the inter-governmental diplomacy."

"You better watch your ass, Bascom," Riley said, "or one of those big dogs will bite it off."

The KNP headquarters in downtown Seoul was a seven-story monolith with a horseshoe-shaped driveway. Ernie and I pulled up in his jeep. Two young cops, their blue uniforms sharply pressed, blew their whistles and snapped a white-gloved salute. They would've opened the doors for us but the jeep didn't have any doors, just an open-sided canvas roof. One of the cops promised to watch over the jeep, but Ernie waited as he parked it a few yards away from the entrance. Satisfied, we pushed through the big glass double doors.

Fan-driven air whooshed through the foyer. I inhaled deeply, catching the familiar odor that seemed to permeate every Korean office building: cheap burnt tobacco and fermented cabbage *kimchi*. The soles of our shoes clattered on a tiled floor. Behind a circular counter another cop sat along side a young female officer, her jet black hair cut in bangs. A sign above them said *Annei*, information.

Off guard duty now, I hoped permanently, Ernie and I were wearing civilian clothes: namely the coat and tie that are required garb for all 8th Army CID agents. The idea was a cockeyed one. The honchos at 8th Army wanted us to wear civilian clothes so we could blend in, but they didn't want us looking like slobs, so they required us to wear a coat and tie and have our slacks pressed and our shoes shined. In the early 1970s nobody wore a coat and tie—not unless they were either getting married or on their way to a funeral. That plus our short GI haircuts and our youthful demeanor meant we didn't blend in with anybody. We might as well have had flashing neon signs attached to our foreheads saying "8th Army CID Agents. Make way!"

I showed my badge to the two officers behind the counter and told them we were there to see Inspector Gil Kwon-up. The young woman's eyes widened slightly, and without answering she lifted a phone, pressed a couple of buttons, and then whispered into it urgently, swiveling away from us and covering her mouth with her small hand.

"Cute," Ernie said.

The male cop's eyes crinkled.

"Easy, Ernie," I said. "Don't start making passes before we've even gotten through the door."

Ernie reached in his pocket, pulled out a stick of ginseng gum, unwrapped it, and stuck it in his mouth. "You worry too much, Sueño."

Finally, the young woman hung up the phone, turned, and gave me directions in broken English on how to reach the office of Inspector Gil Kwon-up, better known as Mr. Kill. I smiled and thanked her, and she stood and placed clasped hands in front of her blue skirt and bowed her head until her bangs hung straight down. Before we left, Ernie offered her a stick of ginseng gum, but she waved her flat palm negatively and backed away, her face turning red. The male cop glared at Ernie. Ernie shrugged and stuck the gum back in his pocket.

On the way up the elevator, I said, "You embarrassed that girl."

"*Bull*. She loved every minute of it."

When we reached the sixth floor, we stepped into a tiled hallway. Typewriters clattered and uniformed officers scurried back and forth on what appeared to be extremely important missions. I was about to stop one of them to ask where I could find Inspector Gil Kwon-up when a gaggle of men in suits emerged from one of the doors and hurtled down the hallway toward us. The man in front I recognized: Inspector Gil himself.

"You're late," he said. "Come on."

As he rushed past us, he used the American gesture of crooking his forefinger, indicating we should follow. We did. He didn't take the elevator but rather headed for a door marked *Pisang-ku*, emergency exit. We trotted down six flights of stairs. At the bottom we emerged out of the back door of the building into a parking lot crammed with small blue Hyundai sedans. One of them rolled to a stop in front of us and the doors popped open. Mr. Kill gestured for Ernie and me to climb into the back seat. He sat up front, next to the driver. The driver was a female officer with a curly shag hairdo that just reached the collar of her blue blouse. Her flat upturned-brim cap sat snugly atop the cascade of black hair. Ernie was craning his neck to get a better look at her but she kept her eyes strictly on the road as we zoomed out of the parking lot and into the midst of the swirling Seoul traffic.

"This is Officer Oh," Inspector Gil said, without further explanation.

She nodded but did not turn back to look at us.

"Where are we going?" I asked.

"Where else?" Gil said. "To the scene of the crime. The game, as your British cousins so aptly put it, is afoot. We have no time to lose."

"You believe he'll strike again?" Ernie asked.

"Undoubtedly. He has everyone on the run now, doesn't he? He'll want to press that advantage and press it hard."

Even though we'd worked with him before, it always took me a while to adjust to Inspector Gil's fluency with the English language. He'd studied in the States, not only at an international police academy set up to train allied police officers in anti-Communist operations, but also at one of the Ivy League universities. I forget which one. And he read a lot, both in Korean and English and sometimes in classical Chinese.

"Why did you choose us for this assignment?" Ernie asked.

"You chose yourselves."

When he didn't elaborate, Ernie took the bait. "Okay, Inspector, how exactly did we choose ourselves?"

"This morning, when I took control of the crime scene from the Itaewon KNP station, the first thing I did was send my men out to

canvas the neighborhood. At the open-air market, they found a vendor who told them that two Americans had been up at dawn, asking
him if he'd seen something that had been left at his stall last night. He
didn't know who you were or why you were asking, but he told my
man he'd been startled."

"Startled by what?"

"Working in Itaewon, this man sees many Americans walking
back and forth on their way to the military compound. Occasionally
one of them even stops at his stall and purchases some vegetables or
fruit. But the communication is always accomplished by pointing and
hand gestures. This American, the one who asked him questions this
morning, could speak the language of our illustrious forebears. And
speak it well."

"So you knew it was my partner, Sueño, here."

"Do any other Americans in Eighth Army law enforcement speak
Korean?"

"Hell no. Why bother? On compound everybody speaks English."

"Exactly. So I knew it was you two, already investigating, already
on the case."

"That vendor," I said, "did he give you any information that he
didn't give us?"

"He said he felt startled, as if he was staring into the face of a great
ape who could talk."

Ernie guffawed. "Damn, Sueño, I told you to shave before you went
out to the ville."

While Ernie enjoyed his laugh, Mr. Kill sat silently. Officer Oh's
narrow shoulders rose as she swerved through traffic. She said, "*I*
don't think he looks like an ape."

Ernie stopped laughing and stared at the back of her head, surprised she could speak English.

■   ■   ■

Mr. Kill had made a number of changes at the murder site.

First, the *pochang macha* had been roped off, as had the area up the walkway where Corporal Collingsworth had been murdered. Technicians in blue smocks with the word *kyongchal*—police—stenciled on their backs were working both crime scenes: dusting for fingerprints, scraping samples of blood, searching under strobe lights for hair or loose strands of material. The KNP sergeant who'd been on duty last night stood off to the side, explaining to the technicians why he hadn't secured the area earlier and called in forensics: the victim was an American, and therefore he didn't fall under the jurisdiction of the Itaewon Police station. The KNP was red-faced and embarrassed, knowing it was a flimsy excuse and an inaccurate one, technically. Anything that happened off compound did in fact fall under the jurisdiction of the KNPs as the Provost Marshal had previously informed us. However, out here in Itaewon, the local KNPs often let the American MP patrols handle issues involving American GIs. Less paperwork.

Mrs. Lee, the owner of the *pochang macha,* sat forlornly on a wooden crate. I walked over to her.

"Did he come back last night?" I asked.

She looked up at me. "What? The killer?"

I nodded.

She hugged herself and shivered. "No."

"Did you sleep in the cart?"

"Where else? But I couldn't sleep much."

I already knew many of the *pochang macha* owners were virtual mendicants. Their cart was their livelihood and their home. Without it, they had nothing.

She looked up at me, her eyes crinkled. "Will they be done before the evening rush starts?"

"We'll see," I said. I returned to Mr. Kill.

"We'll send what we have to the lab," he said, "and it will be given top priority."

"I don't expect much," I said.

"Why not?"

"This man seems very cautious. Everything is well thought out and he spends as little time as possible at the crime scene."

"Like a trained agent."

"Maybe," I said.

Ernie was wandering around on the far side of the cart. Behind him, an American MP jeep rolled up. I recognized the driver, Staff Sergeant Moe Dexter. Moe leaned out of the window, the usual broad smile on his face. He was one of the shift leaders and he and his men rotated between day, swing, and midnight shifts. Ernie and Moe traded barbs. Laughter echoed across the roadway.

"At the fruit stand in the Itaewon Market," Mr. Kill said, "what was it you were looking for?"

I told him about the totem with the grill of twisted wire and the dead rat.

"You think this might've had something to do with the crime?"

"The dark passageway through the Itaewon Market was the logical escape route. This contraption was set up directly in our path. Anyone walking that way with a flashlight was intended to see it. Then, before dawn, it was taken away."

"What do you think it means?"

"I think there was a message in it. Possibly from the killer."

Mr. Kill asked me to describe it to him in more detail. I did. He listened intently, not taking notes.

The forensic technicians were about done with their work, and Mr. Kill left to have a final chat with them. The MP jeep zoomed off. Ernie walked toward me.

"They find anything?"

"Nothing yet. What did Dexter want?"

"You know him. Just wants to poke his pug nose into everything."

"How are the MPs taking the death of Corporal Collingsworth?"

"They want us to catch the guy."

"Is that what Dexter just said?"

"Not exactly." Ernie stared after the now disappeared jeep.

"Well, what did he say?"

"He said the gooks better not screw this up."

"Does he know Mr. Kill is on the case?"

"Sure he does. Word spread fast."

"And he's the best the KNPs have."

"That cuts no ice with Dexter. He knows what the KNPs are like. If it's not convenient for them, they'll cover it up."

"Not with us around."

"You know that, I know that, but Dexter and most of the MPs don't know that. They believe when push comes to shove, we'll do whatever Eighth Army tells us to do."

"Just like them."

"Just like most of them."

After we finished at the crime scene, Mr. Kill hustled us back into his sedan and Officer Oh drove west on the MSR, past 8th Army Compound and past the ROK Army headquarters. At the Samgak-ji circle, she turned north.

"Where are we going?" Ernie asked.

"I have a lead," Mr. Kill said. "My colleagues have been questioning Korean Eighth Army employees who have recently applied for replacement identification badges. Most of them were innocuous." I started at the word, remembering again that Mr. Kill had polished his English at an Ivy League school. He continued. "The badges were worn or damaged in some way. One man, however, applied for a replacement badge only one day before the murder of Mr. Barretsford."

"You talked to him?"

"Not me, but one of my investigators talked with him at length, and with his wife. It appears that when he came home from a bout of drinking, not only had the badge disappeared from the clip on his lapel but also long blonde hairs were clinging to the material and the jacket reeked of perfume."

"Uh oh."

"The employee admitted that he'd stopped for drinks at an establishment called *Yo Chonsa Gong*."

"What's that mean?" Ernie asked.

I answered. "The Palace of Angels."

"Very good," Mr. Kill said, nodding. "We interviewed the man and his wife last night, so this will be our first visit to the Palace of Angels."

"Do you think he's clean?"

"Yes. He's just a befuddled office worker who drank too much *soju*."

"His wife must be pissed," Ernie said.

"Very," Mr. Kill answered. When the Korean National Police showed up at a respectable person's home, everyone in the neighborhood learns about it. Much face is lost.

Officer Oh wound her way through the heavy Seoul traffic. Near the district of Namyong-dong she pulled right off the main road into a narrow lane. She cruised slowly past bicycle repair shops and cheap eateries and open-fronted warehouses containing electrical parts and used hardware. At a small circle with a huge elm tree in the middle, she pulled the sedan over to the side of the road. Next to a store selling discs of puffed rice sat an establishment with green double doors shut tightly and windows barred with iron grates. A hand-painted sign above said *Yo Chonsa Gong*. The Palace of Angels.

Mr. Kill motioned for Ernie not to try the front door. Officer

Oh stayed with the sedan while we slipped down a crack between buildings that led to a filthy alleyway out back. Empty *soju* bottles in wooden crates leaned against dirty brick.

Mr. Kill pounded on the back door. No answer. He pounded again. Finally, we heard a door slam and then a voice from within. "*Nomu iljiki!*" Too early! Apparently, they thought we were making a delivery.

Mr. Kill leaned close to the door. "*Bali!*" he said. Hurry.

The door creaked open. Mr. Kill slid his foot in and gently shoved the door open with his left hand. A woman wearing a cloth robe, grey-streaked hair sticking madly skyward, stared up at him open-mouthed. He flashed his badge at her.

"*Kyongchal*," he said. Police.

We pushed through the door.

The woman stumbled in front of us down a narrow hallway until we reached a carpeted lounge that reeked of spilled liquor and ancient layers of fossilized tobacco fumes.

"*Bul kyo*," Mr. Kill said. Turn on the light.

The woman wandered over to a bar about six stools long, slid behind it, and switched on overhead neon. The light flickered and then shone red, softly but bright enough to see through gloom. The far wall was lined with vinyl-covered booths with small rectangular tables. Mr. Kill, his hands in the pockets of his overcoat, paced around the room. Finally, he turned to the woman and spoke in Korean. "How many hostesses work here?"

"Three, most nights," the woman replied, "more on the weekends."

"Does one of them have blonde hair?"

The woman, still holding her robe shut tight in front of her, thought about this. "You mean now?"

"I mean three nights ago. A Mr. Choi who works for Eighth Army was here. Apparently, he had contact with a woman with blonde hair."

"Mr. Choi. Yes, I know him." The woman bowed slightly, which meant that Mr. Choi must be a good customer. As a clerk at 8th Army headquarters he wasn't getting rich, so if he was spending freely at the Palace of Angels, that would go a long way toward explaining why his wife was so pissed.

"Who served him?" Mr. Kill asked.

"Na," the woman replied.

"She's a blonde?"

"Yes. She dyed her hair blonde a couple of weeks ago."

Mr. Kill glanced up the carpeted stairs. "Is she up there?"

"Yes, but still asleep."

Mr. Kill glared at her. The Korean National Police have the power to make any bar owner's life more than miserable. All they have to do is claim that their establishment is a threat to national morals and then they have the legal authority to shut them down. The hard lines on Mr. Kill's face showed that he was in no mood to wait for Miss Na to get her beauty rest.

The woman clutched her silk robe more closely. "I'll fetch her," she said.

"Never mind," Mr. Kill told her, holding his hand out to stop her. "I'll do it."

He crossed the soggy carpet of the barroom and trotted upstairs. Ernie and I followed.

The accommodations up here weren't nearly as luxurious as downstairs. There was a tiny bathroom with mold-smeared tile and cracked metal plumbing. At the opposite end of the hallway, Mr. Kill slid open an oil-paper covered door.

Thick vinyl flooring lay hidden beneath sweat-stained sleeping mats and thick cotton comforters. The room reeked of perfume and flatulence. One of the tufts of curled hair sticking out of the comforters was blonde. Mr. Kill pulled back the blanket. The woman beneath wore brown wool long johns. She pulled her legs up and hugged herself. Then her eyes popped open. Instantly, she sat up, her cute figure showing itself even through the thick material.

"*Wei kurei?*" she said in a childlike, whining voice, rubbing her eyes. Why this way?

Mr. Kill spoke to her in soothing Korean. "Miss Na, I'm sorry to bother you." He showed her his badge. "I just have a few questions." The girl continued to rub her eyes and started to rise. "No need to get up," Kill said, holding out his palm. "Two nights ago, you sat with Mr. Choi. I think he drank quite a bit."

"Yes," she said. "Can I go to the bathroom?" Miss Na didn't seem at all surprised to see Mr. Kill in her boudoir. Probably other men barged their way in here at odd hours. The other girls were starting to rouse themselves.

"Of course you can go to the bathroom," Mr. Kill said, "in a moment. Did Mr. Choi take off his jacket or did he wear it?"

"He wore it," she said. "It's cold down there. *Ajjima* won't pay for heat." She hugged herself again and started to rise. "I have to go to the bathroom."

Mr. Kill held her shoulder. "In a moment," he said, "after you've answered my questions."

She hammered a small fist against the wall and spoke once again in her small, whining voice. "But I have to *go*."

"What happened to Mr. Choi's badge, the one that was clipped to his lapel?"

Miss Choi closed her eyes and stomped her foot. "I have to go."

"As soon as you answer my question."

She shook her head in frustration. Silky blonde strands swayed beneath brown roots. "I didn't want to do that," she said.

"Do what?"

"I didn't want to take the badge." She stared up at him as if he were stupid. "But *ajjima* said I had to."

"Why?"

"*Why*? Some man, a strange man, was offering her money. She took it."

"This man asked her to steal Mr. Choi's badge?"

"That's what she said."

"Did you see this man?"

"*No-oo.* Can I go to the bathroom now?"

She pushed past Mr. Kill. He let her go. After poking her feet into plastic sandals, she stomped down the hallway. The door to the bathroom only closed partially so we all stood there and listened to her tinkle. As we did so, the other women scooted away from us, various expressions of suspicion and alarm on their faces. Mr. Kill slid the door shut.

When Miss Na returned, he said, "So while this Mr. Choi was drinking, you slipped the badge off his lapel?"

Miss Na stomped her foot again. "I didn't want to tell you."

"You had no choice," Mr. Kill said soothingly. "You had to go to the bathroom."

The girl pouted.

"How did you get the badge?" Mr. Kill asked.

"It was easy," Miss Na told. "Choi *ajjosi* gets so drunk." Her button nose crinkled.

We left the bedroom and hurried downstairs. The older woman had changed into a long velvet house dress, combed her hair back and sat at the bar smoking. When Mr. Kill walked up to her she said, "He didn't tell me his name." Kill stood next to her, his hands in his pockets, glaring at her. As if discussing the weather, she continued. "He offered me twenty thousand *won* if I would get Mr. Choi's badge for him."

"How did he know Choi would be here?"

"He followed him. But we didn't steal it."

"How did you get it then?"

"We waited until Choi *Sonseingnim* was very drunk and then I had Miss Na ask him if he would give it to us. He did."

"And you sold the badge for twenty thousand *won*?"

"You think I'm a fool?" She puffed her cigarette, blew out the smoke and said, "I sold it to him for forty thousand."

-6-

When we returned to the CID Detachment, Miss Kim handed me a pink phone message printed in her precise hand. The caller was Captain Prevault. As she handed it to me she gazed at me inquiringly, a slight smile on her lips, wondering, I imagined, who this cultured woman was who called. I thanked her but didn't answer her unspoken question.

I found a phone in the back of the detachment that wasn't being used. I dialed. No answer. As the phone was ringing, Riley shouted at me.

"Sueño! Bascom! About time you got your butts back here. You have ten minutes to get over to the ROK MND." The Ministry of National Defense. "They're having a briefing on what they know so far about this North Korean agent."

I set the phone down and walked toward his desk. "What North Korean agent?"

Riley put his hands on his narrow hips, staring at me, letting his eyes cross. "The man with the iron sickle, for Christ's sake. The guy you're looking for."

"They've got him?"

"I don't know about all that. All I know is that the Provost Marshal will be there and the Commander of the Five-Oh-First Counter Intelligence unit and your sorry presence is *mandatory*."

"Mandatory" was a word Riley dearly loved. He caressed the word, filtering it through his yellow, crooked teeth.

"Better belay that, Bascom," Riley said to Ernie, who was lazily pouring himself a cup of coffee. "If you're not there by fourteen thirty hours your ass is grass."

Ernie stirred sugar into his coffee. Ten minutes later we sauntered toward his jeep. I glanced once again at the message from Captain Prevault and stuffed it in my pocket.

A ton of brass sat in the first few rows of the auditorium, the Korean officers looking relaxed, the American officers less so, out of their element in this oddly proportioned building reeking of *kimchi*. The seats were too small for Caucasian bodies. On the stage was a female ROK Army officer wearing a tight green skirt and a matching tunic, a woman so statuesque and beautiful that not one man in the room could tear his eyes from her. Her name was Major Rhee Mi-sook. I'd met her, if that was the right word, during my one and only sojourn into the Communist state of North Korea. There, she'd worn the brown uniform with red epaulettes of the North Korean People's Army and her rank was Senior Captain, a rank that didn't even exist in the South Korean army. As beautiful as she was, she repelled me viscerally. My stomach knotted just looking at her. She'd been pursuing me—or pretending to pursue me—in her capacity as a North Korean counter-intelligence operative. When I managed to escape back to South Korea where I'd been debriefed, she showed up again, this time in Seoul, this time wearing her South Korean army uniform.

I'd reported what I knew about her but I was told to keep quiet. I protested. How could we allow a North Korean intelligence officer to operate in our midst? She was a double agent, I was told, working for the South Korean government, our allies, and only pretending to work for the North Koreans. I was ordered to let it go at that.

They could say she was on the South Korean side but I'd seen her operate in the north, and I didn't believe anyone could fake that much love for the Dear Leader and that much avidity in her work. I had the scars to prove it.

Now that same Rhee Mi-sook was in charge of the hunt—on the ROK Army side—for the man with the iron sickle. Someone with stars on his shoulders—whoever had appointed her to this job—also had stars in his eyes, dazzled by her charm. As I watched her, it was easy to see why.

Major Rhee strode back and forth across the stage on her black stiletto heels, rapping her stainless steel pointer against charts and graphs, speaking every sentence first in Korean and then in sweetly pronounced English.

"There is no doubt," she told the audience, "that the man who murdered Mr. Barretsford and the man who murdered Corporal Collingsworth are one and the same person. And there is also no doubt that he is a highly competent and thoroughly trained professional sent south by the North Korean bandit government to sew dissension between our ROK/US alliance. This," she said, peering into the eyes of the silent officer corps, "shall not be allowed."

The group broke into spontaneous applause.

"What is this," Ernie said, leaning close to me, "a freaking strip show?"

"Quiet," I replied.

"If she starts unbuttoning her tunic," he told me, "these guys are going to go nuts."

Ernie was right about one thing, the ROK Army was pulling out all the stops. They had their best up there delivering the briefing because they weren't taking any chances of allowing a couple of murders to damage the special relationship between South Korea and the US. Too much money was at stake. Hundreds of millions of dollars of military and economic aide passed each year from the American treasury to the ROK government, and if stories managed to make their way into newspapers back in the States about how our brave boys overseas were being brutally murdered by evil foreigners, that could jeopardize the steady flow of cash. Blaming the murders on the North Koreans had the effect of solidifying our alliance. It gave us a common goal. Stop the Commies.

Mr. Kill was not there, nor were any representatives of the Korean National Police. They and the ROK Army worked independently. By the amount of olive drab in the room, however, it was apparent the 8th Army had thrown their lot in firmly with the ROK Army.

Major Rhee was replaced at the podium by a senior officer, a husky middle-aged general brandishing a gold-plated pointer. The ROKs were good enough showmen to keep Major Rhee up on stage, sitting in a straight-backed chair, her long legs crossed and glistening beneath the overhead lights.

When the general had said his piece, the show was over. Officers filtered out. Not one item of hard evidence had been presented, only innuendo, such as the fact that there were a suspected two to three thousand North Korean agents in South Korea, and that their training included wielding mundane weapons like the *naht* and other farm implements. We were reminded they were experts at creating and using false identification, not to mention experts at survival, escape, and evasion.

None of this proved the man with the iron sickle was a North Korean agent. He might be, but also he might not.

The Provost Marshal spotted Ernie and me. When he didn't gesture for us to join him, we made a quick retreat.

Just before leaving the auditorium, I stopped and looked back.

The woman I had known as Senior Captain Rhee Mi-sook still stood on the podium, her arms crossed. Our eyes met. She didn't smile. She wasn't the smiling type. Her face was hard, cold, but hideously beautiful.

After leaving the ROK Ministry of National Defense, Ernie turned left toward the Samgakji Circle and then south toward Han River Bridge Number One. Halfway there, he hung a left and entered the back entrance of Yongsan Compound South Post. An MP I didn't know stopped us at the gate and checked our dispatch.

"You headed to the morgue?"

"Eventually everybody is," Ernie said.

"No, I mean now."

"Why would we go there?"

The MP shrugged. "Seems like that's where everyone's going."

"What do you mean 'everyone'?"

"All the MPs."

He waved us through, Ernie stepped on the gas, and the jeep surged through the gate.

"What the hell was that all about?" I asked.

"There's a lot of hard feelings about Collingsworth. Maybe some people are stopping over there to pay their respects."

"Maybe. Not a bad idea. I want to look at the body again anyway."

Ernie shrugged but turned right after the 121 Evacuation Hospital, heading for the morgue.

There were three MP jeeps parked out front.

"A convention," Ernie said,

He parked and locked the jeep and we walked past the wooden sign stenciled with the words MORGUE, 8TH UNITED STATES ARMY. We pushed through double doors into an air conditioned environment. The white smocked clerk at the front counter checked our badges.

"Collingsworth?" he said.

We nodded.

"Join the crowd. There's a few of them back there."

And he was right. A half dozen uniformed MPs stood inside the cold locker. One of the long metal cabinets had been pulled out of the wall, displaying a shroud with a body underneath.

As we walked down the central corridor, the MPs stared at us. Ernie nodded to them because we knew most of them. All of them had taken off their helmets and tucked them under their arms. Everyone was armed, with black holsters hanging off canvas web belts.

"He was a good man," Ernie said.

They continued to stare, but no one responded. Then, single file, they marched out of the room.

After they left, Ernie said, "What the hell's the matter with them?"

I stared at the body beneath us. "They figure since we're CID we should've caught the man with the iron sickle after the first murder. Then maybe Collingsworth would still be alive."

"We weren't even on the case until this morning."

"They don't give a shit about that."

We were used to hard feelings. From the MPs' point of view, we Criminal Investigation agents got all the glory, and they did all the grunt work. Ernie shrugged it off. He gestured toward the body. "You want to do the honors?"

I took a deep breath, reached in, grabbed the edge of the heavy cotton shroud, and whipped it back.

Collingsworth stared straight up at us, his blue eyes open, shining with light almost as if he were alive. But his skin was pasty, his cheeks slack, and now that the blood had been washed away, the wound was nauseatingly apparent. Like a cloud of gas, the odor reached us: meaty, sour, dead. Grey tubes of flesh stuck out of a slash in the neck. Blood coagulated around the edges of the wound and it was so wide—about four inches—and so deep that every artery and vein and esophageal passageway stood out as clearly as a drawing in *Grey's Anatomy*.

Ernie looked away. "So what are we here for, anyway?"

"Just to see if there's something I missed out at the crime scene. I was sort of hyper out there."

I studied the wound more carefully. It was on the left side of his neck, starting almost at the spine and slicing forward. This was consistent with the wound on Barretsford at the 8th Army Claims office. They seemed to have been delivered so fast that the victim never even had time to flinch, much less raise his hands to ward off the blow. Apparently, Collingsworth heard something, he turned to look back, and the tip of the blade caught him in his neck, the *naht* slicing forward. Simultaneously, Collingsworth continued to turn and flinched backward. This had the untoward effect of causing the blade to slice even deeper into Collingsworth's neck, severing his air passage and the carotid artery. Blood would've gushed out, pumping like a hose spewing water. Some of it would've landed on the attacker, on his coat, on his shirt. The killer must've been standing too close to avoid it, not like at the Claims Office, where he was reaching forward across Barretsford's desk. This time, instead of continuing the attack in a frenzied manner, as he had on Barretsford, the man with the iron sickle backed off. There was only one slice, one wound, but it was a lethal one. He would've known that. He showed discipline, not madness. Knowing Collingsworth was a dead man, he departed immediately, as if concerned about being caught.

I pulled the shroud down further and examined Collingsworth's arms. Untouched. No cuts or bruises. He'd never seen the blade coming.

This was a disciplined and skilled assassination, giving credence to the ROK Army theory that the man with the iron sickle was a highly trained agent. But why had he lingered at the Claims Office? Had he not been sure a fatal blow had been struck? Or was he merely enjoying himself? Enjoying the kill? Or enjoying some other type of emotion? Lust? Revenge? Hate?

"You seen enough?" Ernie asked.

I nodded. He pulled the shroud back over Collingsworth's open blue eyes.

Outside, the three MP jeeps were still parked. A fourth had joined them. When we pushed through the morgue's double doors, all the MPs in every jeep climbed out and strode toward us. We stopped on the steps. Staff Sergeant Moe Dexter took the lead. He had both thumbs hooked over his web belt, and he was leaning back, a big smile on his round face. He was always smiling and always joking, even when he arrested someone. It was the way he dealt with life, the way he defused tough situations and the way he relaxed a miscreant right up to the moment before he jammed his baton in his gut.

"Sweeno," he said, purposely mispronouncing my name. "And Agent Ernestine. How are my two favorite CID pukes doing this fine afternoon?"

"Get bent, Dexter," Ernie said.

"Oh," he said in a falsetto voice. "Are you going to bend me over? How thrilling."

Ernie walked down the steps, and I followed. When Dexter didn't get out of the way, Ernie shoved him.

Dexter staggered back in mock alarm. "Oh, rough stuff. How *could* you?"

The eight MPs followed us to our jeep. Ernie and I were about to climb in but stood waiting for them, staring them down. The smile had dropped from Dexter's face. He stared at us through tinted rectangular glasses.

"When you have a lead on this guy," he said, "you point him out to us. None of this playing footsy with the KNPs, none of this showing respect to their bullshit judicial system. This guy killed an MP." Dexter jammed his thumb over his shoulder. "He was one of our own, and you're MPs too, or you used to be. Once you find him, you turn the guy over to us," he said, "not to the ROK Army, not to the Korean National Police."

There was a long silence. "I can't do that," I said.

"Why?" Dexter said, stepping closer. "Because you're too close to the Koreans? Because you speak their freaking language and eat that foul-smelling shit they put in their mouths? Is that why, Sweeno, because you think you're better than us? Better than regular GIs?"

"There's nothing regular about you, Dexter," I said.

"Not without using Ex-Lax," Ernie added.

Dexter threw his helmet at Ernie. Ernie dodged it but slid around to the front of the jeep, and before anyone could stop them, the two men were trading blows. Dexter's hard left jab slid off Ernie's ear, leaving Ernie close enough to land a right uppercut to the taller man's ribs. I jumped in, holding the two men apart. Some of the more level-headed MPs grabbed Dexter.

"Don't you betray us," Dexter shouted, spewing spit. "Don't you throw your lot in with people who ain't our people. You understand me, Sweeno?"

Without answering, I shoved Ernie into the passenger seat, stalked to the other side of the jeep, and climbed behind the steering wheel. I started the jeep and bulled forward through the MPs, kicking up gravel as I gunned the little jeep out of the parking lot.

I drove to the CID office and got out. Ernie had calmed down a little and he was smiling, trying to pretend Dexter's taunts hadn't effected him. He slid into the driver's seat and told me he'd meet me in the ville at twenty hundred hours. Before he left, I said, "You're not hurt, are you?"

"From that puke? No way." He gunned the jeep's engine and sped off.

Inside the office, both Miss Kim and Riley had already gone home. I picked up a phone and tried Captain Prevault's number. Still no answer. It figured there wouldn't be since the cannon had gone off signifying the end of the duty day. I used Riley's Rolodex and then called the duty officer at 8th Army Billeting. I identified myself, gave him my badge number, and asked for the location of Captain Prevault's BOQ, Bachelor Officer Quarters. He gave it to me. Yongsan Compound South Post, female BOQ 132, Unit 4. A pretty good walk but one I could manage.

A half hour later, I stood in a long central corridor lined with individual rooms and knocked on the door of Unit 4. It took a few minutes but eventually darkness covered the peephole. The door opened slightly, a security chain drawing taut. A smooth-complexioned face peeked out, hair wrapped in a white towel.

"Agent Sueño," she said.

"Yes, ma'am."

"You didn't call."

"I tried."

"Wait a minute. I have to get dressed."

She closed the door. I stepped back and leaned against the far wall. Occasionally, a female officer entered or exited a room down the hall, glanced toward me, and when I smiled went about her business. With my short haircut and my CID coat and tie, I didn't look too threatening.

The door to Captain Prevault's room opened.

She wore blue jeans and sneakers and a light rain slicker over a white blouse. "You ready?" she asked.

"For what?"

"For a visit to a nut house."

She smiled demurely, cocked her head, and walked down the corridor. I followed.

Our destination was in the northwest corner of Seoul, an area snuggled beneath Bukhan Mountain known as Songbuk-dong. The *kimchi* cab chugged up a winding road, past a break in the ancient stone ramparts that had once protected the city from waves of invaders: Chinese, Manchurians, Mongol hordes. Now lovers strolled along it, hand in hand, gazing down at the sparkling expanse of the city of Seoul.

"Where are we going?" I asked, staring out at the darkness.

"A sanitarium," she replied. "What you call a 'nut house.'"

"Sorry about that."

She turned and in the light of a passing street lamp, I saw her prim smile once again.

A sign in slashed Chinese characters loomed ahead and Captain Prevault motioned for the driver to turn left through stone gates. The driveway wound another quarter mile through dense foliage and finally circled in front of an Asian-style building with moonlight reflecting off a tile roof. Clay monkeys perched on the edges, protecting the inhabitants from evil spirits. A yellow bulb in the entranceway illuminated a double front door painted crimson, and all around the light, moths flailed madly.

As I paid for the cab, I inhaled deeply of the tree-scented air until the cab sped off, spewing carbon.

Captain Prevault stood a few feet away, smiling and gazing around her. "It's nice up here, isn't it?"

"Yes," I said.

She turned and walked toward the front gate. I followed. She pounded with a brass knocker. The gatekeeper must have been just inside because within seconds the big red doors swung open. A toothy old man bowed to Captain Prevault, recognizing her. She smiled and bowed back, and then we were walking past the front building and climbing broad stone steps lined with more wooden buildings. Captain Prevault pulled a flashlight out of her bag and switched it on.

"It gets dark up here."

"Where is *here*, exactly?" I asked.

"The National Mental Health Sanatorium. There's someone I want you to meet."

"A doctor or a patient?"

"Both."

The steps stopped in front of a more modern building, one with plate glass windows through which to enjoy the view and a door reinforced with iron bars. Captain Prevault pressed the buzzer. A metallic voice said, "*Nugu seiyo?*" Who is it?

"Leah Prevault, here to see Doctor Hwang."

Without further preamble, the buzzer sounded, and Captain Prevault pushed through the door. For a moment I felt I was back in my element: an administrative office with three desks, a typewriter on a table, a water cooler, a short row of wooden filing cabinets, and papers stacked everywhere. Overhead, fluorescent bulbs glowed.

The man who let us in was young, not much older than a teenager, and he wore a white tunic and matching pants. His open-toed sandals made him look somewhat less than professional. He bowed deeply to Captain Prevault.

"I called for Doctor Hwang," she said. "He should be expecting us."

I'm not sure if the young man understood. His face remained blank, but he turned abruptly and started to walk away. Captain Prevault followed, as did I.

The place was quiet. We were obviously outside of their regular duty hours, and only a skeleton crew would handle the night shift. As our feet clattered on tile corridors, I started to realize this place was bigger than it looked from outside. We turned right and then left and climbed a short flight of stairs until we stood in front of a very narrow elevator. I'd seen them before in downtown Seoul, appearing as if they were squeezed into a building as an afterthought or purposely made tiny to save money. The young man pressed the button and the door slid open a few feet. The three of us stepped into the elevator, crammed together tightly, each of us staring in a different direction so as not to wash our fellow passengers with hot breath.

Our floor said six, and the young man pressed the button for two. The little elevator shuddered and descended into the bowels of Bukhan Mountain. I felt as if I were in a coffin. The elevator wheezed and moved down fitfully. Finally, it slowed, then shuddered, and the narrow doors slid open. Captain Prevault got off first. I tried to wait for the white-smocked technician, but he insisted I precede him.

We stood in a smooth walled cubicle with a single bulb glowing above us. The bulb was incased in an iron cage. There was nothing here that could be broken, or used as a weapon.

Brusquely, the technician hurried down a long corridor. I was expecting "tiger cages" like I'd seen pictures of at the Long Binh Jail in Vietnam or rock-hewn cells like I'd seen before in the Korean "monkey houses." Instead, the technician led us through a double door into a spacious lawn with wrought iron chairs and matching round tables. Beyond that, a gentle slope dropped off into a valley lined with narrow walkways that led to stands of willow trees and small tile-roofed buildings adorned with bulbs blinking merrily in the brisk autumn air. On the far side of the valley, about three quarters of a mile away, the sister peak of Bukhan Mountain rose sharply, its jagged silhouette illuminated now by a low-hanging moon. To the right and to the left, the valley was similarly walled off.

Captain Prevault leaned close to me. "Beautiful, isn't it?"

"It's like a bowl, in the center of the mountains."

"Yes, a safe place for patients to recover. I wish Eighth Army had a similar facility."

"What *does* Eighth Army have?"

"The stockade in Pupyong."

The silent technician motioned for us to sit. Dr. Prevault strolled toward one of the tables but continued to stand, arms wrapped tightly across her chest, turning in slow circles as she enjoyed the beautiful cool evening and the fresh breeze wafting into the valley from the mountains above. Night birds trilled and wings fluttered, even at this late hour.

The technician disappeared back into the building. I studied the light shining from the homes in the valley below us. There didn't seem to be anybody moving about, no central hub of activity. So far, there were no zombie-like mad men shuffling toward us, animated by murderous obsession. I felt safe. It was quiet and peaceful.

The technician reappeared with a steaming brass pot and set it on a white towel he folded and placed in the center of the table. Then, from the pockets in his tunic, he produced two porcelain cups. With his open palm he gestured toward the pot.

"Thank you," Captain Prevault said and sat down primly. The man poured her a cup of steaming barley tea. With both hands, she lifted the cup, sipped tentatively, and then smiled and thanked the man again. He poured me a cup, set down the brass pot, and backed away.

I tasted the tea. Hot, earthy. Little lumps of barley bounced against my lip.

We sat in silence for a while. Finally, I broke the ice. "Who are we waiting for?"

"I told you. Doctor Hwang."

"You also said he's both a doctor and a patient."

"Yes. It's sort of a long story."

"Looks like we have time."

"After the war," she said, referring to the Korean War, which had ended twenty years ago, "there was so much death and devastation, so many orphans and people separated from their families, that no one was surprised by the widespread prevalence of mental illness. But it was more than that. The war had been so intense and so disruptive, turning almost everyone in the country into a refugee or worse. You might say that, in a real sense, the entire country had gone mad."

She paused and sipped her tea. In the valley below, branches swayed and leaves rustled.

"Doctor Hwang did what he could. But there were only a handful of trained mental health professionals in the country. The mentally disturbed were handled in traditional ways, which could mean by medical practitioners or even by shamans, but usually it meant they were handled by the police."

And eliminated by the police, I thought.

Without warning, someone was standing beside us. Startled, Captain Prevault rose. "Doctor Hwang," she said. Involuntarily, her right hand touched her neck.

I stood also.

A small man stood before us. In the ambient light, I could see he was *dei mori*, as the Koreans call it, bald on the top of his head with flecks of grey at the temples. He wore the plain cotton tunic and white pantaloons of a peasant from the Chosun Dynasty. His shoes were rubber slippers with the toe pointed upward. The only part of the traditional outfit he lacked was the broad-brimmed horsehair hat. It was as if he'd been in a hurry and had forgotten to put it on. He was a sturdy man, not fat, not skinny, and his face, although lined, was set in a non-committal, albeit pleasant, gaze. He bowed to Captain Prevault and then regarded me.

"Agent Sueño," Captain Prevault said. "He's the one I told you about."

Without changing his expression, Dr. Hwang performed an elegant bow, straight from the waist. I bowed in return. He didn't offer to shake hands, so I didn't either.

"Come," he said, already heading down the long lawn.

Captain Prevault's eyes widened in an expression of exasperation, but she grinned and tilted her head for me to come along. She gathered up her bag and we followed the quiet little man down into the valley.

We sat on a wooden bench hewn out of a log. Straw-thatched homes surrounded a dirt-floored central courtyard. Villagers stood and squatted, some of them clapping rhythmically as a woman twirled in the center of the circle, with a human rainbow of red, blue, green, and yellow ribbons. She chanted some ancient song and banged on a drum that was looped by a hemp rope over her shoulder. As we sat mesmerized, someone leapt out of the crowd. Women squealed. It was a barefoot man, dressed in white, raising his knees high, as if stepping over knife blades, dancing to the rhythm. He held a brightly painted wooden mask in front of his face, a mask with a huge grimacing red mouth and green eyes flashing evil.

He ran after the woman. She darted away from him but the rhythm of the music grew faster and all around eyes widened and mouths gaped as the demon pursued the shaman. Finally, she stopped and threw her arms toward the heavens and chanted as if directly to the gods. She staggered, gripping her chest, and then struggled back to her feet, as if she had just received a jolt of power. She reached into the folds of her skirt and pulled out a *naht*, a wooden-handled sickle. Using it, she smote the demon, who backed away snarling, twisting out of her reach, doing his best to avoid the slashing blade until he finally crouched and bowed and retreated from the central square. The shaman banged more on her drum, slowed, and then bowed to the thunderous applause of the crowd and skipped away into the darkness.

In the hubbub that followed, an elderly woman appeared with another brass pot of tea and a few dumpling-shaped rice cakes. With both hands, Captain Prevault accepted the tray. She first poured a cup of tea for Dr. Hwang, who sat on a bench facing us.

"We like to live like this," Dr. Hwang said in English, holding a rice cake aloft and gesturing toward the village that surrounded us. "It reminds my patients of a simpler time, a time when we were all children, a time before the war, a time before so much was lost."

"All the people in this village are your patients?" I asked.

"All the people in the valley," he corrected.

"How many, all told?"

"Over a hundred."

"And they were all traumatized by the war?"

"Yes, that's why they are all old, like me."

I wasn't sure what he meant, but I had noticed that so far the youngest person I'd seen was maybe forty. "Do any of them ever leave?"

"Only for medical appointments, or if they're released."

"Who decides when they are to be released?"

"I do."

"But I thought you were a patient here, too."

"I am."

Captain Prevault had been sitting quietly, sipping tea, but she finally spoke up. "The Korean government has a rule," she said. "All government employees must retire when they reach *huangap*, age sixty-one. Supposedly, it's to make room for new blood. Most people think it's so Park Chung-hee can appoint hand-picked people who are loyal to him." Captain Prevault glanced at Dr. Hwang and said, "Excuse me for criticizing your government."

"Not to worry," he said, waving his open palm. "We do it all the time."

Captain Prevault continued. "Doctor Hwang had been working in this sanatorium since the war, and no one else understood the patients like he did. It would've been a disaster for him to leave. So, he petitioned the government and after some bureaucratic paper-shuffling, he had himself committed."

"Committed?" I said. "For what?"

Dr. Hwang smiled. "I, too, was traumatized by the war. I lost my entire family. My wife and daughter were raped by soldiers, deserters actually, right in front of my eyes. Then they castrated my son, all the time demanding for me to tell them where I hid my gold and jewels." As he related this, Dr. Hwang continued to smile evenly. "Of course, I didn't have any gold or jewels. We were starving and anything of value I had ever owned had already been bartered for food. The soldiers knew this was probably the case but performed these atrocities nevertheless. Once they were through with them, they shot my wife and my daughter, and when they tired of my son's screaming, they bludgeoned him to death with their rifle butts. Me, they strangled and left for dead." He pointed to scars on his neck. "But they didn't allow for the resilience of the human body. Some hours later, I started to breathe again, and shortly thereafter I was able to unravel the rope around my neck."

I glanced at Captain Prevault. She was staring at him, her fists knotted in her lap.

"I didn't have time to bury my family," Dr. Hwang said. "As soon as I could walk, I set off after the men who had done me so much harm. Two days later, I found them, in a farmhouse in a village about thirty kilometers away. The farmer, lying dead outside, apparently had a cache of *mokkolli* in earthen jars. The deserters had besotted themselves, after raping the farmer's wife, of course. She was crouching in the kitchen when I entered the farmhouse. She raised three fingers, telling me silently that all the deserters were there. Then she handed me a knife. A thick knife, the type used for chopping turnips. For herself, she kept a thin sharp blade, normally used for slaughtering pigs, had there been any pigs left. I followed her into the living quarters, where she attacked one of the men, and I took two. We stabbed them in the stomach, hacking, slicing. They woke up howling, clutching their bleeding bodies, guts spilling through their fingers like free swimming eels. I wanted their deaths to be slow. I wanted their deaths to be painful. They were."

His smile stayed glued to his face, unchanging.

I glugged down barley tea. After a respectful silence, I asked about the man with the iron sickle. Dr. Hwang gave me his opinion.

"He's either mad or he's a North Korean agent pretending he's mad."

"If you were me, how would you go about searching for him?"

"Well, if he's a North Korean agent, I can't help you. But if he's mad, he might've been a patient of someone at some time."

"Maybe you."

"I thought of that. Ever since Captain Prevault called me, I've been reviewing both my memory and my files. Whoever this man was, he was never a patient of mine."

"How can you be sure?"

"Because I specialize in people traumatized by the war. This man, whoever he is, is so violent and so full of rage, he could not possibly have lived these twenty-some years in our society without having previously come to our attention. This person is new."

"New to the mental health profession?"

"No. New to madness."

"How do you know?

"Because when anyone begins to enact their fantasies with such overt violence, they are not likely to live long."

"Why not?

"Certainly when you see him, you will shoot him, won't you?"

"Maybe."

"No maybe about it. If you don't shoot him, someone else will. I presume at your American army headquarters there are plenty of volunteers."

I thought of Moe Dexter and every other MP walking a beat. "But maybe his psychosis has lain dormant," I said.

"Possible. But unlikely."

"Are there any records we could look at?"

"Not centralized records. Only those that are held privately by individual physicians. Mental health workers are still seen as something odd in Korea. Culturally, my country's views on mental illness are backward. We still see it as something to be ashamed of, something to hide from the neighbors, something that can ruin the chance for a good career or a good marriage. This place was established by the government not out of kindness but out of desperation. After the war there were so many people suffering psychologically, and they were committing so much crime and mayhem, that the government saw the need to get them off the streets. At first, they were incarcerated."

"But then you came along?"

"Yes, I managed to set up this sanatorium as an alternative to prison."

"But there must've been others who weren't allowed out of prison."

"Many others. But of course there were no mental health records kept for them. Only criminal records. Impossible to cull out those who are ill from those who are merely criminals."

I leaned toward him and spread my fingers. "So what can I do?" I asked.

Still smiling, he said, "I'll make some inquiries."

"With who?"

"With anyone who remembers someone who liked to kill with an iron sickle."

I described the totem I had seen in the Itaewon Market.

"You think it was this killer who placed it there?"

"I think so. And then he removed it before dawn, before anyone else could see it."

"Draw it for me."

"Draw it? I can't draw."

"Of course you can." Dr. Hwang snapped his fingers and the same woman who had brought us the tea appeared. He was about to issue an order when Captain Prevault pulled a pad and a pencil out of her purse.

"Here," she said, thrusting it toward me.

Dr. Hwang sent the old woman away. Then he turned to me. "Do it," he said.

I took the pad and pencil from Captain Prevault. At first, I kept drawing it with the wrong proportions, so I'd run out of paper. I kept scratching it out and turning the page and starting again. Finally, the proportions seemed right, or close to right, and after some roughing out the lines and filling them in, I finally had a sketch that looked something like the item I'd seen last night at the Itaewon Market.

I showed it to Dr. Hwang.

"A rat," he said, holding the sketch at arm's length, then bringing it closer. Captain Prevault held up a candle. "And a stand. Made of wood, you say?"

"Yes. The rat was hanging from the top of the grill by its hind legs."

"On the nose of the rat; you've scratched something here."

"Blood."

"From the rat's nose?"

"No. That was one of the weird things. The blood seemed to be from another source. A clot of it, as if it had been pasted to the rat's nose."

Dr. Hwang lowered the drawing to his lap and stared at me.

"You were right about drawing it," I said. "I remember more things about it now. Things I hadn't remembered before."

"What do you think this means?"

"I don't know. It's weird."

"Weird yes, but it has meaning to the man who created it. Very specific meaning. And it is for your eyes only."

"For *my* eyes?" I asked.

"Yes. You've formed a bond with him. You're the one pursuing him. He wants you to know why he's doing all this. That's why he placed it there for you to see, and once you'd seen it he took it away."

"He didn't want to share it with anyone else."

"Precisely."

"But what could a stand with a square grill of wires and a dead rat mean?"

Dr. Hwang shrugged. "It means nothing to me, but it means everything to him. I suggest you concentrate on that. He's trying to tell you something."

"What?"

"When you learn that, you will learn who he is, and you will learn why he's doing these horrible things."

"That totem has something to do with his trauma?"

"It has everything to do with it."

-7-

We still had an hour and a half until the midnight-to-four curfew hit, but rather than taking a cab all the way back to the compound, I suggested to Captain Prevault that we stop somewhere to eat.

"Are you hungry?" I asked.

"Starving."

So was I.

The cab let us off on Chong-no, literally "bell road," named for the ancient bronze bell housed in a temple in the heart of Seoul where the road begins. We walked through a narrow alley that led to Mugyo-dong, a brightly lit shopping district that by night becomes a mecca for young people. The narrow lanes were lined with open-air eateries, pool halls, beer emporiums, and shops selling record albums, and they were swarming with revelers. The odor of crushed garlic mingled with the pungent smell of pork barbecuing on open grills. I always got lost back here, what with so many pedestrian lanes criss-crossing one another in every which way, but eventually we found a joint with an open table. We pushed our way through the crowd and grabbed seats.

"It's so exciting out here," Captain Prevault said, her eyes bright with reflected light.

"You've never been to Mugyo-dong?" I asked.

"Never."

"Then you haven't lived."

"Apparently not."

The waitress, a matronly woman in a full-body white apron, approached us warily, caution hardening her broad face. When I spoke to her in Korean, she relaxed somewhat and pointed to the menu, which was handwritten on a board behind the counter. "*Kom-tang* is good," I told Captain Prevault. "Sliced beef and noodles. Or if you want something spicy with fish in it, *Meiun-tang* would be the way to go."

"The fish," she said without hesitation.

I ordered a bowl of *kom-tang* for myself and *meiun-tang* for Captain Prevault, and a plate of *yakimandu* as an appetizer. She also ordered a bottled soda, and I asked for a liter of OB beer, after making sure they served it cold.

"Some places serve beer warm," I told Captain Prevault as the waitress popped off the bottle cap.

"Have her keep the soda," Captain Prevault told me. "I'll have beer, too."

The waitress took the soda back to the counter and brought us another glass. After pouring the frothing hops, I raised my glass in a toast.

"Thanks for your help on the investigation," I said.

"My pleasure."

We clinked glasses and drank.

I was greatly enjoying Captain Prevault's company. She was a pleasant-looking woman, and intelligent and determined to make something of herself in this world; all traits I admired. But also things that made me feel guilty. Doctor Yong In-ja was in hiding, sheltering our son. But as Ernie had so often told me, I couldn't spend the rest of my life waiting for someone who had turned the page on me and entered another chapter of her life. I had to live.

When her soup arrived, Captain Prevault was somewhat nonplussed by the mackerel staring up at her, but she got over it quickly. I showed her how to use her chopsticks to split the already gutted mackerel in half, pick out the bones, and drop them on the polished tabletop.

"It's okay to drop food on the table?" she asked.

"Sure. The parts you don't eat. They come by with a cloth and clean it up after we leave."

"Everything's so different from the States."

"Yes, very."

If she hadn't been out into Seoul much, she might not have understood how truly different things are. People on the compound interact mainly with Koreans who are fluent in English, who are familiar with American customs and polite enough to show respect for them.

Captain Prevault made me show her the drawing again.

"It's so strange," she said. "I can't figure out what it is."

"Neither can I."

"Maybe you should show it around."

"To who?"

"To anybody. Somebody, somewhere will have an idea of what it is." She used her flat metal spoon to sip broth out of her metal bowl. "Maybe you could have it printed in the *Stars and Stripes*."

The *Pacific Stars and Stripes* was read by virtually every GI and every American civilian in country. We were all starved for news from the States and the *Stripes* provided it. It was a single-fold newspaper with major news starting on the front page and extensive sports coverage starting on the back. In the center were editorials and letters to the editor. One thing it didn't cover, however, was crime. In the military, crime is classified. If the Commander believes you have a need to know, he'll let you know at morning formation, not in some damn newspaper. The only time the *Stars and Stripes* ever covered crime was if the story had already been broken by one of the major news services. Then they covered it as briefly and as noncommittally as possible.

"I doubt the Provost Marshal would go along with that," I said.

"Why not?"

"They're keeping a lid on this thing, as tightly as they can. So far, none of the wire services have picked up on it."

"And the Korean newspapers?"

"They can't print a thing until the government gives them the go-ahead."

"It seems that in a case like this what you need is the public's help."

I shrugged. "What we need and what we get are two different things."

She set her spoon down. "I can't believe you're so passive about this."

"I'm not passive. I'm trying to find this guy. But if I spend all my time and energy trying to get the honchos of Eighth Army to do what they should be doing, I wouldn't have time for anything else. Also," I said, "it would be futile. They're more worried about keeping the American public happy about our presence overseas than they are about a few slashed throats."

"Protecting the empire," Captain Prevault said.

I hadn't thought of the 8th United States Army in Korea as an empire but maybe she had something there. After all, even GIs call it "Eighth Imperial Army."

I found Ernie where I figured I'd find him. On Hooker Hill. He stood in the darkness on the narrow road a few yards away from a yellow street lamp. Three or four Korean "business girls" stood near him, poking him in the ribs.

"I see you've found your usual fan club."

"They can't stay away from me."

Without taking his eyes off me, Ernie lunged to his right and caught one of the girls by the wrist. As she squealed with delight, he pulled her close, turned her around, and swatted her firmly on her round butt. Then he let her go with a warning, waggling his finger at her. She bounced away laughing, pretending to pout.

"You give me money, GI," she said, rubbing her rear end. "*Apo*." It hurts.

"I'll show you *apo*," Ernie replied. "A whole world of *apo*."

Most of the girls on Hooker Hill were teenagers, not much younger than the American GIs. The reason they lurked back there in the darkness was so they could escape into the narrow pedestrian lanes if any Korean cops came by. They were under eighteen, the legal age to apply for a "VD card" in Korea. And without an updated VD card, stamped and approved by the Itaewon Health Service, they couldn't enter the brightly lit bars and nightclubs that lined the main drag of Itaewon.

"What'd you find out?" I asked.

"I've been talking to business girls all night," Ernie said, "here and in the clubs, and to the bartenders and the waitresses. So far, nothing. Nobody saw a Korean man in a black suit, holding something under his coat, with a puffed lower lip and the sniffles, and a funny walk."

Unless they worked there, the bars and nightclubs of Itaewon were off limits to Korean civilians. The ROK government had designated them as for "foreign tourists" only. Since Korea had little or no tourism, the "tourists" were all Amercian GIs.

"We know he passed through here," I told Ernie, "maybe on his way to the *pochang macha* and almost certainly during his escape. If he stopped, he would've been noticeable."

"Apparently he didn't stop," Ernie said. "He just kept moving."

Many people who aren't hookers or nightclub workers or

American GIs do pass through Itaewon—little old ladies walking with canes, commuters on their way to work, kids on their way home from school wearing black uniforms with huge book bags strapped to their backs—but like Ernie said, they just keep moving. If that's what the man with the iron sickle did, it's possible no one noticed him.

I was quiet, thinking over the possibilities, when Ernie said, "How was your date with Captain Prevault?"

"It wasn't a date." He raised an eyebrow. "We went to a mental sanatorium, north of the city." I told him who we'd talked to and what we'd done.

"Did you walk her home?" Ernie asked.

"No. She got off at Gate Five. She insisted she was fine and she'd make her way back to the BOQ on her own."

"You should've walked her to her room. Who knows? Maybe she would've invited you in. A medical doctor over here on a thirteen-month tour—must get lonely for her sometimes."

I was trying to think of a retort, but I gave up and pulled the drawing out of my pocket. I handed it to Ernie.

"What's this?" he asked, twisting it to catch the dim light. "The dead rat?" he asked. "The one we saw tied to that contraption in the Itaewon Market?"

"The same."

"Who drew this?"

"I did."

"Not bad."

"It took a lot of tries."

I took the drawing back from him and showed it to the business girls who had wandered over, curious. One of them crinkled her nose. "*Igot myoya?*" What the hell is this?

"*An boasso?*" I asked. You never saw it before?

"*An boasso.*" They all shook their heads. Patiently, I described the man in the black coat, but they claimed never to have seen anyone matching the description.

We had about a half hour left before curfew. In that time, Ernie and I canvassed the area in front of the road that leads to the Itaewon Market and beyond that the spot where the *pochang macha* was still parked. All we got for our work were negative responses. On the way back to the compound I showed Ernie the alleyway where I'd seen someone who matched the description of the man with the iron sickle.

"Maybe it wasn't him," Ernie said.

"Maybe not." But I didn't really believe that.

We kept walking. The Main Supply Route was almost deserted, metal shutters pulled down and locked in front of all the shops. On the road that veered off toward Namsan Tunnel, a white military jeep cruised slowly by.

"White mice," Ernie said.

They were the branch of government security that patrolled the city from midnight to four, making sure no one violated the national curfew. During that time, they had the authority to stop and arrest anyone on the streets, and if the person tried to flee, they had the right to shoot to kill. After the white mice passed, I turned and gazed back down the road toward Itaewon. A dark sedan, its lights off, sat on the edge of the road across from the Hamilton Hotel.

"Who's that?" I asked.

Ernie turned around. "Don't know. A government sedan of some sort or they wouldn't be out this late."

We hoofed it all the way to Gate Five and once there had to flash not only our military identification to the guard but also our Criminal Investigation badges. It was already fifteen minutes past midnight. CID agents are allowed to break the curfew. If we were regular GIs, we would've spent the night in the MP station.

Once inside the gate, I glanced back through the chain link fence. The same sedan, or one that looked very much like it, cruised past.

I was up early the next morning, even before the chow hall opened its doors. I slipped into the big military kitchen through the back loading dock and talked one of the cooks into letting me fill my canteen cup with coffee from the big metal urn. He waved me away, too busy dumping potatoes into a greased pan to argue. With my hot java, I walked downhill in the darkness through the quiet, tree-lined streets of the 8th Army headquarters compound. The air was cool and calm and the world seemed fresh. I love mornings, especially in this country the ancients had called the land of the morning calm.

At the 8th Army CID office, I used my key to get in and switched on the overhead fluorescent lights. While they were still buzzing, I walked down the hallway to the Provost Marshal's conference room. Records from the Claims Office were stacked on a huge table.

I pulled up a chair, set my tin of coffee down, and started going through them. The CID agents in charge of the search had been thorough. They'd created a master list of the various claims sorted by date, type, and resolution. They were most interested in the claims processed in the last few years that were amongst the twenty or so percent that had been denied. Almost all of the denied claims had been appealed to the full Status of Forces Committee, the final arbiter in 8th Army Claims cases. The vast majority of those appealed had been denied again. I read that stack first, the failed claims, the ones most likely to have left the initially optimistic claimants frustrated, stymied, and maybe outraged.

The claims read like Greek tragedies, almost all of the suffering caused by the collision of cultures between 8th Army GIs and Korean civilians. There were complaints about straw-thatched roofs set on fire by stray mortar rounds, crops flooded by breached irrigation channels, farmers injured by careening American jeeps, underage school girls becoming pregnant at the hands of Americans, old men being assaulted and robbed by bands of rogue US soldiers. And these were the ones that hadn't been sustained. The evidence wasn't there to substantiate the claims so they were turned down. It figured these people would be the most aggrieved, that they would be the most likely to seek revenge. There must've been fifty cases in the pile.

The list was being turned over to the KNP Liaison office. They would further task local KNP precincts to hunt down these frustrated claimants and investigate them to see if they had any participation in the murder of the 8th Army Claims Officer or the throat slashing of Corporal Collingsworth. I riffled through the files, each and every one of them. Nothing jumped out at me.

The rest of the table was stacked with more files, like a small mountain range. These were the hundreds of cases that had been adjudicated in the complainant's favor. So far, there weren't any plans to investigate any of these. But wasn't it possible that someone who'd won their case was still aggrieved because the compensation they received didn't match their loss? Possible, but the ones who'd been turned down seemed the logical starting point.

I sighed and returned to the admin office. Staff Sergeant Riley was in early, as usual, and he'd already plugged in the percolator, and it was busy brewing a couple of gallons of PX-bought coffee. We listened to it bubble.

"You getting anywhere in your investigation?" Riley growled.

I shrugged. "I don't know."

"You better. Your butt is on the line here."

"How so?"

"The Provost Marshal didn't like being pushed into appointing you and your screw-off buddy to this investigation. He wants results.

Otherwise, he'll replace you faster than it takes to type up reassignment orders to the DMZ."

The DMZ is like purgatory, neither heaven nor hell. Just a long line of machine guns, concertina wire, and land mines with 700,000 North Korean Communist soldiers on one side and 400,000 ROK and US soldiers on the other.

"The DMZ? Why would he send us up there?"

"To teach you a lesson about how to follow orders."

"We're following orders."

"But when you're out there," Riley said, pointing at some unknowable distance, "investigating crime, you've got to be able to understand the meaning behind the orders."

"Which is?"

"Don't embarrass the Command. And make sure your investigation comes out where they want it to, which means make sure the man with the iron sickle is a North Korean agent."

"Even if he's not?"

"Anybody who does what he's done *has* to be a North Korean agent."

"How so?"

"Because he's screwing us up," Riley said. "He's messing with the Eighth United States Army."

I should've said something rude back to him. He expected me to. GI etiquette. Instead, I sat silently until the coffee was done and poured myself a large cup. I was halfway through when I realized what I'd missed. I returned to the conference room, pulled out my pad and my pen, and wrote down an address.

The phone rang on Riley's desk. His whiskey soaked voice said, "Yeah?" He paused for a moment and then, "*What* crime site?" He pulled a pencil out from behind his ear and started jotting something on a piece of paper. "They destroyed a *pochang whatta*?"

I set down my coffee cup and had already reached the door before he finished.

"Near the Itaewon Market," Riley shouted after me. "At the crime site."

The *pochang macha* was trashed.

I examined the wreckage. Not only had it been tilted over on its side and then turned upside down, but many of the cooking utensils had been bent and the porcelain serving bowls smashed. Pulverized drinking tumblers lay in glassy circular piles.

Mr. Kill picked his way through the wreckage.

"Someone took their time," I said.

"Yes," he agreed. "They not only turned over the cart, they then used some sort of club to systematically smash everything that was breakable."

"And stomp on the smaller items."

He nodded, agreeing with me. "They must've worn thick-soled shoes."

Like Army jump boots, I thought. "What about Mrs. Lee?"

"She was in a safe place," Mr. Kill replied.

Ernie drove up in his jeep, screeched to a halt, and jumped out. "What the hell?" he said.

"Exactly," I replied.

"Anybody hurt?"

I shook my head.

"The ville patrol must've seen who did it," he said.

We looked at Mr. Kill. He stared steadily back at us. "Your American military 'ville patrol,' as you call it, made no such report. Neither did the KNPs. It wasn't until a citizen walked into the Itaewon Police station about zero five thirty this morning that a report was filed."

"We came by here," I said, "a few minutes before curfew. The stand was intact."

"So this happened sometime between midnight and zero five thirty in the morning," Mr. Kill said. He waited for it to sink in. Then he continued. "Who would be most likely to be out during the curfew?"

"Law enforcement," I said.

Mr. Kill nodded. "Law enforcement," he agreed.

"Where, again?" Ernie asked.

"Sogye-dong," I said. "Behind Seoul Station."

Ernie knew where the main train station was. It was a landmark in the city, a beautiful domed building that had been a gift around the turn of the century from the Russian Czar to the Korean King, back before the Japanese had attained full dominance on the peninsula.

I had the address written in my note pad: *Sogye-dong, 3-ku, 105-ho.* Once we looped around Seoul Station and behind the big railroad yards, I had Ernie slow and pull over. On a greasy wooden board holding up a bicycle repair shop, someone had written, *2-ku, 36-ho.*

"Keep going," I said.

The road was lined with lumber yards and spare parts warehouses. We reached a cross street that seemed a little more prosperous. Off to the right were two-story brick buildings, so I told Ernie to turn right. When we slowed I saw we'd reached 3-ku and the numbers were rising rapidly. Across the street I spotted it: a clean, three-story brick building with a placard that said SAM-IL PEIKHUA SAMUSIL. Literally, March First Hundred Products Office. In Korea, March first was like the Fourth of July in America. It was the day in 1919 when the entire country spontaneously arose in opposition to the Japanese occupation of their country. Not that it did them much good. The world ignored their uprising and hundreds of protesters, including all the movement's leaders, were summarily executed. Beneath the *hangul* sign smaller English letters said SAM-IL CLAIMS OFFICE. This was common practice with Korean businesses. Their

Korean name was often different, sometimes radically different, than their English name.

"That's it," I told Ernie. "Pull over where you can."

Ernie waited until the traffic slowed and then hung a U and pulled over right in front of the building in an area reserved for buses.

"We'll get a ticket if we park here," I said.

"Police business," Ernie replied as he looped a chain welded to the metal floorboard around the steering wheel and snapped it shut with a padlock. As we climbed out of the jeep, people waiting for the next bus stared at us dully.

Ernie straightened his jacket. "What is this place again?"

"I told you. Of all the claim packets submitted to 8th Army, both the ones accepted and the ones rejected, this office submitted the most. About half, maybe more."

"They're mining the US Treasury."

"Yes, but instead of a pickax and a shovel, they're using an Eighth Army Claims Form."

We pushed through the double doors of the building. The foyer was clean, with polished tiles, light brown walls, and another one of those narrow elevators. I read the sign for the various offices. The one we were looking for, Sam-Il Claims, was on the third floor. We decided to take the stairs.

Behind a sliding glass door sat a receptionist. Petite and young, she was a Korean woman with a doll-like face. She stared up at us, surprised. I pulled my notebook out and read off a name I'd written down, the name that had signed most of the 8th Army Claims Forms as the legal representative of the claimant.

"Pak Hyong-ku," I said. "*Uri halmal issoyo.*" We have business with him.

Ernie pulled out his badge and shoved it in front of her face. The leather foldout was almost as broad as her forehead. The young woman blanched. A pink handkerchief appeared in her hand, and then she stood, holding the handkerchief to her mouth and, without a word, scurried away on clattering high heels. Ernie watched her tight skirt until she was out of sight.

"You frightened her," I said.

"Not me," Ernie replied. "It's you speaking Korean. They don't expect that from a big nose *Miguk*. You've got to break it to them gently."

I snorted.

In less than a minute, a Korean man in a baggy black suit appeared in the hallway with the receptionist hiding behind him. He approached us quickly, his dark eyes appraising Ernie and me, his stainless steel, horn-rimmed glasses glittering in the overhead light.

"I am Mr. Pak," he said in English.

I pulled out my badge, flashed it and said, "I'm Agent Sueño of the Eighth Army Criminal Investigation Division and this is my partner, Agent Bascom." I slid the credentials back into my pocket. "I was wondering if we could have a few words with you?"

"Is this about Mr. Barretsford? Such a tragedy. Such a fine man."

I glanced toward the hallway where the tiny receptionist was still hiding. "Is there a place where we could talk?"

"Yes," Mr. Pak said, opening his palm. "This way."

As we passed, the receptionist pressed herself against the wall, trying to make herself as small as possible. Pak spoke to her in Korean. "Bring us tea."

Ernie and I sat on a low, straight couch in front of a coffee table. Pak sat opposite us. Her hands shaking, the receptionist brought in a tray with a porcelain pot of green tea and poured it into three handleless cups. She bowed and backed out of the room. Neither Ernie nor I drank. I let the silence stretch for a while, and then I spoke, in English. "Your man at the Eighth Army Claims Office tells us you're their biggest customer."

"Mr. Ku?"

Bingo.

All Korean enterprises that do business with 8th Army have a Korean civilian point of contact on the inside. I hadn't known who the Sam-Il Claims point of contact was, but he'd just told us: Mr. Ku. This was not a formal arrangement. It was Koreans doing business in the traditional way as they mined the gold deposit that had been dropped into their midst by the 8th United States Army. The on-compound civilian workers received a kickback. In return, they provided intelligence. Information on things such as how much the annual budget of their office was and therefore how much their American bosses were willing to spend. When their American bosses were trying to make a tough decision, these go-betweens made recommendations in their own client's favor. Many of the American supervisors served a tour of only one year. They had no idea which Korean companies to work with. Their Korean civilian workers would take care of all those details, which left the Americans free to socialize with the right people and play golf with the post commander and do all those things that insured their continued employment and prosperity with the 8th United States Army and the Department of Defense.

I changed the subject. "Very few of your claims are turned down."

Pak started to smile but thought better of it and ordered his face to compose itself. "We are very careful about our clients," he said.

"You make sure they're telling the truth?"

He nodded vehemently. "Of course. We check into their claims ourselves. Make sure. Take pictures." He mimed clicking a camera. "Everything okay. No problem."

The more nervous he became, the more his English deteriorated.

"And Mr. Ku always handles your cases?"

By now, Pak had realized his mistake. "I don't know. I think so. That's Eighth Army business. Not my business."

Ernie leaned forward. "You've been submitting claims to Eighth Army for many years, Mr. Pak."

Pak nodded.

"Your business is good," Ernie said. He waved his open palm to indicate the building we were sitting in. "But some people have trouble at the Eighth Army Claims Office. Some people don't get their money. Some people become very angry."

Pak nodded, silent now.

"Someone killed Mr. Barretsford," Ernie continued. "You've been in this business a long time. Who are the people who don't win their claims? Who are the people who might be very angry at the Eighth Army Claims Office?"

Pak sat back, appearing to think about the question. Most adult Korean men would take advantage of this pause to reach in their pockets and pull out a pack of Kobukson cigarettes. Pak didn't. Apparently, he was a non-smoker, unusual in Korea. He sipped on his tea. When he set the cup back down he looked back at us.

"There are many people," he said, "who lose claims. Some other offices, maybe they not as good as Sam-Il."

And maybe the other offices don't have an inside contact named Mr. Ku, I thought, but I didn't say anything. Instead, I pulled out my notebook. Acting as nonchalant as I could, I said, "What are the names of the other offices?"

Pak hesitated but in the end he told me. I wrote down the names of about a half dozen enterprises that also specialized in filing claims through the 8th Army Claims Office. I handed Mr. Pak my card and asked him to call us if he thought of anything that might shed light on the murder of Mr. Barretsford. He promised he would. As we left, the tiny receptionist bowed deeply, relieved to see us go.

Outside in the jeep, Ernie started the engine. "Why ask this guy about the other offices? We have a list of them back at Eighth Army Claims, don't we?"

"Sure. But I wanted him to rat out his competition. In order to head off trouble, he'll call at least some of them and let them know we're coming."

"And are we?"

"No time. I just wanted to rattle their cages. See if any fat vermin scurry out."

"Speaking of vermin," Ernie said.

"Yeah. Let's go see Moe Dexter."

The MP barracks was composed of two thirty-foot high Quonset huts hooked together with an interior framework constructed of sturdy lumber. Ernie and I strode down a long row of double bunks, a few with MPs sleeping in them because of the constant rotating shift work that was part of military law enforcement. The NCOs, buck sergeants and above, had individual rooms on the second floor. We stomped upstairs and marched down a long hallway until we reached the end. The last door, like everything else in the building, was painted green—olive drab, to be exact, the army's favorite color. Stenciled on the door in black paint was a name and rank: DEXTER, M., SSG.

Ernie pulled a pair of brass knuckles out of his pocket and slipped them on, flexing his right hand and making a fist. He popped its heft into his open left palm with a wallop.

"I'm not taking any shit from Dexter," he whispered. "Not today."

He tried the door. Locked. He pounded on it. No answer. He was backing up, just about to kick it in, when an elderly Korean gentleman in flip flops, short pants, and a T-shirt hurried up to us. He rattled a ring of keys.

"No sweat," he said. He held a bundle of laundry under his right arm.

"*Anyonghaseiyo*," I said.

"*Nei. Anyonghaseiyo*," he replied. With his left hand, he located a key, stuck it in the lock, and turned.

The door swung open. Ernie charged in. Nobody there. The bed was unmade and there was a wrinkled set of fatigues thrown on a straight-backed chair and a pair of Army jump boots lying on the thin carpet. I picked up the fatigue blouse. It had the name DEXTER printed onto the nametag. I knelt and examined the boots, turning them over and taking a good look at the soles. Bits of crushed glass were embedded between thick tread.

"You're the houseboy?" Ernie said to the Korean man.

"I'm service man," he replied. Most of the houseboys who worked in 8th Army didn't like the term "houseboy." Over the years they'd picked up on the fact that in English it's demeaning. Somehow, they'd come up with the term "service man."

"What's your name?" Ernie asked.

"Joe."

"Okay, Joe. Where's Dexter?"

The elderly man looked around. "He no go. All shoes still here."

"Except for his shower shoes," Ernie said.

The Korean man nodded. "Maybe he go *byonso*. Take shower."

"Maybe."

I thanked the man who called himself Joe. Ernie and I walked down the stairs and exited through a side door that led to the big cement block latrine wedged between the two giant Quonset huts. We even checked a couple of the occupied stalls but Staff Sergeant Moe Dexter wasn't there.

"He couldn't have gone far," Ernie said.

"That's what makes you a great detective," I said. "Deductive reasoning."

There were two other buildings associated with the MP barracks. They were both normal sized Quonset huts, only one story tall, and they sat on either end of the complex. One was the arms room. We didn't go in there. The other was the enlisted day room. I'd been in it before: privately stocked bar, pool tables, a TV, and a couple of vinyl couches. Ernie and I pushed our way through the unlocked door.

Staff Sergeant Morris Dexter sat in a T-shirt, flip flops, and a pair of green gym shorts on a centrally located bar stool. In front of him lay a baseball cap with the name MOE embroidered on it. He clutched a can of Falstaff in one hand and a shot glass of what looked like hard liquor in the other. A Korean bartender washed glasses behind the bar and two other MPs, both men I recognized from our confrontation at the 8th Army Morgue, sat on either side of Dexter.

When we walked in, they swiveled on their stools.

Ernie said, "You blew it this time, Dexter."

He glared drunkenly, eyes half lidded. Even sitting, he swayed slightly, and he had that mean drunk look that comes when the alcohol makes you hate not only the world but everyone in it.

"Criminal investigation pukes," Dexter said. The words came out moist and slurred. "Protecting the Koreans instead of stopping them from slicing MP throats."

"You were on duty last night, Dexter," I told him, "in charge of the MPs patrolling Itaewon. You decided to take out your frustrations on an inanimate object. Namely, the *pochang macha*."

"The what? You mean that pile of shit cart where that old gook woman sells slimy crud? What do you call it, Sweeno? A *poontang chacha*?"

Dexter's sidekicks snickered.

"Yes, that one," I said.

"Never *heard* of it."

That was the punch line. Dexter and his comrades slapped one another on the shoulders, howling. The other two men were younger than Dexter, his military subordinates. They were both red-faced but not as sloshed as Dexter. If they decided to fight, in their current state, Ernie and I could take all three of them. Especially with the help of Ernie's brass knuckles.

Ernie'd had enough of the banter. "Keep your hands on the bar, Dexter," he said. "Stand up, lean forward, and place your feet shoulder width apart. You know how it works."

Ernie pulled his handcuffs out from behind his back and stepped forward. All three of the MPs stood up, Dexter more slowly because he had to push himself to an upright position and then straighten his back, trying to keep from losing his balance.

I moved off to the left and prepared to leap at Dexter if he resisted. That's when I saw it, sliding out from beneath the baseball cap, an Army-issue .45 automatic. Dexter grabbed the pistol grip and started to turn.

I yelled something. I don't remember what, and ran straight at Dexter.

-8-

The Provost Marshal wasn't happy with us. He stood behind his desk, hands on narrow hips, scowling.

"What happened?" he asked.

"When Dexter went for his gun," I said, "I charged at him. A round went off, scared the crap out of all of us, but by then I'd reached him and knocked him backward over his barstool and then him and me and the two other MPs went down in a heap. I'm not clear on what happened after that other than I kept swinging and when another round went off, we all stopped fighting."

The Provost Marshal turned his scowl on Ernie. "That's when you fired into the mirror behind the bar?"

"Yes, sir," Ernie replied. "I managed to secure Dexter's weapon and then fired it once, just getting their attention."

Colonel Walter P. Brace, the Provost Marshal of the 8th United States Army, exhaled long and slow. "So now two MPs are in the hospital, one with a dislocated shoulder and the other with a concussion, and I have a weapons incident, shots fired during an arrest. And what, exactly, are the charges against Staff Sergeant Dexter?"

"Vandalism with malicious intent," I said.

"Which means?"

"He destroyed a *pochang macha*."

The colonel sat down. "A *pochang macha*?"

"Yes, sir," I replied.

Colonel Brace stared quietly at the blotter in front of him. He started to thumb through some papers but thought better of it. Finally he looked back at us.

"And how about the murder of Corporal Collingsworth? And the hacking to death of Mr. Barretsford? Any progress on *those*?"

"We're still developing leads, sir."

"Leads."

"Yes, sir."

"And the KNPs?"

"Lab reports on the *pochang macha* crime scene should be back this morning."

"There's that word again."

"Yes, sir."

"Did you turn your daily progress report in to Staff Sergeant Riley?"

"Working on that now, sir."

"Not now," he said. "Get over to the KNP headquarters and add their lab reports into your daily. Go on now, get out." He flicked his fingers at us, as if to chase away flies. "Get out."

We saluted, turned, and marched out of his office.

In the jeep, Ernie said, "Asshole."

Ernie parked the jeep in front of the Korean National Police headquarters, and we strode through the front door and past the information counter. Mr. Kill's assistant, Officer Oh, told us he was conducting interrogations and couldn't be disturbed.

"Do you have the lab reports?" I asked.

Her long face flushed red. "Only he can give those to you."

Ernie was about to argue with her, but I waved him off. "Where's the interrogation room?"

She debated whether to respond, but in the end she rose from her chair and said, "I'll show you."

We walked down the two flights of stairs we'd just climbed, but when we reached the ground floor we kept going down. After one flight, we hit a door. Officer Oh pressed a buzzer. A metallic voice said, "*Yoboseiyo, Kim Kyongjang imnida.*"

Officer Oh identified herself and then a buzzer sounded. We pushed through the door. A dimly lit cement hallway stretched into darkness. Doors were imbedded into the walls; holding cells. Officer Oh led us in the opposite direction and opened a door marked *Muncho-sil*, interrogation room. Straight-backed chairs and a counter faced a one-way window through which a red light glowed in a space not much bigger than a rectangular closet. The interrogation was being conducted.

"Where's the popcorn?" Ernie asked.

Officer Oh motioned for us to sit and then she switched on the sound. They were speaking Korean, of course, in low but insistent tones. Mr. Kill was doing most of the talking. Next to him sat a young officer taking notes. What surprised me was the person being interrogated. Ernie and I both recognized her. She was the woman who ran the PX snack stand in the building opposite the 8th Army Claims Office.

"What the hell's she doing here?" Ernie asked.

The woman looked haggard and thin, as if she'd been there for days. Patiently, Mr. Kill asked question after question, and she kept shaking her head, exhausted.

"How long has she been here?" I asked.

Officer Oh looked at me sharply but didn't answer.

"Who else has he been interrogating?"

When she didn't respond, I stood up and walked out of the room. Ernie followed. Officer Oh trotted after us. I continued down the long hallway, stopping at the doors, peering through the peepholes located just below my eye-level. Each of the rooms was well illuminated and had a short wooden bench and a bucket for waste. There were no windows, books, radios, televisions, or phones. Just a cement block cubicle. Even this peep hole, I imagined, worked only one way and would be opaque to the prisoner inside. After examining the first cell, I moved to the next.

Officer Oh said, "*An dei.*" Not permitted. She reached out as if to stop me, but I shrugged her off and kept moving. Ernie followed. We peered into every cell along the hallway and then started back on the ones on the opposite side. Besides the PX snack stand woman and her husband, I recognized the receptionist at the Eighth Army Claims Office, two of her co-workers, and the gate guard who was on duty the morning of the Claims Office attack.

When I was halfway back, Mr. Kill emerged from the interrogation room.

"Agent Sueño," he said, "and Agent Bascom. Welcome."

I strode toward him. "Why are these people locked up?" I said.

"We are interrogating them," he replied calmly, "as part of our investigation."

"But these people are witnesses," I said. "*Witnesses.* Not suspects."

"Can you be sure?"

"But there's no reason to suspect them. No evidence links them to the crime."

"Do you have evidence that proves they weren't?" Mr. Kill asked.

The question stumped me. Ernie stepped in. "How long have they been locked up?"

"Long enough."

"One day? Two days?"

Mr. Kill shrugged.

"You can't just keep people like this."

He stared at us blankly.

I tried to think, get over my shock. I knew the Republic of Korea was a police state. Their president, Pak Chung-hee, was a former colonel who'd taken over the government, promoted himself to general, and, through a polling process most international observers viewed as laughable, had finally won the election for president. There weren't any local police departments run by cities or counties, only one police department run by the federal government: the Korean National Police. They were a quasi-military organization charged with not only fighting crime but also with protecting the country from foreign threats— mainly Communist North Korea—and from internal threats: anyone who had the nerve to challenge the legitimacy of the regime. They did things their way. There might've been human rights enshrined in their constitution but all that was for show. In reality the Korean National Police did whatever they wanted to do, all within the supervision and absolute control of the government officials in charge.

Mr. Kill wasn't taking any chances. This was more than just a murder investigation. It was also an investigation into an incident that could threaten the special relationship between the United States and the Republic of Korea. As such, it would be monitored by the very highest levels of their government. Mr. Kill wasn't identifying suspects. To him, everyone was a suspect.

"Let them out," I said, pointing at the doors down the hallway. "They've suffered enough."

"In due time," Mr. Kill answered.

Incongruously, I thought of how well he spoke English. I don't believe I'd ever heard a Korean use that phrase, "in due time." And then I remembered the lab report. I asked him about it. He snapped his fingers at Officer Oh. She bowed and ran upstairs.

"Go back to your compound," he told us. "When I have more information, I will call you."

"You're not going to release these people?" Ernie asked.

Mr. Kill swiveled on him and his face hardened. "Not your business," he said.

"Well it damn sure *ought* to be our business. These people work for the United States government. They were originally identified as witnesses by Eighth Army law enforcement, and the crimes were committed on an Eighth Army military compound."

"But they're Korean citizens," Mr. Kill said. "They fall under *our* jurisdiction. Not yours." Ernie started to say something but Mr. Kill cut him off. "Your Colonel Brace knows we picked them up. He signed off on it. Didn't he tell you?"

Ernie's mouth started to open, but he quickly shut it again. He glared at Mr. Kill and for a moment I was afraid he was about to sock him in the jaw. But he must have rummaged around deep in the recesses of his reptilian mind and managed to find a modicum of self-control. Instead of doing what I knew he wanted to do, Ernie pulled a stick of ginseng gum out of his pocket, unwrapped it, and popped the gum into his mouth.

As he started to chew, I said, "Come on, Ernie."

Ernie kept staring at Mr. Kill. Deliberately, he wadded up the gum wrapper and tossed it on the ground. Finally, he turned. Together we walked toward the stairs. Before we hit the first landing, Ernie was cursing up a blue streak—part of it in Korean, part in English, and some words I figured were Vietnamese—dredging up every dirty word he'd ever learned.

Painstakingly, I translated the KNP lab report from the scene of Collingsworth's murder, using the *Essence Korean-English Dictionary* I kept on my desk. Some of the words were medical terms and weren't in my dictionary. I asked Miss Kim, the admin secretary, for help, but not all the words were familiar to her either.

"Why didn't you wait for them to translate it?" Riley growled.

"Them?" I said. "How would you be able to trust the translation?"

"What do you mean?"

For Staff Sergeant Riley and most GIs in the 8th United States Army, translation into English was a simple thing, like one plus one equals two. Each Korean word could be replaced with the English equivalent word. Of course, it wasn't that simple. But try to explain that to a colonel who's in a hurry. Most KNP reports probably weren't mistranslated intentionally. More likely, the work was just too difficult for the Korean clerks assigned to the job, and he or she was under pressure to finish quickly and just wrote down what was within reach of their English vocabulary.

I was trying to get it right.

I typed up the final draft and turned it in to Riley, who hand-carried it to the Provost Marshal. All it said, really, were things we already knew. The few fingerprints the KNPs had been able to take off the serving counter and the drinking cups belonged mostly to Mrs. Lee, the woman who owned the *pochang macha*. Two other prints probably belonged to the two customers, who hadn't yet been identified. As Mrs. Lee reported, the perpetrator himself wore gloves. At the murder site, the blood samples were all the same blood type as Corporal Ricky P. Collingsworth, O positive. The color, thickness, and texture of the hair samples were analyzed and appeared to match him and Senior Private Kwon Hyon-up, the ROK MP who'd been briefly knocked unconscious in the attack.

So that was it, nothing much at all. The man with the iron sickle wasn't leaving us anything to go on. He'd worn gloves and long-sleeved clothing, and he knew the crime scene would be analyzed closely so he'd been careful not to leave traces. No traces at all, other than the totem, which he'd later taken away. I pulled the drawing out and glanced at it again. I should've had copies made for Staff Sergeant Riley, the Provost Marshall, and every MP in 8th Army. For some reason, I hesitated. I'm not sure why. Maybe it was because the Provost Marshal had given permission for Mr. Kill and the Korean National Police to pick up and interrogate people who were faithful employees of the US government—and he didn't bother to tell me or Ernie. Maybe it was because of the sympathy he'd shown for Moe Dexter and his crew and the belittling attitude he'd displayed at the risk we'd taken in arresting them. Maybe it was because of the almost drooling agreement I'd seen amongst the 8th Army officer corps when the statuesque Major Rhee Mi-sook lectured them on the dangers of North Korean agents. Maybe it was one of those things, maybe it was all of those things. Whatever it was, I figured I had to hold something back. Like the man with the iron sickle, I decided to hide something under my coat. I'd pull it out at a time when it would provide maximum surprise and maximum discomfort for my enemies.

Who those enemies were, I wasn't quite sure yet. At times it seemed like everyone was.

The phone rang. Staff Sergeant Riley picked it up. He identified himself and listened for a while, saying, "Will do" two or three times. He hung up.

"Sueño!" he yelled, although I was just a few feet from him. "Bascom! You two are to get your sorry butts out to the ROK Army headquarters right now. Report to Major Rhee. While you've been sitting on your sorry asses, someone in this man's army has been doing some work."

"What've they got?" I asked.

"What've they got? They're just about to bust this case wide open. Get over there now. They want the Eighth Army to witness this historic moment in joint ROK/US law enforcement."

"They got him?" Ernie said.

"How the hell should I know? But a big task force is moving out. Be there or be square. Move out sharply! *Hubba hubba!*"

Ernie and I shrugged on our coats. On the way out, Ernie flipped Riley the bird.

Even though she was wearing ROK Army fatigues, Major Rhee Mi-sook looked smashing. The baggy uniform had been tailored to accentuate the roundness of her hips and the smallness of her waist. Raven black hair had been piled atop her head and pinned beneath a camouflage cap.

"You're late," she said.

A row of six ROK MP jeeps followed by an armored personnel carrier were lined up in front of the brick ROK Army headquarters. Like the 8th Army headquarters down the street, the entire complex had been built by the Japanese Imperial Army before World War II, but you didn't mention that around here, or you were liable to get your butt kicked.

"Why'd you wait for us?" I asked Major Rhee.

She studied me quietly for a moment, and then Ernie, letting us take in the full magnificence of her unblemished oval face and the full pouting redness of her lips. Her black eyes were full of hatred, or love, I wasn't sure which. With her, there might not have been much difference.

"We need Americans," she said finally. "We always need Americans. Just follow," she told us. "Don't do anything. Stay out of the way and watch."

Without waiting for a reply, she performed a smart about-face. On the way back to the lead jeep, she raised her right arm and circled her pointed forefinger in the air. All the jeeps and the armored personnel carrier fired up their engines. Ernie and I scurried to our jeep and followed the convoy out the main gate into the busy midday Seoul traffic. When we reached the Samgak-ji Circle, the convoy bulled through all the *kimchi* cabs and the three-wheeled pickup trucks piled high with garlic or shimmering green cabbage and backed up traffic for a quarter mile.

As we drove, I tried to calm the revulsion in my gut at seeing Major Rhee. In North Korea, working as a double agent, her mission had been to hunt me down. She done so and then she'd tortured me, seeming to greatly enjoy her work. If I hadn't been rescued by the Manchurian Brigade, she would've forced me to make a phony confession and might've even had me executed as a capitalist spy. I couldn't forget these things, especially the way her eyes had glazed over as I'd screamed in agony.

She was wearing the uniform of a South Korean officer now, performing important work for the South Korean brass. I was supposed to forget what she'd done up north, that was all part of the spy game they told me, but I still saw her as the serpent in the garden, gorgeous but deadly.

Ernie, as usual, brought my thoughts back to sordid reality.

"So did you get any of that?"

"What? You mean when I was in North Korea?"

He shrugged. "Whenever."

"No time."

"But you have time now."

I shuddered. "She's not interested in me, not in that way."

Ernie barked a laugh. "Are you kidding? She looks at you like a python looks at a rat."

I'm not sure why but that made me even more uncomfortable than I was already. I decided not to think about Major Rhee Mi-sook gobbling me up, which was hard for a minute, until the convoy swerved away from the main road and took a left up a steep incline.

This road was much narrower. The few cabs and wooden pushcarts traveling downhill were forced to pull over and press themselves up against open shops and brick walls to get out of the way. Clumps of pedestrians stopped what they were doing and stared at the massively armed convoy trundling past. Old women wearing short blouses with long ribbons and flowing skirts balanced huge bundles of laundry atop their heads and gawked. They'd seen military convoys before, plenty of them, but they'd never seen a woman—and such an eye-catching woman—in the lead jeep.

We walked along the edge of the slope for about a half mile until we reached a straight stretch of road with a cement retaining wall on the left and a ledge overlooking the western edge of the city. Major Rhee ordered a halt. Armed men hopped out of the armored personnel carrier, all of them holding M-16 rifles. Commands were barked. At either end of the retaining wall were broad stone steps. One squad of soldiers climbed the stairs on the left, the other the stairs on the right. Major Rhee motioned for us to follow. As the soldiers trotted ahead of us, Major Rhee hurried to keep up. We stayed right with her.

At the top of the ridge, there were no more paved roads, just an endless shanty town that had been there probably since the end of the Korean War. The soldiers filed through narrow pedestrian lanes, passing crowded hooches, most of them made of plaster and rotted boards. Toddlers without pants were gently shoved out of the way, chickens squawked, and women squatted in front of huge plastic pans, looking up startled from their chopping of turnips or shelling of peas.

Finally, we came to a halt at a small intersection, at the center of which sat a weathered oak with colored pieces of paper and folded notes attached to it for good luck. Major Rhee spoke to the sergeants in charge of the two squads, pointed down one particularly narrow alley and then walked back to us.

As she approached, she pulled a .45 automatic pistol out of her black leather shoulder holster. She ratcheted back the charging handle, letting it slide forward with a clang. "I'm going in first," she said. "Would you care to come along?"

"We're not armed," I said.

She smiled a lethal smile. "Don't you trust me to protect you?"

The answer was no, but I didn't say it. Instead, I held out my open palm and said, "Lead on."

She turned and stepped into the narrow alley.

The soldiers fanned out into parallel lanes as Ernie and I followed Major Rhee down the center pathway. Overhanging thatched roofs closed in above us, and soon we were stumbling through mud, groping forward in the dark, swatting at spider webs. When we reached another narrow intersection, Major Rhee crouched.

She waited until I crouched next to her, and then she pointed at a wooden gate that looked like it was about to fall off its hinges. Chunks of plaster had crumbled away to expose brick beneath the wall, which was topped with shards of broken glass to ward off thieves. Major Rhee Mi-sook rose and walked toward the gate. At either end of the passageway, ROK Army soldiers waited, weapons poised. I expected there were more troops in back of the hooch, although we were not in position to see them.

Holding her pistol pointed toward the sky, Major Rhee grabbed the string that worked as a pulley to unlock the gate. Metal rattled, but the door didn't open. She motioned with her free hand and two soldiers approached holding a heavy wooden log with iron handles, their rifles strapped behind their backs. She stepped back and, on the whispered count of "*hana, tul, seit*," the soldiers swung the battering ram forward.

The old gate slammed inward. Major Rhee entered first, yelling "*Umjiki-jima!*" Don't move! The soldiers with the battering ram stepped back and men on either side filed in. Ernie and I followed as far as the wooden porch.

The hooch was quickly secured. Soldiers ran around the side of the house, more soldiers emerged over the back wall, and Major Rhee and two soldiers entered through the front sliding doors, none of them bothering to take off their boots, a serious violation of ancient propriety.

Then I heard the commotion from within, like a heavy chest of drawers or a large wooden box had crashed to the floor. Someone shouted and then cursed, and an M-16 round was fired before Major Rhee's voice screeched angrily to cease fire. Ernie and I made it inside in time to see something ram against a wall. A small bearded man swung a short stick—a *mongdungi* used for beating wet laundry— in a broad arc, fighting off Major Rhee and the two armed guards. Children huddled in the corner, two of them, clutching flat cushions to their chests, their eyes wide with terror. The man was screaming, frothing white at the mouth, swinging the heavy wooden stick in front of him.

Major Rhee backed away, shouting orders that she wanted the man taken alive, and more soldiers rushed into the room, holding their rifles forward like shields. Five or six of them pressed up against him. Still trying to swing his heavy wooden stick, he was on the floor, biting and kicking and commanding them to get off of him. Within seconds, his hands were trussed behind his back and a sock was stuffed deep into his mouth. Too deep, I thought. As they dragged him out, saliva poured from his mouth, and he was starting to turn red.

Major Rhee shouted for the men to get out of the hooch and not to touch anything. She watched as one of the squad leaders pulled out a length of rope and securely bound the prisoner's hands behind his back. She ordered that the sock be pulled out of his mouth, and when the man started cursing again, she called for it to be put back in.

"If you want to breathe," she told him in Korean, "you'll behave."

The squad leader roughly shoved the prisoner out of the muddy courtyard.

When they were gone, Major Rhee slipped on plastic gloves and returned to the dilapidated hooch, and with another sergeant's help, she started going through the man's personal belongings.

Ernie and I were being ignored. I stepped outside the gate for a moment, mainly to get away from the whimpering of the children. Not a soul in this teeming jumble of humanity moved. Everyone was hiding. I heard nothing, not even the squawking of chickens; nothing except the flapping of wet laundry in the afternoon breeze. I returned to the hooch.

Major Rhee apparently hadn't found anything of note in the man's meager possessions. She ordered that the walls and flooring be cracked open. While the soldiers ripped the house apart, I asked her what she was looking for.

"Incriminating material," she said.

"Like what?"

"Like a radio to broadcast to North Korea."

"In this dump?" I said, incredulously.

She shrugged. "Or union propaganda."

By decree of President Pak Chung-hee, unions were outlawed in South Korea. All except one: the Foreign Organization Employees Union, which mainly comprised the workers of 8th Army.

"What about the children?" I asked.

"What about them?" she replied.

"Now that their father's gone, what are you going to do with them?"

She shrugged. "They must have relatives."

She turned and walked away from me. I followed. She seemed to be examining the outside of the hooch. Using a bamboo stick she found on the ground, she poked through the overhanging thatched roof. We entered the dark passageway between the back of the hooch and the surrounding wall.

"The man you just arrested," I said, "he doesn't look anything like the man with the iron sickle." Major Rhee didn't answer. "He's short," I continued. "His legs are stunted from malnutrition. He has a beard."

"He could have grown that in the last few days."

"Hair doesn't grow that fast," I said.

Again, she didn't answer.

"What evidence do you have that he's the man with the iron sickle?" I asked.

"He's a union organizer," she said, "and therefore he is our enemy. We'll question him and see if he's the man who did the killing." She shrugged elaborately. "If not, maybe he knows who did."

"You're doing this just to make your bosses believe you're making progress."

She stopped poking with the stick, turned, and pointed her finger at my nose, very insulting in Korea. "ROK Army business is ROK Army business," she said. "You are here just to observe."

"I'm observing all right," I told her. "And I believe you've been observing me. Whose sedan was that last night in Itaewon?"

She snorted an ironic laugh, half turned away from me and then thought better of it. "*Huh.* You think you're so important we would watch you all the time."

"You're worried about what I'm going to find out."

"Like what, for instance?"

"Like maybe the man with the iron sickle isn't a North Korean agent."

"So what if he's not? It doesn't matter to me. I'll catch him anyway."

"So you don't think this man is the murderer?"

"Maybe. We'll see."

"Who's going to conduct the interrogation?" I asked. "You?"

"You've seen me in action," she said. "Don't you think I can do it?"

"I think you can do it very well."

She stepped closer, a half smile angling her face. "So maybe you'll want to watch." Then she slapped me. It was so fast I didn't have time to flinch. I slapped her back. Her face twisted but then she stared back at me, laughing. Before I could stop myself, I stepped forward. She lunged toward me and then I grabbed her small waist, and she was kissing me and pulling me closer to her. I hated her, I knew that, but then I started to react, the biological reaction of all healthy young males. Her fingernails clawed into the back of my neck and her leg wrapped around my thigh; behind that dirty hooch, her soldiers not more than a few feet away.

Suddenly, I realized what I was doing and I pushed her away, wiping my mouth with the back of my hand.

"You no likey, GI?" she said, her eyes taunting me.

I turned clumsily in the narrow passageway and stepped back into the light. Before returning to the front of the hooch, I paused, willing myself to calm down, but it wasn't working too well. Finally the lump in my pants started to soften.

As if nothing had happened, Major Rhee continued her search through the low-hanging thatch.

When I had fully recovered, I returned to the front of the hooch.

Ernie squatted in front of the kids, trying to calm them down. Their eyes were as big as summer pears. He pulled out some ginseng gum, tore one stick in half, and offered each child a piece. They just stared at him, unmoving. He continued to speak soothingly and smiled a lot until one of the little arms darted out, and small fingers deftly grabbed the torn stick of gum.

Outside, a woman screamed hysterically. The wife, I thought, back from the market. She pushed past two soldiers and rushed inside, slipping off her plastic sandals and scurrying toward her children. She knelt and wrapped them in her arms, and they all started to cry. Ernie backed away.

Major Rhee, who had emerged from the far side of the hooch, ordered that they be removed from the premises. Where they were taken, I could only imagine.

Back at the CID office, Miss Kim handed me a phone message. It was from Mr. Pak Hyong-ku, the owner of the Sam-Il Office that did so much business with 8th Army Claims. He wanted me to meet him tonight at about seven at a teahouse in the Sugye-dong area.

"Did he say what it was about?" I asked.

"No. He only said someone wanted to talk to you."

"Someone?"

She nodded. The cannon for close of business sounded and the outside speakers blared out the tinny, tremulous notes of the retreat bugle. I picked up the phone and called Mr. Pak. No answer. It must be nice to be in business making good money. You didn't have to work late.

I'd also received a message from Captain Prevault. She had a lead for me, she said, and she wanted me to pick her up at six with the jeep.

Ernie tossed me the keys to the jeep's padlock. "Don't let me butt in," he said.

"It's not a date," I told him.

"'Pick me up at six.' What else are you going to call it? By the way, you spent quite a bit of time behind that hooch with Major Rhee. Was she interrogating you again?"

"Get bent, Ernie," I told him.

He promised me he would.

When we went outside, three of the four tires of the jeep were flat. Ernie cursed and knelt next to the nearest tire, pointing at a slash in the rubber. Then he examined the other two. Same story.

"MPs," Ernie said.

"Isn't Dexter still locked up?" I asked.

"Yeah, but he's got plenty of buddies."

I handed him the keys back.

-9-

As I approached the BOQ, Captain Prevault was outside waiting. She walked toward me wearing a warm coat and a large bag over her shoulder. At Gate Number Five we waved down a *kimchi* cab heading east.

"Where to?" I asked.

She pulled out a slip of paper with an address written on it. I read it to the driver.

"*Aju molli*," he said. A long way.

I groaned inwardly, happy I'd gotten a petty cash advance from Riley.

We headed east for almost five miles along the blue ribbon of the Han River, spanning the southern edge of the city of Seoul, until finally we crossed the Chonho Bridge and headed southeast. We passed a few cement block housing areas and some tin-roofed factories, then acres of open junk yards, and finally we were back in the countryside; fallow rice paddies interspersed with small clumps of farm houses with wisps of smoke rising from narrow chimneys.

"Where the hell is this place?" I asked Captain Prevault.

"Not far." She pointed to a wooden sign on the side of the road and said, "*Chogi.*" There.

The driver nodded and took the turn.

"You speak Korean," I said.

"About ten words," she replied.

"Do you know how to tell the cab driver to stop?"

"*Seiwo juseiyo.*"

The driver slammed on his brakes and veered toward the side of the road.

"No," I told the driver in Korean. "Keep going straight. She was just practicing."

He nodded, then shook his head. Crazy foreigners.

Captain Prevault held her hand to her mouth, her eyes wide with glee. "It worked," she said.

The road wound up into low hills covered with stands of pine. A breeze bent some of the branches. It would be cold tonight. Maybe this was the end of the fall, I thought, and the beginning of the Korean winter; a freezing winter that howls out of the icy steppes of Manchuria. Finally another sign led us to a gravel parking area in front of a substantial two-story brick building.

"The Japanese built this as a prison," Captain Prevault said.

"What is it now?"

"A home for the criminally insane."

"Still a prison," I said.

"Unfortunately, yes."

We climbed out of the cab. I handed the driver a five thousand *won* note, about ten bucks, and asked him to wait. He said he would.

Inside, we were met by a middle-aged Korean man in a white medical uniform who bowed to Captain Prevault, then to me, and escorted us down a long hallway. The odor of *kimchi* wafted through the air behind him. At the end of the hallway, we descended stone steps into darkness. I touched the walls. They were cold, smeared with moss.

■ ■ ■

The female prisoner sat up, her back perfectly straight, and her eyes wide in the darkness.

"We can't turn on the light," Captain Prevault whispered to me. "She finds it upsetting."

The ambient glow from a yellow bulb at the far end of the stone tunnel was the only illumination. We had descended a full three stories beneath the ground. The woman sat behind a heavy wooden door, but we were able to observe her through a wire-reinforced window made of half-inch-thick glass. As my eyes adjusted to the dim light I could see she was holding a tattered rag doll.

"Why do they have her here?" I asked.

"Murder. She hacked three people to death with a hoe."

"Another farm implement."

"Precisely. But her crime was committed almost twenty years ago, shortly after the end of the Korean War."

"She's so young."

"Yes. She wasn't much more than a child when she committed the crime."

I knew the Korean judicial system made no differentiation between juvenile and adult crime, in part because they saw so little juvenile crime. "So what does she have to do with my case?"

"Maybe nothing. It's her reaction that caused us to think you needed to see her."

"Reaction?"

"To your drawing. Doctor Hwang at the sanatorium took the liberty of distributing the drawing among his colleagues, to see if it meant anything to any of them. He came out here himself and showed the drawing to each of the inmates, under controlled conditions, of course."

"He must've had his suspicions."

"Yes, you might say he did."

"What were these 'controlled conditions'?"

"Physical protection."

"From the patients?"

Captain Prevault nodded. "Many of them are dangerous."

"How about this one?"

"Since she's been incarcerated, she's attacked two staff members. One lost an eye, the other the use of his right leg."

"These were men she attacked?"

"Yes."

"But she's so tiny. What did she do?

"She might be tiny but she has teeth. The jaws of even a small woman can exert up to five hundred pounds of pressure."

"She bit the guy's eye out?"

"And half of the other guy's leg."

"Damn." I looked back at the silent woman with more respect. "What made her go nuts?"

"I've made a copy of her file," Captain Prevault replied. "When we're through here, I'll give it to you."

"When we're through?"

"Yes. Rather than describe her reaction to your drawing, we thought it best if we showed you."

The male nurse joined us, but now he was wearing a square mask with an iron mesh, something like a baseball catcher's mask. He also wore the padded chest and groin protection that karate experts wear in Taekwondo tournaments. On his lower legs he wore shin guards, the kind used in soccer. Two other white-clad attendants joined us. One of them opened the door, and the heavily armored man slipped on thick leather gloves and entered the room. He sat down on a stool opposite the tiny woman. So far, she hadn't reacted at all. The man pulled a sheet of paper out of his sleeve. He placed it on the floor in front of her, propped up slightly with his foot. Then he pulled out a penlight and shone the bright beam on the drawing.

It was my drawing of the Itaewon alley totem all right: the wooden stand, the wire grill-like square, and a rat hanging by its ankles.

The light caused the woman to stir. She glanced at the space alien sitting across from her but seemed completely unperturbed. Then she looked down at the drawing. If I live to be a hundred I'll never forget the look of horror that took possession of her face, as if she'd just seen the sum of all the fears any of us has ever imagined. A scream erupted from her open mouth and became progressively shriller, until it seemed like the intensity of the sound would pierce the stone walls that surrounded her. She leapt on top of her bench, crouching like a monkey evading a lion, her eyeballs riveted to the drawing, waving her free hand, as if clawing for it to go away, her tattered rag doll still clutched against her bosom.

The male nurse switched off the light. He picked up the drawing and backed smartly out of the room. The door was opened just wide enough for him to exit, then slammed shut. With a sigh of relief, the male nurse slipped off the wire mask. His brown face was pale, and sweat poured down his forehead.

Inside the tiny cell, the woman was still screaming.

I dropped Captain Prevault off at Gate Five with my apologies for not stopping somewhere for dinner. I explained I had another appointment. She pretended it didn't matter, but the way her shoulders tightened made me believe it did matter. I asked if she had time for lunch tomorrow so that after I'd had a chance to read the complete file, we could discuss it in more detail. This brightened her up somewhat, and we made a date to meet at noon in the main cafeteria of the 121 Evac Hospital.

After I dropped her off, I told the cab driver to take me to

Sogye-dong. He asked for more money because the meter read almost twenty thousand *won* already, and I handed him another ten thousand *won* note. How I wished the tires of Ernie's jeep hadn't been slashed. I could've saved a bundle.

At the Mobom Teahouse in Sogye-dong, the meter indicated I owed the driver another four thousand three hundred and thirty *won*. I handed him a five thousand *won* note and surprised him by telling him to keep the change. In Korea, cab drivers don't expect tips but I didn't have the time to wait for the change. I was already forty-five minutes late for the 7 P.M. appointment. I walked into the teahouse.

As usual, every pair of eyes looked up at me. Maybe a dozen tables were occupied, twenty customers max. But they were all Koreans as this was an area of town that wasn't near a military compound and therefore wasn't frequented by American GIs. At six-foot-four, I was an oddity in the States, never mind here. They gawked at me, expecting me to do something. None of the staff approached me, so I just stood there, futilely trying to spot Mr. Pak from the Sam-Il Claims Office. Finally, I walked up to the glass counter, behind which sat plastic replicas of delicacies such as chopped squid tentacles and rolls of glutinous rice wrapped in seaweed. The man in a white cook's hat behind the counter had his back to me, and he was concentrating on preparing something, studiously ignoring me. I knew the treatment. I was an American and he wanted me to go away; he might be afraid that talking to me would expose his ignorance of English and possibly provoke a confrontation with an unpredictable foreigner.

I said, "*Yoboseiyo.*" Hello. When I got no response I wrapped my knuckles on the glass counter and shouted, "*Yoboseiyo!*" They want obnoxious American, I'd give them obnoxious American.

The man set down the chopper and turned. I spoke in rapid Korean.

"I was supposed to meet a man named Pak here at seven o'clock. Was he here? Was he waiting for me?"

The man stared at me dumbly as if I were some sort of display in a wax museum, then turned back to what he was doing. I was about to wrap my knuckles on the glass again when a young woman in a black skirt and white blouse hurried out of the back room. Apparently, she'd been alerted that there was a foreigner out front who refused to go away, and she'd been assigned the job of dealing with me. It was a status thing. The cook couldn't be bothered. This waitress could.

She nodded slightly to me, not a full bow, and I proceeded to tell her what I had just told the cook. She seemed relieved that I spoke Korean.

"Mr. Pak?" she asked.

"Yes. He owns the Sam-Il Claims Office," I said, pointing across the street at an angle. "It's not far. He must've come in here before."

"Yes. I'm sure he has. But no one here was waiting for a foreigner." She paused, her smooth face glowing red. "We don't see foreigners in here. We don't know what to do with people like you."

She was becoming increasingly flustered and increasingly incoherent. I too was a little tired of being treated like a stray circus animal. Many GIs would've become angry and caused a ruckus. I knew because I'd seen them in action, and I read the 8th Army blotter reports often enough. Me, I liked to think I took the more cosmopolitan view. Korea is a homogenous society and has been for thousands of years. Foreigners thrust into their midst throw them off balance— at least some of them.

I fought down my frustration, thanked the waitress and walked out of the Mobom Teahouse. *Mobom* means exemplary. I didn't think it really applied.

I stood on the sidewalk. The wind I had noticed earlier picked up, blowing dust down the streetlit road and whirring plastic noodle wrappers about like mad ghosts. In the distance the moon lowered red toward the Yellow Sea. I inhaled deeply of the smog and grime and the chill night air. I loved it here, in the middle of this magnificent city, even when I felt embarrassed and out of place.

A cab pulled up and slowed. The driver leaned toward me. "Where you go?" he said in English. I waved him off. I wanted to stand there awhile, alone, away from the compound, away from Americans, away from the case I'd been pursuing for the last few days. I wanted to think.

I pulled the file Captain Prevault had given me out of my pocket. It was in English and only two pages long. A synopsis, I figured, of the longer Korean file. I'd already skimmed through it. Now I stood beneath a streetlamp and read the single-spaced typing more slowly.

The woman in the home for the criminally insane never had a name. For convenience's sake, the staff at the home had called her Miss Sim Kok-sa, for the Buddhist monastery near where she'd been found. It was a ginseng hunter who found her, in a rundown hut on a remote plateau that had been farmed by an old woman and man. They were the ones found hacked to death with a hoe. The girl was estimated to be about ten years old at the time, and she was just sitting there near the rotting bodies, surviving off of raw grain. The testimony of the ginseng hunter, later confirmed by two local KNPs, led the doctors to believe the young girl had been enslaved by the elderly couple. If she'd been sexually abused, the report didn't mention it. Not unusual in official Korean documentation, since sexuality was not a topic that was discussed in polite company, however widely it was practiced.

The girl was taken into custody, committed, and had been locked up in that small cell ever since. Where she'd come from, no one knew for sure. There had been so much tragedy and so much displacement during the Korean War that no one had taken the time to find out.

The question for me was, why did she react so violently to the drawing of the totem? Had she seen something similar? Is that what had driven her mad in the first place?

The area where she'd been found was near the Simkok-sa Buddhist monastery on the slopes of Dae-am Mountain in the Taebaek Range. I didn't have a map but the report triangulated the position by saying it was located forty-five kilometers northeast of the city of Chunchon and thirty kilometers northwest of the port city of Sokcho. Both of those places I'd heard of, and both of them were out in the boonies.

What did it have to do with the man with the iron sickle? I didn't know. I stuffed the report back into my pocket. Time to head back to the compound. I started looking for a taxi, but before I found one a small man in a tattered suit hustled up to me.

"Geogie! Geogie!" he said, waving at me frantically. He stepped into the light, out of breath. "I'm Ming," he said proudly, as if that were supposed to mean something to me.

"Yes?" I said.

"The man you were supposed to meet in the Mobom Teahouse." He frowned. "Over an hour ago."

"I thought I was going to meet Mr. Pak."

"No, no. He sent me. I'm so glad I caught you." He held out his hand and we shook. "Shall we go in?" he said, motioning toward the teahouse.

"It's late," I said.

He nodded. "Then we won't waste time." He raised his arm high over his head and out of nowhere a cab appeared. "Come," he said. "I'll take you to someone who maybe can help you find this man who is causing so much trouble."

I hesitated, unsure if I should get in, but he looked harmless enough. "Ming isn't a Korean name," I said.

"No." He smiled broadly. "I am Chinese. Born and bred in Korea though." He motioned again for me to enter the cab. I did. The cab sped through downtown Seoul and kept traveling north.

"Where are we going?" I asked.

"Oh, you're going to love this place. Full of lovely ladies."

"Where?" I insisted.

"Mia-ri. You ever been there?"

"Briefly," I said.

"Yes. American GIs don't go often. Too expensive."

"I'm not looking for a night on the town," I said.

"No. Of course not. I just want you to meet someone."

I asked him how he knew Mr. Pak at the Sam-Il Office, and he told me he was a field agent. He scoured the Korean countryside, from Pusan to Seoul and up north to the DMZ, looking for victims who might be eligible to file claims against 8th Army. He particularly made hay when he followed US armored battalions on field maneuvers. They had a tendency to cause much damage. So did the 101st Airborne or the US Marines when they were rotated in for war games. They caused almost as much damage as a division of tanks, some of it interpersonal rather than physical: pregnant girls, broken noses.

"Did you know Mr. Barretsford?" I asked.

He shook his head vehemently. "I'm only a small fish. He was a *big banana.*" Ming dragged the words out, pronouncing every syllable. "So sorry what happened to him."

Ming's English was the English you hear outside of base camps, laced with GI slang, the language of a hustler. I'd seen his type before, but never one who regularly wore a coat and tie. Probably to impress potential clients.

"Who is this person you're taking me to?"

"A very intelligent lady, but somewhat of a pest. She's been bothering Mr. Pak since he opened his office, but there was nothing he could do to help her."

"And I need to talk to her why?"

"Because of her claims."

"The ones Pak can't help her with?"

"Yes, precisely."

"You're just trying to get me to take her off your hands."

"No. It's more than that. Listen to her. Hear what she has to say."

The cab stopped in front of a brightly lit road that sloped gently uphill. Chinese lanterns were strung across the entranceway, and neon flashed everywhere. I'd been here before on an investigation, but I'd seen the place in the daytime when it was drab and lifeless. I didn't remember it like this.

The road was lined with single-story establishments all emblazoned with neon signs written in a combination of the indigenous *hangul* script and Chinese characters. Some of the characters I could read. Printed beneath these flashing red, blue, and gold signs in smaller script was an English translation like Blazing Star Nightclub or Flying Dragon Inn or, my favorite, The Long Life Scotch Corner. In front of these establishments, pouring out the doors, were beautiful young ladies, fully made up, waving and cooing and calling to any likely male. What made it all so stunning and so strange to the foreign eye was that the girls in each establishment all wore exactly the same type and color of evening gown. At one, the uniform was a floor-length, high collared dress with a slit up the side; at another, a mini skirt and a tight blouse displaying pushed-up décolletage. They were a team or, more accurately, a family.

Mia-ri is a playground for men, mostly Korean businessmen. Groups of men, usually executives from the same company or employees of the same government office, entered an establishment as a group and sat on the floor of the party room around a low table, each with a lovely hostess next to them. Food and drinks—and eventually entertainment—were brought to them. The hostesses encouraged the men to engage in drinking games and stuffed food in their mouths, all in an effort to run up the bill. Usually there was one woman in charge: an older woman, a "mama-san" in GI parlance. She and the leader of the group of men would negotiate in advance on a set price for a certain amount of food and drink—and time with the girls. During the frivolity, if that price was exceeded, which it often was, additional charges would be slapped on. This system usually worked, but not always. It was a common site to see a group of inebriated businessmen trying to leave a Mia-ri establishment late at night and the mama-san and the other girls hanging onto their coats arguing about additional charges.

I knew all this, and the only reason I knew was because Ernie and I had once followed an investigation here and witnessed how it all worked. As usual, Ernie'd flirted with the girls and over-promised, and after spending about half a month's pay, we practically had to fight our way out of the Eternal Spring Whiskey Bar, an establishment that had been replaced now, I saw, by the Kiss Kiss Gentleman's Club.

As field agent Ming and I walked up the center of the narrow road, some of the girls waved at us, but mostly half-heartedly. They could see by our shabby clothes and by our demeanor that we weren't the advance guard of some group of up-and-coming executives. We looked odd, Ming and I, out of place, and the girls were puzzled.

"Where are we going?" I asked him.

"Right around the corner," he said, pointing. "The Inn of the Crying Rose."

"'The Crying Rose'? That's a sad name for one of these establishments."

"Yes. She's a strange woman."

Once we turned there was less neon. The joints were smaller, with only a single sign above the door, and most of them had only one or two women standing outside. The Inn of the Crying Rose had none. Ming pushed the door open and motioned for me to enter.

A tiled bar and the mirror behind it were illuminated by a dim light and a few upholstered booths ran along the wall. This was for smaller groups of two, three, or four men, groups who couldn't afford the larger establishments along the main drag. Behind a sliding, oil-papered door there was one party room, dark now, which was large enough to hold a group of a half dozen. A smattering of cocktail tables filled the rest of the space. The music was some Korean lament sung by Patti Kim.

One booth in the corner was filled by three drunken men and hostesses but nobody looked up at us, which was a good sign. Ming hustled me toward a booth on the opposite wall. A waitress holding a silver tray followed, and after we took our seats she bowed and said, "*Muol duhshi-geissoyo?*" What can I get for you?

I ordered beer. Ming ordered tea.

After she left, two hostesses appeared, smiling and decked out in red evening gowns. Ming bowed and told them very politely in Korean that we were there on business, and we only wanted to talk to the proprietress. The girls continued to smile and bowed and hustled into the back room. The waitress brought our drinks. We waited. After five minutes, I said, "Where is she?"

Ming glanced at the booth on the far wall and for the first time I noticed that besides the hostesses another person sat with them. She was an older woman with a fuller figure, not one of the slender wraiths who floated silently through the dark environs of the Inn of the Crying Rose. She was smoking—which the younger women wouldn't do in front of customers—talking to the businessmen and waving her cigarette, jabbing the burning ember like a tiny spear.

"That's her," Ming said. "Madame Hoh."

One of the hostesses leaned over Madame Hoh's shoulder and whispered something in her ear. They both turned and looked at us. Madame Hoh asked the young woman a couple of more questions and when the girl shrugged she was dismissed. Madame Hoh reached for her shot glass and tossed the brown fluid back in one deft movement before stubbing out her cigarette, rising, bowing to the three gentlemen at the table and taking her leave. She turned and walked toward us.

Her face was confused, squinting in the dark, and then her eyes zeroed in on Ming.

She bowed to him, placing both hands demurely in front of her waist. "Ming *Sonseing-nim*." Honorable Teacher Ming.

Ming bowed in return and motioned toward me, speaking in his broken English. "This is Agent Sueño, from Eighth Army. Maybe you talk to him, about your case."

Ming smiled so broadly I could see his back molars.

Madame Hoh stared at him. She was no youngster, pushing forty, and they looked like hard years. Her cheeks were puffed, as were the wrinkles surrounding her eyes. There was suspicion in them, and a hardness. It was clear she wasn't pleased with Ming.

She motioned for us to sit. We did. She adjusted her long silk gown and sat on the straight-backed chair opposite us.

"My case," she said, using English, "is closed." She stared directly at him. "You knew that, Mr. Ming."

"Yes, but it has never been resolved. Agent Sueño here would like to re-open it."

I held up my hand. "I didn't say that."

"Then what do you want?" Madame Hoh snapped.

I sat back. She was obviously irritated and immediately seemed to realize she'd over-reacted. Her shoulders relaxed and she tried again, this time speaking more softly.

"My case was closed long ago," she said evenly. "I have no money to pursue it further."

"I just have a few questions," I said. "I won't take much of your time."

Just then one of the hostesses approached and whispered in

Madame Hoh's ear. I figured it was a pre-arranged move, designed to interrupt long-winded talk and induce customers to order more scotch, or the expensive appetizers these joints served. But instead of pressing us for our order, Madame Hoh rose and bowed again and said, "Excuse me for a moment."

We both nodded and she scurried off.

I turned to Ming. "I thought you said she wanted to pursue her claim?"

He shrugged. "She did. Before."

"How long ago was that?"

He thought for a moment. "Three, maybe four years."

"So maybe now," I said, "she doesn't want to be bothered."

Ming looked abashed. "Maybe not," he said. "I am sorry," he said, more than once.

"Tell me about her," I said.

Her claim, Ming told me, had to do with American GIs. There's a surprise, I thought. The woman, who he called Madame Hoh, had been a girl at the time, during the worst days of the Korean War. For some reason on which Ming wasn't clear, a small contingent of American soldiers had been sent to the remote village where Madame Hoh lived with her family. There had been a misunderstanding between the villagers and the soldiers, according to Madame Hoh. The GIs had reacted viciously. People had been murdered. Madame Hoh had been left an orphan. Because she'd been young, and her memory of the events wasn't clear—and because she was afraid of Korean official-dom—Madame Hoh had never given Mr. Pak at the Sam-Il Office all the details he needed to pursue a claim. A claim had been filed earlier, according to Madame Hoh, shortly after the war, but for some reason known only to the relevant authorities, it had been suppressed.

Ming leaned across the table. "Madame Hoh knew she didn't have enough evidence to reopen the claim at this late date," he said, "but she also believed a detailed claim had once been filed. If Mr. Pak could find that claim and reactivate it, then she'd have a chance at receiving compensation from the Eighth Army Claims Office."

"How much?" I asked.

Ming widened his eyes and rolled his neck. "Who knows? Madame Hoh claimed that the actions of those GIs ruined her life and the lives of many people in the village. If true, it could've amounted to one of the largest claims ever paid out by Eighth Army."

"What happened to the file?"

"That's what caused Mr. Pak so much trouble."

"Trouble?"

"Yes. As soon as he made an inquiry at Eighth Army Claims Office, he received a visit from the Korean National Police. They wanted to know who had told him about this incident and who had told him about the file."

"Did he tell them?"

"No. He refused to reveal the identity of his client."

"The KNPs didn't like that."

"No. Mr. Pak was forced to drop the inquiry. Everything calmed down after that."

"How did Madame Hoh react?"

"She's a strong woman. She said nothing, only thanked him for trying. And one other thing," Ming told me. "One of our contacts at Eighth Army told us of a secret file. A file that contained Madame Hoh's claim, along with others."

"Secret? You mean it's not kept with the other files at Eighth Army Claims?"

Ming shook his head vehemently. "No."

"Then where is it?"

"That's what we don't know."

I sat back, taking this all in, studying Ming's smiling face. "Why are you taking the risk," I asked him, "of telling me about this and introducing me to Madame Hoh?"

He grinned, the sickly grin of someone who's just swallowed a medicine that upset his stomach. "We hope that because you're from Eighth Army, you can find the file and re-open it. Then the KNPs will have no choice but to go along. Where you Americans lead, they follow."

"But if something goes wrong?"

"Then Mr. Pak will send me out in the field somewhere far away, and he will bow deeply to the KNPs and tell them how sorry he is."

"And maybe a little money will be handed over to ease hurt feelings."

"A good relationship with the KNPs," Ming said, "is very important."

We finished our drinks.

Ming glanced back at the hallway where Madame Hoh had disappeared, then turned back and rubbed his hands nervously. Suddenly, he leapt up from his chair, bowing again, and said, "She's angry now but I'll fix it up. You don't worry. I'll fix everything."

With that, he scurried off to the back and disappeared into the same dark hallway.

I sat alone. None of the hostesses approached me, no one asked if I wanted anything to drink. In Mia-ri a man alone was an odd sight, especially an American man alone. Not only did the hostesses ignore me, they didn't even look at me.

I wondered why this Madame Hoh would've pursued a claim aggressively in the past, been denied, and then apparently changed her mind to the point of seeming aggrieved that Ming would bring the issue back to life. The more I thought about it, the more I believed there had to be a good reason and the more uncomfortable I felt.

Did this have anything to do with the man with the iron sickle?

Why did Ming, and his boss Mr. Pak, bring me out here? Just to reopen a case they thought they might make some money on? At the moment, I had no answers.

The back hallway remained dark.

The only sound out here in the main ballroom of the Inn of the Crying Rose was the tinkling of ice cubes dropping into crystal tumblers and the gurgling of scotch being poured. The only smell was the pungent tang of stale Korean tobacco. Still, no one looked at me. I might as well have been invisible. What would Ernie do in a situation like this? Probably throw something, smash a mirror. Instead, I rose and walked toward the back hallway. As I did so, the hostesses and even the customers, studiously averted their eyes.

I entered darkness.

A dark hallway stretched back toward one naked bulb. The reek of ammonia led to the co-ed *byonso*. I walked past it and found a hallway leading to the left. At the end was another doorway with no lettering on it. I tried the knob. It opened.

A single green lamp illuminated a small wooden desk in the corner. Taking up most of the room were two stiff-backed couches on either side of a short coffee table. In the center of the table sat a hexagonal box of wooden matches and two large glass ashtrays. I sniffed the air. No smell of fresh smoke.

A shadow loomed out of the darkness. I raised my fists and was about to punch the approaching figure and then I realized who it was. Ming.

"What are you doing?" I asked, lowering my fists.

"She's gone," he said. "When you came, I hid."

"Why?"

"I don't know. Something's not right."

"Is this her office?"

"Yes."

"Why would she leave?" I asked.

Ming shrugged. He didn't have a reply to that. We walked back toward the *byonso* but now a double door just beyond it was open. I stepped toward it and discovered it was the loading area that led to a storeroom. It was piled high with wooden crates filled with brown OB Beer bottles and the smaller crystalline containers of *soju*.

But there was no truck backed up to the door. One of the doors swung open on its hinges, creaking, as if someone had just departed. I stepped outside. A dark alley stretched before us, lined with walls of brick and cement block.

"She's running," I said. "Come on."

"Better we wait here," Ming replied. "I think maybe I shouldn't have brought you."

I had no time for him. I was already trotting down the alley.

There was only one reason Madame Hoh would've decided to drop her claim—if she had already begun to pursue the resolution of that claim in a different way; a way that she wanted to keep secret. A way that wouldn't stand scrutiny from an agent of the 8th United States Army Criminal Investigation Command.

I had already reached the end of the alley when I saw them, emerging from a cross street. Four men, until a fifth stepped from a shadow behind me. Two of them held clubs. The others had unusually large fists. Brass knuckles, I thought. They were all slender young Korean men. In the dim yellow light from the bulb in back of the Inn of the Crying Rose, I could see their grim expressions, their square faces and high cheekbones.

I was toast, I thought. Unarmed. Alone. But I also knew the worst thing I could do was hesitate. I didn't slow my stride. Instead, I marched straight at them, tossing back the edge of my coat as if reaching for a weapon. I shouted, "Freeze! Eighth Army CID!"

Somehow, I don't think they were impressed.

-10-

I plowed into them like I knew what I was doing. The guy directly in front of me with a cigarette dangling from his lips stared up at me wide-eyed and leapt out of my way. The two on either side of him didn't back up but closed in. I landed a straight left to the jaw of one, pushed the other down, and started running. My goal was to make it back to the well-lit main drag of Mia-ri. The problem was this road didn't lead back to it but veered off farther away. Still, I figured there'd be a cross street up ahead where I could hang a quick left, if I ever made it that far. Their feet pounded behind me.

As I passed trash cans I knocked them into the middle of the road. Unfortunately for me, Koreans have been recycling for centuries, and there wasn't much detritus to slow down my pursuers, just fish bones and apple peels and wilted cabbage leaves. I concentrated on speed. But running was for the little guys, never my forte. Instead, I usually chose to stand and fight but this time the odds were much too long. I spotted an intersection up ahead and churned forward, hearing the maddening clatter of footsteps behind me. Sweat poured into my eyes.

I was a few steps from the road when one of the thugs landed on my back like a ravenous predator and wrapped his forearm around the front of my neck. Struggling to breathe with his weight bearing down on me, I bent forward as fast as I could, tossing him in the air. He flew straight over and then down, smashing on the cement with a crack that, even in my panicked state, I hoped wasn't his neck. Two more thugs hit me, and I lost my footing and went down. I rolled on the filthy road, coming to a halt spread-eagled on the pavement. When the first one came at me, I lifted myself up and butted my head into his stomach. Clutching his arms, I was able to regain my feet, and then I pushed him into the other guy and started punching until another guy appeared at my side, and something poked into my left arm. I decided to punch him too. Both men went down but that's when things got bad.

The rest of the herd was on me now. Kicks rammed into the back of my thighs, but covering my head with my forearms, I moved blindly, punching as I twirled toward the cross street, fighting my way to the safety of a soot-smeared brick wall. Just a few yards ahead, I spotted the bright lights of Mia-ri, which gave me hope. I lunged at one of the attackers, hitting him and knocking his head so hard he reeled backward, and I pushed past him and through their line and started to sprint once again for civilization. The bright lights were no more than ten yards away when it seemed as if two one-hundred-pound sacks of rice landed on my back. I collapsed to the ground, rolling from the kicks, and I managed to wedge myself between crates of empty liquor bottles that had been stacked against a wall in the alley. I grabbed splintered wood, yanked the top crate free from its stack, and threw it as hard as I could at the thugs. The crate swirled through the air, and crystalline bottles flew out and crashed to the dirty blacktop. The hoods backed off enough for me to push myself up against the wall and stand, then I was running through them again, only a few yards now from the main drag. They took more shots at me, but I stumbled into the glare of flashing neon.

Through sweat-smeared eyes I saw people were staring at me, their mouths open in horror. Half-crawling, I dragged my body fully into the light.

Grumbling and cursing, the thugs backed away, leaving me to collapse face down in front of a growing crowd of scantily clad cocktail hostesses and red-faced Korean businessmen. Some of the men pointed and laughed, figuring this was part of the adventure of their night on the town. Still, no one was punching me or kicking me anymore, for which I felt inordinately grateful. Briefly, I wondered where Ming was and then I passed out.

"What the hell happened to you?" Ernie asked.

"What do you think happened?" I said.

"You head-butted a rhinoceros?"

"No. I finally decided to have a little plastic surgery. Alter my nose; tighten the wrinkles around my eyes."

"You look divine, *dahling*," Ernie said.

I lay in an elevated bed at the 121st Evacuation Hospital. Earlier this morning when I roused myself from a pain-killer-induced haze, I took inventory of my body parts. Everything seemed to be working, although everything hurt. The nurse told me I'd been shot full of antibiotics, and I'd received almost a dozen stitches in various parts of my body. They'd been monitoring for internal bleeding, but so far there didn't appear to be any.

"Can I leave now?" I asked.

"Not until the doctor says it's okay."

"When will that be?"

"Morning rounds," she said primly and walked out.

I returned my attention to Ernie. "Where's Ming?"

"Who?" Ernie said.

"The Chinese guy I went to Mia-ri with. What happened to him?"

Ernie looked puzzled. "According to the KNP report, they found you alone, face down on the main drag of Mia-ri, passed out. At first they thought you were just drunk and then they saw the blood."

"Nice of them to be so observant."

"They called the MPs, who called an ambulance, and they carted you back here."

I sat up. "What time is it?"

"Zero nine hundred," Ernie said.

"How long have I been here?"

"Since just after curfew."

"That long? And what took you so long to get here?"

"Nobody told me about it until I walked into the office this morning."

Normally, the MPs would've found Ernie whether he was in the barracks or out in the ville to tell him his partner was in the hospital. Apparently they were still pissed about Dexter being locked up.

I tossed the sheet back and started to slide out of bed.

"What do you think you're doing?"

"We gotta talk to Strange."

"Strange? What'd they knock your pervert screw loose?"

"No. Last night, I learned about a file, a secret file containing claims against Eighth Army that have been suppressed, claims that were never processed."

"Wait a minute." Ernie placed his hand on my shoulder. "You better stay put. Let me talk to the doctor."

"To hell with the doctor."

The morning rounds in a big over-crowded military hospital could take hours. I stood up, the soles of my feet cold on the tile floor. I stepped toward the open closet where I saw my clothes hanging, and when I was about halfway to my destination, an earthquake must've hit. The floor rolled, and I remember thinking this was strange because Korea doesn't have many earthquakes and then the room grew dim, and the lights popped out, and the next thing I knew I was diving through the eternal ether. Everything was dark. Very dark.

Strange sat with both elbows on a Formica covered table in the 8th Army snack bar. A black plastic holder with an unlit cigarette dangled between his thin lips. Cruelly bloodshot red orbs bulged behind his green-tinted shades.

"Had any strange lately?" he asked.

"Can it, Strange," Ernie told him. "We're here on important business."

"The name's Harvey."

"Okay, Harvey. You heard my partner's question. Now answer it."

The doctor at the 121 had held me a couple more hours for observation, but in the end he decided I had not received a serious concussion and had probably only been dizzy because of blood loss. He told me to take it easy for the next few days, to drink a lot of fluids, and to refrain from heavy lifting. If I experienced any pain aspirin couldn't help, I was to report immediately to sick call.

"They need the bed," Ernie told me as we walked out of the hospital.

Military doctors aren't worried about being sued, and they figure most of us healthy young GIs are about as rugged as plastic soldiers anyway. We take a beating and keep on ticking. I was stiff and sore but otherwise functioning.

"What was the question again?" Strange asked.

"Eighth Army Claims," I said. "They have a file of every claim for damages made by Korean civilians against the Eighth United States since the end of the Korean War. However, it has come to my attention that there is another file, a secret file of suppressed claims.

Claims that have been deemed too embarrassing to the Command or too damaging to see the light of day."

Strange's lips tightened. His cigarette waggled. "Who has this file?" he asked.

I slammed my open palm down on the table. "Christ, Harvey. That's what I'm asking you."

He glanced around the snack bar, making sure no one was listening. They weren't. The place was bustling with almost a hundred GIs in uniform and a smattering of Department of Defense civilians on their lunch breaks. Conversation was pitched at a controlled roar.

Strange leaned toward me. His long brown hair was oiled and slicked back neatly over his bald spot. "SOFA," he said.

"What?"

"The Status of Forces Committee," he said a little louder, more insistent. He glanced to either side again before turning back to me. "They review those types of reports before deciding whether or not to turn them over to the Eighth Army Claims Office."

I'd known the SOFA Committee, which was made up of ROK Army and US Army personnel, arbitrated the appeal process for rejected claims, but I hadn't realized they also secretly vetted the claims before they were even allowed to go to the Claims Office. "How do you know this?"

He leaned back. "How do I know anything that goes on at Eighth Army? I pay attention."

"You snoop," Ernie said.

Strange's cigarette drooped. He looked offended. "That's a dirty word."

"Your favorite kind."

"So this Status of Forces committee," I said, "they're the ones who make the decision to suppress certain claims."

"Who else?" Strange replied. "The Commander doesn't get

involved. He wants deniability in case the shit hits the rotating wind machine."

"Has it ever?"

"No way." Strange scoffed. "Mr. Cool who runs the country would never allow it."

Ernie said, "Where do they keep these files?"

Strange looked around the snack bar, almost swiveling his head in a complete circle, to see if anyone was watching or listening. Luckily for us I don't believe anyone was, because it would have been obvious Strange was about to tell us a secret. Strange liked everyone to know he knew more than they did.

Well, usually. "I don't know," he whispered.

"What do you mean you don't know?" Ernie asked. "You run the classified documents distribution center. You're always bragging you know everything that's going on in Eighth Army."

"I do," he said.

"But you don't know this?"

"I know what I don't know," he said, tapping the side of his head.

"Can you find out where the documents are?" I asked.

"It depends."

"Depends on what?"

"Have you had any strange lately?"

Ernie groaned. We knew what that meant. Strange wanted to be told an elaborately obscene story of illicit sex in graphic detail and in return he'd spill his guts concerning the secret 8th Army claims file. A pervert in charge of classified documents. Somehow, it made sense.

This was my cue. I rose from my chair and hobbled over to the snack bar serving line. Taking my time, I grabbed a sturdy porcelain mug and pulled myself a cup of steaming hot java from the stainless steel coffee urn. At the register, I paid the middle-aged Korean lady twenty-five cents. She didn't hand me my receipt. I was about to open my mouth and ask for it when she said, "No more free refill."

"When did this start?" I asked.

"Today."

The price of everything was going up. I glanced at the table. Apparently so was the price of Strange's cooperation. He was leaning forward to hear the elaborate story Ernie was making up. From time to time Strange frowned and asked a question. Ernie sighed and kept talking. I stood off to the side and waited. I didn't really want to hear all this. Finally, when my coffee was about half gone, Strange rose and slunk out of the Snack Bar. I rejoined Ernie at the table.

"You okay?" I asked.

"Nothing a hot shower won't fix."

I had just finished my coffee when a siren went off, a huge wailing sound, then stopped. Everyone in the Snack Bar had frozen. And then a cannon fired and the wailing started again, louder this time.

"Alert!" someone shouted. More voices joined the chorus. Virtually everyone in the snack bar, especially those in uniform, was on their feet, grabbing their hats, wrapping toast and doughnuts in napkins and shoving them in their pockets, gulping down final glugs of orange juice or milk or coffee, slipping on their field jackets, and heading for the door, some at a trot, most at a flat-out run.

The wailing of the siren had taken on a pattern, three long bursts and one short.

"Move out," someone said.

A regular muster alert was one thing. Every soldier assigned to the 8th Army headquarters was required to report immediately to his post of duty. Once there, the time he arrived was logged in, and once the entire unit was accounted for, the unit strength was phoned in to the higher headquarters. A move-out alert was worse.

We were to assume our unit was already on a war footing, and we were to first put on our combat gear and check out our weapons at the unit arms room before reporting to either our posts of duty or our assigned defensive positions. Once there we'd be given the order as to whether or not to move out—load up our trucks or jeeps and whatever vehicles our unit was assigned, leave Yongsan Compound, and head to the boonies.

"At least there's no incoming," Ernie said. That is, no rounds being lobbed by Communist long-range artillery from the northern side of the DMZ.

"Not yet," I said.

Pandemonium had broken out and then subsided, and by now the snack bar was virtually empty. Slowly, Ernie stood up, slipped on his jacket, and said, "After you, maestro." I nodded in thanks. He walked and I hobbled up the hill toward the 8th Army Criminal Investigation Detachment. Riley was waiting for us.

"Where the *hell* you guys been?"

We were on night guard duty again, patrolling the shadowy perimeter of the 8th United States Army Headquarters South (Provisional). At least that's what the hand-painted sign above the main entrance said. What we were really patrolling was three or four acres of jumbled canvas tents in a punchbowl of mud. If we had elephants and tigers, we'd be a circus. We already had the clowns.

One of them emerged from the darkness, stepped beneath the glow of a yellow bulb dangling from a wire, and approached us as we made our rounds.

"Look lively there," he growled. "Don't stand around like a bunch of Marines."

It was Staff Sergeant Riley. He had his M-16 rifle slung over his shoulder. He was wearing baggy fatigues, combat boots and a field jacket two sizes too large for his narrow shoulders. His camouflage-netted steel pot sat on his head tilted at an angle.

"Who appointed you king of the guard post?" Ernie asked.

"Somebody's gotta make sure you pukes maintain the integrity of the perimeter."

"Maintain the integrity of this," Ernie replied, showing Riley his favorite finger.

We were tired. It was 8th Army's second day in the field, and we'd been out walking guard duty all last night and tonight since evening chow. It was almost midnight.

"You're supposed to be spread out," Riley said. "Not standing around shooting the shit."

"We already chased away all the Commies," Ernie said. "They're sixty miles north of here up on the other side of the DMZ."

Eighth Army's field headquarters was set up in this rural area about thirty-five kilometers south of the city limits of Seoul. Theoretically, on this side of the Han River, we'd be less vulnerable to an initial North Korean assault—if the Communist regime up north ever actually decided to invade. Once our brave forces repulsed them—and no one thought we wouldn't—we were still close enough to Seoul to return to Yongsan Compound and continue normal operations.

"What about infiltrators?" Riley asked.

"What about 'em?"

"North Korean commandoes can sneak across the DMZ and attack our positions at any time."

"Hey, Riley," Ernie said, "this is not a real war, okay? We're not in 'Nam anymore. All this is make-believe and as soon as the brass has had enough of playing tin soldier we'll be allowed to pack up and go home."

And maybe I'd be able to continue my investigation, I thought, but I knew better than to say anything to Riley, especially about the secret claims file. For now, we had to keep our suspicions to ourselves. If I told Riley, he'd tell the Provost Marshal. Maybe the PM didn't know about it—he probably didn't—and maybe he wouldn't take any action to thwart our plans if he did find out. Maybe. But I couldn't take that chance. I had to see that file without 8th Army's knowledge. I couldn't take the chance they would see the death of Mr. Barretsford and even the murder of Corporal Collingsworth as the acceptable price of keeping their secrets.

In the mess tent yesterday, Ernie'd found out from Strange that the file we were looking for was called the Bogus Claims Register, and it was held in the classified file cabinet of the Status of Forces Committee's Secretariat. We knew where their offices were, not far from the 8th Army headquarters building itself, and Strange said the files were locked in secure cabinets in the Secretary's office, which in turn was locked behind an iron-barred door. And of course, the entire complex was protected at all hours of night and day by armed guards. That was all Strange would tell Ernie.

Staff Sergeant Riley was about to open his mouth and point out another defect in our military bearing when footsteps tromped through mud.

An MP approached, wearing the same fatigues and steel pot we were, his M-16 slung over his left shoulder. He was a big man, and I thought I recognized his silhouette. As he came closer, moonlight shone in his face. Moe Dexter, freed now from his brief incarceration and cleared by the Provost Marshal of any charges stemming from the vandalizing of the *pochang macha* or threatening the use of a firearm against us. He'd been warned to watch his conduct, but all punishment was withheld, and he was returned to full duty.

"Well," Ernie said, bristling, "look who got a clean bill of health from his parole board."

"Better than having the creeping crud like you, Bascom."

"At least I don't stick it to my asshole buddies," Ernie replied.

I thought the two men were about to come to blows, but Dexter stopped his advance, stared hard at Ernie for a moment, and turned and aimed his gaze at me. "You better get your butt in gear, Sweeno, and take this asshole with you."

"I only see one asshole around here, Dexter," I said.

"We'll see about that once you're finished with this little detail. The Provost Marshal is screaming for you two back in the Command tent."

"What happened?"

Dexter pointed to a hill that loomed on the opposite side of the valley. "There's a signal truck up there."

In the dim moonlight, I could just make out the shape of a boxy truck holding up an antenna.

"Yeah?" I said.

"And apparently while you guys have been standing around with your thumbs up your butts, our signal troops have been having themselves a party, brought in a girl and everything."

Outside the perimeter fence, from dawn until well after dark, enterprising farm families had set up wooden stands selling fruit and bottled soda and *ramyon* packaged noodles and half-liter bottles of *soju*. GIs weren't allowed to leave the concertina wire that surrounded the compound but somehow transactions were made. In addition to the innocent stuff, at night some pimps and mama-sans brought in girls. They were mostly hidden out in the weeds, waiting for GIs to sneak through the wire or, if they were authorized to drive out of 8th Army bivouac area on a supply run, to stop beside the road.

Riley squinted at the moonlit hill. "Up there?" he asked.

"Whaddid I stutter? The Provost Marshal wants Sweeno and Bass Comb to investigate, immediately if not sooner."

Ernie rolled his eyes but started to march toward the Command tent. I pointed at Riley and Dexter. "You two," I said, "are now officially on guard duty."

"I can't do that," Riley sputtered.

"Yes you can," I replied. "The perimeter is yours."

Without waiting for further argument, I turned and trotted away.

Rain had held off all evening, but as if to punish us for our sins, it started up just as we were ready to leave the perimeter of 8th Army Headquarters South. The dirt road to the signal truck was extremely steep and difficult to drive under the best of conditions, but now it was much too slippery. We had no choice but to hump it up the hill.

"Did you bring a rain parka?" Ernie asked.

"Naw, it's still in my duffel bag. Didn't think we'd need it."

"Me neither."

The rain soaked my fatigue jacket and pant legs. Water trickled off my steel pot and dribbled down the back of my neck. The mud, meanwhile, sloshed over the top of my boots. After a half hour of steady climbing, we were three-quarters of the way up the hill. We stopped for a breather.

Below, the canvas tents that looked so buoyant in the afternoon breeze were now weighted down by the rain and looked like a field of soggy mushrooms. A few lamps flickered here and there but for the most part 8th Army headquarters was fast asleep.

"How did they get the girl up here?" Ernie asked.

"Probably picked her up in a jeep, drove up during the day when the road was still passable."

According to what we'd been told at the Command tent, the signal truck on Hill Number 143 was tasked with relaying communications from Seoul down to 8th Army Headquarters South. They had just made their routine hourly commo check when the radio man in the

Command tent heard a woman's voice in the background. Shortly afterward all communications were cut off. The communication boys down in the valley hadn't been able to raise them since. What the Provost Marshal was worried about was that the two signal men assigned up there had brought the girl and maybe a few bottles of *soju*, and figuring everything would be quiet, they were now passed out drunk and not relaying military communications. The Chief of Staff was hopping mad and so Ernie and I had been dispatched to check out the situation.

Other than the rain and the mud, it was nice to have a diversion from the boredom of guard duty. After a five-minute rest, Ernie and I resumed our climb up the hill.

When we came to the last rise, the rain had slowed. I couldn't see over the edge, so I signaled Ernie to stop. The only sound was the steady plop of rain into mud. No birds. No wildlife scurrying through the brush. I thought I heard some sort of humming background noise and figured that to be the generator. We crossed the rise. The signal truck was still not readily apparent. A few small lights blinked but they seemed to be coming from a bramble of trees.

"Camouflage nets," Ernie said, pointing at a peaked shadow. At that moment lightning flashed and we crouched low, holding onto our steel pots. The lightning had hit somewhere on the opposite side of the valley, but in that split second of light I could see the boxy truck and the cut brush leaning up against it. Huge nets hung overhead, held up by aluminum poles.

Thunder rumbled across the valley and, as if the lightning had been some sort of key to the locked sky, the rain clouds opened, dumping an angry torrent on the muddy hills.

I leaned toward Ernie. "The main lights inside the truck are off."

"They must be asleep," he said, "or passed out."

"Come on."

It wasn't easy reaching the truck because of the brush, and I had to duck under the camouflage netting, holding it aloft for Ernie so he could get through too. Meanwhile, of course, the rain seemed to be doing everything it could to thwart our progress. Drops hit the ground like pellets, splashing mud two or three feet high. Finally we reached the canvas overhang on the side of the truck.

"Just like back home in the trailer park," Ernie said.

Things weren't right; it was too quiet. Ernie and I both sensed it, which was why we were being cautious. We had expected to find the lights on, two guys drinking and laughing and maybe a Korean business girl squealing, and we'd barge in on them and slap them sober and call back to the Command tent. Later the two pukes would face either court-martial or at least Article 15 non-judicial punishment. But that wasn't how things were looking.

Fold-down metal steps led to a door at the back of the truck. I placed myself to the left and reached for the handle. Ernie stepped off to the right, unslung his M-16, checked the safety, and when he was ready, he signaled for me to go ahead. I twisted the door open so as not to make any noise. Inside the truck it was dark except for the low ambient glow of red and yellow lights coming from a communications control panel. Without walking up on the steps, I leaned forward and peeked into the truck. Too dark to see anything. The smell was metallic and burnt, like the smell from a soldering iron. I stepped up on the steps, and as I did so I slid my hand along the inside wall, searching for a light switch. I didn't find one. Instead, I reached in my pocket and pulled out a flashlight. I didn't switch it on right away because I didn't want to make myself a target. I stood inside the doorway, letting my eyes adjust to the darkness. I made out shapes. Two rows of electronic equipment, metal stools, supplies piled on the ground.

It was Ernie who saw it first. He tugged on the bottom of my fatigue pants and pointed to the puddle on the floor just in front of the door. Water, I thought, and then I saw it was dripping off the edge of the doorframe too slowly. I inhaled. Blood.

Without thinking, I hopped out of the truck. Ernie snatched the flashlight from me, switched it on, and aimed the beam into the depths of the truck. What I had thought were supplies were two soldiers in fatigues, on the floor, covered in blood, not moving.

Beneath the truck, something splashed. It scrabbled through the mud, then I caught the sound of squelching footsteps on the far side of the truck.

Ernie backed out and slammed the door shut. He darted to his left, I ran to the right. As I did so, I slipped my M-16 off my shoulder and, hands shaking, moved the bolt forward, chambering a round. At the edge of the truck, I crouched again, but only briefly. Whoever had run from under the truck had dashed into thick brush. Rain-laden branches quivered at his passing. I darted forward, Ernie crashing into the brush on my left, scanning ahead with the flashlight, but soon I motioned for him to turn it off because I could hear the footsteps moving across the plateau of Hill 143. We both stood still in the darkness and the rain. The rainfall was just a steady patter now, and footsteps sloshing through mud could be heard clearly, but they had stopped about twenty yards from me, as if whoever was ahead of us realized we were listening. Keeping the flashlight off, Ernie and I moved forward like two hounds stalking their prey.

The footsteps moved away from us, stealthily, as if hoping we wouldn't hear.

Ahead beyond the brush was a field of boulders. There were at least two dozen of them scattered across a checkerboard pattern. Briefly I wondered about glaciers moving across the Korean peninsula eons ago, pushing up hills, leaving behind massive chunks of granite. We moved forward, crouching at each boulder to wait and listen. When

I heard nothing, I'd burst around the huge rock, aiming my M-16 straight ahead.

The first two times I saw nothing but empty air. What if this guy was escaping? If he was moving quietly enough, he might already be on the far side of this field and running downhill toward freedom. To hell with safety, I thought. I started moving forward faster, taking my chances, ready to swivel at the slightest sound and fire a round into the face of whoever this bogeyman was.

Ernie and I had both spontaneously decided to chase the culprit, but what if one of the GIs back in the signal truck was still alive? What if one of them was breathing his last at this very moment? What if a well-placed tourniquet could have saved his life? I didn't think so. There had been such a huge pool of blood on the floor and the bodies had seemed lifeless. But what if we'd been wrong?

I shoved these doubts out of my mind and pressed on, stepping past the huge rocks quickly, swiveling from side of side. But it was this worry, this self-doubt, that led to my momentary lapse. Lightning struck. It came from behind me, many miles away, but it was enough to make me flinch and turn my head slightly and just as something darted through the rocks off to the left of my field of vision. I swung my rifle, opened my mouth, and shouted "Halt!" But as I did so, the thunderclap struck, rolling across the valley and drowning out any sound a mere human could have made. After the first flash of movement, the lightning had left me blind, but I darted forward anyway, ramming into the side of a rock, and then I saw it, dark and venomous, like a snake flying through the night, heading right at me. I crouched, feeling a whoosh of air from the reptile wing as it passed my face. Something metallic clanged into rock. I turned and fired my M-16 into the darkness. And then footsteps churned, panicked, through the mud.

My eyesight came back as I pulled myself up.

Ernie was tromping through the mud toward me. "What happened?"

I pointed to the rock next to my head. He switched the flashlight on. A dusting of freshly ground rock clung to a three-inch gouge.

"Christ," Ernie said. "That would've taken your head off."

Footsteps tumbled away through the rocks. "Come on."

We ran.

We had finally reached the edge of the boulder field, the sloshing feet only a few yards ahead of us, when I heard a thump. Someone whimpered. I stood still, listening, and then I took two steps forward. The whimpering again.

Whoever was out there had stopped, and they were so terrified at our approach that they were incapable of keeping quiet. Ernie closed in. I pointed to where I thought the sound was coming from and motioned for him to shine the flashlight on it. He did.

Brush rattled. Then someone was running again. I broke into a full-out sprint, crashing through the brush, shouting "Halt!" in English, forgetting for the moment how to say the word in Korean. Whoever was in front of me went down in a heap. I was holding the M-16, aiming at the sopping pile of rags in front of me, shouting for him to put his hands up, not caring whether he could understand me or not, ready to blow his freaking head off.

It was Ernie, strangely enough, who motioned with his open palm for me to lower the rifle. And then I saw what was in front of me. Bare legs poking out of a huge Army field jacket. The sturdy calves and creamy thighs were hairless, the rear end covered only by a wrinkled miniskirt.

The person huddled inside the jacket whimpered again and then a small hand appeared through the loose green material. It held a short-handled sickle. Ernie snatched it away, handed it to me, and then grabbed the small hand and hoisted the person upright. Long black hair hung down loosely, covering her face. Sweat matted strands were back-handed from cheeks, and then we saw her face. Full-cheeked, smooth, wide frightened eyes. She was about nineteen, I figured.

I examined the sickle. The razor sharp tip was dented in front, boulder dust still clinging to it.

I looked back at the girl. She was staring at her hands, clutching and pulling on her fingers. Her feet were crossed, her shoulders hunched. She was completely ashamed of herself. She ought to be. She'd just come about three-quarters of an inch from chopping my fool head off.

By the time the truck arrived, the sun had reached halfway toward its highest point of the day. The rain had stopped, but the mud was still so thick that there was no way an ambulance could make it up the hill. They had to send a two-and-a-half ton truck and the only one available was loaded in the back with wooden crates of high explosive artillery rounds. A couple of medics and a few MPs had marched up earlier, and they helped us roll the two dead GIs into body bags and hoist them up onto the ammunition crates in the back of the deuce-and-a-half. The rest of us clambered in back and in as low a gear as possible the driver started back down the hill. We slid about halfway down the road, but the guy at the wheel was expert enough to turn into the skids and we managed to reach level ground without rolling over.

The KNPs had already taken the girl.

Before they arrived, I'd had plenty of time to interview her. Her name was Shin Myong-ok. At least that's what she told me. Even though Korean citizens are required to keep their national identification cards with them at all times, she didn't have hers. She'd left it down in the valley with her mama-san, who'd brought her and five other girls out to the field to make some money from the small legion of 8th Army GIs who'd suddenly plopped down in their midst.

Ernie offered her water from his canteen, which she accepted gratefully along with a stick of ginseng gum. We sat beneath the awning on iron stools I'd brought outside of the signal van. Even in the huge field jacket, she shivered in the cold.

I asked her why she'd tried to kill me.

She bent at the waist and buried her face in her knees for what seemed like five minutes. Finally, she sat up, eyes moist and started to explain that the kind gentleman had told her American soldiers were coming to take revenge. Her only chance, according to him, was to protect herself with the iron sickle. He'd left it with her for just that purpose.

I slowed her down and made her start from the beginning. She did.

Just before sundown, the mama-san had bought them all bowls of noodles in the local village, and after dark they'd carried their blankets and a thermos of warm tea out into the brush on the far side of the perimeter of the 8th Army encampment. They sent two girls at a time to linger near the concertina wire and call for GIs to join them in the brush. When a GI worked up the courage to wriggle through the wire, he would disappear with the chosen girl and another girl would take her place. So it would go through the night; the mama-san collecting the money, the girls lying on the blankets, pulling up their skirts, and spreading their legs for the smelly Americans.

Except this night it was different. Early in the evening, before they'd laid out their blankets or sipped on their first cup of green tea, a "kind gentleman" arrived.

"Why do you say he was kind?" I asked.

"Because he smiled at me," she said. "And because he gave me this."

She reached into the pocket of her miniskirt and pulled out a coin. I asked her if I could examine it, and she said yes. It was bronze. I twisted it in my fingers and shone the flashlight on it. It was an old coin, from the Chosun Dynasty, according to the inscription. On it was a picture of Queen Min, one of the last members of the royal family to resist the plans of the Japanese Emperor to colonize her country.

"She was a brave woman," I said, handing the coin back to her.

"Yes. And the kind gentleman told me to be brave."

"Did he give you anything else?"

"Yes," Miss Shin replied. "He gave me that."

She pointed to the iron sickle, which Ernie had wrapped in plastic and placed on a metal stool.

-11-

The murdered GIs were identified as Specialist Four Anthony Ertagglia of Queens, New York, and Private First Class Roosevelt Hargis of Mobile, Alabama. Back in the Command tent there was zero sympathy for the fact that Ernie and I had been up all night. As soon as we arrived, we were badgered for as many answers as we could give in our depleted state. Eventually, Ernie took over the jawboning and I was given some time to type out my report. I slipped away and sat at a wooden field table with a Remington typewriter, rolled a sheet of paper into the carriage, and got all the facts down while everything was fresh in my mind—or as fresh as could be expected under the circumstances.

Miss Shin Myong-ok had told us the man she called the "kind gentleman" had appeared out of the weeds on the far side of the encampment.

"Did anyone else see him approach you?" I asked.

She didn't think so.

He'd been very polite to the mama-san and even bowed to her. She'd made a place for him on the largest blanket, and they'd sat and Miss Shin had been the one to serve him tea from the large thermos.

"Did you ever share your tea with GIs?" I asked.

"Never," she replied, shocked at the idea.

The mama-san thought at first that he was the type of Korean man who liked to partake of the charms of GI business girls. Mostly, the girls who hung out with American GIs were shunned for fraternizing so shamelessly with foreigners, but there were always a few perverts around who craved forbidden fruit. As it turned out, that wasn't what he had in mind. What he wanted, he said, was help in approaching a couple of Americans who worked in the signal truck atop the hill. He had a business proposition he wanted to make to them. He was vague about what the proposition was, but he implied that it had to do with the valuable equipment in the truck, equipment not available in Korea. He wanted to purchase it from the Americans for cash and, although he didn't say so, it was obvious to Miss Shin and the mama-san that he'd sell the equipment on the black market at a huge mark up. Everyone would profit. The GIs could claim the equipment had been stolen and the American military would replace it. However, due to military security, he couldn't get near the American GIs to make this very sensible business proposition. That's where Miss Shin came in.

He offered the mama-san enough money to cover Miss Shin's earnings for the entire evening. Her job would be to accompany him to the top of the hill and approach the Americans. With her pleasing smile and the help of a couple of bottles of *soju*, she would gain access to the truck and then ease the way for the gentleman to join the party.

According to Miss Shin, the mama-san didn't believe a word of it. She believed the man was up to no good, but on the other hand he was offering cash, twice as much as Miss Shin could've expected to earn in one evening. The mama-san accepted. Miss Shin had no choice but to go.

I asked her if she thought this man might hurt her.

No, she didn't think so, because he appeared to be such a kind gentleman.

I asked her if she thought the mama-san cared one way or the other if she was hurt or not.

She lowered her eyes and wouldn't answer.

These girls are literally purchased from poor farm families. The mama-san and the other girls in the group then become their new family. As in all Confucian families, the young owe unquestioning obedience to their elders. The elders, in turn, are required to make wise decisions on the behalf of the young. To hear it suggested that in her "family" this sense of responsibility ran only one way filled Miss Shin with shame.

The climb up the hill had been grueling. When they finally reached the top, the kind gentleman had been very solicitous to her and fetched her water to wash up. He encouraged her to walk alone the last few yards to the signal truck. He handed her the brown sack with the two bottles of *soju* and told her to bow and smile and when she gained entry to the truck to open the door after twenty minutes or so. He'd be waiting outside.

"He promised me extra money," she said.

"For what?"

"For getting inside and for opening the door for him."

"Did he want you to tell the Americans he was there?"

"No. He was very clear about that. His entrance into the truck had to be a surprise. He told me not to worry about that part. He would take care of everything."

"Did he?"

Again, she lowered her head.

By mid-afternoon, Mr. Kill, the Chief Homicide detective of the Korean National Police, had arrived at 8th Army Headquarters South, as had Major Rhee Mi-sook of the ROK Army. Major Rhee commanded a lot of GI attention in her exquisitely tailored fatigues as she strutted down the metal slat walkways lain in the mud. The Provost Marshal entered into a private conference with her, then, separately, did the same with Mr. Kill. Both of them wanted a copy of my report and access to the signal truck, which they were provided. Neither Ernie nor I were allowed to talk to either of them as the Provost Marshal wanted to handle this sensitive issue himself. Eighth Army was both embarrassed and enraged that two American GIs had been murdered right under our noses. There was even some whispering that the CG was considering relieving Colonel Brace as 8th Army Provost Marshal. But that was just talk. Nothing official had come down.

Both Major Rhee of the ROK Army and Mr. Kill of the Korean National Police inquired as to why the two lead CID agents on the case, me and Ernie, were pulling guard duty rather than continuing our investigation. At least, that's the word I got from Riley. The Provost Marshal would have never told us such a thing directly.

The reason we'd been put on guard duty was that the entire 8th Army was on move out alert. That meant, in military parlance, that everybody was required to participate. Everyone had to check out a rifle from the arms room, pack up their field gear, pitch in to hoist portable equipment onto the back of trucks, and be prepared, for once in our rear-echelon lives, to act like soldiers. The very few people excepted from this team effort were excused only because they were next in line on the duty roster—Staff Officer at the headquarters, medics at the emergency room, a skeleton crew back at the 8th Army Commo Center, and a handful of MPs assigned to physical security around Yongsan Compound. Other than that, no matter how important your regular job at 8th Army headquarters might be, you were doing the duffel bag drag and heading for the field along with every other swinging dick assigned to the command. No exceptions. And if the 8th Army Commander and the 8th Army Chief of Staff and the 8th Army Provost Marshal had to go, then a low ranking schmuck like a CID investigative agent was *definitely* going. For 8th Army to have allowed Ernie and me to stay behind and continue with the investigation would've been tantamount, in their minds, to admitting that our jobs were more important than theirs. This would never happen in a hierarchical military organization. That is, until the man with the iron sickle struck again.

That's when the 8th Army honchos were overruled. The special relationship between the Republic of Korea and the Unites States was in danger, and the 8th Army Commander better do something about it. The word came down from on high; maybe from the Ambassador, more likely from the US Army Pacific Commander himself: get your people out there and arrest the man with the iron sickle.

What the Provost Marshal did in response was send Ernie and me back to Seoul, with specific orders to cooperate with both the ROK Army and the Korean National Police to capture or otherwise put out of commission the man who was causing so much disruption.

Or, as he put it, to "Pop a cap into the son of a bitch."

Ernie and I were booked a ride on the next thing smoking. In this case, it turned out to be an empty fuel truck headed for Seoul. Ernie and I sat up front with the driver, our duffel bags stored in a narrow compartment behind the seats.

"Free at last," Ernie said.

"Free to have our butts busted if we don't find this guy."

"Don't sweat the small stuff, Sueño."

Ernie never worried about anything, not that I could tell. I admired him for it because I was a constant bundle of anxieties; anxieties he never failed to tease me about.

"Why do you think the Provost Marshal wouldn't let us talk to Mr. Kill?" he asked.

"Because Eighth Army had already lost enough face. The PM didn't want to make it worse by letting a VIP talk to a couple of enlisted pukes."

"And Major Rhee?"

"He wanted her all to himself."

"They all do." As soon as she'd arrived, the Chief of Staff and half the officers who worked for him found time to join in the conference.

We were heading back to the world of electricity, hot showers, clean clothes, and chow you didn't have to spoon out of a can. That was good enough to make Ernie happy.

Me, I was happy about that part, too, but I was still thinking about Specialist Four Anthony Ertagglia and Private First Class Roosevelt Hargis and what they looked like when we stumbled over their bodies in that signal truck. Blood everywhere. Grey tubes sticking out of their necks. And I was thinking about what the Chief of Staff was going to say when he wrote to their next of kin. I hoped he'd be able to say that the man who murdered their son or their husband or their brother was under arrest and rotting in a Korean prison.

Either that or rotting in hell.

I decided that as soon as we arrived on Yongsan Compound, I'd head straight for the Military Police arms room and exchange this unwieldy M-16 for a .45 automatic. Whatever it entailed, the work we would be doing in the next few days, or maybe the next few hours, wouldn't be done from a secure distance. It would be up close and personal. Of that much, at least, I was sure.

The 8th Army Staff Duty Officer was Major Woolword. We knew him briefly because he'd appeared on the MP blotter reports a few times for being drunk on duty. The only reason he hadn't been kicked out of the service with a bad conduct discharge was because the 8th Army Chief of Staff had a soft spot for him. They'd served together in the same unit in the Korean War. Woolword still had a few months to go until he could retire at his full rank of major. Knowing he was useless, the honchos had moved him up on the duty roster and left him behind at the almost deserted 8th Army headquarters in Seoul. He was being assisted by an efficient Staff Duty NCO by the name of Ervin, whose main job was to make sure that Major Woolword stayed sober. The third soldier assigned to staff duty was a KATUSA driver. KATUSA stood for Korean Augmentation to the United States Army, and they were usually rich Korean kids whose parents paid for a cushy assignment for them during their mandatory three-year tour in the military.

Ernie and I waited outside 8th Army headquarters until Sergeant First Class Ervin left the building for evening chow. When he was two blocks down the road he turned left, heading toward the 8th Army mess hall. We'd already been there to catch some chow ourselves. The usual waitress service was cancelled, and only two cooks manned the shorter-than-normal serving line. But they had a grill turned on, the chow was hot, and the coffee was steaming.

Ernie and I emerged from the bushes and approached the main door of the 8th Army headquarters building, flashing our badges to the two security guards. We were back in civilian clothes, but not the coat and tie normally required. Since there was no one around to keep an eye on us, we'd changed into our running the ville outfits: blue jeans, sneakers, a long-sleeve shirt with collar, and a nylon jacket with fire-breathing dragons embroidered on the back.

Major Woolword sat at his desk watching the Armed Forces Korea Network on a portable television. Some sort of game show, a rerun from about ten years ago. He looked up as we entered. In the corner, the KATUSA driver put down a Korean comic book, looking guilty.

Ernie and I came to the position of attention in front of Major Woolword's desk and saluted. We knew he liked being treated with respect rather than as the hopeless drunk he really was. Ervin wouldn't be gone long, so I got right to the point.

"We need the keys, Major, to the Office of the Secretariat, SOFA Committee."

I knew he was confused by the acronyms but his sagging, wrinkled face tried to look serious. And sober.

"Keys," he growled. "What for?"

"An investigation, sir," Ernie said, trying to appear as obsequious as possible, which wasn't easy for him. "The Chief of Staff sent us to check out some files, and he told us to talk to you personally."

"Fred? How is the old son of a bitch?"

"Fine, sir. And he speaks very highly of you."

"He ought to. I pulled his butt out of enough trouble. Did I ever tell you about the fire fight we ran into down near Gongchang-ni?"

We had to find the keys and get what we needed quick, before Ervin came back from chow. Nobody could enter a secure building and take classified files without express written permission. We'd considered coming back at night and actually breaking into the SOFA office, but that would be too risky. Korean security guards periodically patrol the halls at night, and the fact that the files had been stolen would be obvious once 8th Army returned from the field. Better to take them clean. Even copy them if we had time. What we were hoping for was to befuddle Major Woolword's booze-fogged mind.

I interrupted his reveries. "I'll find it in the key box myself," I told him.

"Sure," Major Woolword said. "Right over there."

Ernie leaned toward him. "You were in command of an infantry unit, sir?"

"No," Woolword replied. "Not infantry, a supply unit. But believe-you-me, in those days when the Pusan Perimeter was collapsing all around us, everybody was an infantry soldier."

"Even the Chief of Staff?"

"You bet. But he got caught with his pants down." Woolword

started to laugh. In short order, his laughter turned to coughing, and he bent over, grabbed a metal trash can, and spit phlegm so hard it sounded like a BB ringing a bell.

I knew where the Staff Duty Officer's key box was from pulling night duty. The idea was that every set of keys for doors and filing cabinets was numbered and listed in a log book, and a spare copy was kept in the Staff Duty Officer's key box. That way, in an emergency, authorized personnel could gain access to any nook or cranny in the vast 8th Army headquarters. I opened the door and fumbled through the huge wall-mounted cabinet. Some of the keys were laid on the lowest shelf, not hanging from a peg as they should be. Others were obviously out of place. The box probably hadn't been inventoried in quite some time. Not reassuring. I scanned the five typed pages of log, found the SOFA Committee, and located a ring of keys on the correct peg. Quickly, I stuffed it into my pocket.

So far so good. I hoped Ervin was a slow eater.

As I walked past Major Woolwoord's desk, I flashed Ernie the thumbs up sign. He'd keep him talking. I'd try to find the file Strange had called the Bogus Claims Register.

According to Miss Shin, Specialist Ertagglia and Private Hargis hadn't been interested in the *soju*, but they'd definitely been interested in her. She smiled and bowed, and they'd let her in, allowed her to sit on one of the stools, and even offered her some of the C-rations they were sharing. Fruit cocktail in a green can, she told me. They had a canvas cot wedged into the back of the van and that's where she figured she'd end up, but for the moment they were happy to have somebody *ooh* and *aah* as they slipped on earphones and dialed knobs and went through their usual communications routine. The boys seemed to be maneuvering about who would be first with Miss Shin, and they hadn't even worked their way around to offering her money yet when, after she figured twenty minutes had elapsed, she'd opened the door.

"He was different," she said.

"How so?"

"He seemed taller. Bigger. He stood up so straight. And for the first time I saw the sickle in his hand. He didn't hesitate. He pushed past me, and swung the sickle first at the dark one."

"Hargis?"

She shrugged. "I don't know their names. The GI was surprised, his mouth open when the blade slashed across his throat." She covered her eyes with her hands.

"Did you scream?"

"I don't know. I think so. So did the other GI, the white one. He tried to reach for something, something behind the blinking equipment, but his earphones jerked his head back, and he stumbled over one of the stools, and before he could grab whatever he was trying to grab, the man leapt over the dark one and sliced the blade across the white one's throat." She covered her eyes again. "I tried not to look. There was blood everywhere, and then he dragged me off the stool and pulled me outside. I fell down the steps. That's when I hurt my arm." She cradled her elbow. "I thought he would kill me, too. I kept trying to hide my throat."

"Did he hurt you?"

"No. He knelt beside me."

"What did he look like?"

"He was calm. Very calm. As if he'd just completed some important job. And he had turned into the kind gentleman again, the one I'd known before, waiting for me to recover from my hysterics."

"Did you?"

"Yes. I had no choice. I didn't want him to kill me, too."

"What did you do?"

"I asked him why he had killed them. He said they deserved it for what they'd done."

"Did he explain what they'd done?"

"No. He told me he had to leave. He told me to wait there and someone would come. If it was a Korean, I should ask for their help. If it was an American, I should run because they would surely kill me. Then he did an odd thing."

"What was that?"

"He wiped the blade in the grass and turned the handle of the sickle toward me and offered it to me."

"You took it?"

"I had no choice."

"Why not?"

"I didn't want him to use it on me."

"Did he say why he wanted you to have the sickle?"

"Yes. He said it was made in Korea. A traditional instrument used by our ancestors. If I used it with a pure heart, my ancestors would give me strength, and I would never be hurt."

"And that's why you used it on me?"

"I was frightened."

"So was I."

She looked away.

There were about a dozen keys on the large metal ring. I went through them quickly and opened the front door of the Status of Forces Committee Office of the Secretariat. I listened for footsteps down the hall. None. I closed the door behind me and used the flashlight sparingly, keeping it pointed to the floor. There was a reception area in front with some chairs and a small desk and behind that another room with another handful of desks. Off to the right a door opened into a conference room with seating for about a dozen. The office of the director was locked. I fumbled through the keys again and opened it. No file cabinets, only a desk bigger than all the others and a few leather chairs in front with a mahogany coffee table. To the left, ominously, was an unmarked door covered with an iron grate.

I looked through the keys. Only one was long with an unusual shape. I tried that first. The heavy door swung open. I stepped inside, feeling I was far enough from the outer hallway to switch on the overhead light. A row of filing cabinets, all of them padlocked with an iron rod running through the metal handles of the drawers from the top to the bottom.

Which one?

I stooped and studied the labels. Numerical—the Army filing system, with numbers assigned to broad subjects like security or logistics or personnel. At the end of each fiscal year, most files were retired, placed in cardboard boxes, and retained on site for five years. After that, if protocol was followed, they were to be shipped to the main Army Records Center in St. Louis. The idea was that an entire history of US Army activities could be recreated by these well-maintained records. I stared down the long row. Where was the file I was after?

What had Strange called it? The Bogus Claims File.

Shuffling through the keys again, I unlocked the cabinet containing the security files. I slid it open. Rows of manila folders, each affixed with a typed label. I riffled through them. Nothing saying "bogus." Maybe that's not what they called it, not officially anyway. I searched through the other subject titles to see if anything matched. Nothing. Then it dawned on me. If 8th Army never wanted this file to see the light of day, and if they never wanted a permanent record made of it, then they wouldn't keep it here. I was looking in the wrong place.

I left the room, relocking the door, and stepped behind the big desk. There it was. A small two-drawer cabinet made out of wood, not the government-issue grey metal like the other filing cabinets, but something more fancy, like maybe somebody had bought it out of the PX at their own expense. This one had a wooden peg in the top handle that said PRIVATE.

Again I fumbled with keys. None of them worked. It figured. If the officer in charge of the Status of Forces Committee Secretariat wanted to keep something away from prying eyes, he'd keep the keys himself.

I searched the desk, pulling open desk drawers and ignoring photographs, personal letters, a shoe shine kit, and the electric razor in the bottom drawer. Again nothing. I pulled out each desk drawer, looking under it. On the third one I found it, taped to the bottom with brown tape almost the same color as the desk. I ripped the key free, replaced the drawers, and tried it in the cabinet. It popped open. I pulled out the top drawer. I had just found the letter B when I heard voices outside and footsteps approaching down the hallway. Did they know I was in here? I couldn't be sure. Nothing I could do about it now. I tried to ignore the rapidly approaching footsteps and concentrate on what I was doing. I was too close now to stop. I kept searching, and then I found it, exactly as Strange had predicted. A file marked: BOGUS CLAIMS, CONFIDENTIAL, EYES ONLY (DO NOT COPY).

My original plan was to copy the information and replace the file. That wasn't going to work this time.

I pulled the file out. It was thin, thinner than I would've imagined. I relocked the cabinet, tossed the key in the top desk drawer, stood up, and stuffed the file inside my pants snug against my back. I tightened my belt to make sure the file didn't fall.

Outside, the footsteps came closer. Subconsciously, I checked the .45 in my shoulder holster. Then I pulled my hand away. These people weren't my enemies.

I walked around the large desk and reached for the door knob, pausing to listen. There was an argument of some sort. One voice was

Major Woolword's. Whose the other was, I couldn't say, but I'd soon find out. I opened the door and stepped outside.

"Hold it right there!"

A black Sergeant First Class in pressed fatigues was crouching and holding a .45 automatic with both hands, pointing it straight at me. An overhead fluorescent bulb had been switched on and ambient light glimmered off a neatly trimmed mustache and a nametag that said "Ervin."

I raised my hands to my side, slowly.

"There's no *need* for this," Major Woolword said.

"The Major's right," I said. "No need."

I was working on keeping my voice steady. The gaping maw of the barrel of the .45 mesmerized me, a black hole trying to suck me in. Where the hell was Ernie? And then I heard his voice, down the hallway. Shouting. More footsteps and then two MPs were barreling toward us, Ernie at their lead.

"Hold it, Ervin," Ernie said. "Put the gun away."

When Sergeant Ervin saw the MPs he straightened up and, much to my relief, lowered the .45. Everyone was shouting at once. Apparently, as soon as Ervin returned from chow and the KATUSA driver told him that Major Woolword had allowed me to take some keys, he'd pitched a fit. Ernie told him to can it but couldn't stop Ervin from pressing the alarm button on his desk, which alerted the MPs. When they arrived, Ernie did his best to head them off by explaining we were on official business, and while he was doing that, Ervin grabbed his weapon and, with Major Woolword in tow, made a beeline for the SOFA Office. Actually, he was just doing his job. Ernie and I had no business rifling through files without the express permission of the Chief of Staff or his designated representative. Our ace in the hole was Major Woolword. If he admitted Sergeant Ervin was correct and we weren't supposed to be doing what we were doing, then he would look like the incompetent he was. Luckily, his exaggerated sense of pride kicked in.

"Hold on now, Sergeant Ervin. I authorized these men access to the SOFA Secretariat, and I believe my authority holds sway here."

"No it does *not*, sir," Ervin replied. "The Staff Duty Officer isn't allowed to grant access to any of the offices in Eighth Army without the express permission of the Chief of Staff."

"Fred? I'll call him. I'm sure he'll back up my judgment on this one."

Ervin believed Major Woolword had been snookered, but he also realized the good Major wasn't going to back down. Ervin grumbled about making an entry in his log, and I believed he would, and I also knew that by tomorrow morning the Provost Marshal would be aware of the entire incident. He'd want an explanation. One he wouldn't get, not from me, because Ernie and I would be incommunicado by then. I handed the keys back to Major Woolword. He snatched them from my hand.

"Thanks for your cooperation," I said.

Ernie saluted Major Woolword, who snapped to attention and returned the salute smartly. As we left, the MPs and Sergeant Ervin were still bickering amongst themselves.

"You think Major Woolword will sneak out now for a drink?" Ernie asked.

"After all this," I said, "who could blame him?"

We knew we didn't have much time. Cooler heads than Major Woolword would soon realize what we were after; namely, the Bogus Claims File. They'd be worried sick over what we'd do with the information and they probably would put out an all points bulletin for the MPs to take us into custody. What we'd done was illegal. We'd pilfered a personal file. Even though I hoped it would provide us with important leads, we hadn't properly requested permission to search the files. Worse, we threatened to blow a hole a mile wide in the façade of integrity of the honchos of the 8th United States Army. Claims against the military are required to be adjudicated in an open and legally prescribed manner. To suppress claims was illegal under both US law and the Status of Forces Agreement. But in this case, the SOFA Committee itself had been the ones to illegally suppress certain claims they deemed too dangerous. Since the SOFA Committee is composed of both US and Republic of Korea officers, not only was the American side guilty of a cover up, but so were the ROKs.

Great. Now they'd both be pissed.

Ernie and I sat in a Bachelor Officer Quarters day room reading the file.

"Christ," Ernie said. "We did all this?"

The file contained allegations of various types of mayhem that ranged from negligent to sadistic. For example, a three-year-old was run over and killed by a military convoy transporting top secret material up to Camp Page in the mountains near Chunchon. The convoy consisted of four huge trucks with canvas-covered cargo on flat-bed trailers. The fact that this claim was suppressed didn't surprise me. It was widely rumored that nuclear-tipped tactical missiles were deployed near Chunchon. Of course, the 8th Army denied that rumor, so this case had been filed away. Whoever lost their three-year-old was just out of luck.

Other claims had to do with secret maneuvers, special forces units on clandestine missions on or near the Demilitarized Zone or down south near coastal areas. One of the things that makes Korea different from the States is there are civilians everywhere. In the States we have huge military reservations in the badlands of Texas, in Oklahoma, in the deserts of Nevada and Arizona and California, places where civilians aren't found—unless they're an old sourdough with a burro. The military can pop off armaments with impunity. Korea, on the other hand, is an ancient country and every bit of arable land has long since been occupied. And since the devastation of the Korean War people have been so poor they've been willing to venture into live-fire exercises to collect the spent brass from bullets and artillery shells in order to sell it to metal dealers. When kids are hurt this way, it usually results in a claim being filed, but not when the exercise is classified. Not when its object is to violate the cease fire agreement between North and South Korea and infiltrate areas north of the MDL, the military demarcation line. Then the claim is crushed.

The file was composed of typed onionskin, stamped FOR YOUR EYES ONLY. There were probably a dozen sheets. Not much when you considered more than twenty years of military operations. Especially when you compared them to the hundreds, maybe thousands, of claims that had been processed.

As I read each sheet I handed them to Ernie. He soon tired of the exercise. "They got anything to drink around here?"

Ernie wandered down the hallway toward the kitchen. The BOQ was completely deserted. All of the officers were probably in the field at 8th Army Headquarters South. Ernie returned in short order.

"Nothing in the refrigerator but *this*." With a thumb and forefinger he held up a cup of yogurt, glaring at it with lip-curled disgust. "Not even one freaking bottle of beer. This is a female BOQ, isn't it?"

I nodded. "Captain Prevault lives here."

Ernie tossed the yogurt into the trash, making the metal can clang. "So you were hoping to see your girlfriend," he said.

"No," I replied. "I just thought her room would be a good place to leave the file. Here," I said, handing him one of the onionskins, "look at this."

Ernie grabbed the sheet and read it quickly. Then he whistled. "Damn. When did this happen?"

"The date's up top there."

He studied it. "During the Korean War."

"Right. But the claim wasn't filed until almost ten years after."

"Why'd they wait so long?"

"Good question. Another good question is why did Eighth Army bury the claim?"

Ernie handed the sheet back to me. "You are so naïve. Do you think they're going to admit to *this*?"

"They didn't do it. It was done during the war, by an isolated unit surrounded by the enemy. All bets were off."

"In your opinion. Try selling that back in the States."

Ernie was right. The public back in the United States would never understand such a thing. And at a higher level, the US government would never want to hand a propaganda coup to their Communist enemies behind the Bamboo Curtain. I pulled out my notepad and copied all the facts I needed off the Report of Claim. Then I ripped out a sheet of paper and wrote a note to Captain Prevault, asking her to keep the file in a safe place until we could discuss it. I placed all the onionskins, along with my note, back into the manila folder, then walked down the hallway to her room and slid it beneath her door.

Outside the BOQ, from the slightly elevated terrain of Yongsan Compound South Post, the bright lights of downtown Seoul glittered in the distance.

"What now?" Ernie asked.

The evening was still young, not even twenty-one-hundred hours.

"After what I just read," Ernie continued, "a drink would do me good."

"Then let's do some more work at the same time."

"Like where?"

"I'm armed now," I said, patting the .45 under my jacket. "And I have back up. Namely you."

"Who do you want to kill?"

"I don't want to *kill* anybody. But maybe we should pay another visit to Madame Hoh, the beauteous *gisaeng* house owner in Mia-ri."

"Sounds good," Ernie said. "Booze and beautiful women. Just the kind of work I like."

And just the kind of thing, I thought, to take our minds off the report we'd just read. It was stomach churning and unbelievable. Americans wouldn't stoop to something so low, would they? Would anyone ever be so desperate? This crime was not a part of modern warfare, or at least I hadn't thought it was.

When we hopped in the jeep Ernie drove faster than usual, zigzagging madly through the swerving Seoul traffic, following the signs past the Seoul Train Station, beyond the Great South Gate, around the statue of Admiral Yi Sun-shin and finally through the narrow roads that led toward the bright lights of Mia-ri. We were both quiet on the drive, trying not to think of what we could not stop thinking about: a crime as old as humanity itself.

Cannibalism.

We parked the jeep near a *pochang macha*. I half expected to see Mrs. Lee, the owner from the Itaewon *pochang macha*, when I peeked through the hanging flaps. Instead, I saw a startled Korean man with a square face and a wispy beard, and I offered him a thousand *won* if he kept an eye on our jeep. He readily agreed and pocketed the money like Houdini palming a playing card.

Mia-ri seemed more lively than ever. Maybe it was the contrast to what we'd seen in the signal truck and what we'd read in the Bogus Claims File, but Ernie was about as animated as I've ever seen him, which was plenty animated. He kept stopping as we trudged up the narrow road, grabbing hold of the heavily made-up young women in the clinging silk gowns, wrapping his arm around their slender waists, cooing into their ears. They laughed and toyed with him, happy to see a young GI but at the same time wary; being warned off by their mama-sans in favor of large groups of businessmen in suits.

"*Tone oopshi*," one of the old mama-sans went so far as to say. He doesn't have money.

Still, the girls liked Ernie and his playful attitude—they weren't much more than kids themselves—and he seemed to have an ample supply of ginseng gum, which he handed out to the red-tipped fingers of the laughing young prostitutes. I kept him moving up the hill. Finally, we stopped at a stand that had a supply of Jinro *soju* bottles, and Ernie bought a half-liter. The vendor popped the top off and Ernie downed about a fourth of the fiery rice liquor on the first swallow. He gasped and handed the bottle to me. I wiped off the lip and took a modest sip. My throat convulsed. Rotten stuff. I handed the bottle back to Ernie. He took another large swig.

"Easy, pal," I said. "We have a long night."

"Maybe *you* have a long night. I'm going to have a drunk one."

Ernie always acted like the things we saw didn't faze him. He would hold everything at bay for a while but finally, as if a dam broke, he'd go on a bender. If he was going to get drunk tonight there was nothing I could do to stop him. Besides, now that I'd managed to hold down the shot of *soju* I'd taken, it was starting to warm my stomach and feel pretty good. I took the bottle from Ernie and held it a little longer this time.

We rounded the corner to the Inn of the Crying Rose, the bar Mr. Ming had brought me to before. It was dark, the neon sign turned off, looking sad and forlorn amongst all the blinking neon surrounding it. I tried the wooden door.

"Locked," I said.

"Try knocking." Ernie pounded on it. While we waited for an answer, he drank down the last of his *soju*. Then he pounded again, and we gave up and walked to a dark crack between the buildings.

"Can you fit through that?" Ernie asked.

"Sideways," I said.

Ernie motioned with his open palm. "After you."

I slid into the narrow passage first. The ground below was muddy and pocked with rocks and broken glass and other types of filth I didn't want to think about. Finally, I popped out in back of the building. Ernie appeared right after me, brandishing his empty bottle of *soju*.

"Let me at 'em," he said.

The alcohol was already doing its work.

The back door of the Inn of the Crying Rose was locked just as tightly as the front. "Looks like she closed up shop," Ernie said.

"Apparently."

We went back around to the front but this time took the long way, walking down to the end of the block, turning toward the main drag, and then doubling back.

"This is where they caught you?" Ernie asked.

"Back a few blocks," I said. "I had to run up here and then with all these people walking around, they left me alone."

"We could go back there and try to find 'em," Ernie said.

"Maybe later," I said.

He whooshed a left hook into the air. "I'm 'bout to knock me somebody the hell *out*." The booze was hitting him hard because we were tired. After returning to the barracks this afternoon and cleaning up, we'd gone right back to work.

I stopped in a noodle shop near the Inn of the Crying Rose. When I started asking questions, the owner waved his hand in front of my face and refused to answer. I tried a ladies' boutique a couple of doors down that was just closing up for the night. This time, the well-dressed owner was more willing to talk.

"She sell everything," she told me in heavily accented English. "Go away. Say her brother come back. Want her leave Mia-ri."

"Her brother came back from where?" I asked.

She shook her head. She didn't know. She also didn't know where the woman known as Madame Hoh had gone.

"Maybe you ask owner."

"The building owner?"

She nodded.

"Who is it?"

202 ▪ MARTIN LIMÓN

She pointed across the street. The man who owned the noodle shop.

Ernie and I sat down and ordered a bowl of noodles. We were famished. When Ernie was about to order a bottle of *soju* to go with it, I told him to wait.

"Wait for what?"

"Let's get this job done first," I said. "Then we can kick out some jams."

"I'm ready to kick out the jams right now," he replied.

But he went along with my program. A rotund teenage girl, probably the owner's daughter, served us two bowls of *kuksu*, steamed noodles with scallions and some sort of sea life floating around. We ate quickly. After slurping down the last of the broth, I told Ernie the plan.

He nodded enthusiastically. "And then we can drink, right?"

"Right."

When it was time to pay up, I flashed the girl my CID badge and demanded to see the owner. Her eyes widened but without a word she turned and fled to the kitchen. In less than a minute, the owner, the man who had waved his hand negatively before when I asked about the Inn of the Crying Rose, strode up to the counter.

"Over here," I said in English, pointing at the area beside our table. The man hesitated.

"*Bali*," I said. Quickly.

He scurried over. Apparently the waitress had told him about our badges. He stood narrow-eyed, staring down at us.

"How long had they been selling it out of the bar across the street?" I said in Korean.

"Selling?"

"Don't act dumb. You know what they were selling. I asked you how long?"

He shook his head.

I sighed elaborately. "You must've known."

"I knew nothing." He was getting worried.

"Everybody knew," I said, "The whole neighborhood knew. How is it possible you didn't know?"

"I didn't know," he said stubbornly.

Ernie slammed his fist on the table, the empty bowls rattled, and he leapt to his feet. "What kinda bullshit is this?" he said, glaring at the smaller man. I stood also, sticking out my arm as if to hold Ernie back.

"You say you didn't know about it," I said. "Then show us. Give us the keys."

I held out my open palm. The man looked confused. "Do you want us to call the Korean National Police?" I said.

That seemed to make the decision for him. He whipped off his apron. "*Jom kanman*," he said. Just a minute.

Within seconds he returned with a set of keys clutched in his fist. We followed him outside and down the two doors to the Inn of the Crying Rose. I held a penlight for him as he shuffled through the keys. Finally, he located the right one and stuck it in the lock. He turned, and the door popped open. Together, we entered.

It was quiet in there, and musty.

"Where are the lights?" I asked in Korean.

"In the back," he replied.

We made our way past empty booths and cocktail tables with chairs upturned on top of them. Finally, we reached the bar.

"What were they selling?" he asked.

"It's better you don't know," I said. "Why did she leave in such a hurry?"

"Something to do with her brother," he told me.

"Where did she go?"

"I don't know. Her hometown. She didn't tell me where it was."

Koreans, through accent and mannerisms, can always tell what part of the country another Korean is from. "What part of the country?" I asked.

"The east coast, I think. Kangwon-do."

Ernie slid open the beer cooler. "Shine that light over here," he said. I did. Empty.

"Nothing but tin," he said. The shelves behind the bar were similarly bereft of any liquor.

The owner found the lights and switched them on. They weren't bright, just a low red glow suffusing the main ballroom. I groped my way toward the back, past the empty storeroom, and finally to the door that opened onto the office. I stepped inside, to a small wooden desk, and searched the drawers. Empty, except for a few wooden matches, some awkwardly-sized Korean paper clips, and two broken pencils.

I returned to the bar.

"She cleaned out totally," I told Ernie.

"Yeah. Not so much as a tumbler of *mokkolli*."

At the mention of the Korean word for rice beer, the owner glanced at Ernie curiously.

"There's one spot we haven't searched," Ernie said.

"Where?"

"The cloak room."

He pointed toward the Dutch door next to the entrance. It had been dark when we walked past it.

"Come on."

The owner followed.

I shoved the top part of the door open and groped inside for a wall switch. There wasn't one. I fumbled with an inner latch and pushed open the lower part of the door.

"Above," the owner said.

I reached up and waved my hand around until I found a string. Gently, I pulled down. A bulb ignited the room. There were no coats on racks, not even any coat hangers, but sitting in the center of the room, perched on a wooden stool was something Ernie and I had seen before.

The totem. The same one we'd seen in the Itaewon Market on the day when Corporal Collingsworth had been murdered. The same wooden stand, the same wire rectangle rising above, but this time there was no dead rat dangling by it's feet. This time there was something else tied to the wire. Something that took a while for my eyes to bring into focus. Something slathered in blood, blood that had dripped down the rectangular wire and further along the wooden base of the contraption and puddled in a yard-wide lake of gore at the bottom of the stool.

It was a head.

The head of Mr. Ming, the man who had once been the top-earning field agent for the Sam-Il Claims Office.

We didn't return to 8th Army until noon the next day.

By that time, the compound was alive with trucks and jeeps and vans, all ferrying personnel and equipment back from the field, away from 8th Army Headquarters South and back to the civilization of the Yongsan district of southern Seoul. The field exercise had been called off. Ernie and I were more exhausted than we thought possible. We drove straight to the 8th Army snack bar and parked the jeep.

The place was packed. A lot of people were after some hot chow. Ernie and I stood in line at the grill, and he ordered a hamburger and fries, and I ordered two bacon, lettuce, and tomato sandwiches. When we finally paid for our lunch, it took us ten minutes of waiting to squeeze into a vacated table up against the wall. We were only a few feet from the jukebox and somebody had put on "Break It to Me Gently," which was one of my favorite songs.

Ernie said, "You like that?"

I nodded.

"You would," he said.

I wasn't sure what he meant by that but I didn't really care because I was too busy eating to pay him much attention. I'd just chomped into my second sandwich when a pair of combat boots appeared next to our table. Small combat boots. I looked up.

Captain Leah Prevault stood next to us. I started to smile but then caught myself. The look on her face was more than grim, it was enraged.

I started to say something but before I could even get out a greeting, her small hand swung from her side and landed on the side of my face. The sound bit into the air around us and all activity stopped. No more murmuring of voices, no more clang of porcelain on tableware. For some reason, even the jukebox chose that moment to shut off and whirr between records.

All eyes turned toward us. Even Ernie seemed shocked.

"You betrayed us," Captain Prevault said.

"What?" I stammered.

"Doctor Hwang," she said. "And the patients at the Mental Health Sanatorium. You betrayed them all. *All*!" she shouted.

I was dumbstruck. I had no idea what she was talking about. "What?" I said.

"They arrested them all!"

"Who did?"

"I don't *know*! You know. They came with trucks and arrested Doctor Hwang and rounded up all the patients and took them away and now the entire valley is empty. I stopped by there on the way back from the field. There are military *guards* out front. They wouldn't let me in until I insisted and finally they showed me. They're all gone. For purposes of national security, they told me. You had them *arrested*!"

"Wait a minute, lady," Ernie said, standing up and holding out his hands. "My partner didn't have anybody arrested. I was with him all last night, and we didn't go near this place, this 'sanatorium' you're talking about."

"Then his friends did it!" she said. "You have to do something about it. They're not *criminals!*"

And then she was crying. I finally stood up and tried to comfort her but she slapped my hand away, staring at me with a face full of rage, and turned and trotted out of the snack bar, knocking over somebody's coffee on the way out.

As we were about to climb into the jeep, Strange appeared.

"Had any *strange* lately?"

"Can it, Harvey," Ernie said. "We're in no mood for your bullshit."

"Who's talking about bullshit? I've got the real deal for you."

"What deal?"

Strange looked both ways. "Keep this under your hat," he said. "You two were busy at Eighth Army headquarters last night."

"So?" Ernie said.

Strange stepped closer and lowered his voice to a whisper. "They know about the Bogus Claims File. They know you have it. They want it back."

"They'll have to ask nice," Ernie said.

"They know that," Strange said. "Technically, the file doesn't exist so they know they can't arrest you for taking it. But there are all sorts of other charges they can bring you up on. Entering a restricted area, for one."

"The SOFA Secretariat's Office?" I said.

"*Exactement,*" Strange said. "Not to mention anything else they feel like making up."

Strange was right. The Uniform Code of Military Justice uses such vague language and covers so many broad areas of behavior that, when directed, the JAG office can charge just about anybody with just about anything.

"So maybe we'll give it back," I said, "after the investigation."

"They want it now."

"People in hell want ice water," Ernie said.

"Then you better make yourself scarce," Strange said. Like a hound sniffing danger in the air, he stepped away and turned his back on us. Within seconds, he was rounding the corner toward the snack bar and in the distance we heard a siren blaring.

Ernie jumped in the driver's seat and started the jeep. I got myself in the passenger seat just as he shoved the little vehicle in gear. We spurted out of the parking lot too late. The MP jeep spotted us. I glanced back. Staff Sergeant Moe Dexter was at the wheel, one MP on his right and two more crouched in the backseat. All of them were armed with M-16 rifles, except for Dexter, but I'm sure he had a .45 on his hip.

Ernie slammed the jeep into high gear, and it surged forward. As we neared Gate Number Seven, a Korean guard marched out into the roadway, holding up his open palm, ordering us to halt. Ernie stepped on the gas. At the last second, the guard leapt out of the way.

Horns blared as Ernie skidded into the busy midday traffic. *Kimchi* cabs, three-wheeled trucks, and the occasional ROK Army military vehicle made way as Ernie careened out of Gate Number Seven and headed east on the Main Supply Route. Moe Dexter and his boys barreled after us, siren blaring, only a few yards back.

"Where are you going?" I shouted.

"Itaewon."

"It's too crowded," I said.

"That's why I'm going there."

Ernie swerved past cabs, darting into and out of oncoming traffic, once even leaping up on the pedestrian walkway to get around a slow moving truck. I held on and prayed.

An old woman with a cane, impervious to the swirling machinery around her, tottered across the roadway. "Watch out!" I shouted. Ernie slammed on his brakes, swerved to his right, downshifted, and once past the elderly *halmonni*, surged forward once again.

Moe Dexter wasn't nearly as deft. He slammed on his brakes in time to avoid murdering the old woman, but then he laid into his horn, thereby insulting a respected elder. I turned in my seat to watch. Pedestrians started shouting at him. One *kimchi* cab driver got out of his car as if to confront the four burly Americans, and a truck loaded with garlic nosed in front of Dexter's jeep. Dexter ignored the taunts, backed up, and then slammed his front fender into the side of the *kimchi* cab. He twisted the little vehicle out of the way, the driver screaming and cursing at him all the while. And then Dexter was after us again.

"About two hundred yards back," I said.

"He's still coming?"

"Still coming."

Ernie turned right and entered the narrow road that passed through the heart of Itaewon, past the UN Club, the Lucky Lady Club, the Seven Club, and finally the King Club. He hung a left up Hooker Hill. We passed a few middle-aged housewives with huge bundles of laundry balanced on their heads. They weren't too mobile carrying that much weight and with only a few feet of clearance on either side of the jeep, Ernie had to slow to give them time to get out of the way. When we reached the top of the hill, Ernie turned right up a gradual incline that was even narrower than the road running up Hooker Hill. I looked back and glimpsed Moe Dexter barreling uphill after us.

"He's still coming?" Ernie asked.

"Still coming."

We passed one alley leading back down to the nightclub district and then another. On this second one, Ernie turned right. Immediately, our pathway was blocked by about three dozen young women milling about in front of an establishment with a sign that said *Hei Yong Mokyok-tang*, Sea Dragon Bathhouse. Caressing both sides of the Korean words were two brightly painted mermaids, smiling past long blonde tresses.

Ernie could've avoided this alley, but he'd purposely slowed and inched forward into the crowd. Ernie tapped his horn playfully, waved at the girls, and blew kisses. Most of the girls carried metal pans containing soap and shampoo and other toiletries balanced against their hips. And they looked great. Their straight black hair was held up by metal clips, and many of them wore short pants with either T-shirts or pullover sweaters with no brassieres beneath, their full natural jiggle on fleshy display. Other than the bars and nightclubs themselves, the Sea Dragon Bathhouse was the main social gathering place for the Itaewon business girls. Here they could meet during the light of day, trade gossip, and catch up on which establishments were hiring waitresses or hostesses or barmaids and who amongst their exclusive clan had landed a rich boyfriend or, better yet, a GI who would marry them and carry them back to the Land of the Big PX. Still holding on to the steering wheel, Ernie leaned to his left, reached into his pocket, and pulled out an industrial-sized pack of ginseng gum. Quickly, he started handing out sticks to grasping hands.

Behind us, Moe Dexter and his MP cohort rounded the corner.

"Don't let them through!" Ernie shouted. I repeated what he'd said in Korean, adding, "The MPs have arrested a Korean woman."

As our jeep passed, the girls clustered helpfully behind us. Moe Dexter was honking his horn, but it wasn't working. Angry business girls stood in front of his jeep and on the sides, taunting the MPs, shouting at them to go back to their compound. Pent-up rage at having been humiliated by members of law enforcement, of having always to show their updated VD cards, of being busted for selling the gifts GIs gave them on the black market—all of these emotions bubbled quickly into anger, and in this large gathering the business girls of Itaewon finally held the power. Cursing and red-faced, Moe slammed the palm of his big hand on the jeep's horn and held it down, screaming at them to get out of the way. This seemed to make the girls even more determined. They pressed forward in front of the jeep, and Moe Dexter was forced by the growing crowd of female pulchritude to come to a complete halt.

At the bottom of the hill, we rounded the corner. Ernie stepped on it, and in a few seconds we'd reached the MSR. Ernie turned right and really let it rip, slamming on the brakes when he had to, giving it the gas when he could, showing the skills he'd developed during his years in Asia. Within seconds, we passed Hannam-dong and turned right until we reached Chamsu Bridge. Ernie crossed it heading south, and soon we were on the wide open roads running parallel to the Han River in the district known a Gangnam, literally River South. There were a few high-rise apartments along the waterfront but not many. Straw hatted farmers worked the fields that stretched on the long inland plains to distant hills. It was as if by just crossing the bridge, we'd been transported back in time. I even spotted a tired-looking ox pulling a plow.

I turned in my seat and studied the road behind us. From here, I had a clear view of Chamsu Bridge.

"No jeeps," I said, turning back around.

"We lost 'em,"

"*You* lost them," I said, "with the help of a few business girls."

"I have always depended," Ernie said, "on the kindness of business girls."

■   ■   ■

We found Mr. Kill three stories below ground in the interrogation room of the Korean National Police headquarters. When he emerged, his tie was loose and his sleeves were rolled up. He looked exhausted.

"What do you want?" he said.

"The National Mental Health Sanatorium. What happened? Every patient there was arrested."

"Not arrested," he said. "They were just taken in for questioning."

"Like the other witnesses were taken in for questioning?"

He shrugged.

"Have they been released yet?"

"Some of them."

"How about the director, Doctor Hwang?"

"He's been particularly uncooperative."

"Why shouldn't he be?" Ernie said. "He hasn't done anything wrong."

Mr. Kill looked down the hallway and then back at Ernie. "This isn't the States. We do things the Korean way." He pointed his forefinger at Ernie's nose. "We do things *our* way."

Ernie bristled. I stepped between them.

"Okay," I said. "We can't talk you into releasing these people but you can at least tell us what you've learned from them."

"Not much. Other than they're all a bunch of Communists."

"You mean literally members of the Communist party?"

"No. I mean in the way they obstinately oppose the goals of President Pak Chung-hee."

"That's it?" Ernie said. "That's why you're holding them?"

Mr. Kill placed his hands on his hips and his face hardened. "How about your investigation? What have you found?"

"Not much," Ernie said.

Mr. Kill nodded, as if that was the answer he expected. "So if you'll excuse me."

He returned to the interrogation room. We watched him go. Silently, we turned and trudged back up the steps.

"Nobody really seems to want to solve this thing," Ernie said. "They're just using the iron sickle murders as an excuse to resolve old grudges."

"Mr. Kill could solve it if he wanted to," I said. "He has all the resources of the Korean National Police at his disposal and yet he continues to concentrate on peripheral issues."

"So what does that tell us?"

"It tells us that they want *us*, Eighth Army, to solve it."

"Why?" Ernie asked.

"Because the KNPs don't want to touch it."

"And why would that be?"

"Because they're afraid."

"Afraid of what?"

"There's only one thing in this world the Korean National Police are afraid of," I said.

Ernie looked at me, waiting for the answer.

"Politics," I said.

We passed the information desk in the main floor lobby. A few uniformed officers stared at us, and there was a lot or murmuring.

"I don't like it," Ernie said. "Maybe Eighth Army put the word out to be on the lookout for us. Let's get out of here."

I agreed.

Without incident, we reached the jeep in the parking lot and rolled into the busy streets of Seoul.

Ernie swerved past a careening *kimchi* cab. "Should we go see Major Rhee?" he asked.

"I don't think so. For all we know Eighth Army's charged us with the crime of absconding with classified documents."

"The Bogus Claims File isn't classified."

"No, not officially. But they might be pissed off enough not to worry about legal niceties."

"So what's our next move?"

I thought about the totem we'd found at the Inn of the Crying Rose. KNP forensic technicians had removed the head of Mr. Ming and taken samples of the blood and other shreds of flesh that had fallen to the floor. The totem itself was made not of wood from produce crates, as I'd originally assumed, but of sturdier stuff. Unlike when we'd first seen it at the Itaewon Market, I had a chance, finally, to study it closely. The wood seemed old and brittle and it was stenciled with faded black lettering, in English: 4038 SIG BN (MOB), which meant, in military bureaucratese, the 4038th Signal Battalion (Mobile).

"Let's make a few phone calls," I said.

"Where?" Ernie asked.

In downtown Seoul there weren't many places to park. And if we did find a public phone I'd need ten *won* pieces to pay for the call; the wait to be transferred to the 8th Army telephone exchange could be as long as twenty minutes.

"Let's go to the RTO," I said.

There, at the 8th Army Rail Transportation Office at the Seoul Train Station, we'd not only have access to phones that were already hooked up to the 8th Army telephone exchange, we'd also have access to Western-style toilets and a small PX snack stand where we could grab a cup of hot coffee.

Ernie nodded.

Five minutes later we rolled up to the brick façade of the 8th Army RTO just to the right of the huge dome of the Seoul train station. No one paid any attention to us as Ernie made a break for the latrine and I grabbed the receiver of the government phone on the ticketing counter. Next to it, chained to a metal pole, was the 8th Army phonebook. I didn't need to look up a number. I dialed Riley.

"Where the hell *are* you?" he said.

"Who wants to know?"

"Whadda you mean 'who wants to know?' You know who wants to know. The freaking Provost Marshal."

"We're working on the Barretsford case."

"You've got leads?"

"A few."

"So what were you doing in the SOFA Secretariat's Office last night?"

"Was that us?"

"According to Major Woolword it was."

"That old drunk?"

"Hey, it's in his log, and Sergeant Ervin and a couple of MPs are backing him up."

"So why's everybody so worried about us being in the Secretariat's Office?"

"You weren't authorized to be there."

"Who gives a rat's butt about that? You want this guy with the iron sickle caught, don't you?"

"Yeah, but the Provost Marshal don't like you two snooping around in places you're not supposed to be."

"So he sicced Moe Dexter on us."

"He didn't sic nobody on you. He put out the word that he wanted to talk to you."

"So there's no warrant for our arrest?"

"Not yet."

"Doesn't it seem odd to you they're making such a big deal out of this when we have a killer on the loose?"

Riley was silent for a while. "I suppose it does," he said, his voice subdued, sounding almost reasonable for a moment.

"I need you to look something up for me. The Forty Thirty-eighth Signal Battalion Mobile. Who are they? Where are they stationed? Anything you can find out about them."

"Why?"

After he promised to keep it under his hat, I told him.

"A *totem*?" he said.

"That's what I'm calling it."

"Left at the site where Collingsworth was murdered and also this Chinese guy."

"I told you to keep it under your hat."

"Oh, I can do that. For now."

I hung up on him. Ernie was back, rummaging around the PX snack stand, asking the cashier if they had any ginseng gum. They didn't. I reached in my wallet and pulled out a slip of paper with Captain Prevault's office number on it. It rang and rang.

I set the phone down, walked over to the snack stand and ordered a cup of coffee. Before I could pay for it, the big swinging doors burst open. Two ROK Army soldiers in combat fatigues entered, M-16 rifles leveled, both of them crouched, narrow-eyed, swiveling the barrels of the rifles from side to side.

The American NCO behind the ticketing counter burst out of his office.

"Hey!" he shouted. "No ROK personnel allowed in here. This is Eighth Army. You *arra*? Eighth Army. You *bali bali karra chogi*!" Leave quickly.

A half dozen more ROK soldiers burst through the door. Two of them hopped over the ticketing counter and shoved the irate American NCO back into his office. I heard scuffling, and then somebody went down.

Ernie and I were both armed but neither of us reached for the .45s in our shoulder holsters. Instead, we stood with our hands out to our sides. More ROK soldiers searched the latrine, the small waiting area, and the other offices of the RTO. Once the area was secure, the word was passed back and then two soldiers held the doors open. I think I had been half expecting it to be Major Rhee Mi-sook who strode into the room.

As usual, she looked smashing in her tailored fatigues and her highly polished combat boots. She surveyed the scene, grinned, and barked an order. Two straight-backed chairs were brought from the office behind the ticketing counter and set down in the center of the small waiting room. Major Rhee pointed a polished nail at them.

"Sit!"

A half dozen M-16 rifles were pointed at us, so we sat. Ernie crossed his arms and slouched. I maintained an attentive posture.

"You boys have been busy," Major Rhee said.

"Idleness is the Devil's handmaiden," I said.

"What?"

"It's good to be busy," I replied.

"Yes, it's good. What have you found out so far about the man with the iron sickle?"

"He's a very bad boy," Ernie said.

"I didn't ask you," Major Rhee replied.

Ernie shrugged and turned his head away. She looked back at me.

"We believe he killed a Chinese man named Ming," I told Major Rhee. "Apparently a woman who owned a bar in Mia-ri called The Inn of the Crying Rose was an associate of the man with the iron sickle. She's gone now. Disappeared."

"What makes you think it was him?"

"The MO," I replied. When she stared at me blankly, I said, "The method of operation. In the previous murders he cut the throats of his victims. This time, he sliced the head off completely."

I didn't tell her about the totem, nor about the Bogus Claims File. What I was telling her is what she could've found out from the KNPs on her own.

"What's your next move?" she asked.

"Our next move," Ernie said, "is to have a cup of coffee."

She smiled at this, a radiant smile. "May I join you?"

"Naw. I like cream and sugar with my coffee. Not five fifty-six millimeter ammo."

"Oh, sorry about that."

Major Rhee barked an order. The combat soldiers arrayed around the RTO assembled in front of the swinging doors and then, as a unit, marched smartly outside.

"A beautiful woman," Ernie said, "should always make an impressive entrance."

Major Rhee ignored him. The three of us took seats at one of the two Formica-topped tables in front of the snack stand. The cashier, a middle-aged Korean man, scurried out from behind the counter, bowed in front of Major Rhee, and said, "*Muol duhshi-gessoyo*?" What can I get for you?

This is something he never did for GI customers.

She ordered green tea, but the man profusely apologized and told her they only had the American PX-bought tea called "Lipton."

She told him that would be fine and the cashier hurried off.

"Hey!" Ernie said. "What about me?"

He ended up getting his own coffee at the counter as usual. I already had mine. Once the three of us were reseated, Major Rhee lifted her steaming white Styrofoam cup and said, "Here's to justice."

"Oh, yeah," Ernie said. "Justice. That's what we're all about."

She gazed at me steadily. "Eighth Army is upset with you."

I sipped my coffee and stared at her unblemished face, reminding myself what she'd done to me while wearing the uniform of a North Korean Army Senior Captain. It hadn't been pretty, and it had nothing to do with justice.

"I understand you've been seeing a woman," she said.

Ernie cast me a wry grin.

I stared at Major Rhee and raised one eyebrow.

"A highly educated woman," she continued. "A doctor. You seem to be partial to them."

"Why do you care who I see?" I asked.

She raised and then lowered her tea bag. "Who you see is important to this investigation. You believe the killer with the iron sickle might have been at one time a psychiatric patient. You're investigating that angle. You're also investigating the various claims processed through the SOFA Secretariat. Good thinking, I'd say. Once you find an intersection, you might find your man."

"And we might not," Ernie said.

It was Major Rhee's turn to shrug. "That's the risk one takes."

"What do you want from us?" Ernie asked.

Major Rhee sipped from her cup, leaving a lipstick smudge along its edge. "I want to be there when you make an arrest. You'll need me." She jammed her thumb over her shoulder. "You'll need the firepower I can provide. This killer has proven he is intelligent and ruthless. You need me and I need you to help me find him. I won't take the credit. I'll leave that to you. I just want to be there on the day when you take him down."

"You want to kill him," Ernie said.

Major Rhee jerked back in her seat. "Not necessarily," she said. "If he comes peacefully, he won't be hurt."

"You don't want him to come peacefully," Ernie continued. "For some reason the ROK Army wants him shut up. They don't want a trial. They don't want to hear what he has to say. They want him dead."

Major Rhee's face flushed red. "Don't *you*?" she shouted. "Don't you want him dead? He murdered an American civilian, a fellow MP, and two innocent GIs in a signal truck. Isn't that enough reason for you Americans to want him dead also?"

The ranking sergeant of her infantry squad pushed through the double doors, holding his rifle pointed toward the ceiling.

"*Naka!*" she shrieked. Get out! The man backed out the door.

She stood and loomed over us, pointing her red-tipped forefinger first at Ernie and then at me. "Someday you will need me. Someday soon. And then you will be groveling and begging for my help." She lowered her hand, stared at us, and turned and stormed out the swinging door. As lumber creaked on rusty hinges, I glanced at Ernie. Saliva bubbled at the corner of his mouth.

"Whadda woman," he said.

We finished our coffee and prepared to go, and the NCO in charge of the RTO peeked out of his office behind the counter. When he saw the coast was clear, he walked up to the counter and said, "Next time you guys need to make a phone call, go somewhere else, okay?"

I finally reached Captain Prevault at her office.

"Thank God you called," she said.

"What's wrong? What happened?"

"Remember Miss Sim, the woman at the home for the criminally insane, the one who panicked when we showed her your drawing of the totem?"

"Yes, I remember."

"She's been taken."

"Taken by who?"

"By a very forceful Korean man. He barely said anything, but he wouldn't take no for an answer. And a Korean woman was with him. 'Flashy' is how the staff described her."

"They just walked in and took this woman who'd been there for years? Didn't anybody try to stop them?"

"Yes, one of the male attendants confronted them. Grabbed the girl on the front steps and wouldn't let her go."

"What happened?"

"As soon as he touched her, Miss Sim dropped her rag doll and scratched his eyes so severely he had to be taken to surgery. Then the three of them left."

"Have the KNPs been called?"

"Yes. So far they've done nothing."

"I'll go up there and check it out."

"Take me with you!" When I didn't say anything, Captain Prevault softened her voice and said, "I'm sorry about what I did in the snack bar. It was wrong of me. I realize now that none of the arrests at the Sanatorium were your doing."

"What makes you so sure?" I said coldly.

There was a long pause. Finally, she spoke in the voice of a little girl. "I know you couldn't."

She was right about that.

I sighed, turning my head so the sound of it didn't reach the receiver. "We'll need to move quickly."

Her voice brightened, becoming the old Captain Prevault again. "I'll be waiting in front of the one-two-one."

I told her we'd be there in twenty minutes and hung up.

-13-

We crossed the Chonho Bridge heading south, Ernie driving, Captain Prevault bundled in a cold weather parka in the back seat. I pointed the way as Ernie wound up through wooded hills and finally pulled into the gravel parking lot in front of the home for the criminally insane. Three white-uniformed staff members were waiting for us on the stone steps.

They took us to Miss Sim Kok-sa's cell and explained how the man and the woman had arrived in a *kimchi* cab and the driver had waited for them. They claimed to be relatives, and then without permission pushed their way to Miss Sim's cell. When the attendant refused to unlock it, the tall man pulled a wickedly-sharpened sickle from beneath his coat and threatened to slice the attendant's throat. The man unlocked the door, and to everyone's surprise, the girl seemed to recognize the two people. Her eyes widened and she started to scream. That's when the fancy woman slapped her, told her to shut up, and barked orders at her to stand up and do as she was told. Amazingly, Miss Sim complied, docilely, as if she were accustomed to taking orders from the woman. Like a convict on her way to the gallows, she followed them up the stairs, and when the head attendant confronted them, Miss Sim dropped her doll and, at the fancy woman's orders, attacked him fiercely.

They showed us the rag doll.

"She left this?" Captain Prevault asked.

"She didn't want to but the fancy woman ordered her to leave it."

"But previously she would fight anyone who tried to take it away from her?"

The staff nodded.

Captain Prevault turned to me. "She knows them," she said.

"Who?"

"The people who took her. Miss Sim knows them and feels she has no choice but to follow their orders."

"Why would she feel that?"

"I'm not sure. But it probably has something to do with the trauma that landed her here in the first place."

"What are they going to do with her?"

"God only knows."

I thought of what they'd done to Mr. Ming and to Collingsworth and to the two GIs in the signal truck and to Mr. Barretsford.

"We have to find her," Captain Prevault said.

I agreed.

One of the staff members had the presence of mind to jot down the license plate number of the *kimchi* cab that had carried them away. They'd given it to the KNPs but my guess was it wouldn't do much good. Most likely, the pair had the driver take them to some densely populated area of downtown Seoul, and from there they'd either catch another cab or hop on a train or a bus. Still, I would've liked to talk to the driver, but that would mean contacting Mr. Kill, locating the investigating officers, and making an appointment, and all that would take time. Also, I no longer trusted Mr. Kill's motives. I trusted him as a man—if he promised me something, he'd deliver. But notably, so far in this case, he'd promised me nothing. I believed he was working under tight orders from his superiors. What exactly those orders were, I couldn't be sure. But I suspected someone higher up in the government was monitoring every move we made and when—and if—we found the man with the iron sickle, then the next step would be taken out of our hands. I discussed this with Ernie.

"Screw them," he said. "We can take this guy down on our own."

I agreed with him. I wasn't too anxious to lead anyone—even a serial killer of American GIs—to an ROK Army or Korean National Police slaughterhouse.

Ernie, Captain Prevault, and I drove back to Itaewon. At a noodle house near the edge of the nightclub district, I spoke to the proprietor, and paid her 500 *won* for the use of her phone. It took only about ten minutes to reach the 8th Army telephone exchange where I gave the operator the number. Riley answered on the first ring.

"Where the hell are you?" he asked, as usual. "I've been waiting here past duty hours for your call."

"Nice of you."

"I'm a considerate kind of guy. I checked with the Eighth Army Historian's office about this Forty Thirty-eighth Signal Battalion. It turns out they were disbanded shortly after the Korean War because there was some sort of a scandal involving a subordinate unit of theirs, namely Echo Company. It appears that during the fighting, when the two million or so Chinese 'volunteers' swept down the Korean peninsula, Echo Company was separated from the main body of the battalion. They broadcast for a while, relaying signals, but then their transmissions became intermittent and eventually they stopped transmitting altogether. They were called 'the Lost Echo.' Even their equipment was lost and never recovered. The official history carries the entire unit as being lost in action."

"Where?"

"Where what?"

"Where were they lost? What was their last known position?"

Paper rustled. I imagined Riley shuffling through his notes. He was angry with me for keeping him from the bottle of Old Overwart in his wall locker, but when Staff Sergeant Riley did a job he was thorough.

"Here it is," he said. He read off the coordinates.

I jotted them down. "Where the hell is that?"

"Somewhere in the Taebaek Mountains. About thirty klicks inland from the port of Sokcho, which is where the Forty Thirty-eighth was disembarked from a Navy transport ship."

"Thanks, Riley. Anything else?"

"Only that the guy at the Historian's office says if you find any artifacts concerning the Lost Echo, don't get any bright ideas. They're official war relics protected under the Status of Forces Agreement. They have to be surrendered to Eighth Army as soon as they're found."

"Thanks for the warning."

"Any time." I was about to hang up when Riley shouted, "The Provost Marshal wants your butt in here tomorrow morning at zero eight hundred."

"That might not be possible."

"Might not be *freaking* possible? You better make it possible, Troop. That's a direct order from your commanding officer."

"We have a lead."

"What kind of lead?"

"Maybe the final lead. I have to go somewhere. I'll call you when we get there."

"Where? Where the hell are you going?"

I hung up on him. I didn't want to take any chances that the Korean National Police Liaison Officer would be notified as to our destination—or worse yet, that Major Rhee Mi-sook would. I pulled out my notepad and started to write down what I knew.

Sim Kok-sa wasn't her real name. She'd been named for the Buddhist

Monastery that sat on the slopes of Mount Daeam, where she'd been found after chopping two elderly people to death with a hoe.

The landlord of the Inn of the Crying Rose had told me that Madame Hoh, the proprietor of the Crying Rose, was originally from the east coast province of Kangwon-do.

"The Lost Echo" had disappeared thirty kilometers inland from the port of Sokcho.

Finally, the file we'd pilfered from the Status of Forces Secretariat office contained a claim having to do with a military unit in the Taebaek Mountains; one of the claims that 8th Army, and the ROK government, had tried so desperately to suppress.

I explained this to Ernie and Captain Prevault. "I believe they've gone to the Taebaek Mountains," I said. "They're taking Miss Sim back to where they came from, to where all this started."

"Why?" Ernie asked.

"The man with the iron sickle wants us to know all this killing has to do with the Lost Echo."

"He also wants us to know," Captain Prevault said, "that he's desperately angry about something."

"Like what?" Ernie asked.

"Whatever happened up there in the mountains. Whatever happened to cause this young girl, Miss Sim Kok-sa, to go mad and chop two people to death with a hoe."

"And for the man with the iron sickle to kill four Americans."

"And one Chink," Ernie said.

We stared at him. "One *Chinese*," Captain Prevault corrected.

Ernie shrugged.

"That brings up a good question," I said. "The earlier victims were all Caucasian. In fact, he studiously avoided hurting the Korean MP on the ville patrol with Collingsworth. So why murder Mr. Ming, a fellow Asian?"

"He wasn't Korean," Captain Prevault said.

"But he came here as a child and grew up here and spoke Korean fluently and acted like a Korean."

Captain Prevault shook her head. "Still not the same. These people, the man with the iron sickle and the 'fancy' woman, for whatever reason, have a set of rules. Koreans aren't harmed, foreigners are. This Mr. Ming was, in their eyes, a foreigner."

"They did hurt the ROK Army MP in Itaewon," Ernie said, "and the attendant who tried to stop them from taking Miss Sim."

"Not fatally," Captain Prevault.

"But either of those attacks could have been fatal," Ernie replied. "In fact the attendant was hurt pretty badly."

We all nodded. No question these people were dangerous to anyone they encountered.

"It won't take the KNPs long to come to the same conclusions we have," I said.

"They don't know about the Lost Echo," Ernie said, "or about the Bogus Claim File."

"They'll figure it out soon enough. Everything this man with the iron sickle has done is designed to lead us to the Taebaek Mountains."

"So aren't we walking right into his trap?"

"Maybe."

Ernie frowned, thinking it over. Captain Prevault looked back and forth between us, sensing our indecision. "We have to go," she said.

"Why?"

"Because of Miss Sim."

"What will they do to her?"

"I'm not sure. I'm not sure why they even want her. But whatever the reason, it's important to them. What they're doing is commonly called 'acting out.' They're trying to teach us something, teach the world something, and Miss Sim is about to play an important part in this drama."

"As a sacrifice?" Ernie asked.

Captain Prevault hugged herself. "God, I hope not. Not now. Not when we're on the verge of finding the key to her mental illness, the events that precipitated her trauma, and therefore a possible cure. If we don't rescue her now, she'll be lost forever."

"Either that," Ernie said, "or dead."

At the BOQ, Captain Prevault packed a duffel bag with her winter field gear and returned to the jeep in record time. We drove to the other side of the Yongsan Compound, and Ernie parked at the far end of our barracks, where the floodlights had long ago sputtered out. We told Captain Prevault to wait quietly, and we'd be right back.

There weren't many GIs in the barracks, just a few hanging around the beer machine, dropping in thirty-five cents, and watching greedily as a cold Falstaff fell out. They didn't even notice us as we walked past. Ernie pulled out his key and entered his room, and I continued down the hallway to mine. I flipped on the light, found my duffel bag and shook it out, and started stuffing wool fatigues, a field jacket, and a parka into the bag. I debated about whether or not to bring my Mickey Mouse boots, inflatable severe winter foot gear, but in the end decided against it. Combat boots and rubber overshoes would give me more mobility. When I figured I finally had everything, I tossed the bag over my shoulder, relocked the door, and hurried down the hallway. Ernie was waiting for me. We exited the barracks and stepped into darkness.

I should've been expecting it, but, like an idiot, I wasn't.

The fist caught me on the side of my head. Reflexively I crouched and moved to my left. More punches came at me, but now I had raised my hands and was able to deflect most of them. In the glare of light from the fluorescent bulb in the hallway, I glimpsed a contorted face coming at me—pasty skin and a pug nose under the black helmet: Moe Dexter.

Ernie was shouting and other voices were shouting and then the thunderous report of a round from an automatic weapon echoed into the night. For a moment, everything was quiet. The punches stopped raining down on me. I used the time to brace myself against the cement-block wall of the barracks, to balance myself in an upright position, to try to focus my eyes. Ernie had his flashlight out now, shining it into the faces of Moe Dexter and the three other MPs in fatigue uniform who stood behind him. Ernie's .45 was out and he was pointing it right at them.

"Back off," he growled. "Back off or I'll plug you where you stand!"

Dexter raised his hands to his sides, grinning. "What's the matter, Bass Comb? Doesn't your boy Sweeno want to play fair?"

"You'll play fair when I pop a fucking forty-five round in your face," Ernie told him. "*Back off!*"

The four MPs did.

Ernie helped me to the jeep. Captain Prevault still sat in the back seat. "I tried to warn you," she said, "but two of them held me here. One of them put his filthy hand over my mouth."

"Drive!" Ernie said.

It took her a moment to understand. She climbed into the front seat. Ernie pulled the passenger seat forward, and I dove into the back seat, still dizzy from the initial blow. Ernie lowered the front seat and sat down, all the while keeping his flashlight and the barrel of his .45 pointed at the MPs. Captain Prevault wasn't sure where the ignition was. Ernie pointed it out to her.

"I've never driven a stick shift before," she said.

"Move the seat forward."

She did.

"Now put your left foot on the clutch." She seemed confused. "That pedal to the left of the brake. That's it. Press down on it." Ernie shifted the gear shift into first. "Now let up on it slowly."

She did. We lurched forward. The four MPs, including Moe Dexter, backed away. When we reached their jeep, Ernie told her to stop. He hopped out, still keeping his weapon trained on the MPs, and walked around the MP jeep and systematically shot out all four of their tires. As an afterthought, he shot out the spare bolted to the rear. Then he fired a round at them. They ducked and took cover.

Ernie hopped back into the jeep.

"Drive!" he said.

She did, haltingly at first, with the little vehicle shuddering and stopping and then speeding up. Finally, we were out in Seoul traffic.

"Don't you want to take over from here?" Captain Prevault said.

"You're doing fine," Ernie replied.

Her small hands gripped the huge steering wheel. I would've felt sorry for her, driving her first stick shift at night in the maddening Seoul traffic, but my head was pounding too hard to worry much about driver's ed. I lay down as best I could in the small canvas-covered seat. Somehow, amidst all the honking and commotion and swirling beams from headlights, I passed out.

Ernie leaned back from the passenger's seat and shook me awake.

"Are you all right, pal?"

I sat up. "Where are we?"

"Out in the countryside. Not too far from the Taebaek Mountains, I don't think."

My head throbbed like a marching drum. "Dexter's not following us, is he?"

"Naw. That asshole is only good on compound or in Itaewon when he's got a bunch of MPs around him. If he hadn't sucker punched you, you would've kicked his ass."

"Right," I said, although I didn't believe it at the time. "Do you have any aspirin?"

Ernie didn't but Captain Prevault, still driving, searched her purse. She pulled out a bottle of Tylenol. I thanked her and popped down four of them, dry.

"We should stop somewhere," she told Ernie, "and have George checked out. He might be suffering from a concussion."

"Him?" Ernie said. "He's got the hardest head in Eighth Army."

"It's not a joke," she insisted.

Ernie glanced around at the dark rice paddies surrounding us. "You see any clinics around here?"

Ernie told Captain Prevault to pull over to the side of the road. A good chance for a piss break, I thought, which is what we would have normally done, but with Captain Prevault there, I hesitated. She sensed what we were thinking.

"Go in those bushes over there," she said. "I'll stay near the jeep."

So Ernie and I relieved ourselves about ten yards away while Captain Prevault squatted in front of the jeep. An occasional vehicle cruised by but no one paid any attention. In Korea, the natural functions of the body are seen as just that, natural functions. No one pays them any mind.

When we were done, we climbed back into the jeep. Ernie asked me if I wanted to drive, but I told him no. I wasn't ready for that yet. We rotated into our usual positions: Captain Prevault in the back, Ernie driving, me in the passenger seat.

"You did a good job," I told her, "getting us out of Seoul."

"Thanks. It's not something I want to do again."

I pulled out the Army-issue maps I'd already stuffed in the glove compartment. Using a penlight, I studied them. The coordinates

Riley had given me, the last known position of the Lost Echo, were only a few kilometers from the Buddhist Monastery known as Simgok Sa, the monastery that had been used to christen the nameless child Miss Sim.

"When we reach the town of Yang-ku," I told Ernie, "we best see if we can gas up. I don't think there'll be much chance beyond that."

"There's not much out here already."

As it turned out, about a dozen kilometers up the road, at an intersection of three country roads, a big neon sign flashed *Sok-yu.* Rock oil. A gas station. We stopped and I spoke to the attendant in Korean and asked him if there'd been any other people up here this evening from Seoul heading into the Taebaek Mountains. He looked at me as if I were mad. I didn't press the issue. When I paid him, I flashed my badge and told him if anyone asked if Americans had come this way, he was to tell them no. He continued to stare at me blankly.

"*Arraso*?" I asked. Do you understand?

Finally, he nodded.

I don't think I'd intimidated him, but I still believed he'd keep his mouth shut. Refusing to get involved, in the States, is seen as shirking your civic duty. In a police state it's the smartest way, and sometimes the only way, to survive.

With a full tank of gas, the three of us hopped back into the jeep. Ernie checked the nonexistent traffic and we drove off into the night.

-14-

By early morning, we had reached a village known as Im-dang. Ernie looked pretty tired, so I told him we should rest and find some chow. He didn't disagree. Captain Prevault slept soundly in the back seat, her face leaning up against one of the canvas duffel bags.

The side of my face still hurt. I touched it gently. Bruised. I probably looked like hell. My headache had been alleviated somewhat by the Tylenol Captain Prevault had given me last night, but it was throbbing again and I didn't have the heart to wake her just for that. She snored softly.

"Where the hell are we going to find chow out here?" Ernie asked.

The village was composed of rickety wooden buildings lining either side of the main road. There were a few signs painted on rotted wood but they said things like GRAIN WAREHOUSE or PAK'S FARM EQUIPMENT. Finally, at the single intersection in town, I spotted the flag of the Republic of Korea hanging from a metal pole on a cement-block building. The local KNP headquarters. We cruised past slowly. No one looked out. Apparently, they were still asleep. A few yards down the road, I spotted three *kimchi* cabs parked in front of a sign that said *Unchon Siktang*. The Driver's Eatery.

"Pull the jeep around the corner," I said. "We'll eat here."

Ernie found a place to park the jeep out of sight of the KNP office and padlocked the steering wheel to the chain welded to the metal floor. I woke Captain Prevault, and she looked around groggily.

"Chow time," I said.

She rubbed her eyes and climbed out of the backseat. As we walked toward the eatery, she did her best to wipe the sleep from her eyes and straighten her hair. Once she had it properly arranged, she pulled her field cap down low.

"Do you think they'll know I'm a woman?" she asked.

"I think they'll figure it out," I told her. Even though she was shapeless in her fatigues and combat boots, Ernie and I still towered over her.

The glass in the sliding door was smeared with steam, and when I slid it open and ducked through, the clatter of metal bowls, wooden chopsticks, and porcelain cups stopped abruptly. All eyes turned toward me. I was used to this, and I was not going to let it stop me. The aroma of onions and garlic and hot peppers bubbling in a huge vat alongside chunks of beef made my mouth water. Unfortunately, all of the small tables were taken, but I stood my ground. A woman who I figured to be either the proprietress or a waitress glanced at me and then looked away, as if I represented a problem she hoped would go away on its own. Ernie and then Captain Prevault bumped in behind me.

"No place to sit?" Captain Prevault asked.

"Not yet," I replied.

Ernie scanned the room. There were fewer than a dozen customers there, most of them workmen wearing jackets, at least three of them the drivers of the cabs parked outside. Ernie spotted a table that was round and big enough for the three of us. Only one man sat there. Ernie took a couple of steps forward and motioned to him. The man was studiously ignoring us, his nose buried in his soup.

Ernie slipped through the crowd and wrapped his knuckles loudly on the round table. The man looked up from his soup, startled.

Ernie pointed outside. "You drive *kimchi* cab?" The man stared at him with blank surprise so Ernie mimicked both hands turning a steering wheel. "You drive?" he asked. "Outside?"

The man shook his head negatively and turned back to his soup. Another man rose from a smaller table near the wall and stepped up to Ernie, smiling and motioning toward one of the cabs outside and nodding and pointing at his own nose.

"You?" Ernie said. "You're the driver?"

The man nodded, smiling broadly, sensing a cash-paying fare.

Ernie patted him on the back and put his arm halfway around the man's shoulders and then motioned to me and Captain Prevault. "Come on over here," he said. "This is the *ajjoshi* who drives the cab."

We walked over, not sure what Ernie was up to. When we approached, Ernie swiveled away from the smiling driver and grabbed the mostly empty bowl and cup and spoon and chopsticks that had sat on his small table and lifted them over to the larger round table. Ernie motioned for me and Captain Prevault to sit at the small table he had just cleared. We did. Then Ernie motioned to the driver and together they sat down at the larger round table, joining the morose man who glared at their intrusion.

We waited and within a couple of minutes the rotund middle-aged woman who I believed to be the proprietress approached us, a worried look on her face. When I greeted her in Korean and asked her what they served, she visibly relaxed. In fact she was so relieved we wouldn't have to wrestle with sign language that she started speaking faster than I could follow. I asked her to slow down and she did. It turned out they had *komtang*, sliced beef in noodle broth, and since you could usually rely on that to be edible wherever you went I ordered a bowl for myself, as did Ernie and Captain Prevault. Ernie also ordered a chilled bottle of Sunny-tan orange drink. Captain Prevault and I stuck to barley tea.

The morose man got up and left, so we all slid over to the larger table. This time the driver grabbed the bowl and chopsticks the man had left behind and shoved them out of the way. Now we were comfortable and the driver beamed with joy at having stumbled into such august company. Captain Prevault nodded at him and smiled occasionally, adding to his glee.

"*Yoja i-eyo*?" he asked me. Is she a woman?

Koreans are more frank than Americans about matters of sex.

"Yes," I told him. "A woman soldier."

"She's not very pretty," he told me.

I translated none of this until Captain Prevault, still smiling, asked me what he said.

"He said this is the first time he's ever seen a female American soldier."

She smiled back at him and nodded.

The steaming metal bowls of *komtang* arrived along with an array of small dishes: rice, cabbage *kimchi*, and *muu-maleingi*, dried turnip slices. We wolfed down the soup and the rice and the cabbage *kimchi*, but when Ernie tried one of the slices of dried turnip he spit it out on the table.

"What the hell is this?"

I told him.

"Who would want to dry a turnip?" he asked. "Isn't it tasteless enough to begin with?"

Captain Prevault tried the *muu-maleingi*, chewed thoroughly and said, "Not bad."

Ernie frowned.

When we were done, I paid the proprietress and we left. The driver followed us outside. He scurried in front of us, reached his cab, and popped open the back door, waving with his hand for Captain Prevault to enter first.

Ernie waved his open palm at the driver.

"No need there, papa-san. I drivey jeep. You *arra*? Jeep."

When we breezed past the driver, his face soured. Placing his hands on his hips he walked after us a few paces. When we turned the corner, he was right behind us. Ernie leaned into the open door of the jeep and popped open the padlock. As we started to climb in, the driver screamed at Ernie.

"Okay, okay," Ernie said, continuing to wave his open palm in the irate man's face. "So you lost your seat at the chop house. Tough shit. Life's a bitch."

Ernie offered the man a stick of ginseng gum. When he refused to accept it, Ernie groaned and pulled out a thousand-*won* note, two bucks. This the driver accepted. He bowed and smiled. As we drove away, the man stared after us, hands on his hips.

The Simkok-sa Buddhist Monastery sat on a craggy granite cliff surrounded by rolling grey clouds. The roads were treacherous, slippery with mud, and Captain Prevault and I held on for dear life during the entire ride. Ernie, however, seemed to be having a wonderful time, zooming around curbs, downshifting up inclines, slamming on brakes, steering into skids, acting as if the entire rock-hewn road had been especially designed for his driving pleasure. When we finally pulled into the gravel clearing in front of the main gate of the temple, Ernie turned off the engine and Captain Prevault and I climbed out to pay homage, at last, to solid ground.

Together, we walked to the edge of the cliff. Somber mist billowed gently between the distant peaks of the Taebaek Range.

Captain Prevault inhaled deeply. "It's beautiful up here," she said. "And the air is so clear."

Most of these monasteries had been here for centuries. Some of them predated the Chosun Dynasty, their founding stretching back to an ancient time when Buddhism had been ascendant in the politics and cultural life of Korea, before the first king of the Chosun Dynasty established Confucianism as the official state religion. The strict precepts of Confucius had long ago taken control of Korean social structure, and although they were still revered by the people, Buddhist monks were definitely not the dominant power anymore.

"Why are we starting here?" Captain Prevault asked me.

"My experience has been that these monasteries are the repositories of local knowledge and local history."

"What about the Korean National Police? Like that KNP station we passed in Im-dang?"

I wasn't sure how much I should tell her about the feuding I suspected between the KNPs and the ROK Army. Instead I just said, "The Korean National Police in some areas of the country are seen not as law enforcement but rather as arms of the occupying government."

"I thought Pak Chung-hee was popular."

"He is, in Seoul. Out here, not so much."

Ernie was checking the oil in the jeep. I suspected if we waited long enough a delegation would emerge from the Simkok-sa Monastery, and I was not disappointed. The big wooden doors beneath the crimson arch creaked like bones and then popped open. Two men walked out, both bald, both wearing saffron robes.

Captain Prevault and I stepped forward and bowed to the men. They bowed in return. The level of education in Buddhist monasteries is very high and more often than not when I'd encountered monks here in Korea they could always produce at least one of their number who could speak English.

"Good morning," one of the monks said. "Welcome to Simkok Temple."

He was a youngish man, thin but strong, maybe in his late thirties. The monk next to him was considerably older, with blue pouches beneath sad eyes.

"Thank you," I said. I pulled out my identification and handed it to him. He glanced at it and handed it back. "I am Agent Sueño from Eighth Army headquarters in Seoul." I introduced Captain Prevault as a military psychiatrist and Ernie as my assistant. He wouldn't have liked that but he was out of earshot, still fussing with the jeep, content to let me handle the boring parts of our job.

I told the men about the young woman we called Miss Sim, how she'd been abducted from the home for the criminally insane and how we were anxious to find her. We also told them about the man and the woman who had abducted her.

"Why would Americans be interested?" he asked. "The crime, as I understand it, involves three Korean citizens."

I agreed. Then I went on to explain about the man with the iron sickle, the Americans who had been murdered and why I believed the man had been systematically leading us to this area of the Taebaek Mountains.

"The Lost Echo," the monk repeated. "Very poetic."

"Yes. Have you heard of it?"

"I haven't." He turned to the older man and they conversed for a while until the younger man said, "Excuse us," and the two of them walked away. Captain Prevault and I waited, out of earshot.

"Do you think they'll help?" she asked.

"We'll find out."

The two returned and the younger man spoke. "Our master remembers the farm couple who was murdered by a young woman with a hoe." The monk shook his head. "Tragic. And he also remembers the hardships of the war, the winter when the Chinese invaded, the Americans suffering and dying along with Koreans. He remembers it all."

"Does he remember the Lost Echo?"

"He remembers something like it. On that mountain." The monk turned and pointed. "On that ledge on the southern slope."

"I see it."

"That's Mount Daeam. The Americans set up their signal equipment there. Later, when the Chinese came, they took the equipment down and hid."

"Where?"

"I'm not sure, exactly."

"Were they ever seen again?"

"Never. Only rumors."

"What sort of rumors?"

"Superstitions, really. Some of the farm people hereabouts claim that on certain nights, when there is a full moon, they can hear the strange foreign sounds of the Americans, like a whispered conversation, floating on the wind."

"Do you believe it?"

The monk shrugged. "All things come within the purview of the Lord Gautama Buddha."

"Where is this farm you were talking about, the one where the two elderly people were murdered by the young girl?"

The monk asked for some paper and pencil and offered to draw me a map. Instead, I pulled out my tactical map and spread it out on the hood of the jeep. Only dim sunlight filtered through the heavy overcast, so I aimed my penlight at the map while the monk studied the multi-colored contour lines. He was a bright man. It took him only seconds to say, "Here, this is our position." He pointed to the military symbol for a Buddhist temple, a red inverted swastika. "The farmhouse is at this end of the valley, in the foothills between us and Mount Daeam."

"Not too far from where Echo Company had set up their equipment."

"As the crow flies, yes," he said, surprising me once again with his mastery of English colloquialisms, "but very far indeed if you had to make the climb."

"You couldn't go straight up from the valley to that cliff, could you?"

"No. There is a narrow path that winds far into the mountains and then a less traveled path that leads back to the cliff."

"You've hiked those areas?" I asked.

"Often."

"Have you ever heard the whisperings of the Lost Echo?"

"When I meditate," he said, "I hear only the whisperings of eternity."

It was almost midday when we reached the valley that stretched between the monastery and Mount Daeam. Already we were hungry again, and I realized that in our haste to get out of Yongsan Compound we hadn't planned this trip very well.

"We should've brought a case of Cs," Ernie said. He was referring to canned C-rations.

"Too late now."

"Maybe we should stop at one of these farm houses," Captain Prevault said. "See if they'll fix us some lunch. We could pay them." She was hungry too.

"Not a bad idea," I said. "Up there," I told Ernie pointing forward. "Pull into that area in front of the pig hut. Don't get too close to the main house, though."

"Why not?"

"I don't want to scare them. This is a military vehicle after all."

Ernie did as I asked. I told them to wait, and I walked toward the straw-thatched farmhouse. Smoke trickled from a sheet-metal pipe. Eventually an old woman tottered out, wearing a long woolen skirt and a short traditional silk blouse with a blue ribbon. She stared at me, her wrinkled face scrunched against the pale rays of the afternoon sun.

"*Anyonghaseiyo*," I said, taking a step forward.

She nodded back noncommittally.

I told her we were hungry, and we were looking for some place to eat. She told me there was no place around here. When I pressed her she told me about the Driver's Eatery back in Im-dang. We didn't want to go there. I offered her money if she'd fix lunch for the three of us. She brightened at that.

"It will only be soybean soup and *kimchi*," she told me. "And my rice is brown."

I told her that would be fine. She was a trusting woman, and we didn't set a price. Twenty minutes later she carried a low wooden table out of her kitchen and set it on the long wooden porch that ran the length of the farmhouse. We sat cross-legged on the porch and ate, lifting the bowls to our mouths and shoveling in the unhusked grain. The soybean soup had no meat in it and that was okay, but the cabbage *kimchi* was sour, as if it had fermented so long it was turning to vinegar. Still, we ate our fill. When we were done I asked her where the *byonso* was and while Captain Prevault used it and then Ernie, I spoke to the woman in private. I described the farmhouse in the foothills at the end of the valley that we were looking for. She knew all about it. It had been abandoned for years and was probably overrun now by field mice.

"Can you give me directions?" I asked and I started to pull out my field map, but she stared at in horror. I realized the interminable squiggles meant nothing to her, so instead I encouraged her to describe the route in her own way.

"Follow the road about two *li* until you reach the creek that flows south past the stand of elms. On the far side of the trees will be a wooden footbridge. Be careful crossing it because it hasn't been repaired in years, and last year a boy fell in the creek while he was fishing. Follow that pathway up into the hills, and you will find the farmhouse where the old people used to live."

"How far into the hills?" I asked.

"Until the land becomes too steep to farm."

She seemed nervous with my questions. In fact she seemed nervous about the whole business of the abandoned farm. I asked her if she'd ever been there.

"Not since the war," she replied.

"Why not?"

She studied me as if I were an idiot. "They come out at night."

"Who comes out at night?"

"Them. The two old people. Many have seen them at night, crying and complaining and wailing." Then she hugged herself, shivering even though the wind hadn't picked up. "Demanding justice."

I pointed over my shoulder to Daeam Mountain, toward the cliff where the monks believed Echo Company had once set up its signal equipment. "How about that cliff up there?" I asked. "During the war, Americans were there. Did you know that?"

"Yes, I knew. They were famous."

"Famous, why?"

"Because they were the only people with food and medicine and heating fuel."

"Did you ever talk to them?"

"No. Absolutely not."

This seemed to make her angry so I didn't press it. "Do you know how I can get up there?"

"You can't get up there." She saw my puzzlement and then added, "Not alone. You'd need someone to guide you."

"Why?"

"The woods are too thick, there are too many obstructions, and there is no direct pathway. You'd have to know the way. And if you got lost, the tiger would take you."

"Tiger? There are no more tigers in Korea."

"Huh, that's what they say."

I considered this. This woman seemed to believe Siberian tigers still stalked these mountains, but according to the books I'd read, no tiger had been spotted in South Korea since the late 1950s. Still, there was no point arguing with her.

"Do you know someone who could guide us up there?"

"There's only one person." She paused for a moment and then said, "Huk Sanyang-gun."

I didn't have my Korean-English dictionary with me, but I believed *huk sanyang-gun* meant "the black hunter."

"He hunts tigers?"

She looked at me as if I were a child. "The tigers protect what he hunts."

"So what does he hunt?"

"The most prized possession in these mountains."

And then I knew what she meant. "*Insam*," I said.

She nodded.

Wild ginseng, sometimes called royal ginseng, was prized far above the value of the cultivated ginseng grown in the lowlands. One gnarled old red root could make a man rich. Ten thousand US dollars in Hong Kong was a low price for the prized medicinal herb, and I'd read that in private sales particularly venerable roots had gone for even more. In Asia, ginseng was considered to be a magical tonic, able to make the old man young again and the young man wise. Ernie believed it, which was why he was always chewing ginseng gum, although I hadn't noticed him wising up any. The difference between a stick of ginseng gum made from the mass-produced version of the herb and a slice of the flesh of an authentic royal ginseng root was the difference between a copper penny and a Spanish gold doubloon.

"How can I get in touch with this Hunter Huk?" I asked.

"You can't get in touch with him," she told me. "If you're pure of heart and you pray for him, he gets in touch with you."

The old farmhouse was located right where the woman told me it would be. The afternoon was getting late and the shadows were long. We wandered around the ruin, searching for anything of interest but finding nothing. Ernie didn't say anything, but I knew what he was thinking: Why the hell had I brought them out here? I was starting to question the wisdom of it too, but I reminded myself we had to keep searching for some sign of the man with the iron sickle, the fancy woman from Mia-ri, and the mental patient known as Miss Sim Kok-sa. It had all started here for them, and I believed they'd return. Up here, in these isolated communities, certainly someone would spot them if they showed up.

"Over here," Captain Prevault said. She stood atop a small man-made earthen hill. "Is this a burial mound?" she asked.

"I think so." It was covered in weeds, not well-tended lawns like the vast burial mound areas that surround the city of Seoul. I climbed the mound and she pointed to a rotted wooden board lying on the ground. It was slashed with black ink.

"Can you read it?"

I knelt and swiped off part of the dirt. Chinese characters, two rows. Names, I thought. I pulled out my notepad and copied them down. The first character I could read: "Kim," the most common family name in Korea. The next two characters would be the given names, probably of the husband since he would normally be listed first. The second row of characters probably represented the woman's name. She had only two characters, the first a word I couldn't decipher but was probably her family name, and then only one character for her given name. It made sense. In Korea, wives don't give up their names when they marry. Below the names were Chinese numbers and the character for "year."

"Two people," I told Captain Prevault. "Probably the two people buried in this mound. The husband's family name was Kim. The year was 1951."

"Over twenty years ago," she said. Then she paused and added, "It's them."

It was dark now and the road was narrow and there was no sign of light anywhere in the universe except for the headlights of the jeep.

"That darkness up ahead," Ernie said, "is Mount Daeam."

"That's where Echo Company is," I said. "Somewhere on that mountain."

"And you believe our unholy little trio should make a pilgrimage up there."

"Not a pilgrimage," I said. "The man with the iron sickle wants us to go there."

"So we're going. You see any place to stop and get a chili dog around here?"

Captain Prevault said, "We should've brought tents and sleeping bags."

"And a diesel heater," Ernie added.

"Okay," I said, "I didn't think this through. But we were sort of in a hurry to get out of Yongsan Compound." Ernie snorted. I continued. "Most of the places I've traveled in Korea have always had some sort of civilization. I didn't expect these mountains to be so full of nothing."

"No bathhouse," Ernie said, "no *yoguan*, no chop house, no *mokkolli* house, no nothing!"

"All right, Ernie," Captain Prevault said. "He gets the point." Then she added, "Why don't you pull into that Howard Johnson's up ahead."

Ernie did a double take and she startled giggling. Then I was laughing and so was Ernie, and then we were all gliding through the night in our little jeep in the middle of the Taebaek Mountains, happy for once, not complaining about being hungry or tired or cold. Happy to be alive—unlike the couple in that cold earthen burial mound—and able to laugh and complain about the hand we'd been dealt.

By morning we were grumpy again.

We'd slept all night in the jeep. Ernie had found a place to pull over and even though he would've liked to have kept the engine running so we could keep the heater on, he'd turned it off to conserve fuel. We'd bundled ourselves up as best we could in every piece of field gear we'd brought and managed to get a little sleep—not much, because of the biting cold. Captain Prevault fared best. She curled up in the back seat on top of the mostly empty duffel bags and slept like a housecat on a fluffy couch.

I awoke first and stepped outside the jeep and stretched myself. Then I walked to the edge of the clearing beside the road. A creek gurgled at the bottom of an incline. I walked downhill, squatted next to the water, and washed my face. I found an isolated area downstream above the water line and did my business, digging a hole and covering it up like the Army field manual tells us. Soon Ernie and Captain Prevault were up and following my pattern. I'd brought a toothbrush and a razor blade but figured I'd wait for hot water before trying to scrape the stubble off my chin. Once we'd all performed our morning toilette, we climbed back in the jeep and Ernie drove off. I studied the map.

"The closest village," I said, "to the last known position of Echo Company is up ahead about three or four klicks."

"What's it called?"

"I'm not sure if this is a name or just a description."

"What is it?"

"I-kori."

"Which means?"

"Two roads."

"They didn't put a lot of thought into that name."

And when we reached the village, we realized why no one had.

"There's nothing here," Ernie said.

Captain Prevault leaned forward, her hands on my seat. "That looks like a cattle pen," she said.

"Or a pig pen," I corrected. I doubted there was a lot of high-end livestock up there.

"And chicken coops," she said.

"Yeah," Ernie replied, "but they're all empty."

"Let's talk to that guy, up there."

I pointed. Ernie slowed the jeep next to an old man pulling a cart along the side of the road.

"*Anyonghaseiyo*," I said.

The man grinned and nodded but didn't stop walking. Ernie kept pace with him.

"*Yogi-ei I-kori iei-yo*?" Is this Two Roads?

He nodded.

"No one lives here?"

He shook his head.

"During the war," I said, "I understand there was an American army unit nearby." His face remained impassive. Then I said, "Do you know where I can find Hunter Huk?"

The old man stopped his cart. Ernie slammed on the brakes and backed up a few feet. As I waited for the old man to speak, I noticed his cart was full of edible plants, probably pulled from the edge of the stream that ran parallel to the road.

"Hunter Huk?" he repeated. His voice was reedy and tattered, as if he'd used it for far too many years.

"Yes," I said. "Hunter Huk."

The old man shook his head. "Who told you of him?"

"A woman down the road." I pointed back from where we'd come. "She told me he was the only one who could lead us to the cliff where the American military unit had once set up their equipment."

The old man nodded. "That's true enough." We waited for what seemed like a long time. "I wouldn't advise you to look for him."

"Why not?"

"You can only find him in the mountains, and it's cold up there."

I nodded.

"And once he finds you, he always exacts a price."

"What kind of price?"

The old man shook his head once again. "Too high of a price. Go back to Seoul. Leave these mountains alone."

"We are determined to climb Daeam Mountain." I pointed toward the cliff the monks had originally told us about. "How do I get up there?"

"By helicopter," he said. His face was straight; it wasn't a joke.

"If I walk, how would I get up there?"

"You are in I-kori," he said. "The road you are on now is the first road. The second road is the one you just passed. It leads into the mountains."

"Have you been there before?"

"Never."

"Why not?"

The man shook his head once again and grabbed the handle of his cart. "Go back to Seoul," he said and started walking away.

We tried the road. Ernie drove along its unpaved surface. It was bumpy and uneven, but the US Army jeep was designed for just this type of terrain. Each of the four tires had its own independent suspension so the tire on the left could be in a ditch and the tire on the right could be elevated over a bump. They weren't connected by an inflexible axle. This made moving forward possible and Ernie was a good driver, but we knew the main danger when driving a jeep over rough terrain was its inherent instability. GIs were constantly driving jeeps too fast and taking corners too sharply and thereby turning their jeeps over. Ernie wouldn't do that, I hoped, but the road was becoming progressively more treacherous. And steeper. And then we were winding in and out of stands of pines, and the road wriggled up Daeam Mountain like a cold-weather serpent. Periodically I spotted the cliff that was our destination.

We must've reached an elevation of at least a thousand feet when we finally hit a dead end. Ernie climbed out of the jeep and surveyed the obstacle. It was a wall of earth and rock.

"This looks man-made," he said.

Even though it was covered with vegetation, I agreed with him. It appeared the rock cliff behind had been blown up with explosives for the express purpose of causing this avalanche. "They wanted to block the road," I said.

"Did a good job of it, too."

I glanced upward. If I backed up about twenty yards, I could just make out the eastern edge of the cliff that had once been the home of Echo Company. Using my Army-issue compass I took a reading on the direction.

"Can we make it up there before dark?" Ernie asked.

"I think so," I replied. "If we hustle."

I started to tell Captain Prevault to wait there for us when she cut me off and said, "No way. You're not leaving me here. I'm going with you."

And so the three of us packed up our gear, climbed carefully over the rock wall, and started humping our way up the last couple of miles between us and the old home of the Lost Echo. Halfway up, I tossed a newspaper-wrapped package to Captain Prevault. She opened it, looked inside, and said, "You've been holding out on us."

Ernie glanced at the package and said, "*Kimpap*. You bought it from the old woman at the farmhouse?"

"I figured we'd need a little extra on the road."

We stopped in a clearing to rest for a while and wolfed down one tube each of the glutinous rice wrapped in paper-thin seaweed, saving the rest for dinner. I drank deeply from the water in my canteen, and then we stared back up the trail.

The view from the cliff was breathtaking. It was apparent why Echo Company had picked this spot to set up their signal equipment. Far to the left, fading out of sight in the thick mist, was the eastern coast of Korea, and if I calculated the azimuth on my map correctly, there would've been a straight line of sight to the US Navy vessels anchored off the coast of Sokcho. To the right, the valley stretched away far to the north, probably to units operating on the enemy side of the 38th Parallel. The valley below looked like a panorama set up by giants. Tiny little people moved between tiny little houses, and smoke rose from chimneys like wavering threads of black silk.

"The top of the world," Captain Prevault said.

"That's what it seems like."

We still had maybe an hour of daylight, and I didn't want to waste it. Systematically, we searched every square foot of the scalloped shelf of the cliff, a natural formation that was about the size of a regulation baseball diamond. We paid particular attention to the back wall because there was an overhang there that would've protected the Americans from rain, snow and, with any luck, incoming enemy artillery.

We found a number of items: old K-ration tins, a P-38 handheld can opener, a moldy brass belt buckle, a couple of rounds of M-1 rifle ammunition, and a brown combat boot that was so worn it had a hole in the sole and rips in the leather near the ankle.

"So a US Army unit was here," Ernie said. "So what? It proves nothing."

No, it didn't. But I was still convinced the man with the iron sickle wanted to bring us here for a reason. What it was, I still couldn't be sure.

"It's too dark to go back now," Ernie said. The sun was almost down.

"So we spend the night here," I said.

"But tomorrow," Ernie said, glaring at me, "we return to the jeep and get the hell back to civilization."

He was tired of being cold and hungry, and I knew Captain Prevault was, too. So far, we had nothing to show for our little excursion, which would be hard to explain back at 8th Army headquarters.

With Captain Prevault's help, we gathered firewood and Ernie dug a pit beneath the rock overhang. Using my old Boy Scout skills. I managed to start a fire, and soon it was a roaring affair. Ernie stacked up enough firewood to keep it burning all night. Captain Prevault cut some vegetation and, using one of the duffel bags as a cover, made herself a tidy little bed. Ernie and I did the same but our constructs were somewhat less neat. Then we sat down around the fire and Captain Prevault handed out the last few rolls of *kimpap*. It tasted delicious. I washed it down with plenty of fresh spring water from my canteen because with all this hiking and all this work, I'd become more dehydrated than I knew.

We told a few listless stories, avoiding ghost stories, and this time, I believe I was the first one asleep.

The moon was high when I awoke, my bladder full. I arose from my lumpy duffel bag bed and tossed a couple of thick branches on the fire, which crackled with appreciation. I made my way to the far edge of the cliff, stepped behind a quivering poplar tree, and started to do my business. I was trying not to splash too loudly into the mud when I noticed movement off to my left. The edge of the cliff there didn't end in a rock wall but continued through low vegetation back to the forest that stretched away up the mountain. I didn't have my .45. The shoulder holster was cumbersome and difficult to sleep with so I'd taken it off and placed it on the ground next to me, but when I'd risen to take a leak, still half asleep, I'd forgotten to bring it with me.

Whatever was moving out there in the bush, I told myself, couldn't have been a Siberian tiger, or it would've been much more stealthy. Then I saw a flash of white moving away from me, from tree to tree, and when it stepped into a moonbeam, I saw it clearly.

Miss Sim Ok-sa, wearing her white hospital gown, glanced back at me fearfully, stumbling through the brush. No time to go back and alert Ernie or Captain Prevault. Within seconds she'd have disappeared into the immensity of the forest. I also didn't want to yell for help because that would only frighten her more. All these calculations were made with the speed of thought and before I knew it, I had tucked myself back into my pants and was shoving my way through the forest, moving quickly in the wake of the little mental patient.

She was surprisingly fast. But the rustling she made and the branches whipping behind her kept me on her trail. I became more reckless, running at almost full tilt, trying to make sure I didn't stumble over any gnarled old roots or stub my toe on low-lying rocks. Luckily, I'd been sleeping in my full fatigue uniform along with field jacket and my laced-up combat boots, but already I wished I'd brought my winter cap and my hooded parka to fight the mountain chill.

I followed her through the thick forest until suddenly I found myself in a moonlit meadow. Grass stretched before me, ankle high, forming an oval about the size of two roller skating rinks. I stood at the edge, scanning the glowing night, expecting to see Miss Sim running through the field with her white gown billowing behind her. Instead, I saw nothing. She was gone.

I couldn't believe it. I knew she had emerged right where I was standing. I searched the brush around me, finding nothing, until finally I retraced my steps about ten yards back into the forest. No sign of her.

Maybe I'd just imagined it. Maybe it hadn't been Miss Sim at all. Maybe I'd been so overwrought at the idea of bringing Ernie and Captain Prevault all the way out here for no good reason that I'd started to imagine reasons. I shook my head and put that aside. I'd seen her. I knew I'd seen her.

I walked out into the meadow and turned around. Nothing but a calm, cold evening in the middle of the Taebaek Mountains.

I sighed and started back. I stepped into the forest just where I'd left it. For the first few yards I walked forward confidently. And then I reached a large elm tree and tried to remember if I'd passed it to the right or to the left. No matter, such a minor deviation shouldn't throw me off much. I stepped to the left. I didn't recognize any of the trees farther in, but I wouldn't have been looking at them from this angle, since I'd been coming from the opposite direction. I turned around to see if that would help me orientate myself. It didn't.

I returned to the large old elm tree. I touched its bark, enjoying the reassuring reality of its rough edges, and told myself that I should sit down for a moment and think this through.

That's when it dropped on me; from up above, something dark and heavy and as large as a man. Before I could look up to see what it was, I felt a jarring in my skull, as if my head had been suddenly crunched between the prongs of a giant nutcracker, and the world and everything in it went black.

■   ■   ■

I was cold.

So cold that I thought I'd never been cold before. Cold had supplanted every inch of my flesh from the top of my head through my face, down my neck, along my chest and my back, through my shriveled testicles and on down my legs to my feet. But that was just the start. Then it seeped inside. My bones were nothing more than carvings of ice, and my heart and my lungs and my liver were snow puffs clinging to glassy ribs.

Something slapped the side of my face. It felt good. Warmth. Again, something slapped the opposite side and my eyes popped open.

A woman. An upside down woman. Mentally, I tried to focus, turning her right side up, trying to think through the caverns of my frozen misery, noting the long black curly hair and the thick lips and the disappointed eyelids. Madame Hoh, the fancy woman from Miari, the woman who'd owned the Inn of the Crying Rose, the woman who'd sicced a pack of local punks on me; the woman who, I believed, had been responsible for Mr. Ming's losing his head.

I also realized something else. She wasn't upside down, I was.

I realized this because of the screaming pain in my ankles. At least one part of my body had feeling in it; an excruciatingly painful feeling, but a feeling nevertheless. A rope, or maybe a thick wire, was biting into my ankles, keeping me from falling to the floor.

Madame Hoh leaned toward me until our noses almost touched. Her breath reeked of stale tobacco. "Hello, baby," she said. "How's it hanging?"

I couldn't reply. I wasn't sure if my throat would work. There seemed to be phlegm bulging through it, following the downward course of gravity. And when I tried to open my mouth I wasn't sure if my jaw or my lips were moving. Everything was too cold for feeling.

With her long red nails, Madame Hoh caressed the side of my face. I was grateful for the tenderness—and for the warmth.

"Can't talk? I understand. You just relax, baby." She leaned back. "That's it. Spit it up. Get it out. That's a good boy."

I coughed and choked and spit out as much phlegm as possible. As I did so my stomach muscles knotted so I could raise my head just a little. I was in a cave. There was light coming from an oil lantern behind Madame Hoh, and I was suspended against something boxy and metal. When I stopped coughing I looked up along the length of my body. I was naked, I could see that, and I was right about my ankles. They were bound in what appeared to be a thick hemp rope. Beyond that was some sort of wire, metal rods, and an antenna-like contraption. I relaxed my stomach muscles and gazed at Madame Hoh. She was smiling. Then she said in Korean, "*Arraso*?"

Do you understand?

And suddenly I did. I started to buck, flailing my body against metal like a hooked fish fighting for life.

It was the totem. That's what it had been all along. The wood from an old ammo box had been used to replicate the boxy shape of a US Army signal truck, a truck that had once belonged to Echo Company of the 4038th Signal Battalion (Mobile). And the wire contraption above the totem represented the antenna which Echo used to so diligently relay signals. And me? I was the rat dangling from a string. The dead rat.

Madame Hoh started to laugh—more than laugh. She shrieked with glee. And then someone was beside her, someone shoving her out of the way. Someone I recognized. I'd seen him in the alley in Itaewon, taunting me, daring me to come after him. And of course I couldn't have mistaken him because of what he held in his left hand. It was the man with the iron sickle.

In his other hand he held a narrow bottle. It was red, or filled with a red liquid. His hand twisted and I saw the label. The bottle and its contents were familiar to me. I saw them on every table in every mess hall since I'd been in the army. They were one of those manufacturers who'd landed a government contract decades ago and had been tenacious enough—and influential enough with Congress—to never let it go: Little Demon Hot Sauce, with a grinning red devil wielding a pitchfork on the label, fumes rising from the coals of hell.

The man with the iron sickle screwed the cap off the bottle, tossed it aside and, as Madame Hoh grabbed the back of my head and held on, he tilted the snout of the bottle into my right nostril and poured. Liquid pepper ignited the tender linings of my sinuses. I screamed and yelled and bucked, trying to snort and wheeze the burning flame upwards, out of my nose, but gravity kept it roiling inexorably into my skull, searing all the tender linings behind my eyeballs. Madame Hoh held on with surprising strength, and the man with the iron sickle continued to pour until the contents of the bottle had plunged deep into my nasal cavities. I coughed and retched and water poured from my eyes.

Despite the pain—or maybe in an attempt to avoid experiencing it fully—my mind was still evaluating evidence. I thought of the old couple at the PX snack stand, about how they'd said the man with the iron sickle sniffled as if he had a bad cold. Now I knew why. Somewhere in his distant past his sinuses had been violated by just such a treatment as I was receiving, leaving permanent damage. And I thought of how Mrs. Lee, the owner of the *pochang macha*, had told me about how he walked as if he were traipsing on egg shells, as if every step was painful to him. My livid ankles knew the genesis of that additional peculiarity.

If I felt any satisfaction in this analysis, it was soon swallowed up by another blast from the surging pepper. I coughed and screamed and cursed a company that would use a little demon as their logo.

Then I saw the iron sickle, held in his hand. He stepped toward me, raised it, and as he swung, I flinched. The rope gave way. I crashed head first to the ground. Dazed, I rolled on my side, raising my knees toward my chest, spitting and coughing and using gravity to cleanse my nose of the viciously burning fluid.

They were using candles now. Madame Hoh sat on a stool beside me, smoking blissfully, as if enjoying her cigarette after a fine meal. The man with the iron sickle sat opposite her, hands on his knees, the sickle dangling from relaxed fingers. Gently, with a soothing voice, Madame Hoh began to talk.

"They came in the fall," she said. "We watched them march in their sturdy combat boots, crushing dried leaves beneath the thick soles, and we watched as they set up their equipment and laughed at us and pointed and tossed bits of chewing gum and candy to us children. We all squealed in delight."

Hot sauce still drained from my nose, and I fought to breathe.

"And then they set up their equipment," she said, "and yanked a long cord, and their generator rumbled to life, and the little metal cabin lit up with light. And some of the GIs set up guard positions with sandbags and others—I believe their commander—marched down into the village, one of them holding a rifle trained on us gawking country folk. We were simple then. We knew nothing of electricity and none of us had ever spoken into a phone and the idea of refrigeration was not something we'd even imagined.

"The officer dictated the terms. None of us would be allowed inside the perimeter of the campground they were setting up, and we were under no circumstances to leave the area of our little village without checking with him first. The elders complained about this because some of the men and women had to carry their produce down into the valley to sell. And the officer replied that until they moved on, there would be no more trips to the lowlands.

"And so we acquiesced because we'd seen other soldiers, South Korean soldiers, in the area, and when they gave orders the punishment for not obeying those orders was death. But we also knew the snows were coming, and the punishment for not bartering in the valley and bringing back grain to store for the winter was also death. So at night, with the approval of the elders, some of the young men sneaked out with A-frames strapped to their backs and made their way clandestinely into the valley.

"And then the sapper came. A North Korean, alone, separated from his unit. But he had a canvas belt filled with explosives. He sneaked close to the American lines, set up his lethal devices, and somehow ignited them, destroying the truck that stored their diesel and burning to death six GIs. Then he disappeared into the night.

"The Americans erupted in a frenzy, shooting into the black sky, screaming for help, and their commanding officer took charge. He led the men as the flames were doused and supervised the salvage operation. All night long, the burned soldiers screamed. Even down in the village we could hear their cries of agony. Finally, only one was left. Even though his voice was hoarse and singed by the fire, his hideous screams continued. None of us slept that night. Neither, I'm sure, did any of the GIs. Just before dawn, we heard a single gunshot and the screaming stopped. A squad of soldiers led by their commander left their encampment and within minutes they were in our village. Everyone was ripped out of their homes: men, women, and children."

Behind the man with the iron sickle, flames licked out of a pit. They'd started a fire. I squirmed toward it, hoping for some warmth that would stop the chattering of my teeth. With her left foot, Madame Hoh kicked dust toward my face. I stopped.

"Unfortunately," she continued, "at exactly that moment, two young men with grain sacks hanging heavily from their A-frames trudged up the last incline of the trail. The GIs arrested them immediately, and the interrogations started. The elders denied that any of us had anything to do with the explosion and told the commander about the North Korean commando, but he didn't believe any of it. From that moment on, we were kept under constant surveillance, allowed to do nothing without the permission of an American soldier. The snow came, thicker than we'd seen in years. The GIs were grumbling about trouble they'd heard about over their radio, trouble to the north. Apparently, the United Nations advance into North Korea, all the way to the border with China, had been stalled and now they were in retreat.

"'Joe Chink,' the GIs told us. 'Joe Chink.' That's all they could think about. Massive legions of Chinese Communist soldiers were on their way south, but the men of Echo Company had to stay put and relay communications. But soon they ran out of fuel for their generators, and all transmission stopped. The commander saved just enough diesel to power their truck so the company would be able to drive out of the Taebaek Range. But it was too late. The roads were impassable, clogged with snow and ice. So the Americans waited, holding us as their hostages. Their slaves. The GIs grew bored. Soon they were bothering the unmarried girls. When that wasn't enough, they had their way with the married women. When husbands protested, they were beaten. And then they started turning their eyes on the younger girls, the ones who hadn't become women yet.

"Their food ran out and still it snowed. Americans and villagers both grew sick and died. They were buried in snowdrifts, preserved for later burial. The ground was frozen too hard to dig into. And then the commander died. We're not sure how. Some say he was murdered by his own men. While the GIs weren't watching, our people began to leave—those who were strong enough to walk through the twelve-foot-high snow drifts. The weak ones stayed behind and grew weaker. All the food was gone, including the grain and the canned goods the Americans had brought. Then one of the GIs pulled a body out of the snowdrift. He chopped it with an axe and charred its flesh over an open fire. Some told him to stop, some threatened to kill him, but in the end they all ate. And still the snows fell. There was no more power now, the last of the diesel had been used, and all communication with other military units had been lost. One by one we all escaped except for two old people who would bring the GIs victims. They would tell their fellow Koreans in distant villages about how rich the Americans were and about how they had medicine and food and heating oil, and then those people would follow them to the American encampment. But instead of being allowed to beg for penicillin to save the life of a loved one or to plead for a can of beans to stave off starvation, they were turned over to the GIs and slaughtered like swine and devoured."

Madama Hoh paused.

"And those two," I said, coughing as my ravaged throat became accustomed, once again, to speaking, "they were the couple hacked to death by Miss Sim." My voice was a croak.

"Her name is Ahn," she said. "And yes, she was a good girl. She stayed with her parents until the end and even accompanied them to the American encampment. When her mother realized they had been betrayed, she fought while her daughter escaped."

"So she hid in the woods," I said, "and heard her parents plead for their lives."

"And heard their final screams before their throats were cut and smelled the smoke from the sizzling of their flesh."

No wonder she'd gone mad. "What about this?" I said, nodding toward my bound feet and arms. "Why this? Why are you treating me like this?"

"We are treating you the same way my older brother was treated when he was caught stealing a can of beans by the GIs. Back when there was still food. They stripped him naked, strung him up by his feet, and poured hot sauce down his nose. You, we cut down after less than an hour. Him, they kept hanging all night."

I'd heard of similar punishments in wartime. Veterans sometimes bragged about it.

"But why do it to me?"

"To show you."

"Show me what?"

"What you need to know."

"For your claim?"

Madame Hoh puffed on her cigarette. "We're beyond that now."

"But you did put in a claim, for yourselves and for the other victims of this atrocity."

"Yes. One of the young men who carried the A-frame, who was older than us, found a lawyer after the war and filed the claim. But what good did it do us? Miss Sim, as you call her, had already been locked away in the mental hospital. The lawyer who filed the claim was threatened, a pistol put to his head. The A-frame man ran away and was never seen again. My friend here, my older brother who cared for me and tried to protect us all, was convicted of treason against the state."

I didn't believe he was her literal brother. Koreans often refer to someone as their "brother" or their "sister" if they're close friends or have been through a tribulation together.

"They put your 'brother' in jail?" I coughed, spitting up dried remnants of the hot sauce.

"For twenty years. They said he was a Communist."

"Why?"

"Because he was party to the claim."

"And you?"

"The KNP officer in charge of our case sold me to a brothel."

"How old were you?"

"At that time, fourteen."

"And your brother?"

"Sixteen."

"They gave him twenty years when he was sixteen years old?"

"They claimed he was the one who led that North Korean commando to the American encampment."

"Was he?"

"No way. He was just trying to survive, like the rest of us."

"What happened to his family?"

"Both his mother and his father were suffering from starvation and too weak to move. That's why he tried to steal the beans. When he failed, they died."

"And your family?"

She looked away. Finally, tears streaming from her eyes, her pudgy face contorted in rage, she said, "What do you think happened?"

Angrily, she threw her cigarette to the ground, stomped on it, and walked away. The man with the iron sickle walked forward and stared down at me.

And then I heard his voice for the first time. It was rough and gravelly and devoid of emotion—no fear, no hatred, no resentment— except for an overwhelming plaintive quality. In a matter of fact way, as if to clarify the record, he wanted to justify himself. In my experience in law enforcement, that desire to confess and explain it all to someone is a strong one. With this man, the words came out in an overpowering rush. Maybe it was because he'd never before encountered an American who could understand him, who could speak Korean. I nodded and listened, saying a brief word occasionally, in order to encourage him to continue.

He told me that the man in the claims office had been killed to show how wronged Korea had been by Eighth Army. He hadn't enjoyed it but it had to be done. The MP was murdered simply to show people that American law enforcement was not invincible. Despite being part of the greatest military power in the world, they were just men. The GIs in the signal truck were similarly slaughtered as stand-ins for the Lost Echo who had engendered all this misery. And then he told me what he planned to do next. He didn't name a specific target, but he said everyone would be shown soon. What he meant by that I wasn't sure, but I knew better than to ask questions. Then he walked away, leaving me alive. I studied the dark corners of the cavern, my ankles aching. As far as I could tell, there were no more bottles of Little Demon hot sauce.

-15-

The flames in the fire pit had subsided, and the cave was even colder than before. Everything was perfectly quiet, not even a mouse scurried through the dust. The only light was a dim glow off in the distance. Somewhere out there it was daylight.

My hands were still tied behind my back, but at least I was no longer dangling by my ankles. There was no pain in my legs, and I knew that was a bad sign. All feeling was gone—maybe all life. The thought of losing my legs and living the rest of my life in a wheelchair was more than I could bear.

I listened again, hearing nothing, convinced now that Madame Hoh and the man with the iron sickle were gone. Why hadn't they killed me? Maybe it was because death would be slower and more painful this way. And maybe they wanted to leave a message to whoever might happen upon my body in future years. What exactly the message would be, I was too hysterical right now to understand.

Or maybe the reason they left me alive had to do with the continuing drama that Madame Hoh and the man with the iron sickle were constructing. In recent years the ROK government had started inviting Korean War vets back to the country, both to thank them for protecting their nation from the northern Communists and to show off the economic progress the Republic of Korea had made. Additionally, it was a smart public relations move designed to continue the flow of US military and economic aid. The government picked up the airfare, hotel bills, and other expenses of the foreign veterans who were thus honored. They were greeted by high-ranking ROK government officials and feted with tours of industrial parks and museums and the peace village at Panmunjom and even an evening of entertainment at the big nightclub at Walker Hill. In other words, the veterans and their wives were treated like royalty. Before each of these confabs the ROK government published a list of the names of the vets and which country they were from and which unit they had been assigned to during the war.

This time, there was a veteran from the 4038th Signal Battalion (Mobile). His name was "Covert," as the man with the iron sickle had told me. He might not have been from Echo Company, but it didn't matter. He was close enough. I'd asked what he planned to do to this man and he told me he and Madame Hoh would decide when the time came.

Exactly when all this would happen, I didn't know. In fact I'd lost all sense of time. I wasn't sure how long I'd been in this God-forsaken cave. It was all agony to me. All I knew for sure was that if I didn't get myself out of here, I'd die.

My feet didn't look good. They were swollen and black and blue, and suddenly they started to hurt. It was a frisson of electricity at first, like sticking my toe into a live socket, but then it became gradually worse, growing like a symphonic crescendo. I wanted to massage my lower legs, maybe work some blood toward the ankles, but my hands were still securely bound behind my back. I tried to stand. It wasn't possible. Not only were my feet screaming with pain when I placed any weight on them, my toes and my instep and the entire foot had no feeling whatsoever; they were just part of the generalized agony. Even if I could've withstood the pain, I probably wouldn't have been able to balance myself upright on such lifeless stumps. Instead, I scooted through the dust on my butt.

At the end of the signal truck was a short metal fold-down stairwell. I studied the edge of the steps. On the interior the metal hadn't been beveled to a machined smoothness. It was bumpy and appeared sharp on some edges. I twisted myself face down, lay beneath the stairs, and shoved my bound hands up to the interior edge of the steps. Pressing as hard as I could, I started to rub the hemp rope against the rough edge. I rubbed and rubbed, and the rope, I sensed, was growing warmer, but it wasn't giving. I crawled out from beneath the stairwell and slid around the cavern, searching for something else, anything, that I could use to cut the ropes that bound my hands. Against the cavern wall, some of the rocks jutted out. It looked to me like this cavern, natural to begin with, had been widened with explosives. Probably the men of Echo Company realized they had to find a place to hide their signal truck and their other equipment from the prying eyes of scouts that ranged ahead of the main units of the Chinese "volunteer" army. They'd blown this opening, rolled everything in here, and hunkered down for the remainder of the winter. I tried not to think of their food supply.

I found a particularly jagged rock, but the sharp edge was a few feet off the cavern floor. Somehow, I had to stand to reach in. I sat with my back against the wall, pulled my feet up as close as I could, and tried to sidle myself upright into a standing position. I couldn't control my lifeless feet, but that didn't stop them from hurting whenever I placed any weight on them. Still, it had to be done. I kept pushing myself upright until I propped the rope binding my hands against the rock. Slowly, I slid my arms up and down, leaning into it, feeling the sharp granite begin to bite. Even though the temperature in the cavern was at or below freezing, I was in so much pain that sweat poured off my body as I worked. I sawed and sawed and finally the knotted strands of hemp rope popped loose. I brought my hands in front of my chest and tossed the last of the offending fibers into the dust.

I rubbed my raw forearms. My triceps were cramping up on me. Quickly, I plopped down in the dirt, stretching my arms and fingers as I untied my feet. Now I could stand, barely, and I had the full use of my hands. What I needed was something to support my weight so I could begin to perform something that would resemble walking. I fell back to my knees and crawled toward the fire pit. Warm embers glowed. I stuck my nose toward the warmth and blew gently, and it flared red in response. Fuel. I had to find fuel. I scrabbled in the dim light until I found a few loose branches that had probably been dropped when the fire was built. I broke them into shreds and gingerly fed them to the fire, blowing air on the embers as I did so. Gradually, the strips of wood started to smoke and then one of them leapt into flame. Carefully, I added wood until I had a fairly good bonfire going.

I began to range around the cavern.

The Army survival manual tells you that when you're in a tight spot, even when time is running short, it pays to plan. I knew I needed food, water, and warmth—not necessarily in that order. I found my clothes wadded up and left in the dirt near the signal truck in a soggy lump. I started with the underwear, holding the briefs and the T-shirt up as close as I could get them to the fire, letting them dry. When they were a little less damp, I slipped them on, hoping my body heat would continue the drying process. I stood up, tested my aching ankles, and managed to hobble my way toward the light. Beneath a rock shelf, I stared out into a grey, overcast morning. Everything sloped downhill, into snow-covered trees and then into impenetrable fog. No sign of Madame Hoh or the man with the iron sickle, only frost-crusted footprints leading away from the cave and downhill. Moving quickly, I managed to gather twigs and dried branches near the rocks surrounding the cave entrance. By the time I returned to the little fire, I was shaking so badly, I could barely control my hands. Still, I fed the fire until it blazed brighter than ever. I warmed myself.

I spent the next hours tending the fire and drying my clothes. But I had another chore here in this rock-hewn mausoleum. One I'd been putting off.

I had to inspect the interior of the signal truck of the company known as the Lost Echo.

I wandered down Daeam Mountain for two days. I was completely lost and only followed the contours of the mountain as they led me downhill. On the second night, I collapsed. I had replaced my first walking stick with a better one that gave me more support. Even though my feet hurt like hell, they were functioning now, and I had high hopes the pain was a sign they were healing. Still, I was hungry and thirsty and desperately cold, and the inner linings of my sinuses bothered me, still raw from the Little Demon.

I needed shelter. Before I'd left the cave, I'd commandeered an old canvas tent flap and, using a rock, sawed a hole in the middle. I slipped it over my head and used it as a poncho. Even though it was heavy, it helped keep me warm and as dry as possible in this wintry world I was trudging through. I'd also found a box of flares. It figured the men of the Lost Echo wouldn't have used them because they were busy hiding from the Chinese, not trying to draw attention to themselves. There were also some old dried up candles. Most of them crumbled beneath my touch but a few were still serviceable.

I found a fir tree with a branch broken from the weight of the snow. Using my walking stick, I pelted it until most of the snow was gone. Then I gathered some more twigs and made a thick bedding beneath the overhanging branch. I crawled in. Shoveling together a pile of earth, I stuck one of the candles atop it. Then, striking one of the three flares I'd brought with me, I lit the wick. Now I had a shelter. One that wasn't too cozy but at least it would keep me from freezing to death. I dropped a handful of snow into a canteen cup I'd salvaged from the signal truck and held it over the flare. When the snow melted, I drank it all down and then melted some more. Finally, I lay on my side, curled around the flickering candle.

I wondered what had become of Ernie and Captain Prevault and if they'd started a search for me, but before these thoughts could formulate coherently, I passed out.

I felt the footsteps before I heard them. They were soft paddings in the night. And then there was something warm above me, hovering. I lay completely still, afraid to move or even to breathe. Something snuffled and then I felt the warmth lowering, the warmth of a very large body. Something touched the lobe of my ear, something like an exquisitely thin wire. And then another. The breath was hot now. Meaty, with a vague wheezing underlying it. A cat. I was sure of it. An enormous cat. So close its whiskers were poking into the side of my head. I refused to move. I would not move. The feline breathed into my ear, deciding, I believed, whether I should live or die. It took a long time in its deliberations, an eternity. And then, like a living dream, it stepped away, ever so quietly, like a fleeting thought. For another long time, I continued to lie perfectly still and then, for some unfathomable reason, I was asleep again.

When I awoke, my candle was out. I peered through hanging branches. A few feet away from my little shelter, a man squatted on his haunches, studying me. He wore a tunic and loose pantaloons tied at the ankles; both appeared to be made of buckskin. His headgear was a woven straw conical hat with a low brim that shadowed his eyes. Large calloused hands hung loosely over his knees.

"Don't move," he said.

I studied him. He wasn't armed as far as I could see and his facial expression was benign, not threatening.

"Why not?" I asked.

"You'll crush them."

"Crush what?"

"The family." He pointed with a thick-knuckled finger. "The grandfather is right next to you, the younger generation between your feet."

Carefully, I lifted my head. Then I realized what he meant. Directly in front of me, poking up from between loose branches, was a sprightly looking plant, about six inches high, with sturdy green stems and bright green leaves. At its base was a thick gnarled root of a reddish hue. Between my feet were more green shoots, smaller, younger than the venerable fellow right in front of my eyes.

"*Insam*," I said. Ginseng. Literally, the people plant.

The man nodded.

Carefully, being sure not to damage any of the plants, I sat up and shoved the hanging branch out of the way. I studied the man's rough visage. He was slightly amused with me, obviously at home squatting in the middle of this vast forest.

"You're Huk Sanyang-gun," I said, playing a hunch. The black hunter.

He didn't nod but stared right at me. "That's what they call me."

"Is that your real name?"

"Now it is." With his open palm, he motioned at the plants surrounding me. There were more of them, of all sizes and apparent ages, like a clan of little green people. "They like you," he said.

"Like me?"

"Yes. That's why they've allowed you to find them."

"But I didn't find them. I was exhausted last night and there was this broken branch here so I used it for shelter."

"Yes," he said. "You must be worthy."

"Worthy of what?"

"Of finding the royal ginseng."

"*I'm* worthy?" I said, pointing to the center of my chest.

Amused, Hunter Huk nodded.

"How about you? You found them, too."

"I found you," he corrected me. "You've been tromping through these woods for almost two days. I figured you weren't going to get out alive if I didn't help you."

"Couldn't you have come earlier?"

He shrugged. "I was busy."

"With what?"

His eyes widened. "You're not the only one who has things to do."

I leaned forward and rubbed my swollen ankles.

"You need to get to a hospital," he said.

"Won't this *insam* cure all my ailments?"

"Don't make fun," he said, frowning.

I figured he was right about that. I was depending on him to save my life.

"There was a tiger here last night."

He smiled. "There are no tigers in these mountains. Once they roamed freely and protected the ginseng but now they are gone."

"I saw one," I said.

"You saw it?"

"Well, I didn't open my eyes."

He smiled again, more broadly this time.

"Can you get me out of here?" I asked.

"Yes," he said, "but you'll have to walk."

"I can do that," I said, grabbing my walking stick.

When I stood up, he said to me, "Which one do you want?"

"What do you mean?"

"The *insam*. They presented themselves to you. It would be an insult now not to harvest one of them."

"Only one?"

"Only one. Greed would also be an insult."

I studied the green plants poking up between the sparse grass and the damp leaves. "Honestly, I wouldn't know what to do with it."

"You don't have to use it yourself. Give it to someone you respect."

I thought of someone. "Which plant would be best?" I asked.

"The oldest is the most valuable," Hunter Huk said, pointing to the grandfather plant, "but the entire clan will grieve if you take him. Better if you take a young man, one who is strong and covets adventure."

I studied a few of the medium sized plants. One of them stood off by itself, slightly elevated on a clump of turf. "That one," I said, pointing.

"Good choice," Hunter Huk said. He pulled a short curved dagger from beneath a leather belt that cinched his buckskin tunic to his narrow waist. He turned it and offered the wooden handle to me.

"Will you show me how?"

He knelt near the plant. Leaning gingerly on my staff, I joined him. "Carve through the earth around the edge and dig deep so as not to damage the roots. If you pull him up whole he will survive longer and once the outer husk dries, the flesh of the root will still be full of vital juices."

I did as I was told, widening the churning of earth at his direction. Finally, I pulled the plant up whole, root and all. It appeared to have legs and arms and even a stumpy kind of face. Hunter Huk handed me a small leather pouch, and I placed the plant inside and knotted it with a drawstring. I tried to hand it to him but he waved it away.

"Keep it," he said. "It is yours now."

I stuffed the plant in the large upper pocket of my fatigue blouse.

"Come on," Hunter Huk said, motioning for me to follow.

At the edge of the clearing, he turned and bowed three times to the small family of plants. I did the same.

Hunter Huk motioned toward the valley below. About a mile away sat the intersection I recognized as I-kori.

"How can I thank you?" I said.

"By giving the *insam* to someone who is worthy."

"I will."

I looked back at the road. There was a military vehicle there, a jeep. Maybe it was Ernie. When I turned back to say goodbye, there was no one there. I glanced at the opening in the woods. Were the branches quivering? They seemed to be, but I couldn't be sure.

I hurried downhill.

As I approached the jeep I realized it was painted a darker green than the olive drab color favored by the US Army. This was the deep pine-colored hue of the ROK Army. I hobbled forward as fast as I could. The hourglass figure that emerged from the passenger seat was unmistakable. Major Rhee Mi-sook waved at me and smiled. For a moment, I wanted to turn and run, but I realized I wouldn't get far. Instead, I tossed the walking stick aside and strode as confidently as I was able straight toward her.

My beard was a growth of a few days now, and my fatigues were muddy and damp. I must've stunk to high heaven. I saw all this on Major Rhee's face. Her cute nose twisted and she pointed me toward a three-quarter ton truck that was racing toward us from up the road.

"Ride in there," she said. "I'll interrogate you later."

"I have to get in touch with Eighth Army," I told her. "Now."

"What is it?" she asked.

But when I stepped closer, her nose twisted more severely this time, and she held the back of her dainty hand up to her face as if to ward off germs.

"Never mind," she said. "We'll talk about it later."

"Do you have a radio?"

"No. But there's a phone not far from here."

The three-quarter ton truck arrived, and she motioned for me to get in. As she returned to her jeep, I climbed in back with three ROK Army soldiers. They scooted as far away from me as they were able. I wasn't happy about being under the control of Major Rhee, but somehow I had to communicate with 8th Army and let them know about the threat to the veterans who were gathering at Walker Hill.

About a half mile up the road, we screeched to an abrupt halt.

The ROK soldiers started cursing and grabbed their rifles. I braced myself against the wooden stanchions of the truck and hauled myself upright. A roadblock. Korean National Police armed to the teeth. The cops all wore combat boots and khaki uniforms, and they were all armed with either M-16 rifles or big .45s strapped to their hips. One of the vehicles even had an M-50 machine gun mounted on it—an M-50 machine gun that was trained right on us.

Some of the soldiers raised their weapons as if preparing to return fire. As fast as I could, I clambered out of the truck and crouched low.

I heard shouting. Major Rhee's voice. Another voice shouted back at her, one I recognized. Mr. Kill. They were speaking so quickly and both of them were so enraged that I couldn't understand everything they were saying, but I picked up enough. Somehow, the KNPs knew I was there. They wanted to take custody of me and return me to 8th

Army. Major Rhee was having none of it. I was in her custody now and that's how it would stay. Neither side was backing down.

I wasn't too crazy about being argued over as if I were chattel, and I was also worried that whoever I ended up belonging to would lock me up. I wasn't sure exactly what was going on, but it was clear that the ROK Army and the Korean National Police were each determined to control the situation in their own way.

My memories of what Major Rhee had done to me when she'd been posing as a Senior Captain in North Korea made up my mind. I didn't want that to happen again. With as much dignity as I could muster, I marched forward, stiff-legged, lurched past Major Rhee's jeep and started to walk toward Mr. Kill.

She grabbed me in a neck lock. I was too weak and off-balance to resist. She pulled me back and somehow a pistol appeared in her hand. The bolts of a dozen KNP M-16 rifles were released and clanged forward. Behind me a smaller number of ROK Army rifles did the same.

"He's mine," Major Rhee screamed.

Her face barely peeked over my left shoulder. The pistol grazed against the right side of my chin.

I willed my mind to concentrate, to try to parse what they were screaming at each other. Mr. Kill was shouting that he knew her game. She wanted the man with the iron sickle to keep murdering Americans because she wanted the US to leave the Korean peninsula. Major Rhee shouted back that it would be good riddance.

Without thinking, I threw myself backward. She wasn't expecting it, and she wasn't strong enough to keep from crumbling beneath my weight. The KNPs surged forward. The next thing I knew Mr. Kill had ripped the pistol from Major Rhee's hand, and she was screeching at him a long list of invectives. Many of the words in Korean were completely new to me. Three of the KNPs jerked me to my feet and dragged me toward one of their waiting vehicles. I half expected a round to burst into my back, but in the end everyone held their fire.

As we drove of, Major Rhee was still screaming.

"I need a radio," I shouted at Mr. Kill as we raced away. "Or a telephone."

"We have one."

He sat in the passenger seat of the small sedan, his assistant, Officer Oh, driving. He flicked a switch and stretched a cord toward me in the back seat.

"Touch the button when you want to talk," he said. "Who do you want me to contact?"

The CID office in Seoul didn't have a radio but the MP station did.

"The Eighth Army MP station," I said.

He punched in some numbers. A staticky speaker crackled to life. A familiar voice said, "Eighth Army Headquarters, Military Police."

"Grimes," I said, "they took you off guard duty."

"Sueño?" He sounded as if he was amazed. "Where the hell are you?"

"With Mr. Kill, heading toward Seoul. You have to relay a message to Riley at the CID."

"Shoot."

"Be sure to let Agent Bascom and Captain Prevault know I'm safe, and I'm on my way back to Seoul. If they were searching for me they can stop."

"Got it."

"And also let them know that they have to get someone out to Walker Hill."

"Walker Hill?"

"Right. The resort area on the eastern end of Seoul. There's a threat to the Korean War veterans who are out there."

"What kind of a threat?"

"The man with the iron sickle. He's after one . . ." I tried to continue talking, but we were behind a line of hills now and the connection had been broken. I handed the microphone back to Mr. Kill.

"Walker Hill?" he asked.

"The man with the iron sickle and his accomplice, Madame Hoh, they're on their way now."

"What do they want?" he asked.

"Revenge."

When we emerged from the hills, Mr. Kill managed to make contact with KNP headquarters in Seoul. He gave crisp instructions, and I had no doubt that within minutes the resort hotel at Walker Hill would be swarming with cops. Whoever this American veteran from the 4038th Signal Battalion was, he'd be safe.

I leaned back in the seat, completely exhausted.

Officer Oh handed me a small can of guava juice. I thanked her and tore off the pop top and drank the contents down in two gulps. Then I closed my eyes. The siren was on now and we were making excellent time back toward Seoul. We'd be there in an hour, I thought as I fell asleep.

The Sheraton Walker Hill Hotel was completely surrounded by armed Korean National Police. A line of black Hyundai sedans was parked behind the sentries, and I figured a few ROK government VIPs were there, probably making speeches to the American veterans. We pulled up in front and a liveried doorman opened my door. He jerked back when he saw me. I looked like what I felt like, a mountain man who hadn't washed in a week. As we clambered out of the car, I noticed a white van with a red cross emblazoned on it. An elderly American was having his blood pressure checked. They really were treating these guys like royalty.

Mr. Kill escorted me through the glass door. My muddy boots slapped on polished tile. We walked up to the long check-in counter, and a number of gorgeously made-up young women bowed to us. When Mr. Kill flashed his credentials, a black-suited duty manager appeared in front of him, almost as if by magic. Mr. Kill deferred to me and I started to talk.

"Amongst the American guests," I said, "there is a veteran whose unit during the Korean War was the Forty Thirty-eighth Signal Battalion. We must locate him immediately." Without being told, one of the young women in a business suit produced a check-in register and flipped it open on the counter. The list of American names was traced with polished nails. In the right column were their unit designations.

"Walton," the manager said. "Mr. Covert P. Walton. He's in room sixteen fifty-two."

Within seconds, Mr. Kill, Officer Oh and I were in the elevator punching the 16th floor button. When we arrived, Officer Oh took the lead, pulling her small pistol out of her waistband as she did so. The door to Room 1652 was open. We barged in. Two maids, both with white bandanas tied around their heads, looked up from snapping sheets. Their mouths fell open. Officer Oh asked where the American guest was.

Terrified, the two women said they didn't know. They'd reached this room about ten minutes ago, and the sign asking for room service was dangling from the outside handle.

Officer Oh ordered them to drop everything and to step outside. They did. She checked the room, in the bathroom and even under the bed, but Mr. Covert P. Walton was nowhere to be found.

We went back downstairs to the lobby. Mr. Kill called some KNP officers over and gave them instructions to search the foyer and the dining room and the shopping boutiques and to check the identification of every foreigner they encountered. As soon as they found Mr. Covert P. Walton, they were to escort him back to the main lobby. When they bowed and scurried off, Mr. Kill and Officer Oh and I looked at one another.

"You should sit down," Officer Oh said.

But something was bothering me, I wasn't sure what. When we had reached the main lobby, I'd glanced outside through the big glass doors and seen the reassuring presence of the doormen and the KNPs standing guard. For some reason, something seemed missing. And then I realized what it was.

"Come on," I said.

Mr. Kill and Officer Oh followed me outside. Her sedan was still parked there, in a place of privilege only allowed for the vehicle of the Senior Homicide Inspector of the Korean National Police. Mr. Kill stared at me curiously, as did Officer Oh. Everything looked normal; everything except one thing.

"The Red Cross van," I said. "There was a woman inside, wearing a nurse's uniform. I only saw her back. I imagine there was a driver up front and I spotted an elderly American in back."

"They're gone," Officer Oh said in English.

Mr. Kill cursed. He ran toward his sedan, flung open the passenger door, and leaned in and switched on the radio. Immediately, he was ordering an all-points bulletin for the missing Red Cross van. Officer Oh questioned the doormen and the KNP officers standing guard. They all confirmed the same thing. As soon as we'd stepped inside, the back door of the van had closed, and they'd driven off.

"Did the American get out?"

Not everyone had been watching but the few who did said he hadn't. They'd assumed he needed medical attention and he'd been taken away for that reason.

We checked with the hotel manager and asked who had authorized the Red Cross van. He didn't know. He assumed it had been part
of the government effort to provide first class service to the visiting
Americans. He made a few phone calls, and everyone he talked to
denied having authorized the van. Within minutes the posse of KNP
officers returned from their search of the hotel. They'd talked to many
foreigners, most of them veterans there for the conference and they'd
checked every passport, but none of them was Mr. Covert P. Walton.

-16-

I returned to Yongsan Compound.

Ernie and Captain Prevault had also returned by now, and we met at the CID admin office. Despite the rawness of my physical presence, Captain Prevault hugged me.

"We searched everywhere for you," she said. "The KNPs didn't help at first but then when Ernie insisted Mr. Kill in Seoul be notified, they started to cooperate."

"How'd you find out I was okay?" I asked.

"I called Riley," Ernie said. "The MPs got your radio message."

Riley said, "The Provost Marshal wants to talk to you, trooper. *Now.*"

"Shouldn't I change first?"

"*Now!*" Riley repeated, pointing down the hallway.

I bowed to the inevitable. Before I left, Ernie said, "Give me the keys to your wall locker. I'll go to the barracks and get you a change of clothes."

I checked my pockets. "I lost them. But Mr. Yim has a set. And there's an extra pair of boots under my bunk."

"I'll get 'em," he said and hurried away.

Captain Prevault squeezed my hand. "Good luck in there," she said.

■   ■   ■

It was a routine ass chewing. Even the Provost Marshal realized that if Ernie and I hadn't broken free of his controlling hand, we never would've flushed out the man with the iron sickle like we had. Still, now the 8th Army faced the problem of having a civilian murdered right under its nose.

"Where are they?" Colonel Brace demanded.

"Maybe they've returned to Mia-ri," I said. "Madame Hoh has contacts there." I thought of the thugs who'd chased me. "Mr. Kill already has the KNPs checking that out."

"Where else might they have gone?"

"After that, they could be just about anywhere, sir. I'm sorry I blew it."

If Ernie could hear me, he'd accuse me of brown-nosing. Apologizing to a field grade officer is something he'd never do. But I did feel regretful. At every step so far the man with the iron sickle had outsmarted us.

"What's wrong with your nose?" he asked.

"A cold," I said.

"And your feet?"

"My boots are too tight."

The Provost Marshal shook his head. "Get some rest," he said. "Change clothes. Then get back here and be prepared for whatever we have to do."

I stood up and saluted.

As I limped down the hallway, I was thinking of a long shower and a change of clothes and a nap in a bunk with clean sheets. But instead when I reached my desk, I opened the top drawer and pulled out the hand-carved radio dial that had been left beneath the totem. I wasn't sure but I believed I knew now why it had been left for us to find.

I stepped toward Riley's desk. "Who do you know at the Signal Battalion?" I asked.

"To do what?"

"To give us information. Old information. Somebody whose been around a long time."

"Grimaldi," Riley said. "That old DAC has been here since MacArthur was a boy scout."

"Call him."

Riley did. Then he handed the phone to me. Mr. Grimaldi was the Department of Army Civilian who ran the signal battalion repair shop. I described the carved dial to him and he explained that when signal equipment was lost or destroyed during the Korean War it was often replaced by jerry-rigged items. And then I described the numbers on the dial and the deep notch at a certain frequency.

"Armed Forces Radio," he said. "They were the only outfit broadcasting during that first winter of the war. Everyone was listening to it, hungry for news. Knowing where the Chinese were— or weren't—could save your life."

"Thanks, Mr. Grimaldi," I said, not knowing what good this phone call had done me. But before I hung up he said, "After we re-took Seoul, they set up a permanent station for a while."

"Permanent? They weren't in mobile trucks?"

"Not for a while at least."

"Where'd they set up?" I asked.

"In one of the few buildings in Seoul left standing. The Bando Hotel."

I thanked him and slammed down the phone.

Ernie returned and I changed into a dry set of fatigues and a polished pair of combat boots.

"You still stink," he told me.

"Thanks."

We hopped in his jeep. "You need some rest," he told me.

"Yeah, but first we're going to the Bando Hotel."

"What's wrong with the barracks?"

I explained it to him.

"Sort of a long shot," he said.

"Sort of," I agreed.

Before we pulled out of the parking lot, Captain Prevault hopped into the back seat. "You're not leaving without me," she said, "not after all this."

We didn't have time to argue.

The concierge at the Bando Hotel held his nose as he talked to me but when I explained what we wanted he led us into an elevator and took us straight to the top floor. From there we walked up a flight of stairs that opened onto the roof. The Bando was ten stories high and during the Japanese occupation it had been the tallest and most luxurious hotel in Seoul.

"Here," the man said, motioning with an open palm. "We set it up as a tourist attraction. A shrine to the only radio station functioning during the Korean War." He frowned. "Now see what they've done."

Equipment was smashed, along with a glass display case, and photographs had been ripped from the wall.

I picked up a placard written in English and Korean. It explained that after the Inchon landing, the 8th United States Army had re-taken Seoul and the first Armed Forces Korea Network radio station had been set up atop the Bando Hotel. It was from here that General Douglas MacArthur broadcast his call for Kim Il-sung and the leadership of Communist North Korea to lay down their arms and surrender. Unfortunately, they hadn't, and once the Chinese entered the war, Seoul had been retaken by the enemy and the war had dragged on for almost three more years.

"When did this happen?" Ernie asked.

"Maybe one hour ago. Many people come and go through lobby. Somebody come up here, do this."

All remnants of this glorious little shrine had been ripped to shreds. I thought I knew why. During those horrible days with the Lost Echo, the one link the suffering GIs would've had was the AFKN radio broadcasts. Even the Koreans would've heard it constantly, since all civilian radio stations had been abandoned because of the war. Just listening to it must bring back horrible memories for them.

I described Madame Hoh and the man with the iron sickle to him and then asked if they'd seen these people with an elderly American.

He thought about it. "Maybe."

We rushed back downstairs. Two staff members remembered seeing three people who matched that description, about the time the AFKN shrine had been trashed.

"How about the older American?" I asked. "How did he look?"

"Frightened," the front desk clerk said, "but I thought it was just because he was not used to Korea."

We walked outside and stood on the busy sidewalk.

"So where are they now?" Captain Prevault asked.

A big PX Ford Granada taxi pulled up and two Americans climbed out. Then I thought of something—what the man with the iron sickle had said to me, about people would be "shown." Before the cabbie left, I leaned in the passenger window and asked if there had been a party of three, two Korean and one American, picked up here within the last hour. He didn't know but Ernie flashed his badge and made him call dispatch. After some discussion, the dispatcher confirmed that a party matching that description had been picked up in front of the Bando about a half hour ago.

"Where'd they go?" I asked.

"Yongsan Compound," the driver said.

"Where on Yongsan Compound?"

He conferred with the dispatcher. He clicked off and looked at us and said, "The AFKN Club."

We ran to the jeep.

AFKN, the Armed Forces Korea Network. They'd long ago stopped broadcasting from downtown Seoul and now had their own studio complex near 8th Army headquarters on Yongsan Compound.

"They have an American with them," I told Captain Prevault, "so that and being in a PX taxi will get them through the gate."

"Don't they check everybody's ID?"

"Yes, supposedly. But the gate guards are aware of the veterans in country. They're given special privileges."

"The other two can be signed in as guests," Ernie told her, "unless they already have phony ID."

"Won't the guards know to be looking for Mr. Walton?"

"Maybe," I told her. "But it's unlikely that word has reached the gate guards yet. Besides, nobody's expecting them to head for the compound."

Captain Prevault sat back with her arms crossed.

"So what are they going to do at the AFKN club?"

"All their suffering had to do with signal, with communications, with broadcasting," I said. "Now they have one of the signalmen who was a member of the same battalion as the Lost Echo. Madame Hoh and the man with the iron sickle know they're going down. They just want to go down big."

"In a blaze of glory," Ernie said.

"Something like that."

"But why?" Captain Prevault asked.

I didn't have time to explain all I'd learned in that cave. "They have reason," I said.

Ernie flashed his badge to the gate guards and gunned the engine of the little jeep all the way along the winding road that led to the top of the hill above the Yongsan Main PX where the AFKN complex sat. Besides the television and radio studios, AFKN also had a barracks and a small Quonset hut set aside as their all-ranks restaurant and nightclub. The AFKN Club.

By the time we barged into the main ballroom, the AFKN Club was mostly empty. The lunch hour rush was over. We made our way to the far side of the building and crossed a well-tended lawn to the main broadcast facility. We walked down a hallway lined with radio broadcast booths, checking each one as we went, getting startled looks from at least one GI disc jockey with earphones enveloping his head. Finally, we reached the TV studio.

A bulb atop the big camera glowed red. The lights on the sound stage were on, bright and hot. Slumped behind the camera was a GI in fatigues, his throat cut, lying in a puddle of blood. On the stage, sprawled over the news anchor desk, lay a man I recognized. He was the one who read the officially-sanctioned world news to us every night in a deep monotone. The side of his face rested in a puddle of gore.

"Back here," Ernie shouted.

The engineer at the broadcast control panel was still alive. With paper towels she'd grabbed along the way, Captain Prevault stanched the blood on the side of his neck.

"The bleeding isn't arterial," she said. "He'll live."

He croaked something. I leaned closer. "What?"

"The camera," he said.

"What about the camera?" I asked.

"Turn it off. It's on. We're broadcasting live."

Broadcasting death was more like it.

▪ ▪ ▪

The MPs shut the compound down. Nothing moved but I had little hope that we'd find them. A quick inventory by the AFKN First Sergeant revealed that one of their mobile broadcast trucks was missing. I immediately called Mr. Kill and left a message with Officer Oh. She'd relay a description of the truck, and the license number, to the KNPs.

"Do they still have Mr. Walton?" she asked.

"Yes," I answered, "as far as we can tell."

I was exhausted but Captian Prevault kindly brought me a cup of hot coffee from the AFKN Club. Ernie and I allowed a gaggle of MP investigators to start interviewing anybody who might've seen anything.

"Okay," Ernie said. "They've made their statement. First with Mr. Barretsford, then with Collingsworth, and again with the two GIs in the signal truck."

"Now they've graduated to live TV," Captain Prevault said.

"So where are they now?" Ernie asked.

"Koreans don't watch it," I said.

Captian Prevault touched my forearm, concerned.

"Don't watch what?" Ernie asked.

"They don't watch AFKN. Not during the day anyway."

On weekdays, the two Korean television stations weren't allowed by the government to start broadcasting until five P.M.

"Okay," Captain Prevault said slowly. "The Koreans, most of them, aren't watching."

"They didn't see the murder," I said.

"No, they didn't." She squeezed my arm tighter. "You need rest."

"That means," I continued, "that they'll want a big venue where the Korean public will be watching."

"Like a Korean TV station?" Ernie asked.

"Maybe. But I don't think so. Not now. The KNPs will be alert for that."

"Then where?"

"Someplace big," I said. "Someplace grand."

Captain Prevault tore open a small bag of saltine crackers for me. "Eat," she said. I did. Before I had finished chewing, she brought me a cup of water. I drank it down.

An army sedan pulled up outside. Somebody ran through the front door. Boots tromped down the hallway.

"They found them," Riley said, pushing through the double swinging doors of the broadcast station. I'd never seen him so excited or his face so flushed, except when he was halfway into a fifth of Old Overwart.

"They found who?" I asked.

"The man with the iron sickle. And that broad. They've got the old goat, and they're threatening to kill him."

"Where?"

Riley looked at a pad of paper he held in his hand. "Someplace called Kong Ha Moon."

"In downtown Seoul?"

"Right in the heart of downtown Seoul."

Riley meant Guanghua-mun, the Gate of the Transformation of Light.

Ernie and I hurried outside to the jeep. Captain Prevault slipped in the back seat.

"You can't go!" Ernie shouted.

"I'm going!" she said.

He cursed and slammed the jeep in gear, and we were heading out of Gate Seven, turning left toward the road that leads through Namsan Tunnel.

■   ■   ■

In the last few days, while I'd been wandering around the Taebaek Mountains, the secret of the man with the iron sickle had seeped out to the Korean public. The story hadn't appeared in official news outlets but word of mouth had spread, especially amongst those groups who, against all pressures, opposed the military regime that ran the country.

Sejong-ro, the main road leading down the center of Seoul, past the towering statue of Admiral Yi Sun-shin, was lined with protestors. Up ahead loomed the huge edifice of Guanghua-mun. Many of the protestors waved signs saying "Yankee Go Home" and other things written in Korean having to do with stopping the rape of Korea and not allowing foreigners to abuse our people any longer. They might not know the exact details of what had happened with the Lost Echo but they could read between the lines. Similar incidents had occurred at other places during the war and the man with the iron sickle was making it abundantly clear that he wanted the Americans to leave. The KNPs were having trouble holding back the crowds but regular traffic had been rerouted. Ernie had to flash his CID badge at the KNP roadblock. Still they wouldn't let us through. I explained in Korean that Mr. Kill would be waiting for us. Someone radioed ahead and within a couple of minutes, a whistle blew and the white-gloved KNP pulled back the barricade.

An AFKN mobile broadcasting van sat at the foot of the three-story stone gate known as Guanghua-mun. In granite relief, valiant masses of workers, farmers, and soldiers strove toward the light above that was freedom. A rope ladder with wood slat footholds hung in front of the inspiring fresco. A platform used by painters and cleaners had been pulled out of reach all the way to the top. Above it, peering down at us, stood the man with the iron sickle and next to him, crouching, smoking her usual cigarette, was Madame Hoh.

We parked and climbed out of the jeep. Captain Prevault looked up. "They'll fall," she said.

"Better if they do," Ernie replied, "when you consider what the KNPs will do to them."

Mr. Kill walked up to me. "You can't see him because he's tied up and lying down. But they used the platform to haul the American up there. We've spotted him from our helicopter. It's an elderly man who matches the description of Covert P. Walton. They're saying they want a copy of their original claim published in the *Chosun Ilbo*, this afternoon's edition, or they'll toss him off."

"They already told you that?"

"Yes."

"Is the government going to allow it?"

"Impossible. But the ROK Army is lobbying hard for it."

"The ROK Army?"

"Why do you think Major Rhee has been tailing you all this time? Her faction in the command structure wants the Americans out. And this story, this 'Lost Echo' atrocity, is just the sort of thing to turn public opinion in their favor."

"But we support the ROK Army," I said. "Why would they want us out?"

"So they can go north."

Then I understood. The ROK Army wanted to be free of the controlling influence of the American government so they could convince the people of South Korea that they should invade the communist north and reunite the country.

"So Major Rhee could've stopped this guy," I said.

"Maybe." Mr. Kill nodded. "We think she knew more than she was letting on."

A massive intake of breath erupted from the crowd. We looked up. Leaning precariously off the stone edge was a young woman.

"Miss Sim," Captain Prevault said. Her real name, as I had learned from Madame Hoh in the cavern, was Ahn, but I didn't have time to explain that now. The man with the iron sickle grabbed the girl by the scruff of her neck and leaned her out into the air. The crowd screamed but he held on and pulled her back to safety.

"He's threatening to drop her first," Captain Prevault said, her face screwed up in anxiety.

"It's a bluff," I said.

"How can you be sure?"

I didn't have time to tell her all I'd learned in the Taebaek Mountains, about how these three people had suffered at the hands of the men of the Lost Echo and about how I believed they would always stick together. The man with the iron sickle was just trying to increase the pressure to publish the story of the Lost Echo atrocity and thereby permanently destroy the legitimacy of the American presence in Korea.

I didn't believe he'd murder Miss Sim but I had no doubt he'd murder Covert P. Walton.

"I'll climb up there," Ernie said.

Mr. Kill looked at him in horror. "They'll kill you."

"We can't just stand here," Ernie said. "They have an innocent American up there. We have to do something."

"What about the helicopter?" I asked. "A sniper could take them out."

"We thought of that," Mr. Kill said, "but once we start firing it would be an almost impossible shot to kill them both instantly. And if we don't, the survivor will throw the American off."

"So we have to deal."

"Yes, but my President won't deal. He never deals with terrorists."

I knew that to be true. North Koreans commandoes had put similar pressures on the ROK government in the past to no avail. Civilian casualties were just part of the deal as far as the ROK government was concerned.

Captain Prevault grabbed my muddy sleeve and stepped close to me, completely unheeding of my rank odor. "You have to save her," she said. "We know now what we're dealing with. A program of treatment could cure her. She's so young."

Ernie walked toward the rope ladder dangling about ten feet above the ground.

"I'm going up," he said.

Mr. Kill snapped his fingers and three KNPs hustled over toward Ernie, standing between him and the ladder.

"What is this shit?" Ernie said. "Somebody's got to do *something*!"

"I'll go," I said.

"What good will it do?" Mr. Kill asked. "They'll just kill you along with the people they already have up there."

"I have my forty-five," I said, patting the shoulder holster Ernie had given me before we left Yongsan Compound.

"You'll never get a round off."

"I'll reason with them," I said.

"How?"

"I talked to them before," I said, "two nights ago in the Taebaek Mountains."

"And they let you live?"

"Yes. I believe they have much they want to say to the world. If I can convince them their story will get out, maybe they'll listen to reason."

"But the government won't let their story get out," Mr. Kill said.

"It's already out," I said, motioning toward the protestors lining the street, "at least partially, and I'm an American. I can get their story out."

"Your superiors will court-martial you."

"Maybe."

"No *maybe* about it," Ernie chimed in.

"It's worth a try," I said.

Mr. Kill thought about it. He looked up at the top of the Gate of the Transformation of Light. Finally, he turned to me. "Are you *sure* you want to do this?"

"I must," I said. "After what the soldiers of the Lost Echo did, someone has to make it right."

"No one can ever make it right," Captain Prevault said.

"We can try."

Mr. Kill nodded and the KNPs stepped away from the ladder. I walked toward it, wondering if it would hold my weight. Maybe. Maybe not. Only one way to find out. I jumped as high as I could, grabbed onto the lowest wooden crossbar, and pulled myself up.

My feet slipped more than once. They hurt like hell and the feeling in them hadn't completely returned. Mucus dripped from my stinging nose. I did my best to place the soles of my combat boots squarely on the center of the wooden steps, but the nerves that should've relayed sensation were faulty. To compensate, I held onto the crossbar above me for dear life. I kept at least one foot and one hand firmly gripped to something at all times. I refused to look down, but by looking up I could tell I'd made progress. I was already about halfway up the three-story wall. Occasionally, a face peered down at me. Once it was the man with the iron sickle, then it was Madame Hoh. They knew I was coming. If they decided they didn't want to talk to me, all they had to do was take that razor sharp sickle and cut the rope. But they didn't. Not yet.

I was about three quarters of the way up when the ladder slipped. I dropped about six feet and at first I was sure I was going to plummet all the way to the ground but suddenly the rope jerked to a halt. I held on with both hands but my gimpy feet slipped off into space.

The crowd below screamed. I managed to regain my footing and breathe deeply and steadily for a few minutes before daring to look back up. Now they were both looking down at me, the man with the iron sickle and Madame Hoh. She's the one who cupped her hand around her mouth and shouted.

"The gun," she said. "Drop the gun."

I felt the .45 tucked snugly in my shoulder holster. I looked back up at them. Both were scowling. There was no question; if I didn't drop the gun they would cut the ladder. I didn't even have time to scurry back to the ground. I was too high and it would only have taken them a few seconds to slice the rope that stood between me and sudden death. For the first time I looked back down. Ernie and Captain Prevault and Mr. Kill were gazing up at me with worried looks on their faces.

With my free hand, I undid the buckle in front of my chest. Then I shrugged and let the leather holster slide into the air. I watched it fall.

When I had first opened the door to the Lost Echo signal truck, an odor had hit me that I'd never before encountered. Certainly, it was the odor of death, of that there was no doubt. And it was of a musty nature that told of ancient things crumbling to dust. I pulled the door fully open and stepped inside. The control panel on the right was slathered in mildew. How it lived in there, I didn't know. Where did it get moisture? And then I realized where: from the five men sitting on steel chairs, some of them with their heads tilted down in shame, some leaning back and gazing up at the roof. Nothing more than papery skin and brittle bone, their fatigue uniforms hanging off them in strips. Teeth poked out, no longer hidden by lips or even flesh on the face. Eye sockets were filled with desiccated cobwebs. The floor beneath their feet was dark, stained. Some of their neck bones had been sawed almost in half. From the scraped mud it seemed that the men had been dragged in there, one by one. Probably the survivors of the winter of starvation, those who'd managed to feed themselves. But they'd been hunted down, one by one, and lined up in the truck like the good signalmen they were. Finally they were no longer a threat to the good people of the Taebaek Mountains.

I pushed my way through them all the way to the back and hunted amidst the bones for the chips of imprinted metal I knew I'd find: dog tags, with their names, ranks, blood types, and religions on them. I stuffed the clinking tin into my pocket.

Someone, somewhere, would like to know. And then I left.

Ernie and Mr. Kill backed away as the .45 clattered to the ground.

I looked up. Satisfied, the two faces disappeared.

When I reached the ledge, there were no hands to help haul me to safety. I reached out as far as I could on the flat stone surface. Pushing up with my legs, I leaned forward, hoping my weight would tilt me to safety, and then I slithered onto solid stone. I hugged the flat surface, feeling the firm body of the ginseng plant pressing against my chest. I wriggled forward until I was sure I wouldn't fall. Then and only then did I look around me. At the far end of the long stone rectangle squatted the man with the iron sickle. Behind him sat Madame Hoh and Miss Sim. Behind them, bound, gagged, and bug-eyed, lay Mr. Covert P. Walton.

"Let him go," I said. "You can keep me instead."

The man with the iron sickle shook his head. Madame Hoh lit another cigarette.

"You'll never get out of here alive," I said. "What's the point?"

"The point is," Madame Hoh said, "the world must know what happened on Daeam Mountain."

"They'll know now," I said, motioning toward the growing crowd of demonstrators below us.

"Pak Chung-hee won't let it appear in the *Chosun Il-bo*."

"He can't stop it from appearing in American newspapers. Stringers from *AP* and *UPI* are already down there interviewing people."

"*AP*?"

I explained about international wire services. When I was finished, Madame Hoh said, "How do you know they'll write about it?"

"Because of him." I pointed at Mr. Walton. "They'll interview him, and he'll talk about it, and then they'll interview me, and I'll tell them everything I've seen."

"Your army will let you do that?"

They wouldn't but I lied. "Yes. I'm an American. Our rules are different."

The man with the iron sickle, apparently, understood enough of what we were saying to be skeptical. He shook his head and said, "*An dei.*" No good.

"You've accomplished what you need to accomplish," I said. "The story of the Lost Echo will be in every newspaper in the world before the day is out. Let her go, at least."

I pointed to Miss Sim. She snuggled closer to Madame Hoh.

"Here," I said. "I have something for you." I reached in my pocket and pulled out the leather pouch. I placed it on the flat stone surface and slid it across to Madame Hoh. She picked it up, unlaced the bag, and the stem of the plant popped out. Reverently, she lifted the *insam* plant out of the pouch. Holding it with both hands, she showed it to the man with the iron sickle. He eyed it suspiciously. Then she turned back to me. "Where did you get this?"

"After you left, I escaped from the cavern and wandered down the mountain. I fell asleep and when I woke up, this plant was there at my feet. At first, I didn't know what it was but Hunter Huk helped me harvest it."

"You met Hunter Huk?"

"Without him, I'd still be in the mountains."

"And you want her to have it?" She motioned toward Miss Sim.

"Yes. It will help pay for the treatment she needs. Captain Prevault, an American psychiatrist, has already arranged for her to be treated by Doctor Hwang Sun-won, one of the most famous doctors in Korea." I didn't know if this was true but it could be. "She needs to get out of here alive," I continued. "And so does he." I pointed at the terrified Mr. Walton. "They are innocent."

Madame Hoh flicked her fingers at me, ordering me to back up. I did, crawling. She kept flicking her fingers until I was on the far side of the top of Guanghua-mun. She leaned toward the man with the iron sickle and whispered urgently. His eyes narrowed in suspicion, glaring alternately at me and then at the ginseng Miss Sim held reverently cradled in her arms.

They conversed, arguing, until finally it appeared they'd come to a decision. Madame Hoh motioned for me to return. I did, sliding on my butt as fast as I could. She opened her mouth and started to say something when her head exploded.

I leapt forward. Another sniper round zinged through the air, probably from one of the high rise buildings two or three city blocks away. It was a masterful shot but now Miss Sim was screaming, and Mr. Walton was bucking his body up and down like a terrified fish. The man with the iron sickle turned toward the rope ladder and started to hack at it.

I leapt at him. But I was too slow. When I shoved off with my lame feet they didn't propel me forward with as much strength as I expected. He twisted back and raised his sickle. The blade caught my shoulder and dug deep through flesh into the bone. I surged forward, not yet feeling the pain. He tried to pull the sickle back but it was stuck now in the cartilage of my shoulder. I landed on top of him, and we slid closer to the edge. I jammed my forearm into his throat, and he leaned away from me and suddenly I was staring down into space and the screaming crowd some three stories below. He kneed me in the groin. I scrabbled back, grabbing at the wooden handle of the sickle, both of us pulling on it, the sharp blade burrowing deeper into my flesh. Finally it popped free and blood gushed out. The two of us had our hands on the sickle, rolling away from the edge but then tumbling together toward the opposite side. I planted my left foot on the smooth surface and his weight rolled over on it. The pain that jolted up from my foot almost blinded me, but we didn't roll off the ledge. He'd managed to wrench the sickle from me now, and he raised the gleaming blade into the air, and then a white apparition appeared at his arm. Miss Sim. She grabbed his forearm just in time to deflect his swing, and I leaned to my right and the blade clanged onto hard stone. He turned back and stared at her in astonishment.

"No," she said. "He's good. He gave me this." She was crying and clutching the *insam* against her chest.

He twisted his head and another shot rang out. This one caught him flush in the neck. He stared open-mouthed at Miss Sim for a split second, and then his eyes darted to me. He appeared confused. A crimson bubble of blood bulged out of the hole in his neck, spurted violently and then dwindled to a stream. I shoved him away and now he didn't resist. His body tumbled farther than I had intended. Still clutching the iron sickle, he tilted over the stone edge of the Gate of the Transformation of Light and, his eyes locked on mine, plunged backward into space.

The crowd below screamed. I grabbed onto the hysterical Miss Sim and, holding her tightly, crawled toward Mr. Walton. I held one of the ropes that bound him and told him to breathe deeply.

"You're safe now," I told him and repeated the same thing to Miss Sim in Korean.

-17-

A month later, Ernie and I were back on the black market detail. At night we prowled the ville. I was healing up nicely. The stitches had been taken out and the memory of how cold I'd been in the Taebaek Mountains, and how much pain the bottle of Little Devil hot sauce had caused me, was mercifully beginning to fade.

Mrs. Hoh's claim had never been published in the *Chosun Ilbo*. The government hadn't allowed it. A few stories had been published by the international news services about the killing atop Guanghua-mun and the protests but they only got part of the story, not nearly the full extent of it. An officer from 8th Army JAG, accompanied by Colonel Brace, had appeared beside my hospital bed the day after the incident, informing me that the claim was classified and I was being ordered not to reveal any information about it under threat of court-martial. He slipped a statement under my nose saying I'd been duly informed and told me to sign it. I refused. Both officers left in a huff. Still, I knew better than to reveal classified information. Years in the federal penitentiary in Leavenworth, Kansas, was not something I ever wanted to experience.

Captain Prevault extended her tour in Korea. She said it was to supervise Miss Ahn's care, which she did in her spare time. I believed her but I also liked to think that I had something to do with her decision.

Moe Dexter and his MP sycophants knew that Ernie and I had been the ones to flush out the man with the iron sickle but he was still blaming us for the deaths of Collingsworth and the GIs in the signal truck and at AFKN. He didn't taunt us to our face though, instead he whispered behind our backs. That, I could live with. What bothered me was the change in policy for the ville patrol. The size was doubled to two MPs and two ROK MPs, and a backup jeep with the patrol supervisor, usually Moe Dexter, sat nearby at all times.

It was a Saturday night, just after end-of-month payday, when a fight broke out at the King Club between some 8th Army Honor Guard troops and a handful of infantrymen on three-day pass from the DMZ. Moe and his band of MPs waded into the crowd, batons swinging. Two guys were hospitalized with concussions, another figured to lose an eye.

Ernie and I arrived just as the injured GIs were being wheeled out by medics. A business girl was screaming at Moe, cursing at him for hurting her boyfriend.

"He no do *nothing*," she screeched.

With the back of his hand, Moe slapped the girl hard. She fell backwards and crashed to the ground, her skull bouncing on tile.

Moe started to laugh, as did his buddies.

Maybe it was all I'd been through and maybe it was because I was fed up with Moe Dexter using his official position to exercise his sadism. Before Ernie could stop me, I ran at him.

One of his buddies shouted. Dexter swiveled.

I let loose with a jab. It caught him on the shoulder but Dexter stepped back in time to avoid its full force. Like the bully he was, he seemed surprised anyone would have the temerity to fight him.

A couple of the MPs rushed toward me but Ernie pulled his

.45 and waved them off. Cocktail tables were pulled back, out of our way.

Moe bounced on his toes, grinning, moving away from me. I followed, jabbing some more but not with as much crispness as I had at first. I was tired. I didn't have to fake that, especially considering what I'd been through in the Taebaek Mountains. I even stood still a couple of times, covering up, and let him hit me. Ernie screamed at me to keep moving and to fight back. I didn't. I let Moe Dexter have his way with me and I could see the gloating in his eyes. He was enjoying himself, savoring his unquestioned dominance and looking forward to the glory of the kill.

The MPs were laughing now and slapping high fives.

Dexter punched me again, and I staggered. He raised his right hand and hopped forward, gleeful at what was about to happen. I backed up. He winged a right at me. I backed up again but this time I planted my rear foot. Moe Dexter let loose with his right, but before it was halfway to me, I jabbed my left directly into his face and his head jerked back, and as I launched my right I saw his eyes blink open, surprise building in his face.

The right landed flush on his forehead, and then I hooked with my left to his ribs and then a left again to the side of his head and finally a cross with my right hand that connected. By the fifth punch I was winging at air. Moe Dexter was down, lying at my feet, his black MP helmet rolling away and finally spinning to a stop next to an overturned cocktail table.

Business girls cheered.

Ernie leaped forward and wiped sweat from my face and spoke into my ear. "Why didn't you tell me you could do that?"

"You didn't ask," I said.

With the graves registration unit, I rode in a two-and-a-half ton truck deep into the Taebaek Mountains. We had plenty of cold weather equipment and tents and diesel space heaters and cases of C-rations but it still took us three days to find the cave. Their faces covered in masks, the recovery GIs pulled the desiccated corpses out of the signal truck. I'd already turned the dog tags over to them.

The men of the 4038th, the Lost Echo, had been missing in action for over twenty years. Now their relatives would know what they'd always known: they were dead. Their families would receive the remains and the dead servicemen would be buried with honors. But some things die hard, as did my memory of C. Winston Barretsford and Corporal Collingsworth and the two GIs in the signal truck and the two dead and one wounded at AFKN. And I remembered Madame Hoh and the man with the iron sickle and I remembered what they'd suffered, and I remembered what they'd been driven to do and I remembered what had caused it.

Captain Prevault told me to try not to think about these things. Someday I'd sleep soundly again, she told me. I made her promise.

-ACKNOWLEDGMENTS-

This book was made possible by three brilliant and accomplished women: Bronwen Hruska, publisher; Juliet Grames, editor; and Jill Marsal, literary agent. Thank you all for your patience and support.